Always
Yellow Roses

by

Lynn Shurr

The Roses Series, Book Three

Always Yellow Roses

COPYRIGHT © 2014 by Lynn Shurr

Cover Art by *RJ Morris*

The Wild Rose Press, Inc.
PO Box 708
Adams Basin, NY 14410-0708
Visit us at www.thewildrosepress.com

Publishing History
First American Rose Edition, 2014
Print ISBN 978-1-62830-466-4
Digital ISBN 978-1-62830-467-1

The Roses Series, Book Three
Published in the United States of America

Dedication

For Julie Robinson and her rebel's heart.

Prologue

Lafayette, Louisiana, 1982

Noreen Courville turned her head aside to keep her tears from falling on the faint brown ink and erasing the words of love. The fragile paper crumbled at the edges and sometimes split along the folds as she removed and read each message from the antique jewel box Rusty had given her as a Christmas gift. He knew how much she loved history, old objects, and ancient words. He would never admit these letters were proof positive—at least to her—that Rusty Niles had once lived another life as a fine gentleman, owner of a vast plantation. But then, he had never suffered from the dreams.

The dreams began when she entered first grade at Mt. Carmel Academy, a venerable Catholic school for girls noted for its excellent academic reputation, long standing traditions, and occasional small miracles. On her first day, she had been frightened of the massive red brick buildings, the nuns' cemetery running along one side of the grounds, and the dark, looming oaks hung with veils of Spanish moss. Ghosts walked here, she was sure. Her mother laughed and tousled her curly black hair.

"Where do you get these ideas, Noreen? This is a holy place where no bad can happen. The Courville girls have gone to school here for generations, and let me tell you, the nuns will curb that overactive imagination of yours."

If anything, the nuns made her imagination grow. Every year at orientation, one of the older girls, a prize pupil, read the history of the Academy to the newcomers. That night, Noreen dreamt of Mother Leontine, tall and imposing as a man, the founder of the school. She could see the ox cart carrying the Sisters, smell the ozone of the storm that delayed them on the hilltop, view the rainbow the Reverend Mother took as a sign to found her school at this site. The woman dying in childbirth, whom she knew to be her own ancestress, Marguerite Courville, scared her awake.

Her mama came running and held her child against her big, comforting body.

"There, there, baby. It's only a bad dream. You know that woman didn't die despite all the blood. She had a baby boy who became your great-great-great—oh, I don't know how many greats—grandfather, Rufus Courville. He's why you are here today. And as for Marguerite, you heard in the story this morning, she became a benefactress of the school. Her husband gave the land for the Academy and built the chapel as a thank offering for the life of his wife and child. You had a wonderful dream, not a scary one."

Easy for her mother to say. From the very first, Noreen knew there was more to the school history than was told. She could imagine Marguerite Courville so easily. The family owned a miniature of the woman painted on ivory. It sat on the sideboard below the large portraits of auburn-haired Rufus and his blonde wife, Marie-Celeste. As Noreen grew to adolescence, she'd studied the small portrait of the young woman. Black curls framed the white-powdered face with two slashes of pink high on the cheekbones. The hair cascaded down from a topknot and lay on fine-boned, bare shoulders above a low-cut, gauzy white gown. Marguerite's lips were red and her eyes narrow, black, and foxy. She held her head proudly, much too proudly.

Noreen had this woman to thank for her own mess of unruly black curls. They both had dark eyes, but her own were big and brown, more like cow eyes, her sister Estelle said when she wanted to tease the baby of the family for getting attention by having nightmares. "Boohoo, Noreen with your big cow eyes," Estelle would taunt.

Noreen had none of the fox in her and knew she would never be as slender as Marguerite was portrayed. She also knew Marguerite to be a liar, but did not fully understand why until puberty clarified her knowledge of what sins a woman might commit. Big, red-haired men rode in on sorrel horses and brought sorrow to her sex.

Once she understood the message, she thought the dreams would cease. Instead, they grew worse. Now she took part in person, Noreen in a grown-up body cinched in by a corset under a full-skirted gown. She held the hand of a dying man who spit blood on the snowy sheets of a canopied bed like the ones found in restored plantation homes. Sometimes, she rode a red horse to meet her lover. At other times, she galloped to her death on a dark steed beneath a full moon and felt the bullet smash between her shoulder blades. She did not care because Rufus Courville was dead and she might as well be.

Noreen read the words once more, the ones causing

her tears.

My Dearest Espy—I love you with all my heart and all my soul. No one can come between us. Meet me in the oak grove this afternoon after the dinner hour. Your most devoted—Rufe.

She knew positively she had been reborn into the Courville family to end a feud, been reincarnated to find her lost love—and he lived on in this life as Rusty Niles. She'd known when she had no proof at all the very first time she met Russ and discovered the true gentleman beneath his rough cowboy exterior. He would laugh off her belief. His obnoxious friend, Bodey Landrum, could make fun of them all he wanted, but Noreen Courville knew the truth.

She placed the note beneath her pillow. That night the cycle of dreams began again.

Chapter One

Southwest Louisiana, 1822

The oxen moved at a slow and steady plod along the Spanish Trail. Old Plato, borrowed from the same pious family who had loaned the nuns the cart and livestock back in Chapelle, flicked his whip against the flanks of the dumb beasts more for form than in any hopes of going faster. He had done his best to make the two Sisters comfortable, padding the wooden seats with thick cotton blankets and rolling up the canvas sides to let in the spring breezes. They wished to consider land for their new school and had turned down speedier forms of transportation. The nuns were educated women who surely knew best, but Plato thought they might have cause to regret their leisurely pace.

Dark clouds churned in the west on this balmy March afternoon. They cast shadows over the pink primroses and yellow-topped weeds growing in the ditches. So far, the road remained easily passable, firm but not muddy after a shower several days ago. Dust stayed at a minimum, too. These ideal conditions would not last long. Plato hoped to see a sign of the plantation house half way to Opelousas where he was supposed to ask for hospitality for the night before the storm struck.

The travelers had started from the hamlet of Vermilionville that morning after a good night's sleep in a fine home. A basket containing ham slices, boiled eggs, fresh bread, a figgy preserve, and a thick-walled jug of cool lemonade had been pressed upon them to serve as their meal along the way. When the sun was directly overhead, they feasted beneath a live oak. The nuns had no qualms about sharing generously with an elderly slave. Viands enough were left over for another meal—fortunate because shortly, the roadway would turn to a thick gumbo of mud and no house came into sight.

The sky blackened, and the wind whipped the veils of the nuns around their faces. Old Plato halted the spotted oxen and lowered the canvas sides as the first fat raindrops splattered on his poor bald head. No use in putting on his battered straw hat. The wind would have taken it away forever. The best he could think to do for his passengers was to urge the oxen up one of the small hills they had been passing for the last hour and take shelter in a grove of native oaks that topped it. He asked permission of the good Sisters to huddle in the wagon with them until the storm passed and of course, they granted his request.

By the time the dark clouds wore themselves out and drifted away in shreds, night had fallen. The elder of the nuns, addressed as Mother Leontine, directed Plato to search for lights on the horizon. When he reported finding none, she declared they would eat the last of the basket's provisions and spend the evening on the hilltop. The ancient, borrowed servant helped the Sisters spread the blankets on the floorboards, then took himself outside and, wrapped in two thicknesses of oilcloth, made himself as comfortable as possible under the wagon. Plato drifted off listening to the Sisters saying their evening prayers.

At daybreak, he called to the nuns, "Come see, come see!"

Not only was the day dawning pink and properly, but a rainbow spanned the sky from end to end, crowning their little hill with bands of colors.

"We have received a sign," said Mother Leontine standing in the wet oak leaves blanketing the hilltop. "This is a place where miracles happen. Here we shall build our school for young ladies and educate them in virtue and in Christ. We must find the landowner at once and make him an offer."

Old Plato scratched his ring of white hair, the sole remainder of a once-healthy thatch, rubbed his bald pate and scraped a hand across his short white beard. Now, how were they going to do that? True, daylight revealed a two-story, frame farmhouse a mile or two down a side road, but the place appeared deserted. No good wife fed the chickens. No husband went to milk a cow in the dilapidated barn. A rider came fast down that road, scattering mud in all directions, but he didn't look likely to stop, not the speed he went along.

Plato was about to make an effort to waylay the passerby by waving his arms when the man slowed and turned his horse directly up the hill. He halted, slid from the saddle and fell to his knees before the towering and stately Mother Leontine, her gray eyes still gleaming over God's gift of the rainbow.

"Sister, please tell me you have a priest in your company."

"Sadly, no, monsieur," Mother Leontine answered in the same finely accented French the gentleman spoke. "Please rise and tell us who owns this land."

The rider arose. He stood shorter and slighter than the Reverend Mother, but made up for his lack of stature with a great deal of pomaded curly black hair, a trimmed moustache, and a small, pointed beard. His bulbous dark eyes beseeched her.

"It is my own, the Courville plantation. Across the Spanish Trail, the land is owned by an American who took advantage of a poor Frenchman. He is godless and unmarried. Forget seeking assistance from Aaron Niles. My wife, she is dying in childbirth. The midwife says if the baby does not come before the noon hour, I will lose them both. Marguerite wishes to make her last confession most urgently, but the nearest priest is in Opelousas."

"We will come and render what aid we can, Monsieur Courville. Sister Francine is skilled in medicine and will do all that is possible. If necessary, I will hear your wife's confession and take those sins upon myself until a priest is found to grant absolution. Take Sr. Francine on your horse. Plato and I will follow." Mother Leontine folded her hands into her sleeves before the frantic husband could kiss them in thankfulness.

"*Merci, merci!*"

Plato gave the man a leg up and with permission lifted the petite Sr. Francine sideways onto the back of the horse. The two disappeared around a bend to the east, moving as fast as the animal could carry them. Plato yoked the oxen and urged them on. The house was not as far off as he had figured. After rounding another of the small hills that had blocked their sight the night before, Plato and Mother Leontine viewed the plantation home but a mile away.

As compact and elegant as its master, the home built in the French style had sturdy brick columns holding up a second floor gallery deeply shaded by the pitch of the roof. This porch was reached by two swooping exterior staircases. As they neared the open front gate, Plato could see a turbaned nursemaid, big and very black, at the foot of the stairs. She pointed out the fading rainbow to the small daughters of the family. The children pretended to look, but their curly heads were cocked toward the screams coming from the upstairs suite. Clearly, they knew Mama was dying, and no rainbow could make up for that. The two girls sniveled into their maid's white apron.

Mother Leontine alighted and went to the children. She bent to their level. "How are you called, petite?"

"Marthe, and I am nine years old. This is my sister, Mariette. She's only seven."

Both girls had their father's eyes underscored with dark smudges from worry and lack of sleep. They looked into the compassionate gaze of the tall nun and sought an answer. "Is Mama going to die?"

"Only the Good Lord knows, Marthe. Sr. Francine is very skilled. We shall see."

"Madame had no trouble birthing these two and the other three over there in the graveyard. Even with her first, it was not this bad," the children's nurse said softly. Her broad face was free of wrinkles, but judging by the tufts of gray wool springing out from under her headpiece, she might have served the mistress for a long time.

"This plantation, far from the city, can be a lonely place. She wanted a townhouse," the slave woman added, as if explaining something of importance.

"I will go to her and pray." Mother Leontine ascended the stairs and entered the bedchamber through its long, glass-paned doors.

"Don't you worry none," old Plato told the little girls. "Dese is holy ladies and dey can do miracles."

Inside, drapes pulled across all windows kept the room close. A small fire burned in the hearth beneath a mantel of black marble streaked with white. Lacy with linens, an empty cradle waited by the bedside. The odor of fresh blood filled the room.

Sr. Francine had drawn back the fine embroidered bed hangings and the mosquito netting. One of the small sharp knives she kept wrapped in bleached linen rested in a basin of warm, pink-tinted water.

"I had to cut her to ease the birth. Now, I will try to move the baby."

Sr. Francine accepted a dollop of lard from the midwife and greased her small hands. The midwife held Marguerite Courville's shoulders to the bed as the Sister, her long sleeves pushed back, groped for the baby's head, cupped it, and tugged. The big round head of the child emerged. Sr. Francine compressed and rotated the broad set of shoulders that had been the real problem all along. The baby boy was born.

The midwife administered the slap of life and a grin bloomed on her dusky face at the infant's lusty cry. "Praise be, Sister. I was too scared to do any cuttin'. If Madame had died by my hand, the Master, he would have sold me off, or worse. Least now, he has a strong son."

She went about attending to the rest of the messy details of birth while Sr. Francine washed her hands and dried them on a hand towel too lovely for the purpose.

The Sister prepared a needle with silk thread. Mother Leontine continued to pray silently from a corner near the fireplace where she observed all.

"Madame, you have a fine son. What will you call him?"

No response came from the bed. Sr. Francine held a silver-framed mirror taken from the dressing table to the mouth of the mother. A small cloud of moisture gathered on its surface. "She lives—for how much longer I do not know. Still, it is God's mercy that she will not feel my stitches."

While Sr. Francine sewed up the wound she had made, the midwife cleaned the child and swaddled him. With the mother nearly gone and unable to hold the infant, she placed the baby in the cradle and rocked it with her foot until he was soothed and sleeping. The three women waited.

"Water," croaked Marguerite Courville. Sr. Francine poured from a painted pitcher into a china cup and held the woman's head while she drank.

"Have I died? Are you the Holy Mother? No, I am unshriven and surely have no place in Heaven." Her dark eyes wild, her long black hair in sweaty tangles on the pillow as white as her face, the small woman in the canopied bed searched the dim room as if the devil awaited her in a corner

Sr. Francine's kind faded blue eyes crinkled. "I am no one's mother, but I strive for holiness—as you must. Come," she beckoned to the midwife. "Let us take this innocent to see his father and allow Mother Leontine to ease Madame's soul."

The Reverend Mother stood by the bedside. "We have no priest with us, but I will carry your confession and contrition with me until one can be found, my child."

She expected Marguerite Courville to say the timeless opening words of the seeker of absolution, but the woman began to ramble. She raised a weak hand toward a small portrait of a dark-haired, delicate boy of perhaps ten.

"That is my son, Francois. He is twelve now and taken off to boarding school in New Orleans this past fall. Last spring, my husband stayed in the city a very long time seeking the best placement. More water, please."

Mother Leontine complied. The penitent continued. "Maxime keeps a mulatto woman in the city. He has another family there. He will not take me to town even for the opera season. I languish here presiding over this house, having his children that die as often as they live."

"That is the lot of all good wives."

"But, I grew bored and lonely. Often, I go out seeking the company of my distant neighbors. We have a newcomer nearby, an American."

"So we have been told."

"He is a big man with red in his hair and eyes the color of American whiskey. He could break Maxime in two." She stayed silent for a moment. "Tell me about my newborn."

"He's a fine, large boy with a big set of shoulders that caused all your difficulties. I did not see the color of his eyes, but he is topped with ruddy hair. Oh, my dear!"

"Forgive me Father, for I have sinned."

****

Sitting at the glossy table in his first floor dining room, a bottle of brandy open before him, Maxime Courville watched his daughters cooing over their new brother, so much larger than they had been at birth, so much fairer of complexion, so much redder of hair. The girls were amused by the baby's auburn tuft and wanted a name to call him. "Rufus," he told them bitterly. "Rufus and Aaron for his saint."

"Mother Leontine, I will take no payment for the oak grove. The old farm is a gift from me, an offering of thanks for the life of my wife—and my son, of course. I will send some workers to begin repairs while you carry Marguerite's confession to Opelousas. My daughters shall be your first students. I am delighted to have you near. My wife is often lonely, and now she will have company, women who will tend to her soul as well. The confession, only you and the priest will know?" Maxime Courville asked anxiously.

"But of course, Monsieur Courville. There is no need to worry." Mother Leontine reassured him, but her sinful burden was so great she wished to finish this discussion, borrow a carriage, and travel posthaste to Opelousas and a priest. She dispatched Plato and his slow oxen with a note to ensure safe passage and many thanks to his owner for the use of the old man's services.

As soon as was seemly after a hearty dinner served on flowered china imported from France, the nuns took their leave. The confession of Marguerite Courville weighed so heavily on her soul Mother Leontine wondered how the wheels of carriage could turn so easily and the horses be so fleet.

Chapter Two

Once Mother Leontine had delivered the confession to the local priest and received the absolution, she experienced a lightness of soul, a merriness of heart, and a new joy in her vocation. She spoke eloquently at every household where the Sisters were invited to dine of the need to educate young women who would be the mothers of leaders and teach in their own gentle way by example.

Consequently, it came as no surprise when the nuns brought back with them a buxom young woman of French and Spanish origins, seventeen years of age, who could read, write, figure, and speak three languages, but wanted finishing. Her mother had passed away at an early age. Her father, a wealthy merchant and cotton broker very much consumed with his work in Opelousas, had neglected to remarry, leaving the child with none but the servants and a male tutor to instruct her. Ramona Viator became the first student recruited to attend Mount Carmel Academy for Young Ladies.

Mother Leontine signaled for the carriage to halt at the base of the small hill where the sign of the rainbow had appeared to her. She wished to offer a prayer for the success of their enterprise on the crest among the oak trees. Sr. Francine accompanied her. Their prayers given, the nuns descended the hill toward the carriage where the darkly handsome and perspiring Miss Viator leaned from a window and worked her fan to provide some relief from the stuffiness inside.

A big man on a large red horse came up from the south on the Spanish Trail. The rider drew up by the carriage and was offering assistance or directions by the time the Sisters came down from the hill to take their charge in hand. Ramona flirted, her large Spanish eyes peering at the gentleman just over the rim of her good lace fan with the ivory end panels. The fan failed to fill the space showing off far too much of Ramona's soft, pillowy bosom as she leaned forward in her inappropriately low-cut gown.

Mother Leontine inserted herself between Ramona and the immense sorrel stallion. One look from her into the animal's eye, and the beast stepped back a pace. Its rider doffed a tall hat revealing the same reddish hair as his mount and bowed low over his saddle.

"Aaron Niles at your service, ladies. I own the plantation t'other side of the road. May I be of some help? We don't see religious people too often out this way."

"Our order is preparing to build a school for young ladies on this land so generously donated by Monsieur Courville. As you can hear the hammers pounding, the farmhouse is already being prepared to meet our needs. This is Sr. Francine and you may address me as Mother Leontine."

"What do you raise on your plantation, Mr. Niles?" Ramona asked in a sultry voice even though she had not been introduced. Her fan still plied the air rapidly across the tops of her dewy breasts.

"Some cotton, cane in the bottom lands, yams and

cattle, Miss…?"

"Viator. Your holdings must be quite large."

"Sizeable, very sizeable."

Mother Leontine cleared her throat so loudly the horse startled. She did not move an inch out of the way. "Pardon. Miss Viator is a ward of our school. The young ladies who attend the Academy will be allowed to entertain guests at tea on Saturday mornings from ten until noon. At no other time shall they mingle. Is that understood, Mr. Niles?"

"Until Saturday, then. I was on my way to inquire about the health of Madame Courville, my nearest neighbor who had some difficulties with her travail."

"Mr. Niles, I can tell you Madame Courville is at death's door and the family wishes to remain secluded at this time. The child, a boy, is quite healthy, however."

"A son. I hope to have one of my own someday, but I do grieve to hear of Madame Courville's illness."

"Only God knows if she will pass through that door and into his kingdom, Mr. Niles. As you said—until Saturday."

Aaron Niles tipped his tall hat again, turned his mount and rode back the way he had come. Ramona sighed deeply, causing her bosom to wobble.

"Mr. Niles has an imposing physique, does he not, Sister?"

"Proper young ladies do not comment on a gentleman's physique," Sr. Francine corrected.

"My maid talked about manly attributes all the time."

"And that is exactly why your father has placed your education in our hands. Study hard, mind your manners, pray, and perhaps God will grant you a husband like Mr. Niles one day. Until that time, sit up straight and turn your eyes ahead."

The nuns accepted the assistance of their driver and reentered the carriage. A short way down the road, they stopped at the farmstead. Maxime Courville, himself, on horseback towering over the workers despite his short stature, oversaw the repairs.

"Sisters, did you manage to find a priest?"

"Most certainly. We also found our first student, Miss Ramona Viator. God smiles upon us."

"But of course. In your absence, Marguerite has made a most miraculous recovery. She claims she could feel the moment her sins had been absolved."

Maxime kept his bulbous eyes on the workers. He pointed with his whip at a slave unloading a wagon full of bricks. "You there, Marcel, take care with those. We might make them on the plantation, but I will not have unnecessary breakage, do you hear!"

Marcel dipped his head and continued to stack the bricks with gloveless hands. Mother Leontine cocked her head. "Bricks for a frame house, Monsieur?"

"A gift from my lady wife. She wishes you to have a chapel built of brick in honor of her salvation. I am to donate a small rose window ordered from France to be placed above the altar. She will send our daughters to school here, she says."

"I see Marguerite is well on her way to healing. May I show you the exact spot to erect our chapel in the oak grove on the small rise?"

****

A month later, Mother Leontine's enterprise received other signs of heavenly favor as she knew the school would. Old Plato returned to them along with his toothless woman, two yellow-skinned, orphaned grandchildren, aged five and six, and his master's daughter ready to be educated. A letter and document arriving at the same time indicated the enslaved family was to be considered as a payment of tuition—"because at the moment, we find ourselves rich in land but poor in cash. While our beloved daughter, Cecile, has received rigorous training at Madame Purdue's excellent Conservatory for Young Ladies in Chapelle, we find she is still given to flights of fancy and somewhat lacking in piety and humility, conditions we feel a year of finishing at your academy should remedy."

Mother Leontine showed no exasperation over the contents of the note. Sr. Francine, standing amidst the muck made by the building, the dust raised by the workers settling on her black robe, could not withhold her opinion. "If you will pardon me for saying, it is quite one thing to have hands owned by our patron erecting a chapel and quite another for the Order to possess Negroes. Not to mention that Monsieur DeVille has sent us the most ancient and the very youngest of his people who will only be a burden added to our endeavors."

From down the road in the old farmhouse, a brisk spring breeze carried along with the dust the racket of Ramona Viator pounding away on the spinet Marguerite Courville had insisted upon donating. Declaring her daughters could practice at the school as part of their education, she'd had her men remove its limbs and hoist the instrument from the gallery outside her parlor into the back of a wagon. Ramona made another egregious error in her elementary music lesson and cursed fluently and loudly in Spanish.

Sr. Francine winced. "I will speak to the girl again about watching her language. But what shall we do about the others?"

She gestured toward a luxurious open carriage. Cecile DeVille sat there impatiently twirling the parasol keeping the sun off of her lily-white complexion with the aid of a veil attached to a fetching straw bonnet attractively tied onto her curls by a pale blue ribbon. The rest of her vehicle, piled high with trunks and hatboxes, held all Cecile was reluctant to do without. The clutch of slaves, however, had followed in a farm wagon bearing only them and the clothes on their backs.

Eyes downcast, old Plato stood by the wagon and pretended not to hear the nuns' conversation until the point when he began to fear he and his small family might be sent back to Chapelle. "Please, good Sisters, don't you send us back. I can raise a garden for you, take care of stock. My woman can cook fancy and plain. She just too old to feed de whole plantation and do up dose big parties anymore. De little ones, dey can feed de chickens, find de eggs, run your errands. Old Missus don't want 'em around no more. Us neither. We goes back, we be sold off separate and cheap somewheres. Please—in de name of God."

Plato dropped to his knees and kissed the hem of Mother Leontine's robe. She hastily motioned for him to rise but thought she caught a glimpse of a smile coming and going on his mahogany-hued face.

"There is no need for dramatic gestures. I had no intention of sending you away. Still, you will have to bide in the barn with the cow for company until a cabin can be built. Thanks to Monsieur Courville, it is quite snug."

"I slept in worse places, Lady Mother, like dat first night we come here. Dis a holy place. It surely is."

"Very well. Sr. Francine, take Miss DeVille to meet Miss Viator. Perhaps her fine manners will rub off on Ramona. Only open a month and four students already. We prosper."

"Six students," said Sr. Francine, who taught the two Courville girls while Mother Leontine exerted her influence on the unruly Ramona. "No child should remain ignorant because of the color of its skin."

"I agree, but go about your mission quietly. We fly in the face of custom."

"Understood, well understood."

****

Cecile DeVille's small, white fingers dashed across the keyboard of the spinet as she performed a spritely piece by Mozart to entertain the Academy's sole Saturday guest, Mr. Aaron Niles. Mr. Niles sat on one side of the rosewood and horsehair settee, a delicate cup of tea balanced on one of his knees, his tall hat on the other for want of any other place to put it. On the far side of the settee, a goodly space between them, Ramona Viator took a sip from her own cup, pinkie finger slightly raised, and engaged him in polite conversation under the eagle-eyed stare of Mother Leontine.

"Miss DeVille plays so very well, don't you agree, Mr. Niles?" The most charming aspect of her comment was the warmth of her French-Spanish accent applied to each word.

"Indeed, she does, Miss Viator, but I somewhat prefer a more rollicking tune like the one you played."

"Miss Viator played a simple piece by Bach, but she does tend to give music her own special interpretation," Mother Leontine commented. "Shall I have Mrs. Plato refill your cup?"

"No, thank you." Niles feared the ancient servant would pour the steaming brew into his lap with her shaking hands. The custard tarts she baked tasted mighty good though, and he said so.

"Mrs. Plato has proved to be more adept in the kitchen than one would have guessed. I know Miss Viator is much appreciative of her hot biscuits and eggs in the morning rather than Sr. Francine's cornmeal mush."

"I would say amen to that as well." Sr. Francine flipped the page of Cecile's music. "I was not blessed with skill in cookery. All the time, the mush is scorched."

Crowded with the spinet, the settee, Mother Leontine's throne-like carved chair, the donated marble-topped table holding the tea set and refreshments, and six sweating human bodies, the small parlor in the front of the farmhouse was stifling on this May day. Very hard of hearing, the old slave woman responded to the nun's gesture to refill her cup. Called "granny" by the yellow children and "my woman" by Old Plato, the nuns had yet to divine her name and had fallen into the habit of referring to the servant as Mrs. Plato, which appeared to be fine with the woman in question. She responded to most speech with a gummy smile and a nod. Afterwards, she would go about cleaning and cooking without letting further directions interfere with whatever she did.

Aaron Niles allowed his eyes to stray from Ramona's doe-eyed gaze to the modest dark blue wool bodice plastered to her bosom. The girl sat stiffly, probably trussed up like the Christmas turkey under her sack-like gown with its neck-hugging inset of thick white batiste and long sleeves covering even the bones of her wrists. Her hands, though, looked strong as if they could rein in a temperamental mount with one yank of the reins. He moved his eyes upward, and he found himself dwelling on how soft her dark, wavy hair, pulled out of its pins, would feel between his fingers.

Miss DeVille finished her piece and rose gracefully from the piano. Aaron Niles rewarded her with a "Bravo" and turned his eyes away from her delicate porcelain doll of a face and figure and back to Ramona's dusky rose cheeks and red lips—which she had obviously chaffed with her teeth while he looked away. Yes, Ramona Viator seemed like a sturdy young woman who would not break if touched, who would not die giving birth to a son.

Aaron Niles stood and placed his cup of now-tepid tea on the marble-topped table.

"This visit has been a great pleasure, I assure you, but I must be on my way. Mother Leontine, a word with you in private before I go if you could spare me the time."

Mother Leontine inclined her head regally and led the way across the hall to the room where she conducted the business of the academy. She took her seat behind a vast desk of dark wood and waited for Mr. Niles to begin.

He cleared his throat, which seemed to have closed up on him. "Ah—Holy Mother."

"Mother Leontine," she corrected gently.

"Yes, indeed. Words fail me at the moment. How to put this—I am a lonely man, an American among Frenchmen who turn their backs on me for no cause at all."

"Is that so, Mr. Niles?"

His ruddy face turned an even deeper color. "Not that I'm free of vices, but I don't believe in the mixing of the races. Why these Frenchies would mount a sow if they had nothing else handy. Excuse me. That was crudely put. What I meant to say is that I am in want of the comfort of a wife. None of my neighbors are likely to offer up their daughters, me not being of the Catholic faith and all. What would it take to make Miss Viator my bride?"

Mother Leontine steepled her fingertips and closed her eyes briefly as if she were taking a moment to pray. Then, she pinned Aaron Niles with a clear, gray stare and stopped his pacing about the room instantly.

"Her father's consent to a courtship, Miss Viator's acceptance of a proposal in due time, instruction in and conversion to Catholicism, and a promise to rear any children of this match in the Faith."

"Is that all? Then, you've got me. When can we start?"

"Miss Viator is to remain with us for the coming year and will complete her education next May. Until that time, you are of course welcome to continue your Saturday visits. Since we lack a priest, I will gladly instruct you in the doctrine of the church. But first, you must obtain the permission of Senor Viator in

Opelousas to court his daughter. I might add that a wife should be chosen for more than—comfort—though that is certainly one of her duties. By next May, Ramona Viator will be a woman highly capable of meeting the demands placed upon a plantation mistress. She will be a paragon of virtue and much sought after as a wife. I might also add that conversion should be a matter of faith rather than need."

Aaron Niles' auburn eyebrows shot up and his whiskey-colored eyes lit. "Exactly why I want to play my hand now. As for the Faith, the infidels spread theirs by the sword. It seems to me the Papists spread theirs by marriage. I'm willing to convert. I will sweeten the pot with two riding horses for the young ladies you tutor, a mule for your boy, Plato, and a genuine brick stable to put them in if you give me the jump on anyone else."

"First, obtain Senor Viator's consent."

"I'll be on my way to Opelousas come Monday. I'll get that consent in writing."

"That would be wise. Until next Saturday, Mr. Niles." Mother Leontine dismissed him like a naughty schoolboy.

Leaving the office, Niles nearly collided with the old granny who was taking the tea tray back to the long room serving as the refectory across the rear of the house. Mother Leontine watched him go with some amusement. She knew Aaron Niles would do all he said, just as she knew Mrs. Plato would give the remaining ginger cookies to her grandchildren who were lurking outside the door of the dining room.

God had given the academy a wonderful cook, and now two horses, a mule, a brick stable, an ardent suitor for the spirited Ramona, and a solution to the problem of Marguerite Courville possibly backsliding into her old ways. The wonders of this blessed place never ceased.

Through the office window, she watched Aaron Niles mount his big red horse and pelt down the dirt path to the road. A carriage turned into the drive. He pulled up to tip his hat to the occupant inside, but Marguerite Courville turned her head away.

Aaron continued on, wondering how he could tolerate an entire year of weak tea and religious instruction unless both were fortified with a swig of Kentucky whiskey afterwards. Snubbed by the French woman, he marveled he had ever found Marguerite Courville so attractive. Compared to the fresh young buds of womanhood in the parlor, she'd looked old and worn as she ignored him, a woman of forty to his twenty-eight. He would have inquired about her health because she'd once meant something to him, but if this was the way Maggie wanted to handle the situation now, so be it. He had a potential father-in-law to approach. Damn, if only he had thought to look for a wife in Opelousas before the nuns got hold of Ramona Viator.

Chapter Three

Mount Carmel Academy, 1823

Ramona Viator stood in the small bedroom of the farmhouse she had occupied for the past year. On her narrow cot, her wedding dress lay with its skirt spread like wings to give her freedom. The Sisters and Cecile, all better with a needle than she, had worked on the gown for the past three months. She had picked the pattern and her father bought the golden silk fabric all the way from Paris. True, the nuns tatted a lace tucker to raise the neckline, which they regarded as immodestly low, but they also created panels of the same lovely lace to overlay the shining material. Aaron would be stunned to see her out of her novice-like schoolgirl clothing at last. Beneath those baggy gowns, her figure, though still voluptuous, had refined with exercise and lighter meals, just as her manners became genteel and ladylike under constant correction.

The crystal beads of the rosary her groom had given her along with a stunning ruby and gold ring when she accepted his proposal hung on the prayer bench at the foot of the bed. She smiled, recalling the moment he had gone down on his knees to beg for her hand in marriage, promising to love, honor and cherish her forever, a nice little play for the Sisters and Cecile to overhear as they'd hovered by the parlor door when

Aaron finally asked to speak to her alone.

None of the listeners knew of the use she'd made of his other gift, the quick-footed sorrel mare with the white star on her forehead. Perhaps Cecile suspected, but for all her superiority, she hadn't told. When the sturdy brick stable with its wonderful arched entries and wide box stalls was completed, Aaron arrived leading the mare, a paunchy gelding and a big, red mule, all, he boasted, sired by his own stallion. The gelding, a disappointment on the racetrack, had lost his balls because of it. The mare, however, could very nearly keep pace with her sire, and the mule was strong if stubborn.

Mother Leontine had assured Mr. Niles that the details of their breeding were unnecessary to convey and accepted the gifts graciously. In anticipation of the arrival of the animals, she hired a Spanish riding master to instruct the girls and oversee this healthy form of exercise. Senor Rodrigo Cortez came with glowing references from a family with four sons living in Nachitoches. Old Plato and the riding master would accompany the young ladies on any excursions outside of the practice ring the servant had cobbled together near the new barn. Why, that marvel of a man, Plato, with the help of some of Aaron Niles' field hands, had already cleared a riding path crossing several of the small hills from the stable down to the Spanish Trail and lined it with sapling live oaks to provide shade as they grew.

Cecile hated everything about horses, their huge bodies, their big yellow teeth, their stink, but she would have done anything to please the dapper riding master, Rodrigo Cortez. Ramona recalled their first lesson in the ring with Cecile half on, half off her sidesaddle as the fat gelding shuffled around the oval. When Senor Cortez commanded a trot, accenting his words with the slightest flick of a whip on the flanks of Cecile's horse to get him moving, she landed in the dust. As Rodrigo offered her a hand up and tossed Cecile back into the saddle with his cupped hands, he'd looked into her cornflower blue eyes and remarked she would need many, many long lessons. Senorita Viator, however, was most accomplished and had his consent to take her exercise outside the ring with the Sisters' permission and the under the chaperonage of Old Plato on his mule.

Brutus, the big red mule, was as mulish as the animals came, which Aaron Niles knew most certainly. While Plato flailed and kicked on his back, Brutus would pause to graze at every clover patch along the way. As Ramona rode over the next small hill, she'd hear Plato calling, "You wait up now, Missy Ramona, you wait up." Down near the Spanish Trail, Aaron Niles passed by every day about that time.

Despite the old adage about not buying a cow when the milk was free, Ramona knew, as a merchant's daughter, a small sampling of the goods often sweetened a sale. On their first chance meeting, Ramona practiced flirting without the fan the nuns had confiscated. As Cecile had shown her, she peered up at Mr. Niles from under her downward cast dark lashes and turned her head modestly away when he clasped her hand and kissed the top of her kid riding glove.

On following meetings, he stripped the glove back and kissed the tender flesh of her palms. Next, came the light kisses on her cheek, then ardent embraces leaving her lips swollen and her breasts throbbing. By the time Aaron got around to unbuttoning her riding jacket and placing a shaking hand over her pounding heart which happened to be covered by her plump breasts, Christmas had arrived. Ramona, never having dismounted from her high horse, went home to preside over her father's holiday table.

Senor Viator was most impressed by his daughter's improved demeanor, manners, and the progress of her courtship by a man of substantial holdings. She had Aaron Niles well and truly hooked. Upon Ramona's return to the Academy and after the completion of an excellent sugar cane harvest and boiling, Mr. Niles presented Ramona with the ring and the rosary.

As for Cecile, she never improved her riding very much and often returned from her long lessons with dust on the back of her habit and throbbing thighs. Still, she waxed eloquent about Master Cortez's skill, his dashing figure in skin-tight pantaloons and his eyes— like the wine dark sea with moonlight upon it. To Ramona, Rodrigo Cortez seemed like all the other swarthy lay-abouts wearing heavy spurs and outlandish clothing who frequented her father's store. While impressive when controlling a mount with his big shoulders and muscular arms, the riding master stood short and somewhat bandy-legged on the ground, not tall both standing and astride like Aaron Niles.

As she'd ripened early, Ramona had developed very quickly a stinging slap with a fan across knuckles of any gropers who got in her way. Her father marveled over the number of fans she had broken in the year before the nuns took her away. When Mother Leontine stripped her of this weapon, she'd felt most defenseless, but soon learned in their company she had no need of it. Even her ardent Aaron had not gone so far he could not meet Mother Leontine's eyes at tea.

Ramona smiled into the large standing mirror Plato and his grandchildren had hauled up to the tiny room for use on her wedding day. No more arranging her hair in the speckled square of glass the nuns allowed for tidiness. She always parted her locks in the center and allowed a few thick waves to frame her face before she pulled the rest of its mass into a bundle at her nape. After being informed that no maids were available to dress her fine blonde hair into ringlets, Cecile cut a wispy fringe around her face with her sewing scissors and settled on a braided style requiring only a little assistance from Ramona to achieve. For all her flighty ways, Cecile could contrive with the best of them.

Today, Cecile would wear a high-waisted pale blue gown edged in ecru lace, and a necklace of enameled forget-me-nots from the trunks the nuns had locked away upon her arrival. She'd greeted the matching bonnet taken from its box like a lost friend. Along with her slow progress in riding, Cecile cared nothing for the academics that Ramona found so stimulating, but her haughtiness decreased.

"Oooh-la-la, but it is difficult to be superior when one is dressed hardly better than the servants," she often told Ramona. Recently, Cecile had begun praying in the new chapel without being escorted by the nuns, a startling improvement.

Ramona bid farewell to the narrow cot, the small armoire now empty of clothes, the plain bowl and pitcher set on the stand under the mirror square. She took a moment to kneel on the prayer bench and ask

God and the Virgin Mary and the Magdalene, figuring she'd need the help of all three, to bless her union with Aaron Niles, to make it fruitful, and to give her the skills to keep her husband faithful. That done, she called for Cecile and the maid the DeVille family had brought along to help the girls with their dresses.

Raising her arms above her head, Ramona felt the gown settle over her like the silken brush of angels' wings. It floated past her undergarments, corset, and petticoats and settled just at the top of her white kid slippers. The maid nimbly fastened the tiny buttons up the back and pulled the ribbon threaded through the lace panels to tighten the dress under the bust before tying it in a becoming back bow. The skirt skimmed Ramona's waist and hips and belled out gracefully, a gorgeous full-blown tulip in form. The bride smiled at herself in the cheval glass as the maid secured the mantilla with mother-of-pearl combs and tucked pure white gardenias into her dark hair.

How glad she was that fashions were returning to a style more flattering to a womanly form than the straight sacks becoming only to young girls with wispy figures like Cecile had she not gained weight at the Academy despite the healthy exercise and long walks to the chapel. Ramona's lone bridesmaid looked stuffed into last year's gown and about to burst out the top of it. Cecile handed Ramona her mother's missal and another white gardenia entwined with the crystal rosary. They formed a small procession with Cecile in front and the maid coming behind to make sure the wedding dress did not snag on the rough wood of the staircase.

At the base of the stairs, Sr. Francine, her blue eyes wide with joy, waited. "The Lady Mother wishes to speak with you, dear child, before you go to the chapel."

In the office, Mother Leontine, a slight smile upon her face, waited behind her desk. "Our first student— my, how you have grown in grace and knowledge this past year, Ramona."

"Thank you, Lady Mother." Ramona kept her eyes on her shoe tips.

"Any man, some better than Aaron Niles, would want you for his bride. Are you quite sure wedding Mr. Niles is your desire, Ramona? Now is the time to speak. Your commitment is for a lifetime."

"I am sure God has ordained this union, Lady Mother. I have felt that way from the first time I laid eyes on Mr. Niles."

"I will say only this—Father Cyprien has doubts that Aaron Niles has made a true conversion." Mother Leontine nodded toward the new priest who had been sent out to hear their confessions and perform the ceremony.

He paced in agitation behind Mother Leontine's desk. Younger than Niles himself, his face blazing red, Fr. Cyprien exclaimed, "I have told the man again and again he need only confess to impure thoughts about his fiancée, not describe them in detail. God forgive me!" The priest sealed his lips with his hands. "But, he taunts me, good Mother."

"Mr. Niles has some rough edges, Mother Leontine, but you have taught me that with time and prayer, I can hone them down. I believe we are well-matched," Ramona said quickly. Be damned if she would be deprived of a lusty groom because of the objections of this skinny-legged little priest.

"So I have felt since your first meeting. Now then, Madame DeVille is waiting in the carriage. She has offered to answer any questions you might have about your marital duties since your own dear mother has departed this life."

"Thank you, but I have no questions." Ramona felt a blush bloom on her cheeks. Its source seemed to come from deep in her loins. As a curious and unsupervised child, she had seen drunken men taking a piss behind her father's store, witnessed the stud her father kept mount mares brought in for breeding and seen her own maid rolling in the hay with the servant who drove their carriage. The maid appeared to enjoy the act of procreation far more than the mares. Ramona had high hopes for her wedding night.

"Very well then, go along. Sr. Francine and I shall walk to the holy place on this most glorious of days to witness the wedding of our first student."

****

The chapel still smelled of new wood, varnish and paint. Just installed, the small rose window given in honor of Madame Courville's salvation shone above the altar and cast its jewels of light on the bride's bowed head, across the mantilla and the combs of mother-of-pearl. While the rest of the chapel had only clear glass windows, God blessed this bride with a day so sunny light lanced across the central aisle as the newly married couple made their exit to the flower-bedecked carriage that would take the bridal pair to a wedding feast being set out on the vast lawn of the Niles plantation. With a prompting from Cecile to open her parasol, Ramona and her groom began their journey west away from the Academy and the Courville house beyond it.

Fr. Cyprien rode with Ramona's father and would accompany him back to Opelousas. The nuns joined the entourage of the DeVille family members who made up the majority of witnesses to the sacred ceremony. One of Cecile's brothers stood up with Aaron Niles since he had no family of his own in attendance. His passel of sisters back in Kentucky weren't willing to endure the dangers of the journey on the Natchez Trace and feared travel by water.

Doesn't matter who comes, thought Aaron Niles, though only one of his French neighbors, the Courvilles, had declined to attend the nuptial feast. After all, Senor Viator purchased their sugar, cotton, and yams, and would expect their attendance at the wedding of his only child—even if she'd had the bad taste to marry an American. Business was business. As their carriage approached the old Frenchman's house sitting on a rise above a bend in the muddy bayou, Niles could tell by the mass of horses, carriages, wagons and buggies strung out in the shade of the oaks lining the road that the Arnouds, Guidrys, Moutons, Arceneauxs and Breauxs had come out in force to wine, dine and dance.

He looked at the house with dissatisfaction, noting the crumbling brick foundation, timbered upper story, the narrow surrounding galleries and staircase exposed to the elements. Leaning toward Ramona, he pledged, "I will build a finer house in the years to come, a temple for my love."

He took advantage of his bride's open parasol to screen them for a moment and pressed a kiss into the nape of her neck where another gardenia gave off a powerful heady scent reminding him of the pleasures of the bed. With luck, the heat of the day, already scorching before noon, would drive off the guests well before dusk.

His house might have been old-fashioned, but the feast Aaron Niles saw lain out before him did not lack. Boards set on sawhorses and covered with fine linens bent under the weight of roasted turkeys, chickens, ducks, and two large, brown sugar-glazed hams. The last of the winter yams had been roasted and whipped and served up with butter and honey or baked into spicy pies. Oysters shipped express in briny barrels from the bay were being shucked and laid out on trays. He'd heard rumors about the powers of the oyster and planned to put away a dozen or more. Beside the pies sat a variety of gateaux, some brought by his neighbors, each cake baked to outdo the others. A strong bourbon punch, flavored wines, and lemonade waited to wash the food down. His cook truly was worth every penny he'd paid for her.

The best Negro musicians Niles had been able to rent struck up a tune as the bridal party arrived, but Fr. Cyprien silenced them and held up a hand to bless the newlyweds and the feast before them. After that, the guests bellied up to the tables and sought a place in the shade to eat.

When the youths began to burn off their heavy meals with dancing, and the over-imbibers slid slowly under the tables or fell asleep beneath the oaks, the nuns prepared to depart after giving the bride and groom a most sincere blessing for their happiness. The DeVille's driver would take them back to the Academy and return for the family.

"A moment, Mother Leontine, I wish to make a pledge to your school—well, to the chapel. I figure on replacing those plain glass windows you got with colored ones showing the Stations of the Cross, the first two in honor of Ramona and me for our wedding and one after that for each child born to us," Aaron Niles told the Sisters.

"You do know there are fourteen Stations of the Cross, Mr. Niles? That is a very ambitious and expensive undertaking."

"Yes, ma'am, I mean Mother, much more costly than a single rose window. I did study my catechism and surely know how many stations there are and what they mean. I figure today I gave up my freedom and Ramona has taken up the burden of me, you might say. Two down, twelve to go," he answered, beaming at his bride.

"I will pray for you both," Mother Leontine replied and took her leave.

Sometime later, many of the male guests, shouting coarse jokes, were poured into their conveyances by disapproving wives and helpful servants. Courting couples, flushed from the obscuring shade of the oaks by their mothers, got sent on their way. Aaron Niles tucked a spare bottle of wine into the crook of the tipsy Fr. Cyprien's arm and wished him sweet dreams and a bon voyage as he heaved the priest into Senor Viator's carriage. His new father-in-law shook Aaron's hand and warned him to be good to his daughter.

"I will be more than good, I assure you, sir," Niles answered with a mighty grin and a gesture to the coachman to be on his way.

Ramona had kissed her father good-bye and gone

in to prepare for the night ahead even though the sun hadn't yet sunk below the horizon. Aaron Niles had every intention of turning in early this evening.

****

In the Master's bedroom, Ramona fidgeted impatiently as a maid helped her out of her gown, untied her petticoats, and unlaced her corset. As she sat to have her thick, dark hair brushed out into becoming waves, she eyed the huge bed behind her in the mirror. The curtains and mosquito netting were drawn back, the fresh embroidered linens turned down on both sides. She recognized her own clumsy handiwork of satin-stitched yellow roses—like the ones the nuns grew on a trellis from Madame Courville's cuttings—adorning the covers of the plump feather pillows. She'd grumbled and sworn under her breath as she'd labored over the dainty items the Sisters insisted she bring to her marriage. How kind of Aaron to pretend the contents of her hope chest were as fine as anything he could buy.

The maid opened that very chest sitting at the foot of the bed and took out the nightgown the nuns had made for their first student. Of fine lawn, the neckline edged in their handmade lace, the nightdress would cover her to the collarbone and the long, full sleeves to the wrist. A row of tiny pearl buttons down the bodice provided a challenge to any groom, especially one with hands as big as her husband's. She knew Aaron's hasty temperament and would hate to see the nightdress ruined.

The room was overly warm even with the drapes pulled to keep out the late afternoon sun. Ramona dismissed the maid who held the gown in front of her waiting for the bride to drop the rest of her undergarments.

"I will do this myself. Tell Mr. Niles I shall be ready to receive him in a moment or two."

Grinning broadly, the dark-hued maid nodded. The two of them had been listening to the impatient groom pacing the gallery for the last fifteen minutes.

"I'm thinkin' he don't need no invitation, Missus, but I'll tell him."

Ramona took the minutes before Aaron burst in to light two candles, drop her remaining covering, dash up the bed steps and pull the top sheet up to her chin. She saw he'd taken advantage of the short delay to retire to his dressing room and fling on his own nightshirt, dressing gown and soft slippers so there would be no need to fumble with his boots and buttons.

As her husband approached the high bedstead, Ramona sat up, baring herself to him. His eyes, the light caramel color of fine Kentucky bourbon, were strangely lit and his mouth hung open as he stared at her naked bosom. The bride, seeing his pole-axed look, covered her chest with her arms but did not take her eyes off of his.

"I am not afraid to be naked before you, Aaron." She revealed herself to him again.

"Nor should you be, my dear." By damn, only the whores of New Orleans possessed such boldness. Her breasts were so plump, so enticingly tipped with nipples erect and rosy with expectation. He could feel his saliva pooling and snapped his jaws shut before it could dribble down his chin. The nuns hadn't ruined his Ramona for bed sports after all.

The eager groom flung his dressing gown over the hope chest and kicked off his slippers, but greatly aware of the tenting of his nightshirt, stopped short of shucking that, too. He knew his organ could be downright scary to small women and wasn't about to make his bride shy away now. Shy! She held out her arms to him, her full breasts squeezed between them. He vaulted on to the springy moss mattress and tossed off his shirt as soon as he lay beneath the covers.

Those breasts, cupping them in his big hands, he suckled them like a baby overdue for nursing. Ramona made small, breathy noises, and he transferred his lips to hers. Since her mouth was already open, he thrust in an eager tongue, a technique he had learned from Marguerite. If there was one thing the French excelled at, that was the art of lovemaking. While Ramona seemed a little startled at first, she caught on to the tongue play before he had even gotten a good start. What could be better than a bride with the hot blood of the Spanish and the innate sensuality of the French? To think, he'd almost bound himself to a pallid Kentucky gal before coming south to seek his fortune.

All the while, Ramona's hands worked their way down his back and across his thighs. Aaron jumped when she took his nether parts in her palms and began to stroke. "Like iron encased in velvet," she murmured.

"If you are ready, my dear, I most surely am. If not, you'd better let loose of what you're holdin'."

"Oh, I am ready, dearest Aaron." She spread herself back on the pillows and beneath the sheet opened her legs.

He couldn't hold himself and took her with one long thrust. She gasped. He froze there, up to the hilt in the woman he adored more by the minute.

"Did I hurt you? I thought it was best over with

quickly."

"Not pain, just discomfort and amazement that we fit." Ramona laughed softly. "Although they didn't say as much, the nuns were quite afraid I had ruined by maidenhead by riding astride as a girl. They stressed the use of the sidesaddle to preserve virginal delicacy. Is this all there is to it, then?"

"Hardly, my dear. Let me teach you the rest."

The mattress sank beneath his weight, and the bedposts beat rhythmically against the wall of their chamber. Nearby servants grinned, put aside their labors, and went to feast on the leftovers. Master would be busy all night long.

While Aaron, breathing hard like a stallion that had run a long course, slept beside her, Ramona Viator Niles smiled into the darkness. An exhilarating beginning to their marriage, she thought.

Cecile had shared Mrs. DeVille's knowledge of deflowering one night when her fellow student crept into Ramona's room to chat, indicating that losing one's maidenhead came accompanied by excruciating pain. Cecile swore her mother had lied in order to keep her chaste. Ramona promised to let her know the truth, but Cecile gave one of her cat-in-the-cream smiles and told her not to bother.

Of course, the way the young men were drawn to Cecile's now full-blown blonde beauty at the wedding feast, her friend would surely be a bride herself by autumn.

When she next saw Cecile, who had gone home with her own family, she would tell her the act was not unlike riding free and fast over an open field and taking a great jump at the end of it. No, Cecile hated horses and riding. She'd have to think of a better way to explain the wild and dizzy sensation to her friend. Hmmm, perhaps this bride would try riding upon her husband in the morning.

Chapter Four

"What a calamity! If the DeVilles take this matter up with the Mother House, we are sure to lose the funds for the building of our convent, the new dormitory and classrooms. They placed Cecile in our care to teach her humility and piety. Now she has run off with the riding master." Sr. Francine wrung her hands over the letter spread out on Mother Leontine's desk.

"Perhaps, we were too proud of our accomplishments and this is the Lord God's own way of humbling us. I accept His will. We shall make things right with the DeVilles," the always-unruffled Mother Leontine replied.

"How is that possible? When the DeVille boys caught up with the couple, they'd already been married by a roving Methodist preacher in New Town. When they asked Rodrigo if he'd rather be shot or hung, Cecile pled her belly. Married by a Methodist and carrying a child. Oh, Mother, how could I have been so lax! I knew Cecile hated her riding lessons and often lingered in the barn making excuses to shorten her time in the ring. Afterwards, she would stay watching Senor Cortez groom the horses. I told her more than once to move along and get washed for dinner. She was always so grimy and disheveled—from falling off her mount, I thought."

"Be still, Sr. Francine. The girl was vain and had

no other man about to exercise her flirting ways. No wonder Senor Cortez took advantage to move up in the world. Still, I bear the blame for not seeing her character more clearly—or his for that matter—for not keeping a better watch, for allowing Ramona to ride outside the ring taking Plato with her. I spent my worry and prayers on the wild child and Aaron Niles, never thinking Cecile so sly as to do such a thing right under our noses."

"Once her condition became known, they beat Rodrigo and left the couple by the side of the road, wholly disowned by the DeVilles."

"Yes, yes, it is all in the letter. We must find Cecile and Rodrigo at once. We will see they are properly married in the church and find employment for Rodrigo and a decent home for the family. We must send Plato to search on the gelding. I will write him a pass."

Plato stood just outside the cookhouse splitting logs for the fire. With his ropey old muscles clenching, he raised the maul and hit the wedge to sunder a piece of dry pecan. Kindling flew. His grandchildren gathered it up and took the wood to their granny who was starting the noon meal. At Sr. Francine's summons, he wiped his face and hands with a bandanna, ran his shoes over the boot scraper, and followed her to the house. Mother Leontine had the pass ready and explained his mission.

"No need to send me off, Lady Mother. I heared dey at Missy Ramona's place when one of her boys come over to bring us some extra beans from deir garden. Mastah Niles ain't too happy about de upset to his honeymoon days. Dere be string beans with ham and nice fluffy biscuits for dinner, my woman says."

"The Lord does provide. You may go, Plato."

"So, our Ramona has taken them in, God be praised," Sr. Francine said.

"She is a big-hearted girl for all her faults and will stand by her friend, no doubt. I shall visit them at once. Have Plato hitch the gelding to the buggy. We will see what can be arranged."

****

The arrangement reached over a table of refreshments offered in Mrs. Niles' upstairs parlor provided the use of an empty overseer's house a mile out on the flatlands to the west and employment for Rodrigo supervising the horse and cattle operation which Aaron Niles previously had seen to himself having more taste for that than for farming.

Mr. Niles was none too pleased. "Do you know cattle?" he quizzed the Spaniard.

"I know cattle. Also the breeding of horses," asserted Rodrigo, his proud beak of a Spanish nose now so sadly bent he whistled when he breathed. He shook Cecile loose from the arm where she clung. The errant couple had not been invited to sit and partake of the sweets and coffee by the master of the house when summoned from the guest bedroom.

Mother Leontine frowned at Rodrigo's crude reference to breeding, but only Cecile colored a bit. Ramona and Aaron Niles took no notice.

"I will contact Fr. Cyprien and ask he suspend the reading of the banns and come to marry you properly as soon as possible. A private ceremony in our chapel would be best. Now that we have settled the matter of lodging and employment, I will write your parents and attempt to restore you to their good graces, my child."

Aaron Niles still looked unhappy. "I have some very valuable stock. If any goes missing…"

"What is more valuable than having extra time to spend together, my love, and my having a dear friend nearby to visit?" Ramona asked, laying her hand over her husband's table-tapping fingers.

His hand gripped hers at once. "Nothing, dear wife, but I would prefer Mrs. Cortez visit here."

"But of course, dear heart." Ramona gave him a brilliant smile telling him he had no need to worry about her seeking out company alone as he'd confessed one night that Marguerite Courville had done.

"Have a seat then, Cortez, Cecile."

Rodrigo accepted a cup of coffee poured, sugared, and creamed by Ramona's hand and raised it carefully with bruised arms to his split lips. Cecile waved the aroma away with a small, white hand. "I cannot tolerate the brew right now."

"A pot of tea for Mrs. Cortez," Ramona called to a servant standing quietly in a corner of the room.

The tea came and Cecile heaped her plate with small cakes and pecan tarts under the disapproving eyes of Mother Leontine.

"Forgive me, but I seem to be ravenous all the time."

All eyes in the group dropped to the small bulge showing beneath her high bodice and loosened stays as she sat, but no one said a word. All for the best until Fr. Cyprien could be summoned.

****

Some weeks later, Mother Leontine consulted again with Sr. Francine. "See here, Madame DeVille writes she is grateful for the assistance we have given her daughter and is joyous that Cecile has been married in the church. She believes her husband will eventually be reconciled with his daughter. Until then, she will send whatever she can spare from her household accounts for the couple through us. Her husband will think they are donations to our cause—which is unharmed. The DeVilles have given out that Cecile met her match in Opelousas and chose to marry quietly here in our chapel and take up residence nearby. Our plans go forward, Sr. Francine, once more."

****

Shortly before the celebration of Christ's birth and just after the first heavy frost browned the grass and withered the gardens, Cecile Cortez was brought to childbed and delivered of a daughter having the father's dark hair and olive skin tones, but possessing eyes of so bright a blue, everyone who saw little Leona Francine thought they would certainly stay that color. When the new mother grew feverish after the hard birth, Ramona Niles brought along a wet nurse with ample milk for two babies from the quarters of Frenchman's Bend Plantation as they now called the place on the rise above the turn in the river.

Ramona Niles sat at her friend's bedside, wrung out and placed a cool cloth on Cecile's brow. Cecile turned her head and smiled weakly. "You are so good to me. I wish my mother would come. Has Rodrigo sent for her? I asked for Sr. Francine when the pains began, but he said he'd had enough of meddling nuns and brought the old granny midwife who lives down the road."

"He should have borrowed our midwife. Louisa is very skilled and rarely loses a child or a mother. I,

46

myself, make sure the bedding is clean and the water hot for washing before each birth as Sr. Francine taught us."

Ramona tried to ignore the condition of the sheets her friend lay upon. While not actually dirty, clearly they had not been fresh before the birth and not changed afterwards as she could tell from the damp, stained places.

"Ah, yes. Cleanliness is next to Godliness, dear, strict Sr. Francine. She still blames herself for my condition, but there is one thing I have learned. If a person is bent on sinning, they will find a way to sin. Oh, and I've learned a second thing—losing one's maidenhead is not excruciating, but giving birth is."

Ramona laughed at this slight jest. She smoothed her hands over her own distended belly. Her child was due in early March. Aaron had wasted little time getting started on the dozen he desired. Ramona shivered, thinking of the dangers and pangs of childbirth. Her own mother had died giving birth to a stillborn child. Her father, ever since he learned he would be a grandfather in the spring, kept assuring his daughter that she took after the Viators whose offspring were numerous and vigorous, a delicate sort of way to silence her fears.

"Here, drink this water. It will help with the fever. I've sent a rider on a swift horse to Chapelle. Your mother will come."

"No, Papa will prevent her. Ramona, you will be godmother to Leona Francine. Promise me."

"I promised months ago. I will care for her and love her like my own."

"That's good, then." Cecile pushed back curls

sweat had plastered to her forehead. "I must look a fright. No wonder Rodrigo stays away, but then, he has shown little interest in me since I became as big as one of his cows. I suspect Aaron feels the same."

"Aaron? Nothing deters Aaron when he wants something, no matter what." Ramona shrugged. "Get well, return to beauty, and Rodrigo will be giving you more attention than you desire. I must go now and see to some business. Rest, dear one."

Ramona stroked Cecile's damp hair until she slept. The young Mrs. Niles wondered if she would have run off with Aaron if he had been merely a riding master. No, she was a merchant's daughter and knew her own worth. She whispered a prayer of thanks to Mother Mary and the Magdalene for allowing her to feel a passion for a rich man—a man she would have eloped with if her father had tried to prevent their marriage.

Giving Cecile's hand a gentle pat, Ramona went out to look for the female half of the pair of slaves she had given to Cortez as a wedding gift. She found the young woman sitting with her feet up in the warmth of the cook shed and chatting with the wet nurse who had Leona Francine suckling at one breast and her own black baby at the other. By the looks of the servant's belly, she was as far along as Ramona herself.

"Molly, I want you to change the bed linens immediately."

Molly lumbered to her feet. "If you says so, Missus, but I can't see why. She still bleedin' and will mess up a clean set. Dat ole midwife weren't too careful with her oilcloths and clumps of moss, neither. She done ruined de sheets I put on jus' last week."

The woman placed a hand to the small of her back

and sighed. Standing, she looked as if she might be expecting twins. Ramona relented.

"If you need more help, have Narcisse come to the big house and ask. This is his child? We will have Fr. Cyprien marry you on his next visit."

"Oh, it Narcisse child, all right, but we done jumped de broom some time back. No need for de priest. De ole granny what come to deliver de Missus say I might be havin' two."

"You shall be properly married in the Faith and your children will be baptized."

"If you wants it so. I be gettin' dose sheets now." Molly trudged off, shaking her red-kerchiefed head over the ways of white folks.

Ramona took a deep breath, as deep as her belly would allow. Always treat those in your care kindly and decently, Mother Leontine had drilled into her head. Cecile had been quite imperious with Mrs. Plato when she'd first arrived at the Academy. That behavior soon stopped when Sr. Francine informed the young Miss that she had to keep her own room tidy, fix her hair by herself, and do other light chores when not busy with studies, piano practice, riding lessons, sewing, or prayer. By such means, one learned humility. Cecile had managed to spend most of her spare time practicing the piano, doing embroidery—or lingering in the stables. Despite the nuns' teachings, she'd been lax as a wife.

Ramona noted the dust on the furnishings and small cobwebs in the corners when she passed through the house. In her condition, Aaron didn't want her to lift a finger and, heaven knew, she had only to raise a hand to summon help of any kind. Spiritually, she felt herself becoming as lax as Cecile was about keeping house. Ramona found a feather duster in the small pantry and began to set the cottage to rights. Tomorrow, she would bring scented candles and a dry potpourri made from rose petals and gardenia blossoms since the frost had killed all the fresh buds in her garden. The smell coming from the sick room was most unpleasant like the stench of meat gone bad.

Once back at Frenchman's Bend, Ramona summoned the plantation's midwife, a dark chocolate-colored woman with arms big and strong enough to birth calves, let alone humans. She always wore a clean white bib apron over her dress and a bleached linen kerchief covering her iron-gray hair. Pleased to be consulted, Louisa nodded gravely. "Dat sound like childbed fever to me. Strong ones fight it off. Weak ones can't. You don't see none of my women catchin' it. Dat ole granny, she ain't clean. No, ma'am, she ain't—but she come cheap. If I was you, I send for de doctor and de priest."

Ramona did just that along with posting another imploring message to Madame DeVille in Chapelle.

The following day, the stench in the room grew worse. Ramona ordered the wet nurse to care for the baby in the other bedroom and reached out to touch her friend's forehead. Cecile did not respond to that gentle touch. Her skin burned with fever and the pulse in her neck throbbed with the rapidity of butterfly wings. Ramona pulled back the blankets piled on to produce a sweat. A sickening, putrid discharge soaked the cotton batting beneath Cecile's hips. As she and Louisa stripped off the sick woman's sodden nightdress, Ramona's eyes widened at the look of her friend's pale, distended belly and puffy, leaking breasts. Louisa took her aside.

"You shouldn't be seeing dis, Missus. Not a first-timer like you. Make you scared and ain't good luck. Why don't you go on out and get dat lazy Molly to make us all a big pot of coffee, now?"

"I take after the Viators, Louisa. We are strong and stout-hearted, do not abandon our friends and will give succor even to our enemies."

"If you say so, Missus."

"I do. But if you would remove the batting, I will fetch a fresh gown from the armoire." Ramona pinched her nostrils shut, found the gown, laid it over a chair, and filled the china basin with tepid water. "I believe we should sponge her first."

With Louisa doing the heavy lifting, they cleaned Cecile's failing body and changed her sheets again. They put water on a clean rag and coaxed their patient to suck, kept cool cloths on her head and dribbled bitter quinine water down her throat as best they could. Reluctantly, Ramona cut Cecile's long, fair hair in hopes that this, too, would help break the fever, and laid it aside for remembrances.

The doctor, persuaded to come after seeing to his own patients by the promise of a goodly fee, arrived from Opelousas in the early evening and expressed his regrets. "Your gal is right, a puerperal fever. She won't last the night, I fear. My condolences. Make her comfortable as you have been doing."

Ramona wept, then pulled her sturdy, round body up straight. "Get Narcisse and tell him to find Senor Cortez at once," she ordered Molly

"Oh, dey both gone, Missus," Molly said as she

poured coffee for the doctor and set down a sandwich for the man. "Done took some cattle into Opelousas to be sold off yesterday mornin'. Must have stayed de night."

"Would that be Rodrigo Cortez?" The doctor paused with the cold beef sandwich halfway to his mouth. "I saw him drowning his disappointment over not getting a son on the first try with the contents of a little brown jug. He sat out front of a tavern catering to his sort. Had I known this was his wife, I would have flung him into the buggy with me."

Ramona raised her dark eyebrows into an expression of doubt. The physician, portly and gray of hair, had eyebrows thick as caterpillars. By the look of his red nose, he was no stranger to the bottle either. She ought to have sent for Sr. Francine. She ought to have asked her husband for help in finding Rodrigo.

"Doctor, when you have finished your meal, would you please summon my husband at the big house on your way back to Opelousas?"

"I am accustomed to sitting out the night with the dying, Mrs. Niles."

"I am sure your services are needed much more in town by the living. Mr. Niles will see you are paid what is owed for your time."

Looking affronted, the doctor swallowed his last bite of beef and bread and banged the coffee cup on the cypress tabletop. "Very well, but I have traveled a long way and expected a bed for the night."

"You are welcome to stay over at Frenchman's Bend if you deliver my message."

Clearly feeling her hospitality lacking, the doctor rose, snatched up his bag and went to his buggy. They saw the last of him as his vehicle jolted away over the frozen ruts in the road.

In a remarkably short time, Ramona heard hoof beats coming toward the overseer's house. Aaron tied up his big, red stallion at the porch rail and bolted inside.

"How goes it with Cecile?"

"Not well. The doctor says she will not last the night. I wish to bring Sr. Francine here for another opinion. Rodrigo and Fr. Cyprien need to come at once and both are in Opelousas. Will you go for them?"

"I'll bring the two men if I have to tie their tails together and sling them across my saddle. I doubt if the nuns will see me if they have retired for the night, but I will send a messenger with a carriage. Ramona, dearest, should you be exposed to this infection in your delicate condition?"

Aaron Niles took a step back when he saw his little wife's expression, most likely learned from Mother Leontine. "Please take care, then. You are my life."

Her face softened. Ramona tugged on his lapels, brought his lips to hers and did something he knew she hadn't learned from nuns. "Go swiftly, my love."

Ramona returned to the sick room where the scented candles and potpourri failed to cover the stench. Her dying friend, unaware of her presence, called out once for her mother and once to the Blessed Virgin when Sr. Francine arrived. None of the witnesses were certain if Cecile mistook the nun for the Virgin Mary or if she saw something where her eyes fixed at the foot of the bed.

Sr. Francine shook her head in sorrow. "The result of a bad delivery, I fear. I cannot repair what has been done. Let us pray for the sake of her soul."

Saying the rosary helped turn the minutes into hours. The plainly furnished house had no clock and Ramona could only gauge the passing of time by the rising of the moon seen through the window. When that orb shone like a shining silver coin glimmering high overhead, the sound of riders barreling down the road came to her ears. She rushed to unlatch the door.

Fr. Cyprien, his skinny legs clad in long underwear showing where his cassock bunched up, rode behind Aaron Niles. Rodrigo Cortez, red-eyed and unshaven, kept pace beside them on one of Aaron's fine horses. Narcisse straggled after the group on a lesser mount. Niles pulled up in front of the house first and lifted Fr. Cyprien and the small case he carried by a strap to the ground. The priest made his way unsteadily inside while Cortez dismounted and clumped across the porch, not bothering to remove the heavy spurs he favored before entering his home. After all, he had no fine carpets to snag, his attitude said. Although Ramona could smell strong spirits on his breath as if he'd had aplenty, Rodrigo bent to unlock a small chest and handed Molly a dusty bottle of wine to uncork. The unhappy husband slumped into a chair at the table where he'd shared meals with his wife when she was well and not so huge and pathetic.

Requesting all the women to leave the bedchamber, Fr. Cyprien went about his holy work. Although Cecile could not answer his questions, he took her silence as assent and gave the last rights to assure the safety of her soul. Relieved, Ramona listened to the words through the cracks in the thin door. Coming from the bedchamber, the priest told Rodrigo in a subdued voice he could go and sit with his wife now. The Spaniard barely raised his head from the table.

Aaron Niles wrested the wine bottle from Rodrigo's hand and gave him a shove from his chair. "Are you deaf, man? Go sit with your wife."

The priest slipped into the chair vacated by Cortez, and Aaron poured him a cup of wine from the half empty bottle.

"Thank you, the ride has made me dry. The child survived the birth?"

"A beautiful little girl whom I have put to a wet nurse, Father," Ramona told him.

"Bring the child for baptism. Life can be treacherous for the very young and you live far from town."

Ramona went to the opposing bedroom and lifted the baby from her cradle without waking either the child or the wet nurse who snored on a cot. Fr. Cyprien opened his small box again and took out the cunningly cushioned vial of holy water from its place beside the sacred oil, the case also containing the host, a small chalice, and a measure of sanctified wine. He performed the rite of baptism at the mother's bedside, again assuming her assent and drawing grudging answers from the father. Aaron and Ramona Niles, he named as godparents and pledged them to see to the spiritual growth of Leona Francine. The baby cried as the water dripped on her forehead, a good sign that the devil was driven out. Her dying mother smiled at the sound and then went to a better place than this house where Cecile DeVille Cortez had learned humility at last.

Ramona took charge of the details of death by

arranging for the plantation carpenter to make a coffin. She and Louisa lined the box in white linen and placed the scented candles at the head and foot. They laid Cecile out in a pretty frock from happier days and covered her shorn head with a lacy cap. Ramona kept a lock of hair for herself and braided and coiled the rest into a box, a keepsake for tiny Leona.

They debated whether to haul the coffin to Opelousas to be buried in holy ground, but Sr. Francine offered a plot in a newly consecrated cemetery adjoining the Academy grounds. A place had been set aside and blessed for the simple burials of nuns and a separate area for seculars. After all, Old Plato and his woman had one foot in the grave already, but their reserved spaces were toward the back. Aaron had a simple square brick tomb erected above the ground in the first row. Cecile's coffin was sealed within it after a funeral Mass said in the chapel by Fr. Cyprien. Ramona ordered a marble plaque to be set in place once the bricks were plastered over and whitewashed.

Madame Deville arrived, supported by two of her sons the next day. She wept at the grave and cried over her grandbaby, then firmly handed the child back to the wet nurse. Her husband would not relent and referred to Leona Francine as being very nearly a bastard. The DeVille boys looked at Rodrigo Cortez with blood in their eyes. That night, their brother-in-law fled into Texas on one of Aaron Niles' best mares.

Aaron wanted to go after him and the DeVille boys were game, but Ramona held her husband in place with soft words and a gentle hand. "Please, Aaron, I want you near me from now until my travail begins. At the first pangs, you will send for Sr. Francine and Fr.

Cyprien, will you not?"

"Whatever you wish, dearest, but I'd put more faith in the skills of the nuns than I would in Fr. Cyprien. He ain't a bad little feller, but I doubt he's man enough to forgive my sins—and you don't have any."

"Untrue in both cases. Aaron, have you been listening to the Methodists?"

"Oh, those preachers had their shot at me back in Kentucky. I'll tell you one thing, though. If God sees fit to take you away from me in childbirth, I'll never set foot in a Roman church again."

"Then, I must be sure to live to a ripe age for the sake of your soul, Aaron Niles."

"I couldn't desire anything more, my love."

****

In early March of 1824 when all the south was aflowering, Ramona Niles gave birth with the greatest of ease to her own daughter. Sr. Francine and Louisa agreed that a youth free of corsets contributed to the success of the matter, just as they were sure that Madame DeVille's old-fashioned habit of corseting Cecile even in childhood had abetted her daughter's death, that and unsanitary midwifery. Aaron Niles bought out the old granny and sent her to live with a daughter in Franklin far from his wife and future children. The wise women commended him for it.

On a full-blown spring day six weeks later, Ramona and Aaron brought the first Niles daughter to be christened in the nuns' chapel overlooking the square foundations of what would become the red brick convent, classrooms, and dormitory of Mt. Carmel Academy, all arranged around a large circular drive. Good as his word, Aaron Niles set in place a third stained-glass window for the occasion. A brass plate mounted into the wall beneath it read, "Given in Celebration of the Birth of Esperanza Maria Niles, March 5, 1824, with Great Hope for the Future by her Parents."

INTERLUDE

Noreen Courville yawned and told her mom she was going to bed early.

"But it's only nine." Her mother immediately placed a hand on her youngest child's forehead to feel for a fever. "Are you sick? You do feel a little warm. Let me get you some aspirin."

"I'm fine, Mom, just tired. I stayed up late last night studying for tests, remember? I only need some rest."

Truthfully, she did feel flushed, but not from that kind of fever. The early dreams had ended. She now existed in that beautiful by-gone era in the form of Esperanza Niles, a lovely young woman with refined manners and the ability to sit a horse sidesaddle and race her red mare across the meadows to meet her love, so superior to her once pudgy, bookworm modern self. That made tonight special. Again, she would meet Rufus Courville and give him her heart.

Okay, so the past wasn't always so wonderful, so romantic. Women did die in childbirth. The descendants of slaves who had chopped cane and dug yams for Aaron Niles now went to Opelousas High. In the town of Rainbow, the Plato family obviously had grown out of some master-slave hanky-panky, maybe rape, maybe not. The violence of the Civil War loomed ahead. She knew her history. She could endure all that was to come for the sake of loving Rufe again.

In the safety of her room, Noreen put on her prettiest nightie and lay on top of her covers, a silly gesture she knew. She had never slept with Rufus Courville nor had she had sex with Rusty. Her father thought he'd driven Russ away. But they still met secretly exactly like Espy and Rufe. With a smile on her lips, she closed her eyes and went to meet her destiny.

Chapter Five

Rainbow, Louisiana, 1841

Rufus Courville first noticed the womanly and exquisite Esperanza Niles in church. Only four days home from abandoning his university education, Rufe figured being dragged to Mass by his mother was the least he could expect in the way of punishment. He stood aside politely to allow his mother to arrange her wide, black rustling skirts to enter a narrow row more suited to nuns' habits and school girl uniforms. She took her place beside Francois, his brother, and Francois' barren French wife. As Rufe waited, the prolific Niles family entered the chapel and began to fill the pews on the opposite side of aisle.

The March sun shone through twelve stained-glass windows showing all but two of the Stations of the Cross and turned the prematurely white hair of Aaron Niles a red fainter than his original auburn. His short, plump wife looked to be in the family way again. Rufe's father had said, "Those Niles, they breed fast as rats," often enough.

Having been gone seven years with few visits home, Rufe didn't know the names of the smallest of the brood who filed in after their mother. He recognized the second daughter, freckled Amalia, and the blue-eyed, black-haired orphan, Leona Cortez, who was around his age. The eldest son, Andrew Jackson Niles, glaring as he passed, seemed to be in fairly good health, fully recovered from the wound in his arm Rufe had given him in a duel fought after the horse races the last time he'd been allowed to visit home from boarding school.

Rufe didn't know the names of two more small daughters and another son of about five and newly breeched sometime during the intervening years. Missing was the sickly second son, Henry Clay, who had long ago succumbed to the mumps brought home and liberally spread by Rufe's brother, Francois, at the age of sixteen fresh from Jesuit school in New Orleans.

Struggling with a restive toddler in her arms, Esperanza Niles brought up the rear of the formation. The little boy squirmed so violently her prayer book went flying, hit Rufe Courville in the shin and dropped to the floor. He stooped, as any gentleman would, retrieved the missal and returned it to the young lady with a slight bow. Their eyes locked. The toddler, a boy still in skirts, escaped by sliding down the slope of her gown and headed toward the altar. Rufe reached out with one long arm, secured the child by his smock and asked, "Yours?"

"No. One of my many errant brothers, I fear. I am a senior student here at the Academy and not anyone's mother—though I hope to be one day. Thank you for capturing Billy for me."

Esperanza blushed, a charming pink glow spreading across her smooth olive skin. Her eyes were as large and brown as those of a beautiful doe he'd shot last autumn. He knew his own light brown eyes must be sparkling gold in the light from the windows as he took in every detail of the woman before him. Certainly, he'd seen the dark-haired girl among the Niles horde before, but she'd changed mightily in figure and in grace while he had been in Virginia surrounded by fair, giggling belles whose minds fluttered as much as their eyelashes.

Esperanza knew she should not be staring directly at a gentleman. How bold and unseemly of her. Still, his eyes were the color of the Kentucky whiskey her father favored. He had hair of dark auburn and skin tanned from being outdoors setting off the whiteness of his smile. She found herself smiling back when she should merely have nodded and lowered her lashes. He was taller even than her father and just as mightily built. The Courville's second son had gone off to the university and returned a man. A second wave of heat passed over her cheeks.

Marguerite Courville hissed, "Take your seat, Rufus. The procession is about to begin."

He glanced toward the back of the church where grumpy old Fr. Cyprien urged the altar boys, one carrying the cross, one with the means for lighting the candles, to move forward. Twins clad in angelic white, the boys bore the unmistakable brand of Aaron Niles—ruddy hair with an added smattering of freckles as well. The nun playing soothing melodies on the organ donated by Rufe's mother, a much finer gift than mere colored glass, Marguerite claimed, struck up the processional. Everyone rose. Leona Cortez reached out and pulled Esperanza and the squirming toddler into the last seat of the row. Rufe went to stand beside his mother.

As Fr. Cyprien preached on and on about avoiding

63

forbidden fruits, they exchanged surreptitious glances across the aisle. Once, when everyone was presumed to be praying with eyes closed, they had stared so long at one another that both were caught with wide smiles on their faces when Father said, "Amen." As Rufe stood aside to allow the women to precede him to the communion rail, he'd brushed elbows with Esperanza—that touch had been almost as good as a kiss in the way it made him feel.

Little chance would a Courville have of being received by a Niles at Frenchman's Bend for a cordial Sunday visit. Every encounter of the two families turned out badly, but Rufus Courville thought he knew a way he might encounter the lovely Esperanza again. Hadn't he often heard his two sisters in their teen years complaining about the enforced healthful exercise required by the nuns at the Academy?

As a boy of ten, he'd hidden in the tall grass along the alley of young live oaks and used his bean shooter to spook Mariette's horse. The animal dumped his sister on her rump. The nun in charge, the fierce Sr. Grazielle who could ride sidesaddle in a habit without showing even the tips of her shoes, demanded that Mariette remount despite her tears and pouting.

Oh, how he had laughed when his sister required a cushion to sit upon at dinner. Oh, how he had cried when his father found out about the mischief and whipped his bottom with a willow switch, all the while shouting, "You spawn of the devil, you might have killed my daughter." Rufe Courville shook off the unpleasant ending of the memory and began to plot a sweeter encounter.

****

The string of schoolgirls walked their horses out of the stable and down the fledgling oak alley on a bright and shining day. Once the muscles of the horses warmed, they kicked their mounts into a brisk trot, then a gentle canter along the packed earth of the trail. The group would approach the Spanish Trail through a grove of much more ancient oaks, ride along that road for a piece, then cut across the meadow, thread through the pine woods and return to the path back to the stable.

From his vantage point behind one of the monstrous old oaks near the road, Rufe Courville easily picked out Esperanza and her sisters from the dozen young ladies taking the air before dinner. Her sister, Amalia, gawky at fourteen, with flaming red hair and the freckles to match and eyes of a lighter brown, had grown to such a height it caused her mother to worry her daughter would overreach any future suitors who came her way, Rufe's sister-in-law mentioned during Sunday dinner.

The assembled Courvilles laughed as they always did at anything disconcerting to the Niles family. Amalia had inherited none of Ramona Niles' dark beauty, the younger sister so unlike Esperanza who resembled her mother, but polished and refined by the tutelage of the nuns. The sisters herded two smaller siblings, eight and ten, before them. All rode red horses with flashy white markings that any man in the area would know Aaron Niles had bred along with his daughters.

Feeling like a mischievous boy again, Rufe raised the bean shooter he'd made from a stalk of bamboo that morning and charged it with a black-eyed pea. With one sharp explosion of breath, he sent the pea flying at

Esperanza's mare. If the horse spooked and took off running, he was well-placed to save Miss Niles. If the animal threw her onto the thick mat of old oak leaves, he could rush forward to help her up. Neither event happened. The red mare reared slightly but steadied under Esperanza's firm hand. He shot again with the same result. Miss Niles pulled her horse up to an old stump in the grove and slid from the saddle.

"Something is bothering Scarlet, Amalia. Please ride ahead with the children and tell Sr. Grazielle I will be along as soon as I check my saddle. My mare might have been stung by a bee."

"You'll be stung by Sr. Grazielle's tongue if you linger too long, Espy. You know the kind of women who wait in the grove and stain their honor with men." Amalia shivered deliciously while her younger sisters began badgering her about the meaning of her words.

"Well, I am certainly not one of those. Go along and deliver my message."

Esperanza checked beneath the girth for sores and around her horse's flanks for stingers. She'd have a time getting back in the sidesaddle without aid, but graceful mounting didn't matter if one was alone. One wasn't alone.

Rufus Niles came down the path on a large horse as black as doomsday. From her place on the old stump, his broad shoulders seemed to blot out the sky and his face bore a grin filled with strong, white teeth same as the one he had bestowed on her in the church. Even though the oaks shaded much of the sun, his eyes had a golden glitter to them. In some ways, Rufe reminded her strongly of her father, the very best man she knew.

"We meet again, Miss Niles. May I be of

assistance?"

"If you would help me to remount, I would appreciate it. Something spooked Scarlet, but she seems to have settled now."

"My pleasure." Rufe dismounted with ease, came to the stump and placed his big hands around her small waist made even tinier by the corset she wore. Before she could protest, he lifted her across the horn of the sidesaddle. In that brief moment he felt the swift beating of her heart beneath two soft breasts pressed against him, and measured her rounded hips against his. Esperanza Niles sat speechless on her mare.

"You said you were still in school. When, pray tell, will you finish your education?"

"In May," she said faintly.

"In May, I will court you openly, but for now, I will make my intentions known only to you. I see no reason why our families cannot resolve an old feud. After all, Francois did not mean to kill your baby brother with the mumps. I caught the disease from him myself when I was four and survived. There is no reason to bear him a grudge."

"Is that what your mother told you? Mine always says God decides whom he will invite into heaven. Little Henry was beautiful but weak in health, so he is better off in the care of the angels. I do not think his death is the cause of their dislike."

"And yet, your eldest brother felt free to disparage my mother, saying she is not as pious and good as I know her to be."

"Andy had barely turned fifteen when you fought. Mama said he was too hot-headed and ought to have apologized for repeating idle gossip."

"Because I was seventeen and a deadly shot, I took care not to kill him, just teach him a lesson. My years in the military academy were apparently good for something."

"That's where you have been these past years—at military school?"

"When I turned twelve, I heard my parents talking. My father quarreled with Mother. He said, 'The pup grows big hands and feet. It is time for him to go. No one in New Orleans will take him for a Courville. It's best he go to Baton Rouge and study soldiering.' My mother wailed, 'You would condemn him to a dangerous and roving life.' 'An honorable life at least,' my papa said."

Rufe made the long ago conversation very amusing by mimicking his father's stern voice and his mother's tremulous cries. He gave Esperanza a rueful smile. "I hated every minute spent at the military academy. There are no bloodthirsty bones in my body, I assure you. But of course, once I completed that ordeal I was packed off to the university when I declined to go to West Point. Not to the Jesuits in New Orleans for further schooling, but all the way to Virginia to Thomas Jefferson's university. Study law or medicine, they told me. I had no taste for either. I wish to be a planter like my father. Since Papa passed away last year, I hoped to be called home to assist Francois, but there seemed to be no need for my presence. And so, I took it upon myself to come unbidden. I am but a poor lamb trying to find its way home."

"Sir, you seem like no lamb to me. More a wolf in the woods."

"Ah, but I am a lamb—in your hands." He placed

one large, warm hand over hers where they gripped the reins tightly.

At that moment, all hell rained down upon them. Sr. Grazielle had doubled back to find her missing charge. "Miss Niles! *Faire attention a moi*! I know the scheming ways of young girls. In the future, you will ride in front with me—after you have done a week of penitence during our exercise time."

"Mr. Niles merely helped me remount, Sister, please…"

"Have we not taught you that it is up to the woman to fend off such advances and remain pure until marriage?"

Sr. Grazielle pointed her riding whip at the placement of Rufe Niles' hands. He had heard this particular nun could turn men to stone like the monster, Medusa, and now he believed it. He might be a worldly young man of nineteen, but he froze in place, fairly sure his hands had gone numb and his privates shriveled for daring to touch Esperanza Niles. Esperanza backed her horse away.

"I meant no harm," he managed to croak.

"That is what they all say." Sr. Grazielle sniffed as she took Scarlet's bridle and urged her from the grove.

Once the two women were gone, Rufe's body began to thaw. He meant what he said. He would court Esperanza in private and ask for her hand in marriage when May came, no matter what anyone did to him. He had other ways to let the young lady he loved at first sight know his feelings, and one of those ways would be faithful attendance in church.

****

How easy it had been to pluck a prayer book

similar to the one Esperanza carried from his mother's large collection of religious materials. Rufe concealed it and the note the missal contained under his coat. All of the other Courvilles were seated in their pew, his mother already on her knees in prayer. He'd had to feign a coughing fit, covering his face with a large linen handkerchief, to delay taking his place by her side.

At last, the Niles family arrived, straggling along with the youngsters wedged between the parents and the older girls. Esperanza again had charge of her youngest brother, a lad called William Harrison after the president. Little Billy, asleep on her shoulder, would provide no distractions this time.

As Aaron Niles passed, Rufe bid him a pleasant 'Good Morning' and received only a curt nod in return. Mrs. Niles gave him a faint and pitying smile as she turned into their row. There was no help for it. Rufe dropped the concealed prayer book to the floor as Esperanza approached, startling her with the noise. Quickly, he scooped up the missal and exchanged it with the one she held loosely in her free hand.

"Allow me. I believe you dropped this, Miss Niles."

"I suppose I did," she answered quickly and took her seat.

Espy knelt to offer a quick prayer. As usual with so many to gather and transport, her family had barely gotten themselves to Mass on time. She paged through the prayer book and found the message folded in the middle.

My dearest Espy—If I may be so familiar, but I cannot think of you in any other way. I was stricken to the heart when first I saw you one mere week ago.

She smiled, her very first billet-doux, a love note from Rufus Courville and so cleverly delivered. Across the aisle, Rufe returned her smile. Familiar to call her 'Dearest Espy'? She remembered all too clearly the feel of his hands around her waist and covering her fingers. She read more of the note.

I believe we can be to each other what Mr. Shakespeare's Romeo and Juliet were to one another and their families—a means of uniting those who feud. Please, I beg of you, meet me in the churchyard this day as soon as you have broken your fast. I will languish in the shadow of my father's tomb awaiting you. I worship you. Yr Most Devoted Admirer—Rufus Courville.

As Rufe looked on gauging her reaction to his words, Esperanza Niles felt her face grow warm. Indeed, her whole body burned. She could only imagine the ways in which Rufe Courville might worship her. She snapped open a fan and began to cool her heated cheeks.

Down the row, her mother bent her head in Espy's direction. Although crammed with nuns, their boarding students and any and all from the neighborhood attending early Mass, the mild air of March kept the sanctuary from being uncomfortably hot. She did hope her daughter, who always thought herself as overly plump, had not been laced too tightly. Young ladies frequently fainted at the communion rail from extreme lacing and the Sunday morning fast. Ramona considered the benefits of being with child were loose undergarments and a small meal before church.

But what if her oldest child suffered from a fever? She'd been blessed to keep nine of her ten children, an extraordinary gift from God, but she had to admit losing

Esperanza would hurt most terribly. The Mass progressed at the pace of a holy snail and she fretted until she could place a hand on her daughter's forehead when the service finally ended. Espy remained cool to the touch and Ramona sighed with relief.

"I have a small surprise," Aaron announced as the servants flooded from the chapel balcony and assisted with the children. "Your mother, Espy, Leona, Andy, Amalia and I will be dining at the Arc-en-Ceil in town today. I have reserved a table."

"Why do we have to eat with the babies?" Nathan Hale Niles complained along with his twin altar boy, Ethan Allen. "Yes, why?"

"Because your manners are questionable. Now you two go along before you have more to answer to than simple rudeness. You are in charge of the second carriage."

The twins whooped and ran to lord it over their younger sisters and brothers. "Bring us some treats. Yes, a treat," they shouted over their shoulders.

"My dear." Aaron offered his hand to his wife and helped her into the first of the carriages. They could have walked the short distance to the burgeoning town of Rainbow—so named for the sign from God that had blessed the founding of the Academy—but Aaron would always treat Ramona like a fragile piece of glass when she was expecting.

Rainbow now boasted a general store across from the new hotel and eatery, which housed families visiting the boarding students on a Sunday. They stopped there first to allow Aaron to purchase in advance of good behavior, a sack of peppermint sticks and rock candy formed on short wooden spindles, for the brood at home. For all his booming voice, Aaron doted on his family and left more of the disciplining to his wife than she cared to do. Espy smiled fondly at her dear papa. Rufe had no reason to fear him.

Crossing the dusty street to the grand Arc-en-Ceil, really no more than a great, boxy building with a gilded false front and two stubby pillars at the entrance, the family entered the dining area to indulge in a meal beginning with sherry-infused turtle soup and ending with a fine cheddar cheese, spiced pecans, liqueurs for the men and tea for the ladies.

Ramona, at the ravenous stage of her pregnancy, did justice to all the courses of the meal, then declared she had eaten too much and needed to return to Frenchman's Bend and lie down for a nap. By the look in her husband's eye, he planned to join her.

Before they could send a boy for the carriage waiting around back, Esperanza spoke up. "I feel the need for fresh air and a brisk walk. Might Leona and I stroll back to the Academy? We will pick the wildflowers and take them to her mother's grave and also to Henry. The carriage could come back for us after taking you home. Please, Mama."

Ramona Niles cocked her head. Espy always preferred riding on horseback to any other form of exercise. She seldom walked if she could ride. Still, her daughter's request was not untoward. Only some nagging motherly instinct prevented her from granting immediate approval. "Very well. Take Amalia and Andy with you, then."

"Mother, I beg of you, do not saddle me with the girls. I had plans to put Petitjean on Red Rover for the race meet this afternoon," Andy Niles, already a sportsman, protested.

"Racing on a Sunday?"

"Only the Methodists object. Father?"

"Who else is racing?"

"I hear that Francois Courville is taking all bets that his big, black brute, Satan, will win with one of his Nigra boys aboard." Andy knew his father well.

"You do say? Considering that, place a bet against Satan for me. Your mother and I need our rest, but I might join you later."

"We will do very well walking without Andy, Mama dearest. Look, even the widows are out promenading on this grand day." Esperanza inclined her head toward two women in black who had retired six years ago to a small house in Rainbow. One called herself a seamstress. The other adorned hats. Neither worked very hard at their trade, and yet horses belonging to local men were often tied up in back of their place.

The yellow gentry strolled as well. Some had been set up on small plantations in the area by their white fathers. Others provided services to the Academy beyond the skills of slaves and had houses in town. None would molest three white ladies walking to the cemetery less than a quarter mile away.

"Very well. Expect the carriage within the hour and be at the Academy gates. Do not make Caesar come looking for you."

"We won't. Come Leona. Come Amalia. It's such a lovely, airy day, don't you think?"

Espy's companions looked at each other behind her back. Obviously, the spring air had addled her brain. They walked along watching Espy flit down the road and pause to break off wildflowers growing in the drainage ditches. She made a big bouquet of yellowtop and pussytoes. They could have gone home and gotten finer flowers to honor Cecile Cortez and little Henry.

With Espy setting the pace, the girls arrived at the churchyard in very little time. They entered through the wrought iron gate encircling the tombs. Leona's mother had company now beside Ramona's third-born child. The nuns' final resting place, set apart, had an entire row of simple white crosses where those not as hardy as the still reigning Mother Leontine lay at peace. In the far rear of secular graveyard, Old Plato and his woman waited for Judgment Day beneath two small headstones.

The grandest tomb by far was a gleaming marble sepulcher with bronze doors which contained the remains of Maxime Courville. Built prior to his demise, this small and perfect Greek temple had room enough to house his wife and children when their time came. Indeed, the coffins of the three infants lost by Marguerite had been moved to dwell therein.

Amalia shivered as she passed through the shade cast by the Courville monument. "Do you think Papa is really going to build a bigger, finer tomb than this? He talks about doing so, but Mama says the place would have to be immense to hold all of us. I hate when they talk about death, so jolly and teasing."

"I believe one must laugh in the face of death or become morbid, Amalia," Leona said, giving a bright blue glance back over her shoulder.

Esperanza had fallen behind quite suddenly and still stood in the shadow of the Courville sepulcher. She talked to a young man, that Rufus Courville, who must have come to pay his respects to his deceased father. He held in his gloved hands a wilting bouquet of thorny, pale yellow roses plucked from a bush planted at the side of the tomb.

"Espy, are you coming?"

"In a moment. Here, take the flowers for your mother." She darted over to press the wildflowers into Leona's hands, then returned to her intense conversation with the younger Mr. Courville.

Leona and Amalia continued on to the end of the long row, said their prayers for the dear departed, and left the flowers. Espy still conversed with the young man when they returned to collect her, but now she held the yellow roses.

When Leona stared at the bouquet, her dearest friend said brightly, "Here, let me arrange these in the urn for your father. Men are no good at such things."

"Thank you. Until we meet again, Miss Niles." Rufus Courville gave a small bow in the general direction of her companions and strode off toward a dark horse tied to the fencing.

The girls continued on toward the circular drive on the Academy grounds where some of the boarders strolled with their visitors. They had time to make two circuits before their carriage arrived. None of them commented on the yellow rosebud tucked into Esperanza's black hair and peeking out from the edge of her bonnet.

****

Each Sunday, Espy managed to fumble her prayer book. Each Sunday, she found a note in its center. She saved these messages of love tied with a ribbon knotted around a dried yellow rosebud and locked into the secret compartment of a case carved with a rose motif and holding a few pieces of fine jewelry given to her by her grandfather. *Abuelo* Viator favored his first grandchild, so like his own daughter, but softer and tamer. He delighted in giving Espy small cunning gifts, spoiling her, Ramona claimed. Esperanza blessed her abuelo for this particular gift. The Niles family had far too many nosy, troublesome children to take any chance of discovery.

Rufe devised many clever ways of meeting, but the last of them proved fatal to their plans. Early in May, two weeks before the senior girls were to graduate from the Academy, Esperanza begged to go riding on a Sunday afternoon because with the heat increasing, the oak grove would be pleasantly shady. Neither Leona nor Amalia had any desire to ride. Her father insisted those twelve-year-old scoundrels, Nate and Ethan, go along because they were destroying the peace of his day of rest by tormenting their younger sisters. He granted them the use of the stallion, Red Rover, who needed some exercise. The boys were to change mounts halfway through the ride so each had an equal chance on the superior horse.

Espy rode Scarlet as they set out for the oak grove. She led the boys to a shortcut across a meadow and feeling a sense of urgency and freedom, abandoned her ladylike posture and bent low over her horse's neck. The warm wind whipped past her cheeks as she raced to meet her love. There he waited just ahead, Rufe Courville on big, black Satan.

Rufe tipped his hat. "Good day, Miss Niles and young sirs. I see Red Rover is out for some exercise."

"He can beat your old nag any day," Nate boasted.

He had won the flip of a coin for the ride out.

"Ah, but he lost to my Satan by a nose at the last race meet. I don't suppose you boys would be up for a rematch?" Rufe tilted his head. "I'm a greater weight, though, so it wouldn't be fair—unless your brother rode my horse."

Nate and Ethan grinned, thoroughly game for the idea. Rufe drew an elaborate course for the race in the oak duff using his riding crop.

"Now, Ethan is it? I expect you to do your best. No letting Red Rover win. Can I count on you?"

"Oh, yes, sir! I won't give Nate an inch."

Rufe tossed the lad into his saddle. Borrowing their sister's beautifully embroidered handkerchief to drop as a signal for the start of the race, Rufe urged the boys on. The two horses took off in a spray of the brown oak leaves recently shed to give way to the spring growth of the trees.

Rufe raised the hankie to his lips and inhaled its sweet perfume, the scent of Courville roses, he thought. He examined the scalloped edges and design of yellow rosebuds. "This is your work, Espy?"

"Yes, mine, newly made."

Rufe tucked the token into his coat over his heart. "Will you get down?"

She allowed him to put his hands about her waist again and lift her with his strong arms to stand beside him. Taught well by the nuns since the age of six, Espy would not normally dismount during their meetings, but the end of her schooling loomed only two weeks away. She tired of being proper. Her heart filled with the urges of the month of May when pagans used to dance around symbolic poles, a rite not celebrated at the

Academy. Rufe would speak to her father shortly and they could court openly. Then, she could allow him certain liberties so far denied.

When his lips descended toward hers, she quickly turned her head. He brushed her cheek in an almost brotherly way, but lingered too long. Then, his lips wandered across to the lobe of her ear where a ruby earring quivered like a small droplet of blood. He nibbled down her neck to the top of her collar where her pulse beat furiously.

"In two weeks, you will allow me a real kiss, dearest Espy. Say so."

"If my father agrees to our courtship."

"And if he does not, we will elope. We will be like Romeo and Juliet. No one will be able to stop us."

"The nuns say that couple ended very badly, both suicides. They kept us to Julius Caesar and The Merchant of Venice, but Leona and I read about the star-crossed lovers in my mother's *Complete Works of Mr. Shakespeare*. I shouldn't like to end that way." Her voice shook as Rufe switched to the other side of her neck and ran his tongue lightly down the skin of her throat.

"Of course not. Our families will forgive us and each other for any past slights."

"That is not what happened to Leona's parents when they eloped. Her mother died in childbirth but six months later and her father hung for a horse thief in Texas the next year. The DeVille family never acknowledged Leona. As you know, my mother raised her."

"Who is filling your mind with such terrible tales?"

"Mama. She took me aside one evening after I'd

been to Madame Cortez's grave to meet with you again. I think she might suspect."

"She is trying to frighten you away from me, Espy. Don't allow her to do that."

"No, she said I'd never given her a day of trouble and was a fine example and, indeed, a second mother to the younger children. She said she trusted my good judgment in all things. We cannot run away, Rufe."

Rufus Courville released their clasped hands and kicked up oak leaves with the point of his polished boot. "Promise me you won't let them separate us!"

Before she could open her lips, the boys thundered back into the grove. In this race, Red Rover won by a neck. Nate was jubilant and Ethan consoling.

"Satan is still a mighty fine horse, Mr. Courville. They are well matched."

"Yes, yes, they are. Here, a half-dime for both of you for being such fine jockeys. Good to have seen all of you. I must be on my way now that you have a safe escort home, Miss Niles."

"The boys will not let me come to any harm, Mr. Courville. Until we meet again."

Nate and Ethan wrinkled their noses over the mushy look their sister exchanged with Mr. Courville. They kept an eye on where he put his hands when he helped Espy back into the saddle, too. When they got home, the boys were fair to bursting with a tale to tell to their parents when they dashed into the parlor of the fine Greek Revival mansion with its twenty-four rooms all set about with white pillars and galleries that had replaced the old Frenchman's house.

"Pa, Red Rover beat Satan this time! That Mr. Courville, the younger one, let us race when we met him in the grove. He gave us both a half-dime. He's not such a bad feller and you should see how he looks at Espy—like he's gonna die if she don't smile at him."

"Doesn't," their mother corrected automatically. "We need to find a boarding school specializing in grammar for the two of you in the fall. You are covered in dust. Go wash."

Ramona couldn't help but notice her eldest daughter had gone directly to her room to change. She looked at her husband who had taken refuge behind the newspaper recently delivered from New Orleans. "I knew it. I will have to talk to Espy again and tell her another story, the one you told me the evening after our marriage."

Aaron Niles crumpled his paper in his hands as if he needed to destroy something near at hand. "About the affair. I will not have my daughter think ill of me. I've sworn to you more than once I did not know the boy was mine. They kept him so close to home as a young child and you know our families don't associate. I noticed the resemblance at his first communion lined up there at the altar with half a dozen others, my own eyes looking back at me and that hair. You said I was forgiven."

"And so you are, but the truth needs to be told to at least one more person." Ramona placed the latest installment of the Charles Dickens tale she had been reading on the arm of the horsehair settee.

"Let me find the boy and threaten his life if he comes near my daughter again. That should scare him off."

"Not if he has your nature as well as your looks. What would you have done if my father had denied your courtship?"

"Put you across my saddle and taken you into Texas."

"Exactly. Esperanza must be told."

"Surely, my clever wife can contrive another way to separate the two," Aaron said, so very good at getting what he wanted when he sugarcoated his words.

"Mandy, go find Miss Leona. I believe she is in her room," Ramona asked the servant who had just entered the room bringing them cooling drinks on this rather warm Sunday afternoon. She fanned herself briefly, thinking how many years had passed since she had broken a fan while swatting a randy man. She'd like to take this one to both her husband and Rufus Courville. Her family was giving her gray hairs faster than she could pluck them out.

Leona came immediately, so lovely with her olive skin and blue eyes set off by black curls. She still wore her Sunday best, a bit wrinkled around the bottom of the skirt. "You wanted me, Aunt Ramona?"

"You weren't resting then?"

"No, at prayer while Espy went off riding."

"Always at prayer. Would you mind breaking your Sunday habit and taking the carriage to call upon Marguerite Courville?"

"On a family day? Won't she find that an intrusion, not to mention odd? I have never called on her before."

"You needn't stay long. I want you to deliver a note I will write shortly. She cannot have any grudge against you, while I might be turned away."

"May I ask if this concerns Espy and the younger Mr. Courville? I have prayed so hard. I've wanted to speak up, but could not betray my near-sister. I have been afraid they might elope. They meet more often than you know and Espy is so smitten. At night, she tells me about their encounters in such ardent terms I blush with embarrassment." Leona wrung her hands as the truth came pouring out.

"Has the boy ruined her?" Aaron Niles roared, his face growing red.

His ward flinched. "Oh, never that! Esperanza believes they will be married soon after we graduate and says Rufus will wait for what he wants most."

"Thank God!" Ramona, feeling weak in the knees, went to her writing desk and penned a message with a slightly shaking hand causing the ink to blot here and there on the paper. Rather than wait for the ink to dry, she sanded over her words, shook the letter clean, folded and sealed the note that meant the end of her daughter's dreams.

****

Marguerite Courville enjoyed the shade of the oak she had planted as a bride. Nearing sixty, she still thought of her home as elegant and airy, not some heavy, white pile set all around with Corinthian columns and fancy pediments like the house Aaron Niles had built for his wife. If only her home had not been so isolated, so lonely, twenty years ago. Now, she had all the company she could wish at the Academy, in the growing town of Rainbow, and from her adult daughters who visited with her this pleasant Sunday afternoon.

Two granddaughters threw a ball for their new puppy. Marthe's eldest boy set up empty wine bottles on the fence posts for Francois and Rufus to practice marksmanship and hoped to get a turn himself. Rufe stripped out of his coat and would soon outdo his elder brother. Francois, so short and lithe compared to his baby brother, would concede grumpily and return to the shade. He had agreed to a friendly contest only after Rufe returned from a brisk ride too full of a nervous energy to settle down, as was often the case.

Marie-Celeste, her daughter-in-law, attempted to capture the entire scene in a watercolor at which she was very skilled—the women sipping mint tea in the shade, the children at play, the men banging away with their pistols in the distance. She had already done a fine rendering of the house. With no children to occupy her time, the trim, blonde woman from the Rhone valley sought other outlets. Marguerite had surrendered the master's bedroom upon the death of her husband, hoping more space and privacy would result in more grandchildren, but to no avail.

Still, Marie-Celeste had taken many of the burdens of running the plantation off of Marguerite's shoulders, leaving her mother-in-law more time for religious activities and good deeds. She knew for a fact Marie-Celeste, for all her lady-like manners, could argue old Viator down to the penny when purchasing fabric for the field hands' annual clothing allotment. Her daughter-in-law was certainly fearless when treating the maladies of the workers as well. Being childless, she could afford to be brave.

One of the servants made her way across the lawn. "Miss Leona Cortez come callin', Madame. She out front in de Niles carriage. You want me to bring her 'round?"

"No, I shall go out to meet her."

Puzzled, Marguerite picked up her walking stick

and told her daughters she would take a short stroll for the good of her stiff knees. The Cortez girl had gotten down, but waited patiently in the shade of the first floor gallery. She wore her church clothes and a rather plain straw bonnet, but the ribbon holding it in place did set off the blue of her eyes. Whatever could Leona Cortez want?

"As you can see, I am not attired for guests, Miss Cortez." Marguerite touched a hand to the plain, black cotton housedress, decorated only with a mourning brooch she had put on after Sunday dinner.

"No need to fret. I will only stay a moment. I admire the way you have trained your lovely yellow roses to grow up the lattice."

"I would be happy to give you a cutting. Will you sit? May I offer you a cool drink?"

"No, thank you. My only reason for disturbing your Sabbath is that my aunt asked me to bring this note and deliver it directly into your hands."

Leona watched as Madame Courville opened the letter. For an elderly woman, Marguerite maintained her looks with a perfumed powder covering the fine wrinkles in her skin, a dab of rouge and a hair dye that kept her curls as jet as they had been in her youth. She may have assumed perpetual mourning, but some vanity remained in her yet. Now, the dark eyes, sunken with age, opened wide in alarm as she read.

My Dear Madame Courville—I beg of you to keep your son from my eldest daughter. You know the reason why. With all urgency—Mrs. Aaron Niles.

Marguerite put a thin hand to her heart and began to sway. The message fluttered to the ground. The servant, who hovered just out of hearing range, moved forward to catch her mistress and move her bodily to a bench.

"Some water for your mistress. Hurry!" Leona ordered as she fanned the pallid, blue-lipped older woman.

A puppy holding the ramrod for a pistol in its mouth tore around the corner of the house. A boy pursuing the dog came next, and after them charged Rufus Courville wearing only breeches, shirt and an open waistcoat. In the midst of the chaos, Marguerite looked into Leona's eyes and whispered, "The note!" Unable to stoop down without giving her action away, Leona moved her skirts over the fluttering piece of paper before the breeze could blow it toward Rufe.

"Mama, are you ill?" the young man asked with concern.

He cast a blaming glance at Leona. She read his thoughts in that whiskey-eyed glare. Her disapproval of his meetings with Espy had been clear from the very start and now she came probably bearing tales and upsetting his mother.

"Miss Cortez, what brings you here?"

"A brief visit. I think your mother needs more than water to revive her. Please, could you find some brandy?"

He had no choice but to leave at once in search of a bottle. Leona reached down and retrieved the note she had secured under one small foot. She held it out for Madame Courville to take, but the woman rested with her eyes closed, head leaning against the stuccoed bricks. Rufe returned all too soon with brandy in a glass. Leona balled the paper in her hand. Marguerite sipped.

"Thank you, Rufus. Merely some heart palpitations. One must expect such weaknesses at my age."

"I must not stay if you are unwell. Please, let me know how you do. I leave you in the hands of your loving son and our merciful Lord."

Leona rose to leave and allowed Rufus to hand her into the carriage at the prompting of his mother. He was so towering and temperamental, exuding the scent of all things masculine, horses and leather and gunpowder and sweaty musk. She had no idea how gentle Espy could not be afraid of him, how her friend from the cradle had controlled him thus far. Remembering her mother's fate, Leona kept herself aloof from the world of men.

The sweat of her palm covered only by a netted glove reduced the note further in size, but once away from the Courvilles, Leona allowed it to unfold again. She could understand that her godmother would object to Rufus as a suitor. The great brute had shot Andy. The families had never gotten along—but for whatever reason?

Chapter Six

Rufe Courville restlessly paced the circular oyster shell drive in front of the nunnery at Mount Carmel Academy. He had no idea why his dear mother had asked him to drive the buggy for this visit to old Mother Leontine. In the regular course of events, she came in the carriage driven by a servant and with his two chattering married sisters to deliver jellies and sweets as treats for the good Sisters.

He had planned to hare off the plantation this Monday afternoon and sit his horse in the deep shade of the oak grove behind the school to watch Esperanza pass. He thought Espy had the best seat of all the female riders. Rufe pictured her face dewy and shining with exertion, her full red lips slightly parted, her warm brown eyes turning his way. She'd be wearing the long, plain dark habit required of all the girls, but he might catch a glimpse of a slim ankle clad in half-boots. As the group cantered back and forth in the shade of the trees to protect their delicate complexions from the broiling sun of this Louisiana afternoon in May, because those silly little cocked hats and veils certainly wouldn't do it, perhaps Espy would fall behind the group. He imagined dashing out of concealment to steal a kiss while Sr. Grazielle rounded the hill.

Rufe kicked an oyster shell with the toe of his shiny boot and lofted it into the air. The shell landed with a puff of white dust several feet away. He took off his hat and fanned his face. The young ladies would soon be done with their ride, dismissed to return to their homes or to their rooms to wash and change before the evening meal. Damn the complexion that went with his auburn hair. Even though well-tanned, he knew he grew red in the face. His wild mane, as Espy liked to call to his locks, would soon be soaked with sweat. What was taking his mother so long?

****

"You do understand my problem?" Marguerite Courville said to Mother Leontine, nodding at the figure of her son pacing back and forth in front of the nun's office window. One of the shells kicked by the lad pinged off the wavy glass and made both of them startle.

"Yes, indeed, my daughter. I do." Mother Leontine sat with her hands tucked into her habit sleeves, ever serene. "I was there at his birth and took your dying confession to the priest in Opelousas. Old Fr. Mathias is gone to his reward now and Fr. Cyprien sits in his place," the nun said, as if feeling her sixty and more years.

"If I had died, I would not have to face this dilemma now."

Mother Leontine studied the young man left outside in the heat. He cut a fine figure—tall, over six feet in height, broad of shoulder, fiery of hair and eye, and in no way resembling his late, short and bulbous-eyed father or his petite, dark mother. If the Courvilles and Niles families ever dared to occupy the same social space, the resemblance to the prolific Aaron Niles, father of the lovely Esperanza and nine other offspring, would be highly noticeable. Thank le bon Dieu they did not. The Niles clan kept company with the Americans, their near Cajun neighbors and some of their Spanish relatives by marriage in Opelousas. The Courvilles socialized only with the old French families of the area and in New Orleans.

Still, there was talk and some time ago, a duel. She had heard her young ladies gossiping about the wound Andy Niles had taken. He bore it so bravely they were certain a group should be formed to visit his sickbed and present him with prayer cards decorated by their own hands. An older circle of mostly French girls couldn't cease talking about handsome Rufus Courville who had passed through their lives as quickly as a blazing comet, only to disappear the next week on a steamboat taking him to far away Virginia for a university education. Mother Leontine silenced them all and admonished them to pray for forgiveness of the sins of idle gossip and impure thoughts.

Turning toward Marguerite, she felt as if she were again speaking to her girls, though she and the woman had nearly the same number to their age. "Nineteen years ago your sins were absolved, my child. You have lived a blameless life since that time. You must believe the Lord Jesus will give you strength to face this crisis."

Marguerite gave a Gallic shrug. "I thought I would go to hell for all eternity. Of course I confessed my infidelity. My husband, out of pride, accepted the child as his own and did not stint in the boy's upbringing or education, but there is no denying I was an unfaithful wife. The Niles boy only said as much. I cannot have Rufus shooting people every time the old rumors arise."

"Have you told your son the truth?"

"I cannot. We are so close, closer than I am to Francois or his sisters. I thought two years at the university would cool his temper, but it seems to have gotten worse. He claims to have no interest in law or medicine and wants to be a planter like his brother and father right here in Rainbow. The other occupations would have confined him to a city."

"Two years among rowdy university students rarely cools the blood, I have observed. I have also observed your son's interest in Miss Esperanza Niles."

"Yes, the second problem, to keep them apart. Surely, Miss Niles has no idea…"

"I greatly doubt her mother has discussed this delicate issue with her eldest daughter. Ramona Niles, my first pupil, possesses an acute intelligence and has grown into a strong woman of great good sense. If her husband did not inform her of his connection to Rufus, I am sure she has figured the situation out for herself. When I arranged her marriage to Aaron Niles eighteen years ago, I did hope her liveliness and quick mind, not to mention her fine physical attributes, would keep him occupied for some time. What a miracle it is that Mr. Niles turned out to be such an ardent and faithful husband."

"A miracle, indeed. I do remember how ardent Aaron could be." Madame Courville let a small, regretful sigh escape her lips, which she quickly covered with the black crocheted mitt on her hand. She had worn nothing but black since the birth of a red-haired son.

Mother Leontine allowed this comment to pass. Marguerite would certainly confess her improper thoughts without prompting before the next Mass.

"I will speak to Ramona. Esperanza will finish her education in a matter of days. She should be taken from the classroom and exposed to a wider society, perhaps in New Orleans where Ramona has an elderly aunt."

"But the season will not begin until autumn. Two young people can get into a great deal of mischief during the heat of summer."

"May is an excellent time to travel abroad before the hurricanes stir the oceans. If Rufus has completed his education, he should be encouraged to go on a Grand Tour of the continent the same as his brother. Did not Francois bring home a bride?"

"He did. The daughter of a Lyons bourgeois to be sure, but very pretty and willing to learn our ways, a great help to me on the plantation. Marie-Celeste must have kin who would welcome Rufe into their homes and introduce him to eligible daughters."

"My thoughts exactly. Two years in Europe may be just what your young man needs. As for Esperanza, her charms will not go unnoticed in the city. This small problem of an inappropriate calf love need not lead to a tragedy."

"As always, you are correct, Lady Mother. Keep me in your prayers. Poor Rufus looks about to die out there."

****

"Mother, I have no desire to be sent off yet again. I've barely been home since the age of twelve. I mean to settle right here." Rufus Courville took a deep breath. "In fact, a certain young lady has caught my eye and I would ask for her hand in marriage." His fingers tightened white on the reins as he urged the buggy horse homeward.

Marguerite laughed with a merriment she did not feel. "Oooh-la-la, a boy who weds at nineteen will regret his choice by the time he is thirty. Going on a Grand Tour is hardly a punishment. In fact, it is a reward you don't deserve for leaving the university, so naughty of you."

"I am not a child. I know what I want. Don't you even care to know her name?"

"In Europe you will meet women of such sophistication and accomplishment that in six months you won't even recall this country girl." Marguerite fanned herself briskly.

"Her name is Esperanza Niles, and there will never be a better woman for me."

"Spoken like a petulant child. Your late father despised Aaron Niles, that crude American upstart with his ostentatious house and dark, Spanish wife. He would roll in his grave if he knew you would mingle our blood with theirs."

"Papa is dead and old feuds must end."

"Francois is not and you are under twenty-one. Do you suppose your brother will give you your inheritance when you offer up an insult to his father? The two of you will end up like that brainless Cecile DeVille and her Spanish lover, disowned by both families."

Suddenly, Marguerite's heart beat wildly. She felt another weak spell coming on at a terrible thought. "Is the girl with child, Rufus?"

"Of course not! I honor her too dearly. Had I known your low opinion of me, I might have stayed in Virginia." He shot his mother an angry glance and saw her wilting back into the cushions of the buggy. The fan dropped from her hand. Rufe whipped the horse to speed its pace home. In the dooryard, he leapt down and carried his mother up to her room, shouting for help on the way. All of her weight seemed to come from the clothing covering a frail, nearly lifeless body. Marie-Celeste and a bevy of servants rushed to his aid and pushed Rufe from the room as soon as he had placed his aged mother on the bed. He paced the parlor, waiting.

"She has recovered for now, Rufe, and wants to speak to you. Please, do nothing to upset her," Marie-Celeste begged, her sincere blue-gray eyes filled with tears.

The women had sponged Marguerite and changed her clothes to a nightdress. As Rufe sat on the top of her bed stairs and took hold of his mother's hand, he smelled the restorative brandy on her breath. Her fingers grasped his with amazing strength considering her condition.

"My dearest son, I ask you one more time to take the Grand Tour. If the girl is true, she will wait a mere two years. And if she is not, better that you escaped."

"Mama, what if the Lord chooses to take you while I am away?"

"That would be His will and not your fault, Rufus. Please, write often and tell me of your wonderful adventures. I will try so very hard to be here when you return."

"I will do as you say."

Heavy boots clumped up the far stairs and along the gallery. Francois burst in on the touching scene. "No one thinks to find me when my mother is near death! I must learn this from the servants. You, little brother, go fetch the doctor from Opelousas. Whenever

I have need of you, you've gone off on some lark. At least make yourself useful now."

With his bulging black eyes, bantam rooster physique and accusing voice, it was as if Maxime Courville had come back to possess his first-born son's body. Rufe flinched, even though having come into his full growth he could have snapped Francois in two. He felt a great temptation to do so—to make up for all the pinches and slaps his brother had given over the years as Rufe grew up. Instead, seeing the worry in his mother's eyes, he stood and left for Opelousas without a word.

****

Young Dr. Owen Maddox had a good horse and was a decent rider despite a rather tall, stooped and reedy physique. He'd studied in London and put in four years under the former physician before that knowledgeable but boozy man had taken a bottle to the grave. Senor Viator had foreseen this event coming for many years and took care to recruit a new doctor for the settlement when on a business trip abroad. Maddox inherited all the costly instruments of the medical trade, but took only a small bag with him on this trip. The symptoms described by the frantic son were easy to diagnose: an aging woman, a failing heart.

****

Ramona Niles received the summons from Mother Leontine early the next morning. On the surface, she was invited to tea. In reality, Ramona knew the Lady Mother would not call her away in the seventh month of a pregnancy, not to mention from the obligations of running a plantation and mothering ten children, which made her social calls rare unless some urgency required her presence. Of course, she must go.

Ramona set aside the accounts she had planned to balance that day. Having a better head and less impatience with figures than her husband, she had taken on that task early in her marriage. They were never in want. Aaron cultivated such a diversity of enterprises that if cotton failed, sugar saved them. People always needed yams, corn and beef. Perhaps, the good Sister had need of funds for the steadily growing academy. Sighing, Ramona resigned herself to the discomfort of a short trip over rutted roads that would test her bladder every mile of the way.

Plato's Jeanette, the yellow-skinned young woman who had become housekeeper in the convent, showed her to Mother Leontine's study where a choice of tea and coffee and some superb little madeleines concocted from a book of French cookery, waited. They were not to meet in the parlor, then. This was a matter of business. Noting the servant also appeared to be with child, Ramona accepted the tea Jeanette poured. Once settled, Mother Leontine dismissed the woman and waited peacefully while her former student sipped the tea and sampled the small shell-shaped cakes.

"Your housekeeper, she is *enciente*?"

"We have seen she is properly married to the Courville's cooper. Francois Courville wanted two-thousand for his barrel maker, far beyond our means to purchase. As devoted as Marguerite Courville is to the Academy, she could not persuade her son to make a donation of the man. Monsieur Courville says his mother squanders her widow's portion on us. However, all Jeanette's offspring will be baptized and remain here with their mother until their Day of Jubilee."

"And when will that be?"

"God knows. Until then, Jeanette and her children are better off in the hands of the order."

Ramona shifted from the awkward subject of slavery. Her own plantation could not run without enforced labor and though she took good care of her people, she had no wish to argue the issue with Mother Leontine. She nibbled at the lemon-flavored cake in her best lady-like manner as the nuns had taught her. In truth, she could have eaten a dozen.

"These are excellent. I must have the recipe for my cook."

"Jeanette's doing. She has her grandmother's talent in the kitchen. When a French culinary book arrived in a box of donations for our library, she seized it at once."

"She reads? But of course. I remember both her and her brother lurking in the rear of the classrooms."

"As eager to learn as you were. You will keep our little secret?"

"Forever."

"Keeping secrets forever is, perhaps, impossible. Some are better not kept. You must be aware Esperanza has been unusually clumsy with her prayer book at Sunday Mass and young Mr. Courville is always ready to return that book—or one like it—to her hands. They have been exchanging notes in this way for some time now. Sr. Grazielle tells me Espy's admirer often lurks in the oak grove when the girls go riding by."

"I am aware of the infatuation, yes."

"Are you aware of the reason why such an attachment cannot be allowed?"

"I am. If Aaron had not confided in me, my own

eyes would have told me Rufus is his son."

"I am greatly relieved as I would not have been able to speak more plainly. Marguerite Courville has agreed to see the lad off on a Grand Tour. He will be gone for several years. In that time, I have suggested Esperanza might find a husband in New Orleans. Surely, she would enjoy a round of parties and a string of beaux in the city as much as any girl her age."

Ramona Niles shook her head. "She is too much like me. Having fastened on this young man, she will not be diverted by dances and clothes and city dandies. Her heart is engaged. If Rufus Courville returns after several years abroad, he will find Espy waiting. Since I sent that note to Madame Courville, I have come to believe only the truth will do. That truth will wound my daughter so greatly I do not know how she will recover."

Mother Leontine moved her age-spotted fingers over Ramona's plump, soft hand. "With prayer and in God's good time, she will overcome this tragedy."

"The trouble being that God's good time is often not swift enough for us. Aaron does not want me to reveal the truth. May he forgive me—as God must forgive him."

****

Ramona Niles was not one for putting off the unpleasant. She took her husband aside and closed the door of the parlor. "Mother Leontine and I feel only the truth will sway Esperanza from making a terrible mistake."

"That blasted nun! What does she know of passion! I will not lose the love of my daughter, do you hear, Ramona? I forbid it!"

Ramona watched her husband grow red in the face. Then, she turned her bulky body and walked awkwardly on her swollen feet toward the door. Her husband could bluster, but she had every faith he would never harm her physically. As she mounted the stairs to find Esperanza, she heard his cursing followed by a crash. Another vase or small table had suffered from his temper.

She paused listening outside of the room Espy shared with Leona. The girls practiced their speeches for the coming graduation ceremony. Leona had been chosen valedictorian and Espy as salutatorian. She was immensely proud of both of them and hated bringing sorrow into their young and happy lives. No help for it. Taking as deep a breath as her belly would allow, she quietly entered the room.

"Mama, listen to Leona's speech. It is so lofty and grand mine seems a sorry thing." Despite the words, Espy's face glowed with the nearness of graduation and her hopes of wedding Rufus Courville.

"I will be glad to listen to both speeches in a short while. Leona, I would speak privately with Espy."

Espy noticed her dear friend's face change from joy to sadness as Leona left the room. "Mama, what is it? Has something awful happened?"

"No. Nor will it. Dear child, sit down. Twenty years ago, your father committed an indiscretion with a married lady from a neighboring plantation."

Quick as her mother, Esperanza understood. "Madame Courville. What Andy heard was true. She wasn't always such a pious woman."

"She is not ours to judge. What matters is a child resulted from that affair a year later. His name is Rufus

Courville, your half-brother." There, as bluntly put as a bullet to her daughter's heart, but done.

Espy's soft brown eyes went wider. Her sweet bowed lips trembled, but no sound came out. She put one small hand over her heart and said at last, "No, that cannot be."

"See them side by side in your mind, dear heart—your father and Rufus—and you will see the resemblance."

Leona's footsteps pattered on the stairs. "Aunt Ramona, come quickly! Uncle Aaron is deathly ill in the parlor. I might have passed right by him if the door had been closed. He cannot move or speak."

Despite all the burdens she carried, Ramona Niles pushed to her feet and went down the stairs as fast as she could. She alerted the household staff and sent Andy to bring Sr. Francine. At the gates of the Academy, her son encountered Plato's Jeanette leaving with a market basket on her arm. He implored her to bring the Sister out of the convent for the emergency.

"Sr. Francine, she's all knotted up with arthritis today, but my man told me this morning the young doc from Opelousas is out checking over the hands at Courville's plantation. Seems Madame Courville had a spell of some kind, but since he came all this way, they asked him to examine everyone else, too. Hadn't been done since the old doc died last year."

"Bless you, I'll ride on." Charging on to the Courville property would be like diving headlong into a nest of vipers, but for his father, Andrew Jackson Niles planned to be as brave as his namesake.

****

Dr. Maddox pushed his spectacles up on his nose

again and looked at the wound more closely. The gash in the slave's ankle might have been self-inflicted in order to get a day's rest in the sick house, but it was not a doctor's duty to say so. He cleaned up the dirt and debris, put in a few stitches which the field hand endured stoically, rolled a bandage around the wound and recommended the Negro stay off his feet for a few days. Owen Maddox had not gotten used to the peculiar institution of slavery, long ago abolished in Britain, and could see no harm in giving his patient some rest.

Francois Courville looked unhappy with the treatment, but called for the next patients, two little pickaninnies who were doing poorly because of a worm infestation. The doctor prescribed a dose of worm-seed oil to be given morning and evening and sent them back to their mother, each one clutching a peppermint for a treat.

"Do not coddle them with sweets or the whole crew will be lining up for treatments. The old doctor knew better. The worse the cure, the less the malingering," Francois growled.

"You insisted I fulfill the contract you had with my partner, though I saw none of that three-hundred dollars you paid him for coming out here twice a year to examine the hands. I am doing so to the best of my ability. Next."

An elderly slave leaning on a crutch was shoved aside as he attempted to enter the infirmary building. Young Andy Niles filled the doorway. "Please Dr. Maddox, you must come quickly! My father has suffered a fit of apoplexy, my mother says."

Owen stood and took up his bag in preparation to go at once, but Francois Courville barred him with an arm across his chest. "Your obligation is here."

"I see no emergencies waiting and will return. In a case of apoplexy, the patient must be bled immediately to restore the body's balance and purify the blood."

"What of my mother?"

"I have given your wife the foxglove leaves to make an elixir for the palpitations. Madame Courville is resting comfortably. She is to avoid excitement and excessive exercise. There is nothing more I do for her. Mr. Niles has the more urgent need."

"If you go, I will give my contract to another physician and you will be without three-hundred dollars."

"Of which I have not seen a penny. Good day to you, sir."

His horse still stood saddled in the shade. He had intended to ride back to Opelousas this morning before Francois decided to wring his partner's services from him. Now, the doctor gladly followed Andy Niles through the thriving little town of Rainbow, past the ladies' academy, across the Spanish Trail and down the rutted road to Frenchman's Bend plantation. Perhaps, he should consider opening an office in the small town if his services were so valuable as to cause a dispute between planters.

His patient lay in a bed fit for royalty. The women of the household had removed his coat and neckcloth and sponged the man's head of thick white hair with cold water to relieve the congestion of the brain. Dr. Maddox could see the telltale signs of an apoplectic stroke in the drooping eye and lip on the left side of the face, the limpness of the left arm. While rolling up the victim's shirtsleeve and applying a loose tourniquet to the arm, he called for a basin to catch the blood. Taking out his thumb lancet from its silver case in his waistcoat, Dr. Maddox inserted the blade into a vein of the sick man's arm, pulling it upright to open a wound large enough to allow the blood to flow freely.

"Your husband is of a choleric nature, Mrs. Niles?"

"Yes, but he barks more than he bites. My poor dear."

"Mr. Niles is a large and robust man. We will need to take sixteen ounces to restore balance to his body. If you do not see some signs of recovery in a few days, I will have to bleed him again."

Aaron Niles' good eye went wide and wild. "N-no." He clutched at his wife with his good hand.

"That is a good sign. He has retained some speech. He must practice to regain control of the muscles of his face. If he can rise from the bed, exercise might help to overcome the malignancy. If God wills, he will walk and speak again. In the meantime, do keep his head cool and see he receives foods mild in nature, none of the peppery dishes people here have a fondness for."

The emergency bleeding done, the tourniquet removed and the wound bound up with lint and a bandage, Dr. Maddox tested the extent of the paralysis with pinpricks down the numb left side of his patient's body and then down the sensitive right.

"B-blast, hurt. Go way!" Aaron Niles made an attempt to push the younger man and floundered, weak as one of his own infants.

"It is imperative that you remain calm, Mr. Niles, or you may do yourself a further injury," Owen Maddox told him firmly.

From the bedchamber doorway, a soft voice said,

"May I come in and talk to Papa now?"

Dr. Maddox swallowed hard, making his rather protruding Adam's apple bob in his long neck. He brushed his unruly brown hair from his eyes and pushed up his spectacles again.

Angels had descended into the sick room in the form of two young ladies. One stood lofty and slim, black of hair and blue of eye, and as untouchable as the Virgin Mary herself. She held the hand of a smaller Miss who possessed large, brown eyes, thick waving dark hair and a lush, full figure like the statue of an Indian goddess he had seen once in the British Museum. He stammered like his stroke victim.

"D-do, come in. The presence of such beauty can only make the patient feel better." There, he'd gotten out a compliment. While other young men had been sowing wild oats and wooing women, Dr. Maddox had been applying leeches and learning to amputate putrid legs. "I am quite finished here."

Ramona Niles tucked in the blankets around her husband's limbs and stepped aside to allow Espy to have her chair. "My daughter, Esperanza, and my ward, Leona Cortez. Come, doctor, I will see to your fee. Would you like to take a meal before your journey or care to stay the night?"

"No, thank you. I ate heartily at the Courville plantation this morning and as Monsieur Courville has dismissed me, I shall return to Opelousas. Send a message immediately if your husband does not show signs of improvement and I will come bleed him again. Do not use the services of a barber or apothecary. In their ignorance, they often damage the nerves and muscles, leaving the patient worse off than before."

Mrs. Niles, despite her delicate condition, saw him all the way to the door and pressed a generous amount of money into his hand. "My husband's life is everything to me. Thank you for coming so quickly. I will send for you if necessary."

The daughter had her eyes and hair, he thought, and probably her gracious smile. He would have to come back to see the patient and Miss Esperanza Niles who had so charmingly taken and kissed her father's hand as tears ran down her cheeks. If her father recovered, the doctor who cured him would earn that smile. In the interim, he could concoct some pleasing phrases and compliments and have them as ready as his lancet. As Owen Maddox skirted the town, Rainbow seemed more and more likely a place to set up a second office.

****

In the bedchamber, Espy stroked her father's hand. "Can you hear me, Papa?"

Aaron Niles turned his head toward his daughter though it took an effort. "Yeth."

She hated hearing the sound of his voice so weak and slurred. "Papa, I understand and I forgive you. You do not need to worry about me. I will not be seeing Rufus Courville anymore. Your health is my only concern."

Aaron tried to smile for his daughter, but only one side of his mouth obeyed. He struggled to find words. They would not come. A single tear trickled from his good eye. It slid down his cheek and into the pillow.

"I was to meet Rufe this afternoon at his father's tomb."

"N-no," he managed and thumped the bed with the

leg that still did his bidding. She understood his fear. How often had he said he would have run off to Texas with her mother if *Abuelo* had denied them the chance to marry, such was the passionate nature of their love? And her father had been an older and more controlled man than hot-blooded Rufus Courville.

"Papa, please be still. Don't hurt yourself. I will ask Leona to take him a note breaking off our—our attachment. He deserves as much. Now, release my hand so I might do that."

He let her go with reluctance. Espy went into the adjoining sitting room and inked a pen at her mother's writing desk. The words did not come easily.

My dear Rufus—Father is deathly ill, and I have heard your mother is suffering from a weakness of the heart. I believe you must understand by now that we cannot be together and must void our promises to each other. I will remain your loving...

She couldn't quite bring herself to use the word "sister". The idea was too new, too full of hurt and sorrow. *I will remain your loving friend, Esperanza Niles.*

She used the sand and then the sealing wax even though she would have trusted Leona with her life. No one else had any need to know of her father's sin.

"Please, Leona, go to the cemetery and give this to Rufe. I should have been there an hour ago. He will be frantic."

"I will do whatever I can to help you, Espy, always."

"You are dearer to me than any of my sisters. Go, now. Call up the carriage."

****

A desperate Rufus Courville paced beside his family's sepulcher. Leona Cortez made her way across the grass, the sound of her skirts rustling causing him look up in hope. Rufe frowned.

"What are you doing here? Where is Espy? I have to tell her my mother is sending me away again—to Europe. It is all a scheme to separate us, I know, but I will write and she will wait. I will be of age when I return and nothing can stop us then!" He raked his hands through his auburn hair as the color rose in his cheeks. His whiskey-colored eyes held a feverish look.

Leona watched his face calmly. The reason why her dear friend could never marry Rufe Courville was as plain to see as the red hair on the man's head. Rufus Courville—the son of Aaron Niles. Espy had always adored her father and admired the likeness veiled by another family name. Poor dear heart.

"She is at home tending to her sick father. I have a message for you." She held out the note, then tucked her hands away as tidily as the nuns after he seized the paper.

He felt the wrongness of the salutation at once. Where were the words My Beloved Rufus?

"They have told her some lie to keep us apart. You must tell her to wait. I will write. I'll send my direction at each stop along the way so she can answer me. Do tell her, I beg of you."

"It would be best for all concerned if you forgot Espy entirely and set your hopes on someone else, Mr. Courville."

Did he see pity in the usually cold features of Leona Cortez? The thought was as unbearable as a life without Esperanza Niles. And now to add insult to injury, here came Francois riding his black horse right up to the tomb.

"No use in hiding here, baby brother. Your trunks are packed and in the carriage. Mother will see you gone today even if we must travel at night to catch the steamer in Chapelle in two days time. You have fallen from her favor at last and I am no happier to lose valuable time escorting you to New Orleans just as the sickly season begins. She does not trust you to make your arrangements and board the ship without someone to oversee your every action. I am sorry Miss Cortez, but Rufus must leave your company at once."

"Go with God, Rufus Courville," Leona said as she turned and made her way to the waiting carriage.

"God has nothing to do with this! There is a devil in the works and his name is Aaron Niles!" Rufe shouted after her, but Leona did not turn back or say another word.

"Baby brother, if you have your heart set on that one, you'll have it broken. Our mother says the nuns want her, and cold as she is, the convent will be a good place for her. The mother of Leona Cortez was a silly slut, I've heard, and now the daughter wants to take the vows. From whore to nun in two generations. It makes me laugh."

"Perhaps, the mother had to fall in order for the daughter to become a nun. Some things are ordained to happen."

"Our mother's piety is rubbing off on you, baby brother. Still, if I wanted to put a stick up the ass of Aaron Niles, I'd seduce the warm-eyed one with the womanly figure, Esperanza. Unlike Marie-Celeste, I'd wager she's fertile as a sow just like her mother."

"Don't speak her name!"

"It would suit me if I never spoke to you again. Now, get on your horse and bid your mother farewell. You will be gone a long time."

Chapter Seven

"Look at them, Leona. Have you ever seen such love? There is Mama, so great with child her travail may begin at any moment, forcing Papa to waltz her around the ballroom in order to strengthen his leg. I hoped for a love like that once and thought I'd found it." Espy pierced the linen pillowslip she embroidered with a needle dragging yellow thread behind it. The pattern was yellow roses, always yellow roses.

She and Leona sat hiding from the heat of the July day in the most shaded area of the verandah. The doors to the long, narrow ballroom stood open at both ends to catch any breeze, the twin chandeliers bagged in cheesecloth to keep off the dust from the road. With Papa ill and Mama greatly expectant, the ball to celebrate the girls' graduation had been cancelled. Mama promised them a magnificent fete in the autumn, but neither desired it.

Moments before her parents had stumbled by counting—one, two, three—one two three—out onto the verandah and around the porch to the other side. The couple now collapsed, laughing, into two dainty chairs sitting by the empty fireplace. Her mother waved a fan next to her perspiring face.

"Uncle Aaron has slowed down awfully. He used to turn Aunt Ramona until she became quite dizzy. Still, he has made a wonderful recovery according to

Dr. Maddox—who seems to visit his patient with great frequency." Leona stole a quick glance at the oblivious Espy.

"Yes, it's good to see Papa getting better. Dr. Maddox takes excellent care of him."

"He comes to see you, you silly goose! All those compliments about your gentle hands, your caring soul helping to heal your father—don't you notice?"

"Most days are simply a struggle to contain my tears, Lee. Forgive me for saying Papa's illness has been a welcome distraction."

"You need more time. That is all. But, my dear friend, now that Uncle Aaron is on the mend, I mustn't delay my entry into the convent."

"Poor Andy, he hoped you would be his bride one day."

"Andy has always been like my pesky younger brother. How could I marry him?" Leona wished she had bitten her tongue when she saw Espy's hand shake and the needle prick her friend's finger. She said quickly, "Ah well, Andy loses me to the Lord Jesus, not some unworthy man. He will get over it."

"You don't believe love is eternal?"

"Only God's love qualifies for that, I think. I will pray for you each and every day, Espy."

Espy tried to smile, but the tears splashed down as she watched her father and mother leaning close together despite the heat. They pored over a bit of paper her father had taken from his waistcoat.

"Now what is this?" Ramona Niles said. "I don't believe I can see straight after our dance. You are improving, or perhaps my belly is so big you can't get near enough to step on my feet."

"I n-never step on your feet."

Oh, how he hated the stuttering, having to dig for words that used to be on the tip of his tongue. His wife rushed to reply. "Oh, really? You were always so exuberant you didn't notice, I think."

He smiled at her, still very aware only one side of his mouth responded. She joked and told him a crooked smile was very dashing. Good Lord, how he loved her. Aaron smoothed the paper as best he could for her perusal.

"Let's see this drawing. Is it our house? What are all these squares across the front?"

"N-no. It ish—is my t-tomb." If he spoke carefully, he could control the slurring.

Ramona crumpled the paper in her fist and threw it over the ornamental screen that hid the empty fireplace. "We have no need for that."

"Like our house, but with a p-place for all, you, the ch-children." He reached his long, strong arm over the screen and retrieved the paper. "C-columns all around, a winged victory atop. C-call it an angel to make the Sisters happy. Start it soon."

"Nonsense. We have no immediate need for a burial place."

"P-please, 'Mona."

He wrung her heart with his words. She took his chin her hand. "Say, Ra-mona, and I might do as you ask." She could feel the muscles of his face bunching.

"Ramona."

"I will summon the bricklayers and order the marble within the month. Now, let's have our dinner. I wish to lie down after the meal. You have worn me out."

Aaron gave her another of his crooked smiles.

****

The eleventh child of Aaron and Ramona Niles came so swiftly and easily around dusk that Louisa, the midwife, barely had time to lay down the waterproof and old, but clean sheets. Glad of the easy birth, Ramona declared, "We shall call her Victoria Claire in acknowledgment of trials overcome in the past year by the grace of God." Sponged of her birth sweat and blood and wearing a nightdress her eldest daughter had decorated with a pattern of yellow roses, she watched her husband goggle over the cradle. He loved all his children so. This made five daughters, and she had to admit, she'd hoped for another son. Girls, they were so much trouble.

****

The letters kept coming—from London, Venice, Athens, even Cairo in exotic Egypt. Though Ramona did not withhold them from her daughter, Esperanza Niles answered not a one. She read them all, each lush description of a foreign place, each vow of love, then bound the letters together with a ribbon and placed them in the secret compartment of her jewel box. They lay there hidden in their drawer beneath the small ruby earbobs her grandfather had given her, and the gold brooch with the glass inset containing a tuft of brother Henry's hair.

Leona had delivered part of Rufe's verbal message back in May. His mother insisted he go abroad. He would not be home for several years.

"And you may be sure that cowardly woman has not told her son of his true paternity. I loathe her for causing you such pain, Espy, but God delivered you in time."

"You know, then?"

"All the world would see the resemblance if they hadn't kept Rufus out of sight for so many years. Now, they have sent him off again instead of facing the truth. Let us pray he never returns to Rainbow."

"Rainbow is his home, too. Have some compassion," she'd said, but Leona had tightened her lips and not answered.

Now, Lee also had gone away to take the veil. That hadn't sat well with Espy's father. He begrudged the church any of his young ladies, though he had been generous in giving the nuns a section of piney woods adjoining the rear of the Academy's grounds. It was a good turpentine lot if the Sisters cared to tap the trees, or they could sell the pines for lumber. The slave Molly's twin girls, trained to be better servants than their mother by Ramona, had gone with Leona as well and would be put under the tutelage of Plato's Jeannette.

On the day when Espy lost her best friend to God, her parents stood side by side in front of the immense mausoleum they were erecting for their eternal rest. Two Italian stonecutters brought from New Orleans to carve the Corinthian capitols for the columns estimated the work would take two years. Esperanza shivered at the thought of her parents' enthusiasm for lying side by side in death. Losing either of them seemed nearly unbearable.

Esperanza wandered away through the graveyard and dropped a few wildflowers on the resting places of Old Plato and his woman. She remembered him as kindly and hardworking and his woman as silent, but doting as she slipped the youngest students gingersnaps when they cried over being taken from their homes to board at the Academy. Rumors abounded that Molly's girls were swishing their tails at his grandson, Jean, who held the place of Number One Man on the Academy grounds and oversaw the work of all the other outdoor hands, just as his sister had control of the maids and kitchen workers. Jean made certain the brick stable stayed as clean as some houses. The rich manure hauled from there nourished the huge vegetable garden and grew monstrous flowers in the beds surrounding the oval drive and the side paths of the school.

The Academy was a wonderful place, a holy place. If she thought her father wouldn't have another episode of apoplexy, Espy might have entered the convent herself, but she knew her vocation to be impure. Leona wanted to guide young women to be stronger, to make better decisions and be more devoted to God than her own mother. Esperanza merely wanted to escape from the pain in her heart her mother kept assuring her would pass. Given her own choice, she would be the first to be entombed in the new mausoleum before she suffered another lose.

Dr. Maddox fretted about Esperanza's declining weight and constant melancholy. He encouraged her with sweets and threatened her with bleeding to correct the imbalance causing her decline, but her Papa would not allow it even though the procedure had saved his own life. Feeling weak because the September day grew very hot and she hadn't eaten breakfast in her misery over having Leona taken in by the nuns, Espy sank down on a stone bench near the wrought iron fence that separated the dead from the living. She barely took note of what her parents discussed with such deadly seriousness.

"I know I will go to hell, Ramona. I don't fear death or the d-devil himself. It's being without you for all eternity that I dread." Aaron Niles put his weak arm around his wife's shoulders and held her close.

"Don't be ridiculous. I drag you to confession often enough. At most, you will do a stint a purgatory for making mock of poor Fr. Cyprien, my love." Ramona Niles reached up to squeeze the left hand that had never regained its former strength.

"He listens to the confessions of nuns and schoolgirls. My repentance must be the high point of his week. He enjoys giving me maximum acts of contrition for minor sins."

"Then, you should not bait him. Never worry, though. I shall find you wherever you go."

"You will be in heaven and I hardly believe St. P-Peter will allow me to enter there."

"Then, I will ask to be sent to wherever you are."

"Truly, you would risk hell for me?"

"I would, beloved, but I don't think it will come to that. Now, I suppose I must confess that to Fr. Cyprien."

"I believe I could be forgiven for the affair. I have tried to make up for it by being a faithful husband, a good father, a kind master—but the boy. There is nothing I can do about the boy. I would have killed him for Espy's sake and I am not contrite about that."

"It's all in God's hands now. Enough of this morbid talk. What do you think of enclosing the tomb and those of Henry and Cecile with a fence of its own in the weeping willow pattern, perhaps the one with lambs beneath the trees? Wouldn't that be lovely?"

****

Letters from his mother always waited at his new address when Rufus Courville moved on to the next city in his tour. He enjoyed her chitchat about Rainbow. Dr. Maddox had opened an office in the town, good because Francois had been ailing ever since his return from New Orleans. The chills and fevers came and went, leaving his brother weak for a long time afterwards. They feared he had the dreaded malaria. She warned Rufe to be cautious of the foul air in the Roman forum and Colosseum known to cause the same disease.

He scanned her words for any news of the Niles family, but all he found was that the old devil, Aaron Niles, had survived his illness, and though he had some impediments, would probably live to a ripe age. In Athens, he learned Leona Cortez had entered the convent just as Francois predicted. No news of Esperanza, no letters in her hand. Her family must be keeping his every missive from her and his own relatives were not sympathetic enough to pass along notes for him.

Rufe was tempted to make a side trip to ancient Egypt. There he would buy Espy a necklace of lapis to go with the one of glass beads he'd purchased for her in Venice. The glassworkers called the pattern millefiori, a thousand flowers, for Esperanza Niles. He'd slipped a bit in his devotion in that city of canals. The courtesans were well practiced and his need grew so great, but he had gone to an Italian church and confessed in order to regain his purity for Espy. A year and six months must pass before he would be welcomed home again.

Rufe wintered in Cairo and took a dhow along the Nile to see the pyramids and the massive ruins of the ancient Egyptians. He saw the very colossus that had inspired the poet Shelley to write his great poem, *Ozymandius*. In his letter to Esperanza, he wrote:

My Dearest Espy—What is made by man soon crumbles. I have seen enough ruins on this tour to make that observation quite forcefully. Only love is eternal—as is my love for you. I know you are prevented from answering my letters, but oh, how I need some sign that you are reading my thoughts and remaining constant. Yours, Always Yours—Rufe

No matter how long he lingered in Cairo, the only mail arriving came from his mother who chided him for departing from his itinerary and spending Christmas among the heathens when he could have gone to Jerusalem and followed in the footsteps of Christ. Francois had recovered with the onset of cooler weather. The grinding of the cane crop was nearly complete and they would ship seven hundred hogsheads of raw sugar to the refinery, an excellent year.

Rufe welcomed 1842 by getting supremely drunk with several other young men who insisted he accompany them to a brothel where the women danced clad only in sheer veils. In the morning, he reeked of a musky perfume and only remembered the whore's long, black hair had reminded him of Espy. Disgusted with himself, he went off to Jerusalem and wallowed in religion for a time. Later, he followed the sun north along the coast of Turkey and engaged Mussulmen guides who swore every hillock and crumbling archway to be long lost Troy even if the inscriptions were clearly in Latin.

Brooding in the footsteps of Lord Byron, Rufe re-crossed Greece and arrived back in Rome in time to attend the papal Easter Mass. For a time, its splendor lifted his gloom. He wrote long and detailed accounts to both Esperanza and his mother of the glories of St. Peter's Cathedral.

Reaching the Alps in June, Rufus Courville wrote again from his guesthouse on the shores of Lake Lucerne that his love was as deep as the blue-green lake and as towering as the mountains surrounding him. If he did not have word from Esperanza soon, he would be tempted to throw himself into the ice-cold water and end his misery. Before he could post this melodramatic nonsense—and he did recognize it as such—his mother's letters caught up with him once more.

With the return of the heat, Francois had suffered another bout of the illness, leaving him drained of the energy needed to run the plantation. Dr. Maddox recommended a long rest and perhaps a trip to the restorative mineral baths in the cooler mountain atmosphere of Hot Springs. Marguerite hinted that taking the waters sometimes cured other long-standing conditions and so Marie-Celeste would accompany her husband and soak in the curative pools. His mother would carry on, missing both her boys, with the help of her sons-in-law and a strong overseer.

Mention of Dr. Maddox caused an idea to form. The physician was a kind soul who went from plantation to plantation caring for the sick, both white and black. Why not enlist his aid in getting a letter to Esperanza? Rufe scribbled the direction on his letter, not to Frenchman's Bend Plantation, Rainbow, Louisiana, but to Dr. Owen Maddox, his office in the same town.

****

Esperanza Niles sat in the shade on the north side of the portico. The heat of the July morning made her palms sweat, leaving little marks on the gingham and causing her needle to slip. The garment was simple enough, an infant's dress for a servant who had recently given birth. She'd already hemmed a pile of diaper cloths in preparation for a visit to the cabin.

Her father, cursing and swearing because he still needed assistance to mount his horse from the left, his weak side, had gone off with Andy and the twins to survey the fields. Amalia, offended because she had not been invited along "all because I might see some half-naked darkies in their presence" had called for her horse and gone to the Academy where she "could do some good and might be appreciated" leaving Espy to finish the task their mother had assigned.

Espy looked up with alarm when Dr. Maddox rounded a corner of the house and came her way. "Is someone ill, Doctor? Did Papa fall off his horse in the fields?"

"I find one of the problems with being a man of medicine is no one ever assumes I have merely come to call. I do enjoy a cool drink in the presence of a lovely lady on a hot day as much as any man." He flushed slightly, perhaps from the heat.

Owen sat in a rocker across from Esperanza and fumbled in his waistcoat, finding first his thumb lancet, then two peppermints, and at last, the paper that had given him an excuse to seek out Miss Niles.

"A letter from abroad curiously addressed to me, but meant for you."

On the outside of the folded paper, Rufe had written, *Kindly forward to Miss Esperanza Niles of Frenchman's Bend Plantation.*

Espy put her sewing aside and reluctantly accepted her mail. The servant who had shown the doctor the young missy's whereabouts appeared with a pitcher of lemonade and two glasses, put the refreshments on a small table and went silently back to her other duties.

"Aren't you going to open it? Please do not wait on my account. On the rare occasions I receive news from England, I am eager to get at it."

In order not to appear secretive or rude, Espy cracked the seal and ran her eyes swiftly over the note. She paled and gave a small gasp.

Dr. Maddox immediately took her hand and laid his fingers lightly on the pulse in her wrist. "Your pulse is rapid. Are you unwell? How long have you been out here in the heat without taking a drink?" He poured the lemonade and held the glass to her lips, steadying her head with his other hand.

"Thank you. It is not the heat that bothers me. Last year around the time of my father's illness, I was forced to break off an engagement to Rufus Courville. He had formed an unhealthy attachment to me and now says he will drown himself if I do not respond."

"May I?"

Dr. Maddox picked up the letter and shook his head. "The key word here is tempted. Although he is clearly a very overwrought young man, I believe he will do nothing of the kind, and if he did, it would be no fault of yours. I have been present at the aftermath of several suicides and the persons involved rarely gave warning or even left a note if they were truly determined to put an end to themselves. Others simply want attention like this callow lad. I met him once. He was nearly overcome when he learned that his mother had a heart condition. It is hard for the young to accept that death comes when it will at each person's appointed time, and as a doctor, I can delay the Grim Reaper only so long."

"You make yourself sound as old as the hills surrounding us." Esperanza, revived, smiled at Owen Maddox. His hands trembled visibly.

"Thirty years loom just ahead."

"My papa was nearly thirty when he wed my mother, newly graduated from the Academy and just eighteen. Here I am, a spinster of nineteen, making clothes for the children of others."

"Hardly a spinster yet. If you would go about more, and as a doctor I recommend this, men would fall at your feet."

"Then, I should have the trouble of having to step right over them."

She made this little joke and waited for his words. Dr. Maddox was so sure of himself in medical matters and so awkward in society she often wanted to protect him from the world. Always kind and well meaning, he had fretted over her health all winter. How he rejoiced when he thought one of his potions had finally restored her appetite and banished her melancholy—when the cure really had been the passage of time and the coming of another spring.

"Oh, of course. Men falling at your feet like plague victims, not a very good turn of phrase, I'm afraid."

"You are afraid too often and need only to speak to me plainly."

"Yes, well. Have you plans for your Fourth of July celebration, then? I thought I might attend the picnic in Opelousas. Dignitaries will be giving patriotic speeches all afternoon, and I hear there will be a public concert, a firing of cannon, and perhaps a few skyrockets. Would you consider going with me? The smoke and noise will most likely keep off the mosquitoes and prevent unhealthy air from gathering if you are concerned about staying after dark." His Adam's apple bobbed up and down as he swallowed after issuing this long invitation.

"Never fear, I am quite well now and would be delighted to celebrate our nation's birth with a person from the opposing side. My family goes into town every year for the festivities and you must join us. Our cook always packs far too much. Papa gives the hands a day off and several pigs to roast and employs a fiddler to keep them busy dancing. It wouldn't do for the Negroes to hear long rants about freedom."

"England may have lost the war but did abolish slavery in 1833. I think your country has some catching up to do."

"The end of slavery will mean the end of all this." Esperanza gestured to the house and the spacious yard studded with oaks and flowerbeds.

"A doctor's wife will never go hungry. I mean a doctor is always needed in good times and bad. We are never without employment, so our families won't starve."

"Speaking of starving, the afternoon meal should be nearly ready. Will you join us? You once threatened to feed me every mouthful of the egg custard you prescribed to build me up if I didn't do it by myself."

"For your own good, my dear Miss Niles."

"Espy. Please call me Espy."

"And I shall be Owen to you."

****

Even the doctor appeared to be part of the conspiracy to keep them apart. Rufus Courville fumed as more time passed with no answer to the last letter. He'd expected some response to be waiting in Paris where he dawdled in the cafés and salons and went to view collections of antiquities looted by Napoleon and carried back to France. He was expected in Lyons by Marie-Celeste's family and meant to spend the winter holidays with them, but he still watched the red leaves fall into the Seine from a table in the Latin Quarter when October came. He finished his wine and his mother's letter.

Francois had improved somewhat in health, but his mother noted no change in Marie-Celeste's condition. If any young woman caught his eye in Lyons, he must be sure to observe the number of children in her family and the health of her mother. She depended upon her dear Rufus to see the Courville name did not vanish from Rainbow, Louisiana. She could not say this any plainer. He must uproot himself from Paris and get on with his journey.

Indeed, he would. He might suffer through Christmas while excess daughters were thrown in his pathway and stay until March when the weather improved, but the second he turned twenty-one, Rufus Courville intended to return to Rainbow and claim Esperanza Niles.

****

As Rufe had feared, his stay in Lyons was dreadful. Not that the Marchands lacked in hospitality or worldly goods. He had a room more than comfortable, even quite luxurious, and the meals were superb. They treated the second son of an American planter like the landed gentry of England or maybe like the aristocracy the French so handily got rid of with their guillotine. Marie-Celeste had sent her family small sketches and watercolors of the Courville estate, the elegant home, the lawns, the colored men and women going about their daily tasks like happy French peasants. Clearly, they would be only too glad to place another of their daughters in the same situation.

When Rufe did not immediately take a liking to Marie-Celeste's youngest sisters, a flat-chested, consumptive blonde and a schoolgirl given to giggling, female cousins had been imported from surrounding towns. Two were brunettes with big white teeth and hips the size of brood mares. Both came from enormous families. If he looked for breeding stock, they would certainly have filled the bill. A twenty-four year old spinster with a lazy eye was taken from the shelf, dusted off and presented for his inspection. Who knew what Americans would find attractive?

Rufe politely danced with them all, exquisitely careful to favor none of them during the Christmas festivities. When Twelfth Night came, he began to long for the rowdiness of Mardi Gras in New Orleans. While at school in Baton Rouge, he and several other senior boys slipped off to carouse in the Old Quarter. The punishment had been worth the crime on their return. He recognized this as a pang of homesickness, the first he'd had, other than his longing for Esperanza Niles. He began to plot his return to Louisiana.

The letter came before he completed his

arrangements. In just another affectionate, chatty missive of several pages from his mother, Rufus Courville finally received news of Esperanza Niles. Grinding season was over, another good year for sugar-making. The weather continued unseasonably warm. She feared Francois might have a relapse. Dr. Maddox was not about as he had wed the eldest Miss Niles on St. Valentine's Day and taken her to honeymoon in his native England. They did not expect the couple back until the end of May and so the good people of Rainbow had to seek medical treatment in Vermilionville. Wanting to show his bride the daffodils that bloomed in April—a poor excuse for abandoning his patients, his mother thought.

Rufe had planned on taking Espy to the warm clime of Italy first and then on to Greece and Egypt. He felt England to be too chilly and damp for a warm-blooded southern girl. He'd dreamt of their wedding eve a hundred times—the two of them entangled on a humid June night beneath the tent of netting covering their bed—and woke embarrassed with himself just as often. But, Esperanza Niles had been faithless and married another.

The Marchands noticed their guest went off his food and later attributed this to a premonition of the receipt of a black-bordered missive coming hard on the heels of the previous letter. Francois Courville had died, taken by a severe bout of malaria not even large doses of quinine could quell. He expired before the physician from Vermilionville arrived. Rufus must come home at once and take control of the plantation before the hands took advantage of the two widowed ladies and began to run off.

Now he should hurry home. Now he was needed—while Esperanza visited England, closer than she had been in nearly two years, as the bride of another man. The Marchands heaped their guest with condolences and gifts for Marie-Celeste: precious pots of goose liver paste, cases of good wine and bolts of silk, some of the vivid colors exchanged for black. They waited to see if Rufus would make an offer for any of their young ladies before seeing him on his way. He did not.

Chapter Eight

Rufus Courville first saw Esperanza Niles Maddox again in church on a June day beautiful enough for a wedding. He'd helped Marie-Celeste and his increasingly frail mother, both dressed in their widow's weeds, into the pew and started to enter the row himself when Aaron Niles, using a cane to support the weak leg slightly shortened by his stroke, came clumping down the aisle followed by his wife. Rufe noticed the lady was breeding again. That man, one side of his face slumping, the other side still devilish, would probably mount his woman on his deathbed. Rufe began to turn away in disgust when he noticed who followed.

There she appeared, his Espy, becomingly dressed in rustling dark blue silk and judging by the loose ties of the skirt and slope of her bodice, also with child. Her brown eyes seemed larger and finer than he remembered and she'd taken on the glow that gave great beauty to some expectant mothers. Behind her walked a tall, stooped man with spectacles and a bushy mustache, his face full of adoration for the pregnant woman. For a moment, Rufe did not recognize Dr. Maddox with his newly sprouted facial hair. The man gave him an affable nod.

Rufe jerked his head toward his mother and Marie-Celeste. Neither had given the slightest hint they knew of Esperanza's return. He had immersed himself in making a sugar crop, work all week and church on Sundays. With the family in mourning, they had few social distractions. Both women knelt in prayer, totally oblivious to his thundering heart.

He presented his back when Espy approached, but the thud of her prayer book hitting the floor forced him to look around. She gestured toward the book and asked softly, "Would you be so kind?"

Rufe bent stiffly, retrieved the missal and thrust it at her. She leaned close to take it and breathed very quietly, "Oh Rufe, your mother never told you the truth."

Her sympathy smarted worse than a blow to the face. Her words were an insult to the one woman who truly loved him. His booming voice filled the nave of the church to its rafters. "Don't speak her name, you lying, fickle bitch!"

If Rufe had thrown a rock through the colored windows and stabbed her in the heart with a shard, Esperanza could not have been more wounded. She stepped back, a hand to her heart, and tangled in her skirts, began to fall. Dr. Maddox caught her in his arms, his expression frozen in astonishment.

In years to come, Rufus Courville would remember every detail of that scene. Behind Espy and her husband, the procession of the Niles family came to a halt. Homely, big-boned Amalia, her face gone pale around its freckles, clutched a toddling little girl. Her two younger sisters, clad in lacy pantalets, pretty dresses and prim bonnets, looked confused and blocked the aisle with their skirts. Behind them, the Niles twins, red-faced, dropped the hands of eight-year old Danny and squirming, four-year-old Billy, who immediately made his escape down a side aisle. Looming over all of them, Andy Niles, come into his towering full growth but not yet completely filled-out, grew livid. He began to push his siblings aside, the gloves he had just removed clenched in his fist, but the challenge did not come from Andrew Jackson Niles.

Aaron Niles, the patriarch, his face turned even redder than his son's, delivered the sharp slap with his good hand. "I'll k-kill you."

Rufe stared directly into those whiskey-colored eyes and prepared to accept the challenge. He saw the moment when Aaron Niles' pupils suddenly widened as if the sky beyond the stained glass windows had gone dark. The big man crashed to the floor.

Ramona Niles shrieked, "No, no! This cannot be!"

Marie-Celeste called out, "Rufe, your mother!"

Confused, Rufe turned toward the pew where his mother lay crumpled against her daughter-in-law. He went to her and looked wildly around for help. Dr. Maddox attended to Aaron Niles, but from the seats at the front of the church where the nuns sang in a choir, he saw old Sr. Francine push up with her knotted walking stick and move toward them. The regal Mother Leontine, her usual serenity shattered, got to her feet as well.

When he seized Marguerite's hand, she opened her eyes, and speaking against the pain breaking in her chest, said, "My dearest son, Aaron is your father. That girl, your half-sister. He and I, we will pass through the gates of hell together."

"Then I should have died at birth and you with me!" Rufe cried out.

The mass of people in the aisle gave way before

Mother Leontine. "Never say that. You do not know the will of God who gave you life, Rufus Courville."

Andy Niles tried to push past the nun, but she turned with a suddeness that belied her years and blocked his way. "And you, Andrew Jackson Niles, will not make this tragedy worse. See to your mother and sisters and think of how they would go on without you."

The young man hesitated, then turned away to put his arms around his sobbing mother. Dr. Maddox held the head of Aaron Niles while Esperanza chafed her father's hands, trying to banish their coldness. The doctor looked up at Mother Leontine. "Dead," he said.

The Lady Mother turned toward Sr. Francine who leaned over the front pew and held the wrist of Marguerite Courville. "Gone," she said.

Chapter Nine

For all the clarity of that scene in the church replaying over and over in his mind, Rufus Courville barely remembered the next few days. He knew he had picked up his mother, so light considering the heaviness of her sin, and carried her from the church at Marie-Celeste's urging. Once at the house, his sister-in-law placed a decanter of brandy and a glass in front of him and went to lay out the body in the bedchamber. By the time he thought to look for his pistols, they had gone missing. When he demanded that the weapons be found and brought to him, Marie-Celeste hushed him as she stopped the clock and covered the mirror in the parlor. She had put them in a safe place, she assured him.

Well, she could not hide all the rope on the plantation and plenty of stout oak trees grew in the vicinity of Rainbow. He'd lived on the bayou all his life and was too strong a swimmer to drown in its warm and silty waters, no matter what he had once written to Espy. Oh God! Just for now, he would drown himself in brandy.

Someone ordered a fine coffin and the hearse drawn by four black-plumed horses from the undertaker in Opelousas. Was it he? Neighbors came and his sisters—his half-sisters—and their families filled the rooms. One of them made sure a servant brushed his black coat, shined his boots and knotted his neckcloth properly into a bow. No one would allow him to ride Satan in the funeral procession. One of his brothers-in-laws forced him into the carriage, sandwiched between Marthe and Mariette, making escape impossible. Mariette's youngest son, a toddler, sat on her lap. The child called Rory took one look at his uncle and bawled, his bright blue eyes swimming with terrified tears. The boy recognized a terrible beast despite the proper clothes when he saw one.

Courville slaves lined the way, bidding farewell to Old Missus by singing one of their dirges, something about a chariot coming. Rufe hazily recalled a gasp when he'd stumbled while helping in carrying the casket to the front of the church for the Mass for the Dead. Afterwards, the family finally let him alone. He stayed by the Courville crypt watching some of the nuns' darkies seal the grave and reset the marble panel previously engraved with his mother's name and birth date and the words "Beloved Wife and Mother", which struck him as very funny. They had only to add the day her son had brought about her death. He did not know how he got home.

Rufe woke late the next morning with a headache and a crisis. His hands shook too hard to hold a razor so he went into breakfast unshaven. When he called for whiskey, he got black coffee and a scolding from Marie-Celeste.

"You are the master now. You, who wanted to be a planter and not a doctor or a lawyer. Jacques Gros," she said, referring to one of the work gang leaders, "has been waiting to see you on an important matter half the morning."

"He gets out of work, doesn't he?" Rufe took the

dry toast offered to him on a china plate.

"Yes, and he risks being beaten by that overseer your mother hired during Francois' illness because he has been gone so long from the fields. Think of someone besides yourself, Rufus. Do not be such a child."

Rufe slammed down his cup with enough force to crack it. "I'll see what he wants, then, before I've eaten!" He stalked out of the dining room to the rear of the house where Jacques Gros waited in the shade of the portico. The huge Negro stood and whipped off his hat. Looking at the ground, he said, "Sorry to bother you, Mastah. Mr. Boutte, de overseer, done whipped Sedonia for not being quick enough."

"What of it?" Rufe rubbed his temples. The sunlight beyond the portico pierced his eyes like the thorns on his mother's yellow roses.

"Well, Mastah, Sedonia los' de baby she was carryin' and died right after out in de fields. Where you want us to bury dem?"

What a ridiculous question! The slaves had their own burying ground and even a small chapel his mother had insisted on building for them. He'd been called from his breakfast for this? Rufe was about to snap out those very words when he noticed Jacques Gros' big eyes now looked up at him hopefully. Slowly, Rufe comprehended Boutte had whipped a pregnant woman for being slow and caused two deaths.

"Take Sedonia and her child back to the quarters. Have some of the old women wash the bodies and prepare them for burial. Tell John Cooper to make up a coffin. I'll send for Fr. Cyprien to say some words in the chapel. We'll ring the bell when it's time to come in for the service."

"We appreciates dat, Mastah, but could you come say dat to Mistah Boutte? He think I'm lyin'."

"Very well. Have one of the boys saddle my horse and bring him round. How did you come?"

"In de mule wagon."

"Fine. You can show me where you were working." Rufe went inside to gulp down his now cold coffee and pour another cup. He wolfed the toast, explained the situation briefly to Marie-Celeste and went to look for his hat. His sister-in-law bid him a very pleasant farewell.

The ride out to the work area jolted his brain while the rays of the noonday sun shot bolts into his eyeballs. If Rufe's mind hadn't been so fuddled with drink, he would have realized most of what he ordered was already being done. The wagon had borne the bodies back to the quarters and the old women washed the dead as he spoke to Jacques Gros. John Cooper had already begun shaping the coffin, but only the Master could call for time off for a service. Later, when the heat burned off the alcohol in his system, he realized this.

The slaves were silently hoeing down weeds in a patch of cane. None of the work gang leaders started up a song to keep the rhythm and make the work go lighter. To Rufe's eyes, the field hands appeared shabbier and thinner than usual. Their clothes were tattered and lash marks showed through the gaps in their rags. Francois had loved bullying the big Negro bucks as he sat on a high horse that gave him stature over them, but his brother hadn't been one to reduce the value of his property through starvation or excessive punishment. This was the work of a man who had no interest in the returns of their labor but worked for a salary and the power the job gave him over others.

Mr. Boutte walked up to Rufus Courville, hat in hand. "I haven't had da pleasure of making your acquaintance since you been home, sir. I'm called Filo Boutte. Maybe, your mother, she had da time to tell you she was pleased wit' my work before she passed."

He held out a dirty hand. Rufe ignored it. "When you hear the plantation bell ring, the hands are to be dismissed for a funeral Mass for Sedonia. They will have the rest of the day off to bury their dead."

"Well now, we comin' up on da noon rest break. Can't we get dis out the way den, and get 'em back in da fields right after? We wastin' daylight otherwise."

"I've given Jacques Gros my word."

"You da master, you can change dat. No sense wastin' a whole afternoon on a dead nigger bitch." Boutte checked the time on a silver pocket watch that seemed a bit ornate for his station in life.

"No sense wasting a pregnant woman, either."

"Got to show da rest. Got to keep dem in line." Boutte wiped the sweat off his forehead with a red kerchief. Out from under the shade of the tree line where he'd been sitting, the sun blazed. The man's sour body odor, stronger than the musky scent of the slaves, rose to Rufe's nostrils. Did the man never wash or take a dip in the bayou?

"I'll speak to Jacques Gros before I leave."

"Whatever you say, sir, but he's an uppity one."

Leaving the overseer to seek some shade, Rufe turned his horse back to the mule wagon where the big man still sat slumped over. "Jacques Gros, how does

Mr. Boutte treat the hands, generally?"

"Guess he be de same as any overseer, Mastah. Maybe, he visit more wit' his friends down by de bayou."

"Social calls?"

"More business, I'd say."

"What kind of business?"

Jacques Gros shrugged. "Buyin' and sellin' business."

"And what would an overseer be selling?"

"Don't know, Mastah. Could be food. Could be clothing."

"I see. Listen for the bell. Lead the hands in when you hear it." Rufe rode off without another word to the overseer.

Back at the big house, he stayed the loading of provisions into a wagon for the hands' meal and asked the cook to ring the bell and call the workers in. All were to be fed before the service.

His own hearty dinner waited for him along with Fr. Cyprien who had been invited to partake before performing the simple service. Rufe had no appetite for the light soup, roasted chicken, steaming cornbread sticks and the last green beans the garden would produce in this heat, nor did he have much stomach for Fr. Cyprien. The priest chattered on about the growth of Rainbow and the need for a true congregational church since the nuns' chapel was becoming too crowded. With the proper donations, a small boys' school might be added to his plans as well. Some people in Rainbow would welcome the opportunity to give contributions that would help to cleanse their souls along with the usual confession and acts of contrition of course. He hoped to see Rufus Courville in church the following Sunday.

It seemed to be a day for subtle conversations. Rufe changed the subject by asking Marie-Celeste if the hands had received the customary two sets of new homespun clothing at Christmas.

"But of course," she answered from her seat across from Fr. Cyprien and next to Rufe, who had slipped into the place once occupied by Francois because that is where the dishes had been set.

"Would the servants use their older clothing and save the new for best?"

"I think not. They prefer brighter colors for their free time and frolics, red silk scarves, striped or checkered material if they can earn enough egg or moss-gathering money to buy it. Besides, by the end of grinding, the old clothes are good for nothing but rags."

"I see. And there has been no change in their rations?"

"I send the same food stuffs as your mother did, extra during grinding. To save time, Mr. Boutte has insisted some of the elderly women come out and cook the afternoon meal at the work site rather than let the hands return to their quarters. That is the only change since Francois died."

"Your late husband was an excellent provider, a generous supporter of my new project," Fr. Cyprien thought fit to add. "Your dear mother, Rufus, willed some of her widow's portion nearest town to the Academy, but I am petitioning Mother Leontine and the Sisterhood for that land on which to build the new and larger church. I have proposed the name St. Leo's. The Lady Mother should find that pleasing, don't you think?" The priest held out his cup for more wine, instantly refilled by a waiting servant.

A custard pie was served, roasted pecans and a sharp cheese offered along with rich, dark coffee. Fr. Cyprien waved away the sweet and had more wine with his savories. Finally finished, he rose to prepare for Sedonia's service.

Since the priest stopped at the necessary on the way to the simple white chapel sitting at the end of the quarters, no doubt taking the time to contemplate the hefty sums he could expect from Rufus Courville, Rufe and Marie-Celeste arrived before the priest and sat awaiting him in sturdy chairs to one side of the pulpit. The slave woman, Sedonia, laid out in a plain pine box lined with worn-out blankets, wore her best purple-flowered gingham and a red silk scarf on her head. The premature infant lay swaddled in her arms.

The chapel overflowed and more of the hands stood outside the open windows. Given the stench of the slaves, the proximity of the corpse and the rising heat, Fr. Cyprien, grown fat over the years, waddled into the sanctuary and hurried to begin. Madame Courville fanned herself rapidly, and he appeared grateful for any breeze she might send his way. The Negroes, as usual, were disrespectful, talking among themselves as he droned away in the Latin they could not understand.

Jacques Gros whispered to John Cooper. "Sedonia, she on her way to de promised land, no mo' work, no mo' beatings."

"White man's talk," John Cooper answered sullenly.

"Fine for you to say, John Cooper. Your woman

owned by de nuns who don't whoop anything but little schoolgirl hands and bottoms. Sedonia, she was mine and so was dat baby. Ole Boutte only whip her to keep me in line. Gotta believe she in a better place now."

"Believe what you want."

"I believe our new mastah gon' be fine, you see."

"All mastahs de same, Jacques Gros. You see."

Fr. Cyprien sprinkled the dead with holy water and signaled that the coffin be sealed. Women began to wail. He held up his hands to silence them and put aside his Latin for a moment.

"This woman has been called to God. She will be rewarded for her obedience and her hard work in the world to come. Rejoice, I say."

He motioned to Jacques Gros and John Cooper, who had whispered throughout his service making him uneasy, to come forward and shoulder the coffin. The two burly men carried it easily out of the church and around to the hole dug into the dense, dark soil of the slaves' graveyard shaded by wild pecan trees and water oaks. The priest said the final words, dropped some large clods of earth on the coffin and told the hands they could return to work.

Rufus Courville intervened. "You may rest this afternoon. In the morning, Jacques Gros will be head man. He will organize the gangs and you will continue working where you left off today. Now, has anyone seen Mr. Boutte?"

"He in de kitchen, Mastah," Jacques Gros called out, but to John Cooper he said, "Tole you so."

The overseer had pulled a chair up to the worn wooden table and enjoyed his coffee and a big slice of custard pie leftover from the dinner of the high and mighty Courvilles while the cook went to the funeral. His mouth was full of crust and filling when Rufus Courville blazed in and fired him without preamble.

Filo Boutte swallowed hard. "But me, I brought in a big crop dis year. Now you say my work's no good."

"I'd say if I took an inventory, plenty would come up missing. I'd say if I take a head count, I'd noticed more deaths and more runaways among the hands than in any previous year. I'd say you better get off Courville land before you finish that pie."

"Da horse, she is mine. Francois Courville give her to me."

"You ride that horse right out of here. Now!"

"I got friends, me. I got family in da swamps. You better not send nobody after me, you hear."

"Go before I find out where my pistols are."

Filo Boutte showed Rufe his back but took the half-eaten pie with him.

****

Evening came. Rufe and Marie-Celeste could hear the singing from the quarters. The music would likely go on all night. The hymns had started out slow and sad but now reached a joyous pitch. They sat listening on the upstairs verandah.

"You did well today, Rufe," the petite blonde woman said, waving away the night insects with her fan. He could just make out the pale oval of her face and the whiteness of her hands against the dark of her mourning gown.

"I thought it would never end. I felt like I was in some kind of purgatory where I'd always be hung over and no one would let me lie down and die."

"The day is not over. I suggest you spend some

time writing letters of apology and condolence to Ramona Niles and Esperanza Maddox—and to your sisters for your behavior at the funeral. Being women, they might forgive you, but don't deliver the messages yourself. The Niles boys are likely to shoot you on sight for insulting their sister and killing their father no matter what they have promised their mother and the nuns."

"Why don't you add destroying my own mother to the list and then give me back my pistols to finish me off?"

"Because I believe the redemption of Rufus Courville began today."

Chapter Ten

Women were one of the great mysteries of the universe—the secrets they kept, the men they chose to love, their ability to forgive—and mean it. Rufus Courville was profoundly grateful for all of that. His sisters replied to his notes with a scolding and a great deal of understanding. He had always been their mother's favorite child and so naturally had taken her death harder. If they knew Rufe to be only their half-brother, neither would ever admit to it.

Espy, gentle Espy, wrote at once to assure him that she did not consider him responsible for the terrible predicament that had caused him to insult her. Both of them had suffered a great loss, but that must be put aside. She and her husband wished only to be his dear friends in the future. Still, Rufe thought he would not call on Dr. Maddox to bleed him any time soon. Her kindness hurt more than calling him a bastard would have—because that is exactly what he was, Marguerite Courville's bastard.

Ramona Niles had not replied. He went to make his confession and present Fr. Cyprien with a large donation for the church project, knowing full well he would never set foot in the nuns' chapel again. He could barely pass their church without recalling the havoc he had wrought there. Once St. Leo's was built, he could return to Mass in a fresh place, clean of memories. Passing the cemetery on his way home, Rufe had seen her, the Widow Niles, standing in front of the ornate mausoleum where her husband lay interred. Her forehead beneath its black veil pressed against the cold marble sealing Aaron Niles in his grave.

Rufe stopped and tied his horse to the iron fence surrounding the graveyard. He walked past his family tomb, thorny with rosebushes wilting in the heat, and forced himself to address Mrs. Niles, first taking off his hat and turning it in his hands.

"Forgive the intrusion on your sorrow, but I-I must say that I am ashamed of my behavior toward your daughter and of all my impulsive actions that led to the passing of your husband. His death is my fault and mine alone." He thought she would snub him entirely and he put his hat back on preparing to leave.

"His own temper killed my husband. You were the most innocent one of all—and so like him, like Andy, like all my sons. I wish you a good life, Rufus. Both you and Andy should have enough work in running your plantations to keep you from coming to blows, but still I will ask you to make the same promise I have asked of him—you will not harm each other."

"My word on it, Madame." Rufe struggled to find an exit from the conversation now that they had reached an understanding. "I see more construction is underway at the Academy, right in the center of the circular drive."

"A last gift from my husband. He commissioned one of the pupils of Emile Duchamp, the French sculptor, to create a statue of the Blessed Virgin and the Christ Child to be placed there in honor of my fortieth birthday. Jean Plato and his men are laying the foundation for it. We will have a dedication and a special Mass when the statue arrives from Chapelle."

"A fitting tribute to a woman such as yourself," he managed to say. He kept his eyes averted from her pregnant belly.

"You might find comfort in doing something similar for your own mother, Rufus." Ramona patted his hand as if he were the one who needed comforting.

"I-I don't think so. Not at this time. The plantation, the work, consumes my energy. Good day, Mrs. Niles and God bless you."

He made his escape as rapidly as he could without breaking into a run. As he remounted to return to his ill-gotten estate, Rufe saw Ramona Niles had resumed her posture, pressed up against the marble as if she wanted to join her husband on the other side.

Marie-Celeste had dinner served when he returned. He had no appetite and would have over-imbibed in wine if his sister-in-law had not had the bottle removed.

Clearly, she had been thinking much farther ahead than he when she said, "I'd like to remain here and fulfill your mother's duties until you take a bride, Rufus. This plantation has been my home for ten years and I have no desire to return to France. I believe my blood has thinned too much in the heat to withstand the climate of Lyons anymore."

She tried to make a joke of it, but he could see she was serious. "You are welcome to stay as long as you want because I have no plans to marry. The cursed Courville name should die with me, don't you think? I'd hate to give my mother her dearest wish that I procreate. But, others might talk about your living here alone with your husband's despicable brother."

"And twelve household servants. Rufus, there will always be talk and I do not find you despicable. Two thousand acres need to be tilled and two hundred people are depending upon you for direction. I will help you with the task."

Rufus took a long look at his sister-in-law. She had to be at least thirty years of age, but having escaped the burden of childbirth, she'd kept her girlish figure and all of her teeth. Her blonde hair had no strands of silver, and if a few fine lines showed in the corners of her serene blue-gray eyes, they gave Marie-Celeste an air of wisdom and patience, especially patience with him. He had no desire for her or any other woman after coming so close to a mortal sin with Espy and the lovely French woman was barren. How perfect.

"We could marry," he said abruptly.

"That would require a dispensation from the Church, Rufus, and I would not dishonor your brother by taking another husband before completing my year of mourning. Let us see how we go along and perhaps in the spring, we might consider your proposal again."

By the way Marie-Celeste tilted her head and gave him a small smile, he had the feeling she'd considered the idea before, perhaps while lying alone in the big, canopied bed in the master's suite while he stayed in the bedchamber of his childhood.

"Until then," he said. "I am sure we can buy a dispensation from Fr. Cyprien."

****

With so much to repair and replace, time passed quickly for Rufus Courville. His domestic life ran smoothly under the guidance of Marie-Celeste and his holidays were spent quietly at the home of his sister,

Marthe. He attended midnight Mass in Opelousas with her family and came back to the plantation to hand out new clothes and small gifts of money for the hands and candy to their children like an old Father Christmas. He failed to notice when his sister-in-law added a white collar to her dress or when she changed from black gowns to gray and lavender.

His first grinding of cane had been good, if not spectacular. He had the new crop muddied into the rows and he'd seen to increasing the drainage as the spring was wet enough to rot the sprouts. He seemed to be riding in mud all day, every day, and needed a complete washing down when he came in for dinner.

Rufe was sluicing himself with warm water in the mudroom when Marie-Celeste came to the door to inform him dinner would be served in half an hour. She usually sent a servant. Grateful he'd kept on his cotton drawers, he reached self-consciously for a towel and the clean shirt folded neatly on a nearby bench. Even his bare feet embarrassed him somehow by being large and white and sprinkled with a bit of auburn hair.

Marie-Celeste looked cool and calm. She wore a full-skirted gray dress with a black velvet ribbon accenting her narrow waist. Simple pearl drops dangled from her small ears and her hair had been done in a most becoming way, a style he'd never noticed before. She didn't turn her eyes away but glanced down at the spot where he clutched the towel in front of his groin. He hesitated, not wanting to drop the towel to put on the shirt. Her gaze swept up across his chest, youthful, firm and well-muscled with its thatch of reddish hair in the center reflected in the mirror he used to comb his hair. She would see he began to blush.

Rufe took his eyes from the mirror and stared over her shoulder toward the windbreak where the Judas trees and dogwoods bloomed. The grass sprouted a tender green and the breeze blew as soft and warm as a feather mattress. In a very short time, he would turn twenty-two.

"Spring has come, hasn't it?" he asked, inanely.

"Yes, Rufus. Spring has come and dinner is ready in half an hour. We have much to discuss. Do not keep me waiting." She went with a swish of skirts, leaving behind the faint scent of lily-of-the-valley.

Rufe remained self-conscious at dinner, but the fact that Marie-Celeste did not stint the spirits for a change did help the conversation along. She told him bluntly of her readiness to give up widowhood and marry him as soon as the Church would allow. She'd spoken to Fr. Cyprien and the priest believed he could facilitate a dispensation for their marriage. He greatly needed funds for the boy's school and a small building to house the Christian Brothers who would do the teaching.

"Do you suppose priests must confess to tippling and venality like the rest of us?" Rufe asked the mistress of his house.

"I believe they are supposed to." Marie-Celeste gave him a coy little smile. "Do you suppose they have a problem with lust as well?"

Suddenly, lust filled Rufus Courville's mind. Even the slice of ham on his plate seemed to be in the shape of a pair of full, pink breasts. He covered the meat with the two halves of the biscuit he had in his hands. During his stay in Europe, he'd battled his passions, trying so hard to be true to Espy, but all those urges had vanished with last year's tragedies. Now, they were back, just like that.

"Yes, well, lust can be overpowering, very overpowering. I should give you a token for our engagement, shouldn't I? A ring? Mama left a case of them behind. Marthe and Mariette took most of her jewelry, but their hands were too big for the rings. Would you like to pick one out?"

"No, I would like you to do that for me, Rufus."

He tripped going up the stairs to the bedrooms and slipped on a rug in his haste, but at last found the jewelry case in the bottom drawer of the armoire in the room where his sisters once slept and where his mother had taken up residence in order to give Francois and Marie-Celeste more privacy. Marguerite's hands had been small and dainty, a source of vanity. Even after his mother adopted black as the only color of her gowns, she'd still worn no less than four rings each day. The case held a dozen.

Rufe noticed the one of gold and rubies he had intended to beg for his engagement to Espy. He tore his eyes away from its brightness. Onyx was too dark for a happy occasion and engraved gold too simple. He settled on a moonstone ringed by seed pearls and set in silver well-suited for Marie-Celeste's coloring and calm demeanor. Hoping he'd chosen well, he took the ring to her and made himself get down on one knee to place it on her finger.

"Why, Rufe, how gallant you are. Did you know in some countries an engagement is considered as good as a marriage?" She smiled down on him.

"Not in this country, I don't think." Her hand stayed very warm while his turned very cold. Rufe returned to his seat and resumed his meal, cutting up the ham into little squares so it would cease to resemble any part of the female anatomy.

"Well then, in some places experienced widows teach young men the ways of the world."

"I know. I went to see the widows in Rainbow when I was fourteen and allowed home for the holidays." He smiled, remembering the kindness and the faded charms of Miss Dulcie who'd gotten him ready and told him what to do.

"Yes, I seem to remember that day. You went out for a ride and came home very pleased with yourself."

Rufe glanced at the two servants standing unobtrusively nearby. He lowered his voice. "Miss Dulcie said I had natural talent and great endowments."

Marie-Celeste leaned close to his face. "Which were probably enhanced by your stay in Europe, no?"

"I tried to stay true to—" Rufe shoved a piece of meat into his mouth and swallowed. "Not as much as one might think."

"No matter. I am finished here. I find the humidity unbearable today and must lie down for a while. Please, complete your meal, but see me before you go out again, Rufe."

He stood to help her from her chair and watched her go, her wide skirts swaying gently around that tiny waist. Rufe Courville finished the meal on his plate. Women's clothes were incredibly complicated and difficult to remove. He figured he had time for the sweet and the savory.

When he went to Marie-Celeste, he found her lying on the narrow day bed at the foot of the larger canopied four-poster she had shared with Francois, the same bed where Rufe had been born. With the curtains only partially drawn, the spring daylight illuminated Marie's unbound golden hair and made her thin chemise almost transparent so the pink of her nipples showed under the cloth. She assumed a pose Rufe had only seen in whorehouses and on dirty French playing cards, one arm behind her head, one leg bent, the other lolling over the edge of the couch. He had no trouble finding the slit in her lacy drawers with his fingers and his mouth and she had no trouble telling him what she enjoyed the most.

Marie-Celeste sat up enough to unbutton his pants and push down his garments while he shrugged out of his jacket and tossed away his waistcoat. She worked her hands under his loose shirt and ran them over his muscles as if she judged a fine piece of horseflesh. Like a stallion, he shivered, eager to get on with it. He straddled the narrow bed with both booted feet still on the floor and entered her. How pleasantly snug and incredibly warm. He'd learned from the widows to take his time and he possessed the youth and stamina to do so. When Marie-Celeste made a small sound and tightened around him, he knew he could let go himself, but he rocked on for a while afterwards. Miss Dulcie had been a good teacher.

With no room for them both on the narrow daybed, he took his sister-in-law, no, his fiancée onto his lap afterwards and held her. She sighed, leaned back against his chest and said happily, "Now, we are truly engaged."

****

As soon as the dispensation came through, Rufus Courville married Marie-Celeste Marchand Courville in a quiet church ceremony using the cathedral in

Opelousas. Only his sisters and their families attended. The celebration afterwards was likewise subdued, given all the losses of the year past. Marthe and Mariette welcomed the union that would settle Rufus down and make Marie-Celeste their sister-in-law twice over. With Marie-Celeste being barren, the Courville lands would eventually come to their children. The solution was elegant and very French. The couple avoided the raucous charivari their Cajun neighbors might have enjoyed and continued on together as they had been doing for some time.

Rufus Courville would have done anything Marie-Celeste asked of him—except go to church in the nuns' chapel. When he was working or at his home where everything stayed under his control, he could forget much of the past. If he had been forced to return to that church, he would have to bear the sight of Espy cradling her infant son and of the Widow Niles whose arms were empty.

Ramona Niles' twelfth child had come early, been christened hurriedly Aaron Edward Niles, Jr. and died the same day. The baby lay next to his brother, Henry, inside the fence adorned with a pattern of willows and lambs surrounding the family mausoleum. The Widow Niles had the last of the fourteen stained-glass windows set in place above a plaque bearing the name of her final son and a single date. Ramona Niles still wore black and probably always would. Gossips said she'd lost the child from grieving too hard for her husband. Others said she had simply gotten too old for childbearing and should have quit sooner. Rufe Courville knew the guilt of yet another loss to the Niles family was his to bear.

When Marie-Celeste took ill, Rufe began to believe himself a curse to all women—his mother, Ramona and Esperanza Niles, and now his wife. She grew lethargic and slept away the afternoons. Worse, Marie-Celeste could not keep down food except for dry bread and hot tea, delicate cold custards and hot broth. He feared she'd fade away and leave him all alone. With the greatest reluctance, Rufe called for Dr. Maddox.

The doctor examined Rufe Courville's bride in her bedroom with two of her women hovering nearby ready with a basin in case she puked or the doctor wanted to bleed her. When he gave Marie-Celeste his diagnosis, a noise like a flock of birds twittering sounded from the bedchamber as all the women giggled. Pacing in the parlor, Rufe Courville did not know what to make of the noise, but Dr. Maddox soon came to tell him.

"Well, sir, it does look like you are going to be a proud papa sometime around the turn of the year."

Rufe lowered his voice so his wife's feelings would not be hurt. "Marie-Celeste is barren. She was married to Francois for ten years and—nothing. Are you quite certain she is not dying?"

"Very certain. I told your brother on more than one occasion her courses were regular and though a small woman, she is very healthy. Her own mother had six children. The fault was his—mumps gone down on him in his youth, but he would not believe me. Pardon me for saying, but Francois tested himself in the quarters often enough to prove me wrong, but you don't see any little mulatto babies on the Courville plantation, now do you? And if you do, they were probably spawned by that rascal, Boutte, after Francois passed away."

"I never meant to… I didn't mean to…"

Dr. Maddox, looking more elated than Rufe, pounded the younger man on the back. "But you are supposed to. Congratulations. The vomiting should go away shortly on its own along with the lethargy. During the next stage, I can assure you Marie-Celeste will regain an appetite. Call me if there is any bleeding or other problems. Otherwise, nature takes care of the rest."

Hands shaking, Rufe found the brandy bottle in the liquor chest. He got a glass and poured, offered the doctor a drink as well. Maddox clinked his portion against his host's tumbler. "To the mother and child," he offered, smiling.

The doctor left still grinning. Rufe accepted his good wishes as sincere, the physician being a mild man, but suspected Owen Maddox felt more than glad that his past competitor for Esperanza's affection found himself married to a very wise and stable woman about to give him a family that would keep him occupied and worried for the rest of his life. Regardless, Esperanza stayed ever in his heart.

****

Gossips who counted backwards on their fingers said the Courville baby had arrived a month too soon. Those with kinder hearts like Esperanza Maddox observed the baby as being very small and that Rufe and Marie-Celeste had married in a timely manner and been blessed by the Church. Old Cajun women, stirring brown sugar into their coffee when they got together for a good chat, thought Marie-Celeste Courville to be *une femme canaille*, a shrewd woman who had kept her place as mistress of the plantation and gained a youthful, virile husband in the bargain.

In the bar of the Arc-en-Ciel where no women entered, the local men enjoyed a drink and a fine cigar, commenting that for a young man, Rufus Courville had done well. By marrying his brother's widow, he had kept both portions of the plantation. Besides, Marie-Celeste was a fine figure of a woman and, who would have suspected, not barren after all. They hoisted a toast to Rufe Courville, one smart and lucky son-of-a-bitch. Rufe heard the gossip and did not give a damn.

Tiny, fragile, and bald as an egg, the baby fit into Rufe's two hands. Dr. Maddox pounded the new father on the back and said the next time he would get a son. To Rufe, his daughter proved no disappointment. She would not carry the family name any further and might even marry one of Marthe or Mariette's sons and so bring the land back to the people who should rightfully own it. He would warn her away from the Niles boys and never let her heart be broken—if the Good Lord allowed such a frail creature to live so long. The infant weighted less than a five-pound sack of flour and yet Marie-Celeste, glowing with her achievement, wanted to saddle the babe with the grand name of Adelaide Elise. He would call her Addy, his little Addy. He placed his daughter back into her mother's arms.

"You see, all I needed was a younger man to make me a mother," Marie Celeste said without thinking. She'd meant to be light and flirtatious, knowing how Rufe had worried during her pregnancy and how he paced the floor outside the bedroom door for the full twelve hours of her labor. Her mind must have weakened with childbirth. After all, she had heard Marguerite's last words and suspected the truth long before that.

Rufe turned away. "We should be more careful of your health, my dear. My mother nearly died in that very bed giving birth to me. A larger child might have killed you. We should sleep apart."

"For now, my love, until I heal and then I will not hear of it," *la femme canaille* answered.

Thinking he had more will power than that, Rufe kissed his wife's lips and presented her with a box containing two necklaces—one of lapis and one of Venetian glass—in honor of the birth.

Marie-Celeste smiled and insisted he put them around her neck at once. Then, she told him to feel behind the mattress and find the hole in the ticking. His hands encountered something hard among the feathers. Rufe withdrew the box containing his dueling pistols.

"At last, I can rest more comfortably," Marie-Celeste told her young husband.

"This certainly explains the escaping feathers when we—ah—performed our conjugal duties."

"Soon to be resumed, my love, soon to be resumed."

INTERLUDE

Noreen knew she would wake with eyes red and puffy from crying in her dreams. Over the years, she had lost Rufus Courville so many times that her own death counted as nothing. She went to breakfast feeling low and bedraggled. Her mother would hint her youngest child needed counseling. Her father would dismiss her distress as silly emotional hormone-driven girl stuff—or more recently, as a stupid teenage crush on that cowpoke she needed to get over. Their opinions did not matter. Even now, knowing Rufe had come back for her in the form of Rusty Niles, she suffered from the parting of over a hundred years ago.

Chapter Eleven

Rainbow, Louisiana, 1863

When Rufus Courville looked into his shaving mirror, he saw his father's face. At the age of forty-one, his auburn hair grew prematurely white along the sides. His features had turned craggy just like the old man's on the day he died of apoplexy in the nuns' chapel. Rufe put out his hand for the towel his body servant held and wiped away the foam of the shaving soap. A prudent southern gentleman shaved himself, no matter how trusted the slave. In these days of tension with Yankee troops advancing across the countryside, one had best to be careful.

Prudent in business, industrious, a good steward of the land and a kind master, these were terms his neighbors applied to Rufus Courville. They'd once said similar words about Aaron Niles whom Rufe had long ago forgiven. After all, despite his best resolve, Rufe had fathered four children he had never intended to sire at all. Two died young, swept away by one the fevers periodically plaguing the bayou country—a small son and an infant daughter buried the same week as Esperanza's only girl child. She still had four thriving sons. Despite the hot blood Marie-Celeste knew only too well how to arouse and his reluctant fatherhood, he had been allowed by God to keep Addy and a son,

Marchand, named for his mother's family.

Yes, he had forgiven his father, but sixteen years passed before he forgave his mother. Rufe slipped into the shirt presented by his man and tucked the tails into his trousers. Because it was easier, he let the servant tie his neckwear into a proper floppy, black bow and put out his arms for his jacket. Today, despite the impinging War Between the States, the shrine given to Mt. Carmel Academy in memory of his mother would be dedicated.

"March!" Rufe called, pronouncing his son's name in the French manner as Marsh. The Americans called the Courville heir, March, like the month of the year. Adept in both French and English like his father, the boy answered to neither when he bothered to answer at all.

Sixteen, and nearly as tall as his father, Marchand Courville was headstrong, impetuous and an ardent supporter of the Southern cause. He had argued with his father only yesterday, pleading to be allowed to join the Confederate army. Perhaps, Rufe thought, he should not have kept his son so close. With St. Leo's operating a school for boys, he hadn't sent March away to board in New Orleans. Now, when he wanted to ship the lad off to the safety of a university in Paris or Oxford, the boy rebelled just like the Southern states. His father had not stayed at the university. Why should he? No, Marchand Courville wanted to remain and defend his homeland.

Despite their disagreement, March decided to answer his father's shout. "Coming, Papa. Addy is already in the carriage with enough flowers to attract all the bees along the way."

Addy, his little blossom—Rufe looked down upon

her from the upper gallery as she sat in the open vehicle. In the warm autumn sunshine, her fair hair shone almost white. She hadn't yet put on the straw bonnet with the wide ribbon matching her blue-gray eyes, eyes much like her mother's. Still petite, though a woman grown at eighteen, Addy had inherited none of Marie-Celeste's practicality. Fey and spritely, she danced and sang her way through life, her mind as delicate as her frame. Often paying no attention to where she went, Addy had been pulled from the pathway of carriages and fished out of the bayou by her father, brother and male cousins on many occasions during her childhood. Miraculously, she had survived, but she did foster a protective spirit, especially in men.

Even from the gallery, Rufe could hear her humming a pleasant tune. The sun twinkled off the small diamond ring she wore on her left hand as she twiddled her fingers against her crinoline skirt as if she were playing the piano in the parlor. Addy's engagement to her cousin, Rory Donahue, could not have pleased him more.

Mariette's youngest boy had inherited his father's deep blue eyes and the Courville's dark, curly hair. Stocky and of average height, Rory had long been one of Addy's protectors. Even at an age when a boy did not want a tag-along relative, especially a girl, Rory had always been kind and watchful of Rufe's daughter. Once, Addy had taken a dare to climb a tree. Up among the branches, she grew too embarrassed to come down when she realized all the boys could see up her pantalets. Rory climbed to her bearing a blanket and brought Addy safely and modestly to the ground. Rufe planned to give the young couple a large portion of

Courville land when they wed. They could build a home and live nearby—if Rory returned safely from the war.

March Courville thundered down the opposite gallery staircase taking two steps at a time on feet so big he had barely grown into them. Tall and broad-shouldered like his father, he possessed a thick head of hair a striking blend of blond and red much envied and admired by women. His eyes had the same hue as his sister's and his fair-complected cheeks sprouted a peachy down that he claimed was growing into a beard. So far, the light facial hair did little more than help cover his tendency to blush when the female students at the Academy greeted him and giggled as he passed. March took a seat in the carriage in the opposite corner from his sister who had placed baskets of autumn flowers everywhere. He barely had room between the purple asters, pink snapdragons and yellow fall roses set off by lacy ferns to stretch out his legs and still leave room for his father.

Rufe Courville joined his family and gave the word to move on to the driver. They progressed to the edge of Rainbow where the white-framed Maddox house sat behind a picket fence covered in sunny climbing roses. He knew Marie-Celeste had given Espy slips from Marguerite's rosebush years ago. The doctor's wife stood in her yard clipping the full-blown flowers and handing them to the basket-carrying colored woman she had received as a wedding gift from her parents a long time past. Even from the road, he could see strands of silver in Espy's hair. Of course, her figure thickened with childbearing, but she looked up at Rufe with the same warm brown eyes and gave him the same sweet smile he loved. After so many years, he still remembered the softness of her dark hair beneath his fingertips as he'd placed a rosebud in her curls. She would walk to St. Leo's for the service bearing yellow roses for the new shrine. After a nod in her direction, he forced his eyes straight ahead.

St. Leo's church sat not much farther down the road. He knew the service should have been held in the nuns' chapel, but had given Fr. Cyprien's gout as an excuse not to go there. Rufe had donated the funds for the shrine to the Academy back in 1861 when his sugar crop exceeded all expectations. He specified the sculptor must be the same used for the Madonna and Child that graced the entry to the school. He wished to honor St. Mary Magdalene in his mother's memory and have the shrine placed in the rear gardens planted on the pine lot given to the nuns when Leona Cortez entered the convent and become Sr. Mary Frances.

Sr. Mary Frances, who stood at ancient Mother Leontine's right shoulder to assist her in any and all ways, had objected, but the Lady Mother held up a hand that at the age of eighty still possessed not a single tremor. Though her once imposing frame had shrunk, her absolute authority had not.

"We do our best to educate young ladies in the way of Christ, but some will stray—as you well know, Sr. Mary Frances. Some may want to return here to find their way again. This is a fitting gift, Mr. Courville, to honor your mother and will be much appreciated in years to come. A wise man learns to forgive himself and others."

"I married a wise woman, Lady Mother. She often reminded me of my mother's love for me and this school. She wanted me to make this gesture. I am only sorry Marie-Celeste did not live to see the shrine built."

"A fine woman, your wife. I could not have chosen anyone better for you," the old nun said rather ruefully. "The storm that took her life—such a terrible tragedy. We offered thanks to God that Adelaide was spared and we have tried to help her with her loss."

The Sisters had helped Addy recover from the death of her beloved mother and the horror of that August day in 1856 when a hurricane swept across Last Island and destroyed the summer cottage Rufe so thoughtfully rented for his wife and daughter. Too busy to take in the Gulf breezes himself, he remained behind, as had March, sick with some minor childhood ailment. The great storm swept inland, flattening the cane crop and foreshadowing the news that came in its wake: hundreds drowned on *Isle Dernieres*, Last Island.

They went to search for their loved ones, Rufe and March, young Rory and Mariette's husband. The body of Marie-Celeste, stripped by looters of her moonstone ring and any other adornments she might have been wearing, they found caught in the rushes of the island and conveyed it home in a lead coffin. No hope remained for the recovery of Adelaide when word of a blonde girl child found lashed to a board and floating in Gulf waters reached their ears. The search party rode to the fishing village and found Addy, swollen from being in the sea and covered with so many mosquito bites she might have been suffering from the chicken pox. She sat dazed in a shanty where a toothless old woman urged her to drink the broth of a fish chowder. Rufe left behind a pouch containing a hundred dollars for the Portuguese family to aid in mending their boats ruined by the hurricane.

"The Lord giveth, and He taketh away," Rufe pondered as he helped Addy, all grown up but still fearful of storms, from the carriage at the front of the church. He entered the pleasant dimness of St. Leo's, genuflected and crossed himself, led the way to the family pew toward the back off the main aisle and allowed Addy and March to enter before him. They lowered the kneeler and said a brief prayer. In that moment, Espy Maddox passed by with her sons and a basket of yellow roses. After all these years, Rufe still knew the sound of her step and the scent of those roses even with his eyes closed.

Oh, he had been widely praised for donating so much money to the building of St. Leo's, which turned out to be squat and wide and solidly put together like Fr. Cyprien in his later years. The windows did not come close to rivaling those in the nuns' chapel except for the one given in memory of Marie-Celeste portraying a fair-haired woman being raised out of rough waters and up to heaven by two angels. Rufe Courville's modesty and devotion in claiming a pew toward the back of the church near that window was often remarked upon.

In truth, from this position, he could see the tender nape of Espy's neck between her bonnet edge and collar as she bent her head in prayer in one of the front rows. After all these years, he still held the idea close that if his mother had not sinned, he might have been born the legitimate son of Maxime Courville and been free to marry Espy. Or, he might have been the eldest son of Aaron Niles and regarded her as merely a sister.

In the past, if he stared too long, Marie-Celeste

would have touched his arm and he'd move his eyes forward and focus on the cross. Once, he'd asked his wife how she could be so understanding.

"Because God has given me everything I have asked for," she replied with one of her seductive smiles. Rufe often missed his wife, had loved her, but wanted no other than the one denied to him all those years ago.

The church filled with women, many wearing black, accompanied by younger children and older men. Mariette and Marthe had come along with their grown daughters. Ramona Niles walked down the side aisle and joined Espy and three of her grandsons. The eldest of Espy's boys, named after his father and called Owney, had already enlisted and gone off to fight the war. Espy's sisters, one an early battle widow, followed towing their small offspring. With their men off at war and marauders of all kinds on the loose, the Niles daughters had come home to the safety of Frenchman's Bend plantation.

The altar boys began the procession and Fr. Cyprien clumped along behind them on his gouty feet. The Christian brothers who taught in the school came next, and then the nuns from the Academy with Mother Leontine supported by Sr. Mary Frances on one side and Sr. Ann Carmel—formerly Amalia Niles—on the other out in front. All took their seats across the front of the church. The old priest would deliver a speech of dedication and a communion before those attending walked to the new shrine for the unveiling and blessing of the statue on this glorious autumn day.

After the usual rituals, Fr. Cyprien droned on about the place of St. Mary Magdalene in the church of Jesus Christ. The priest never warmed to his topic but did a creditable enough job so as not to offend the Courvilles. As he raised the host, the doors of the church slammed open. The gathering gawked at the dusty man with a full red beard, his uniform Confederate gray, who stood there for a moment before taking off a cavalry hat pinned up on one side and adorned with the tail feathers of a fighting cock. The soldier started forward toward the chancel. The spurs on his boots clanked as he walked and made small nicks in the pine flooring. He turned just in front of the communion rail.

"Y'all know me, William Harrison Niles. Some of you call me Wild Billy. I raised a troop of cavalry a while back to defend our countryside. I'm here to tell you the Yankees are coming up from Brashear City. Going to be here in a few days. We plan to join up with the Texicans coming in from the west. Any man who wants a part of this war meet up with me in the oak grove off the Spanish Trail tonight. Bring your own weapon, ammunition, bedroll and horse. We got none to spare. Sorry for the interruption, Father, but I could tell most of the town was here by all the buggies outside. Folks, I'd hide those horses if I were you."

"Will you take communion before you go, Billy?"

Wild Billy Niles answered with a wolfish grin. "Father, I haven't gone to confession since this war started and by now my sins have piled up so it would take too much of your time to hear them all. I do thank you for offering, but the devil is on my tail. I have to go."

Ramona Niles called out softly to her youngest surviving boy. He went over to his mother and bowed his head to accept a kiss on one bristly cheek. "Go with God, son," she told him. Wild Billy strode out the way he had come, awing the lads of sixteen and seventeen who would sneak away in darkness to join his troop that night.

Knowing this might be the last communion for some of the boys seated by their mothers Fr. Cyprien regained his composure and called the congregation to the rail. He seemed only too glad when the short service ended and he could hobble outside on his painful feet and be helped into the pony cart provided for him and Mother Leontine. The celebrants flowed along the main street and turned at the gates of the Academy. They passed the statue of the Virgin and Child and continued around the circular drive, cutting off across the lawn between the dormitory and the nuns' chapel where the priest and the Lady Mother stepped down to be helped the rest of the way.

Academy girls, all dressed in white and carrying candles, met the group and led the procession to the rear gardens. The path they took was narrow and crooked, hemmed in by mature azaleas that blazed with bright pink and deep purple blooms in the spring. Camellia bushes and wild dogwoods still tipped with red berries grew under tall pines. Fallen brown needles cushioned the way. Students were forbidden to come here unless accompanied by one of the nuns.

The statue, brought to its site on another, wider path connected to the Spanish Trail, caused some bushes to be removed and replanted and a few pines sacrificed to its passing. Now, the work of art rested on its pedestal covered by a linen sheet. Reverently, two chosen girls removed the covering while their peers sang a hymn of praise. As the last words sounded in the woods, the shrine of St. Mary Magdalene stood revealed. Silence fell.

St. Mary lay on a couch, her feet bare, her hair free-flowing. A loose robe of many folds draped a voluptuous body. Her head was haloed and her hands were clasped in prayer before her well-developed bosom. Her eyes looked upward as if she would follow Jesus Christ anywhere.

The female students stood with their mouths agape. Grown women placed their hands over their lips in shock, though some might have been smiling. A few older men in the back of the crowd elbowed each other. The pose bore a similarity to a painting over the bar in the Arc en Ceil, only that woman was stark naked and in the throes of lust. Rufe Courville had seen the same picture many times when he conducted business there or met with friends. Color rose in his face.

Before he could speak, Mother Leontine cleared her throat. "This representation of the Magdalene is a wonderful example of the late Greek Classical style. I have seen many such fine pieces in France. I commend the artist and the Courville family for providing such a great work of art to Mount Carmel Academy."

"Indeed," Fr. Cyprien choked out. He began a prayer and circled the shrine, sprinkling holy water about as if he were trying to drive out evil spirits. The little girls, all dressed in white, began another well-practiced hymn. The ladies who had brought flowers came forth and laid their bouquets at the Magdalene's bare feet near the plaque reading, "Given in loving memory of Marguerite DuPont Courville, 1863."

At a signal from Mother Leontine, the girls led the way back up the crooked path to the school grounds. The servants had set out tables under the oaks and were in place to dispense lemonade, small cakes, cookies and tarts. Tiny glasses of sherry passed to the women. The men accepted more full-bodied wines. Fr. Cyprien felt the need for a chair and a large goblet of the Burgundy. The little girls brought him a plate heaped with sweets and he gave them a small blessing in return.

Addy Courville sipped her lemonade and nibbled on a tart. She knew her grandmother only as the person buried beneath her own mother in the Courville mausoleum. "Papa," she asked innocently, "does the statue resemble our *grandmere*?"

"No, of course not," her father answered. He felt himself going red in the face again. "She was a very small woman with dark hair and eyes. I rarely saw her with her hair down or her feet bare, but she was very lovely like you, dear heart."

March Courville snickered. He'd sneaked looks at the painting in the Arc en Ceil many times along with the Maddox boys who were not as adverse to Courvilles as the rest of their family. At a sharp look from his father, March drew away from his relatives and sought out Glenn Maddox, his old schoolmate from St. Leo's. Glenn sat on a low-slung oak branch. He eyed a cluster of Mount Carmel students, young ladies he might be courting in a few years. His two younger brothers, higher up in the tree, spit lemon pips from their drinks down on some disgusted little girls standing in the shade.

"Glenn, you riding with your uncle tonight?" March Courville asked.

"You can bet on it—if I can sneak out without Ma and Pa catching on. You know my daddy has abolitionist feelings and Ma just won't want me out there. She cried all night when Owney went off with Uncle Billy the first time he recruited. I have that good horse Uncle Andy gave me for my sixteenth birthday and I think I can count on Wild Billy for a gun."

"We have plenty of horses, but they aren't sorrels like the ones in your uncle's cavalry unit. Still, I'd like to ride with the Red Horse Troop if Captain Niles would have me. Last time the Confederates came by, they took most of our arms, but we still have an old hunting rifle. There's a French sword that belonged to my *grandpere* in a chest. I used to play with it when I was a child." March stoked the peach fuzz on his cheeks as if it might be coming in thicker now. His gesture drew some giggles from the Mount Carmel girls.

"Oh, most of those red horses have been shot to bits or ridden into the ground. I think they would accept any fast mount. If you could bring some extras, Uncle Billy would be sure to take you."

"I can do that. The stable hands won't stop me. I have my own staircase and can sneak out any time I want. Papa sleeps on the other side of the house. He won't hear me."

"Harder for me, even though I have my own room since Owney left. I might have to go out the window. My Ma hears everything in the night. She's been jumpy since the Union Army took over New Orleans."

"Just like everyone else. See you in the oak grove, then." The two youths shook hands in a manly manner, which brought more laughter from the young ladies observing them. Feeling feminine eyes staring at his back, March Courville straightened his shoulders and stalked back to his family circle.

Adele Charles whispered behind her hand to her best academy friend, Eulalie DuLac, "That March Courville, he's so pretty with all that red-gold hair and dreamy eyes."

"Well, isn't it just too bad he has a crazy sister? I wonder if insanity runs in the family?" Eulalie sniped.

"You'd be crazy too if a hurricane washed you away and killed your mama."

"She was strange before that, always moon-eyed and wandering in the gardens or cemetery picking flowers. And after they brought her back from the Gulf, admit she acted the lunatic. I do mean, who wants to practice the piano all the time? Addled Addy was always the music instructor's pet pupil and the nuns favored her because she was half-orphaned."

"Jealous because you never played as well?"

"Simply saying."

Red crawled up March's neck at the overheard words, but Addy appeared oblivious. Thank God, his father paid no notice. He favored Addy so surely he would have made a scene about the remarks and demanded an apology from the young ladies.

Thunder rumbled in the south and those gathered under the oaks automatically looked toward the sky, still as blue and cloudless as an October day could be. Adelaide Courville gripped her father's arm and quivered. "Is a storm coming, Papa?"

"No, Addy child. It's far away. We have some time to get ready and make ourselves safe. Don't worry."

Rufe Courville had heard that sound before when cannons were fired in demonstrations at the military academy where he'd been schooled for most of his early years. The battle was far off, maybe around

Vermilionville or Carrion Crow, but it would come their way soon enough. He needed to get home and prepare for the invasion. Without worrying the rest of the gathering, he thanked Fr. Cyprien for the service and Mother Leontine for the kind words and wonderful refreshments, signaled to the rest of his family that they were leaving and hurried to their carriage drawn up to the Academy's gates.

As soon as they were on the road, Rufe told March, "Change into work clothes as soon as we get home. I want you to get two of the drovers and some supplies together for camping. You will take the best of the horses and cattle out to that chenier in the swamp where we hunt for deer and remain there until I recall you."

"But, Pa!" March stopped protesting when his father jerked his head at Addy whose face turned toward sound of the distant rumbles. In silence, he had time to think. His father had just made running off to join the battle that much easier.

Back at the house, Addy went at once to her piano, drowning out the storm-like noises with a piece by Beethoven. Music was ever her solace when her nerves started to jitter. Running her fingers across the keys worked so much better than the praying and meditation the nuns advocated.

Rufe Courville began giving orders. "Jacques Gros, fill a wagon with barrels of the salted pork and beef we put up when the weather cooled. Take a load of yams along, too, and place it all in the little glade hidden by wisteria vines near the coulee. Make sure you cover the entrance well. Leave no wagon tracks. Let loose the pigs in the oak groves to make them harder for the Yankees to catch. Same with the chickens and turkeys."

Provisions taken care of, he got out his old dueling pistols—the ones he'd once considered killing himself with—and primed them. The guns were sadly antiquated, but shot true over a short distance. Against his better judgment he let March have the old rifle.

Rufe watched the son he hadn't wanted, but now feared to lose, ride out, flapping his hat at the slower moving cattle and taking one of the dogs to help with the herding. The sun glinted off a piece of metal protruding from March's blanket roll. By damn, if the boy hadn't taken that old French sword as well. Rufe shook his head but didn't stop the lad. He had too much else needing his attention.

Coins and silver valuables needed to be lowered into the cistern. He had to find a good place to hide the jewelry once belonging to Marguerite and then Marie-Celeste and now worn by Addy. The old blanket chest in the bedroom had a false bottom. That should do. When the Yankees arrived, he'd say the rebel army had already confiscated most of livestock, food and money. It was as good a plan as any. Most of his neighbors would be doing the same.

****

March Courville led his men and livestock through the muddy shallows of the swamp and up on to the higher ground of the oak-topped chenier well-hidden by tall cypress and tangled vines. He told the drovers to start a smudge fire to keep off the mosquitoes. They were welcome to make up the last of the real coffee and prepare a meal so long as they kept an eye on the grazing herd of cattle and horses. He was leaving them the dog but had other business to attend to back home. They said nothing when young master put a rope around the neck of one of Satan's best offspring—a mount whose black hide matched their own—and led the beast away through the swamp. They had easy duty, swatting bugs and drinking coffee and listening to the animals cropping grass as the tree frogs sang.

March Courville reached the oak grove near the Academy just after dark. The guards immediately relieved him of his extra horse without a word of thanks. He moved over to where Glenn Maddox sat on a log and was surprised to see the doctor sitting next to his son with his long face buried his hands.

"Your daddy came, too?" March questioned his friend. Glenn motioned they should move away from the hunched man.

"Uncle Billy came by our house. He said the Confederate army had need of doctors and he'd take Pa at gunpoint if need be. After they left, I told Ma I was going to look out for my father. She tried to stop me, crying and fussing the way women do, but I didn't let that bother me. When I arrived here, Pa was angry and told me to get on home and take care of my mother and brothers. Uncle Billy came by and said he should be proud I wanted to do my duty toward the South. If Pa didn't shut up, he'd have him bound and gagged and thrown into a wagon. You have any trouble getting away?"

"No. My father trusted me with hiding the livestock. I brought one of his best racers along with my own. Guess I'll never see that horse again."

"I guess you won't. Some officer will claim him."

Wild Billy himself rode into the grove on one of those big red horses the Niles family favored. One of his men called, "Atten-shun" and the volunteers rose, some with military quickness, others with civilian dalliance. Dr. Maddox did not stand at all.

"I'm Captain Niles of the Louisiana Red Horse Troop. Most of you know me. We're going to mount up and head west to join General Green and the Texas infantry out on the prairie. We'll be riding with Colonel J. P. Major's Cavalry Brigade. We don't have time to teach you much, so stay to the rear and watch the others."

Billy's eyes flickered with red in the light of a single torch. They came to rest on Marchand Courville.

"You the Courville boy? You know your daddy killed mine when I was just four years old. Don't know if I can trust having a Courville in my troop."

March did what his father always told him to do when faced with such rumors at St. Leo's school. He squared his shoulders and looked Niles straight in the eyes. "I believe your father died of a fit of apoplexy and I am very sorry for that—but I want to fight. If I can follow the orders given by a member of the Niles family, I think you can put your trust in a Courville."

A sudden grin parted the rough, red beard of Wild Billy. His smile seemed demonic and demented to the boy, but the captain simply gestured for the new recruits to mount up. "You'll do well enough," he told March Courville. "Your rifle won't be much good a-horseback, but I'll have someone teach you how to use that saber you're dragging in the dust."

His eyes turned toward Dr. Maddox who had stood to defend March Courville with words if nothing else. "And you, brother-in-law, don't make me tie you to a horse. Gather up your box of scalpels and bone saws and come along. You can do more good where you are going than in Rainbow."

****

Marchand was not the only one to light out that night. In the quarters of the Courville Plantation, the slaves talked of the Union Army being just a day or two ride away. "I'm going," said John Cooper. "Union Army can use a good barrel maker, and if dey give me a gun, I fight for my freedom."

"Mastah Rufe always been good to us. We getting old for runnin'." Jacques Gros leaned back against a porch post. He'd learned the trade of sugar-making and was more than a gang boss now.

"Yeah, Mastah been good. He get rich off my barrels and de sugar you make. How you like to have dat money for yo' own? You stay den and see where it get you."

"Won't get me an early grave for sure. What about yo' woman and boys over at Mt. Carmel. You leavin' dem?"

"You tell Jeanette I be back soon's dis war over and de day of Jubilee done come. She be fine wit' de Sisters until den."

John Cooper loaded his tools into a sack along with some provisions for his trip. He'd lay low by day and just keep on a-going south until he saw a blue uniform. Two young bucks and a mulatto gal fathered by the overseer, Boutte, also disappeared into the night.

None of these defections surprised Rufe Courville who did a head count every day and saw his work force dwindling when he needed them most for cutting the cane. What did upset him was the word that March had left the cattle camp and gone God knew where in dangerous times.

Chapter Twelve

November came with its morning fogs settling over the cane fields and the tents of the Union army encamped on the lands belonging to Ramona Niles and her family. She'd urged Andy to depart for Shreveport. He had been elected to Louisiana's succession government and could be hung as a traitor. Nate and Ethan had taken the cattle and horses and most of the slaves into Texas long before Andy rode off. Ramona assured all her sons that she would be fine. Even Yankees weren't likely to shoot an elderly widow—at least, not intentionally.

Foragers preceded this invasion of troops. Ramona understood their need to take her milk cow and the chickens, but of what use were the two crystal chandeliers from the ballroom or a set of parlor chairs to the military? Though she'd delighted in nice things, Ramona had been taught by the nuns that venality was a sin. The Yankees could haul away her luxuries so long as the small huddle of daughters, grandchildren, and servants gathered around her remained safe. They wouldn't starve. Daniel, her fifth son, had taken over Viator's store and brokerage and would see that his mother and sisters ate once this army marched away.

The Union officers were polite enough, apologizing for earlier looting and the inconvenience she would have to endure of having hundreds of men tearing up her gardens because Frenchman's Bend had space and easy access to the Opelousas road. Thinking like a merchant's daughter, she invited these men to dinner and served an adequate meal of roasted wild ducks, baked yams from a freshly dug patch and several bottles of wine the scavengers missed because the vintages had been cooling in the ice house. Her daughter, Olivia—her husband dead at Vicksburg the past summer—refused to join the dinner party and stayed upstairs with her two little boys. Susanna and Victoria, both very nervous, did sit down to the dinner to support their mother.

In return for their hospitality, the women learned to their relief that General Franklin had posted guards around the Academy and given orders the nuns and their charges were not to be molested. Olivia had two daughters boarding there and Susanna one. St. Leo's, emptied of its pews, housed the wounded resulting from skirmishes up and down the bayou all the way to the village of Carrion Crow where General Washburn remained headquartered. The church overflowed with the sick and Ramona remarked she was sure her eldest daughter, wife of a doctor, probably helped there. Perhaps, she should go to help with the wounded, too.

The colonel suggested she would be safer in her own home under his protection than out on roads where snipers from both sides lurked in the trees trying to pick off a general or any other likely target. Her daughters should stay above stairs and not wander about. Ramona, herself, was not intimidated. When she grew too restless, she walked among the troops and saw them not as the enemy, but as the fresh-faced Indiana and Wisconsin farm boys they were. She urged them to write their mothers often and when some confessed to being illiterate, she had her writing desk moved to the front portico and took down letters for any who wanted to give her their words.

This bizarre peace continued until the Confederate army brought up its artillery on the opposite bank of the bayou and began to shell the camp. Ramona, with the aplomb of a commander, had the three household servants remaining tip over the dining room table and move the armoires to block the windows. She padded the interior fireplaces with quilts and nestled her precious grandchildren there whenever a barrage began. Neither side wanted to waste good cannonballs on a house built with walls three feet thick, but now and again a stray shot crashed into its white-stuccoed sides or lodged in one of the tall pillars. Glass broke from the wide windows with each concussion and the women pulled the Spanish moss-stuffed mattresses over themselves until the firing stopped.

No one died inside of Frenchman's Bend, but outside, the Federals opened a trench at the far end of the garden and began laying out their dead in rows. Ramona prayed for those boys as well as her own and hoped a mother somewhere far to the north would receive one last letter to cherish.

****

Srs. Mary Frances and Ann Carmel climbed the narrow brick steps up to the top of the bell tower of the chapel. They carried with them a precious telescope used for the teaching of astronomy. Below them in the sanctuary, their fellow nuns kept vigil around the clock praying for the safety of the students, praying for peace. Mother Leontine, as if her will alone protected the school, could not be persuaded to leave the chapel except for brief rests and light meals.

The Sisterhood fully expected their servants to desert, joining the hoards of slaves who flocked to the Union army. The nuns began to train the students how to milk the cows and till the vegetable garden. The most stalwart girls offered to haul manure from the stables. Their efforts were unnecessary. Not a single hand abandoned the convent or the school. Mother Leontine's policy of teaching the dark children and treating all within the gates of Mt. Carmel with respect and dignity had been reciprocated with loyalty. Jeanette Plato hugged her two boys close in this safe haven and wondered if she would ever see John Cooper again.

Sr. Ann Carmel raised the telescope in her freckled hands, placed it to her eye and scanned the land around Rainbow. To the east, everything looked normal except for the ambulance wagons dashing up to St. Leo's and a small group of blue-coated horsemen riding off toward the Courville plantation. She thought she saw her sister, Espy, delivering another basket of clean rags to the church. Toward the west, however, a haze of cannon smoke obscured the pillars of Frenchman's Bend.

"Oh, Lee," she said, forgetting to address her childhood friend correctly and even forgetting the custody of her hands as she grasped Sr. Mary Frances's arm. "The battle is being fought by our house. Our mother and sisters are in the midst of it. What are we going to do?"

Sr. Mary Frances took the telescope and held it to her steady blue eye. "We will give our report to the Lady Mother and then we will pray with all our might for their safety, Sister." Relenting her formality for a moment, she squeezed the hand of the former Amalia Niles. Careful not to trip over their long habits, the two made their way back to the chapel only to find their Sisters gathered around Mother Leontine who lay collapsed in their midst.

"Don't just stand there! Get Fr. Cyprien. The Lady Mother might be dying. Sr. Ann, bring water."

Sr. Mary Frances knelt on the floor and took Mother Leontine's head into her lap. The old nun's lips still moved in prayer, she thought, until she leaned closer.

"So many things left undone. Sister Mary, I entrust the Academy to you. Things left undone. Things left undone."

****

When the doctor in charge came out of St. Leo's church, Esperanza Maddox handed her donation of boiled rags to an orderly and explained that as a doctor's wife, she did have some medical experience she would gladly put to use. Ignoring her, the officer called to a bored and grubby sergeant who had been assigned to the protection of the medical corps.

"Sergeant Hobbs, we're overflowing in here. Take your men and ride down the road apiece to that plantation house just outside of town. You tell whoever lives there we need more room for the wounded and are commandeering their place."

"What do you want me to do with the folks inside?"

"I don't give a horse's ass what you do with them. Just get the civilians out of the way. If they still have furniture, move it outside on the lower floor." Noting Esperanza's presence, he added, "Pardon my rough language, ma'am."

"My husband is a doctor. I know how to tend the sick. Let me help at the Courville place." She knew Rufe would not abide this invasion well and his daughter was fragile in mind and body. March had gone away with Glenn and Billy. She prayed they were not involved in the battle to the west.

"If you are willing, I'll send you over there with the first ambulance, but let the sergeant make sure the place isn't filled with Johnny Reb sharpshooters before you go."

"I'm sure it's not. Only a widower and his daughter live there."

"Can't be sure of anyone in these times, Missus. Sergeant, move out."

Espy shivered as she watched the soldiers heading toward the Courville place though the November day, now that the mist had lifted, was as mild as that spring morning when she'd first seen Rufus Courville in church.

Sgt. Hobbs spoke to Corporal Dawkins riding by his side. "I do hope that place is crammed with Rebs. We sit here back of the lines when there's a battle going on having no fun a'tall."

Dawkins, a skinny boy from Wisconsin whose fair skin had suffered from sunburn ever since he'd been sent to this ferocious climate, counted himself lucky not to be in the fray. He was no coward, but he'd seen enough bloodshed since enlisting to last him the rest of his days.

As they drew near the beautiful house, he saw a vision—a fair-haired young woman wearing a pale pink dress spread out over a wide hoop. She carried a bouquet of the small yellow sunflowers that grew everywhere along the road this time of year and sang to herself like an angel from heaven, simply as beautiful as any heavenly messenger, too. She seemed to be dancing to her own tune. He heard some whispering from the small group of privates riding behind him and knew they thought she was the prettiest thing they'd ever seen as well.

The angel's eyes widened as she watched the men in blue approach. She looked all dressed up for company rather than for picking wildflowers on an autumn day while a battle raged. Coming closer, Dawkins noted the gown was made of silk, pink and cheerful with its little rosettes lining the neckline and descending in two narrow rows to her tightly laced waist, finer than any dress his mama owned. The angel lady tried to smile bravely, but her entire tiny body trembled like a dove captured by rough hands.

Sgt. Hobbs pulled up and dismounted. Since they'd drawn no gunfire, Sarge probably figured the place to be safe, pretty much deserted like most of the outlying houses they'd passed, their owners fled to the towns for protection. He walked right up to the angel. She stopped her singing and backed up against a wall, making her wide skirt sway up showing her small, slippered feet and dainty ankles covered by white silk stockings.

"What do we have here? One of them real live southern belles, I'm guessing, all done up in fancy clothes. You figure if we tip her over, her cunt will look the same as one on a camp follower? Probably smells better. Bet it's all covered in soft yeller hair."

Dawkins would have blushed if he could have

gotten any redder. The sergeant mocked him, knowing he'd made a vow to his mother to stay pure and away from bad women while in the army. Sarge likely had no intention of hurting the angel lady. He enjoyed coarse humor and frequented the tents of prostitutes and often made his corporal the butt of his jokes.

Sgt. Hobbs grabbed the lady's arm. "Should I tip her, Corporal Dawkins, should I? You probably never seen a cunt before and this one is certain to be real nice."

"Aw, let her go, Sarge," he answered, but the young woman began to scream, crying out, "Papa, Papa!" between her shrieks. She tied to get away and the light fabric of her bodice ripped under the sergeant's grasp, making her panic all the more.

The men, some of them, laughed. Sgt. Hobbs did not see the man who killed him come halfway down the stairs. Tall, broad-shouldered, his auburn hair streaked with white, the planter raised up one of a pair of old dueling pistols, took steady aim and shot. Caught by the bullet in the back of his head, the sergeant's blood and brains sprayed outward across the girl's pale pink dress and stained its rosettes red. Two troopers swung their carbines forward and fired their bullets into her papa. He fell back and slid the rest of the way down the steps, his pistols clattering after him.

"Hold fire, hold fire! I'm the one in charge now," Dawkins shouted. "Miss, is this your papa?"

The young woman continued to scream uncontrollably. Corporal Dawkins dismounted and went to remove Sgt. Hobbs from the bloody bosom of the lady where he had fallen. She trembled so it was as if her wings wanted to take flight. Hating to do it, he shook the angel's shoulders hard.

"Miss, your papa needs you. Now you stop screaming and we'll get him upstairs. Doctors are coming because this house is going to be a hospital fairly soon. They'll do what they can for him. You go on up the stairs with him. I won't let anyone hurt you. I promise on my dear mother's head." He made shooing motions with his hands.

Dawkins thought he heard some ugly snickers. Some of the privates were older than he, but he'd been in the service longer. He lowered his voice to sound more commanding. "You and you, carry this man back upstairs. Put him on a bed. I'll shoot you myself if anyone lays a hand on this lady. The rest of you check the house and grounds for the enemy. If all is secure, report back to me. We need to get these rooms cleared."

His men reported finding only one big nigger back in the quarters and an old colored woman above stairs trying to hide under a bed. The barn held a horse twenty years old or more and two broken-down mules.

"Put that Negro you found to work shifting the heavy furniture. We got to make way for the wounded, but let the man upstairs die in peace. The old woman can help fetch and carry for the surgeons. Get to work. I see the first ambulance heading our way."

****

March Courville and Glenn Maddox led their mounts through the tangled forest along game paths where they'd once hunted. They wore hats pinned at the side and adorned with gamecock feathers they had shared after eating the rooster captured from a Cajun homestead. In only a few weeks, the boys had learned a few basic cavalry maneuvers out on the prairie, the meaning of the bugle calls, the unnerving rebel yell, and the stabbing and beheading of straw men with sabers. Veterans told them hitting a real man wasn't the same since the scarecrows didn't fight back and the sabers never got stuck as they did in real bone and gristle. Now, they were real soldiers and about to find out.

When General Green saw no way to cross the river and get around the Yankee bombardment, Captain Niles had spoken up, saying he knew this land and how to outflank Union forces with a massive cavalry strike to their rear. His nephew knew the way as did Private Courville. Each one could guide a unit of horse through the marshy woods where the bayou bent back on itself, a thicket Union General Burbridge obviously thought impassable. The infantry would follow while their artillery kept firing to cover the noise of the approaching troops.

March and Glenn remounted at the very edge of the woods. For one glorious moment, they raced at the front of the charge when the cavalry burst screaming from the trees and rode into the lines of Indiana soldiers who were already dropping their weapons in surrender. Their horses, better bred and fresher than most of the others, carried the two friends, side by side, beyond the flag-bearers and through the ranks of Union infantry who were trying to lay down their arms, and then beyond. March saw the flash before he heard the explosion. Whether he and Glenn had been hit by their own artillery from across the river or a Union cannon had blown up, he never knew. Glenn and his big horse were gone suddenly. March rode alone through a red mist. A hot piece of shrapnel seared his cheek and he lost his knee grip on his horse. March Courville's last thought for a long while was how embarrassing to fall from his saddle in front of all the other troopers.

****

Captain Billy Niles went to tell his mother Frenchman's Bend had been liberated from the enemy. The able Indiana troops were being marched off smartly to a prison camp while the Confederates confiscated the cannons, supplies, tents—hell, anything of use—and burned the rest. Now, the darkies who had attached themselves to the Union army could dig ditches for the Rebs. He took his nephew, Owney Maddox, with him because he had bad news as well and could not quite face his mama alone.

Enthroned in the only remaining ballroom chair, Ramona Niles sat near the fireplace. Her three daughters made do with wooden boxes for seats at her feet. Strangely, their babies slept exhausted by terror on quilts in the fireplace. Billy thought his mother resembled Queen Victoria, all in black and surrounded by ladies-in-waiting with wide skirts spread. He felt as humble in her presence as a knight who had failed in his duties—because Glenn Maddox was the only fatality on their side in an otherwise flawless attack.

Hat in hand, Billy bowed his red head and told her the troopers had gathered up the body in a blanket and sought a coffin to take Espy's son home for a proper burial, not some anonymous grave in the pit at the garden's edge. They would give one of the darkies a wagon and send the body on since the Union still held Rainbow.

"You should have taken better care of him," Ramona scolded.

"Yes, ma'am, I should have." Wild Billy hung his head lower.

Having been raised by a gentler mother, Owney Maddox spoke up. "It's a war, Granny. People get killed, soldiers, boys, even women. Glenn gave his life for the cause. You should be proud."

Ramona stared at the oldest of her grandchildren, once a clean-shaven young man with eyes as soft and brown as his mother's, now a soldier, black of beard and dead of eye. "I would lose everything before I would have another of my children or grandchildren die in this war, Owney. Keep yourself safe for your mother's sake. My poor Espy."

Then, she astounded them all by asking, "And what of the Courville boy? I heard he ran away to fight the same time as Glenn."

"Wounded in the explosion. We put him in a Union ambulance and sent him back to Rainbow. His family will take care of him better than any military doctor. I'd rather it had been the last Courville than Glenn who died. If March hadn't dashed out ahead, Glenn wouldn't have followed and gotten himself killed," said Billy Niles, trying to make himself feel better through anger and the passing of blame.

"God forgive you for those words. Go. Take care of Glenn's body and come to see me before you leave."

"Yes, Mama."

Two hard men brought low left the room. The widowed Olivia raised her head and dabbed her hankie at her eyes to erase the tears she shed for Glenn.

"The Courvilles are responsible for another death in our family. First Papa, now this."

"How so?" asked Victoria, who had no memories

of Aaron Niles, just stories told by other family members.

Married in the past year, quickly, before her fiancé rode off to war, Vickie worried her new husband would be taken from her as swiftly as Aaron had departed from his family, Ramona knew.

"I remember the day in church when Rufe Courville insulted Espy and Papa had his final stroke trying to defend her. Andy should have killed Rufus that day, then Glenn might still be alive," Olivia said. This daughter had grown harder, too, since her husband's death at Vicksburg.

"I will not hear that story again! Your father's death was God's will." Ramona Niles rose and went out to see what she could do to help the confused and frightened boys from Indiana. As soon as their mother went, Olivia told Victoria the whole story as she knew it.

****

Esperanza Maddox arrived at the Courville plantation on the first ambulance from town. Immediately, she heard the sobbing of Addy Courville coming from the open door of Rufe's bedchamber. A Corporal Dawkins explained to the doctor that in commandeering the building for a hospital, the owner had been shot. Dawkins had promised the distraught daughter that a physician would see to the wounds, one in the chest and one in the stomach, he thought.

"You shouldn't make promises to young women in a time of war, Corporal. Sounds like there isn't much we can do." The doctor started up the stairs. Espy followed.

She'd never been in this room but knew Rufe had

been born here. The story of how Sr. Francine and Mother Leontine saved the mother and child and obtained the land for their school was a legend told to new students each year at the Academy. Now, the man she had loved with all her heart lay gravely wounded in the bed of his birth. Addy, wearing a torn and bloodstained ball gown, wept in a corner. The housekeeper, old Eliza who'd taken care of the girl since her mother's death, had already removed Rufe's shirt and tried to stop the bleeding from his chest as a basin full of bloody rags attested. The other injury below the belt buckle barely oozed at all.

The doctor did a cursory examination. "A bubbling wound in the lung and gut shot. I could remove the bullets, but he won't last the day. Kinder to just let him slip away."

"Then I will sit with him, doctor, and give him what comfort I can. We are old friends," Espy said.

Rufe's eyes opened. "Espy?"

"Yes, Rufe. I'm here."

"Papa, you mustn't die. March is gone and all the servants but Eliza and Jacques Gros." Addy came to the bedside and watched wide-eyed as the doctor applied some bandages to staunch the wounds.

"Yes, I know, my angel. Go to the parlor and play for me, all my favorite songs. That's a good girl. Stay with her, Eliza." His breathing became labored, and his face grayed with pain. In a moment, he heard the sound of the piano as Addy played a soothing melody she knew by heart.

"I do not want her to see me die, Espy."

"Then don't die."

"I don't believe I've been given a choice in the

matter." Rufe coughed and a thin line of blood ran from a corner of his mouth. Espy dabbed his chin with her hanky embroidered with yellow roses much like the one he kept hidden away and still treasured.

The doctor prepared to leave. He handed Esperanza a brown bottle. "Laudanum for the pain. We can use your help—afterwards."

Espy poured a small amount into a cup and held it to Rufe's lips, but he took only a swallow.

"I don't want to sleep until I must."

Espy smoothed back his thick hair and ran her fingers through it—as she'd often dreamed of doing. She'd never seen him other than tightly buttoned into shirt, waistcoat, and jacket. Now, viewing his broad, naked chest with its thatch of reddish hair, she thought how of how it might have been if she'd been able to rest her head right there and hear his heart beating in the night.

A commotion from downstairs distracted her. The querulous voice of Fr. Cyprien announced he had come to administer communion or last rites to any who wanted it. There weren't many takers among the wounded Lutherans of Wisconsin and Ohio.

"Rufe, you should see the priest."

He nodded, saving his scant breath for a last confession. Espy went to the balcony and called to Fr. Cyprien. The old priest inched his way up the stairs on gouty feet. Some of the Union soldiers offered to help him along with the points of their bayonets and he moved a little faster. He looked at Rufus Courville laid out on the big bed and sighed.

"More bad tidings. Mother Leontine has gone to join her Savior. She wore herself out praying for the safety of her school. I barely arrived at the Academy in time to give last rites, and even then, she practically ordered me to leave and see to the wounded. Sr. Ann Carmel took that as a last request and brought me here on horseback. Rides like the devil for a nun."

"Yes, she does. We used to race each other since we weren't allowed to race with the boys, but please, see to Rufe."

"Go outside then."

Espy waited on the gallery. In the short time she'd been here, a surgical tent had sprung up and a small pile of arms and legs built outside its flap. Already covered in gore, the doctor who had bandaged Rufe signaled for the next patient from the Battle of Frenchman's Bend. She recognized that red-gold hair. March Courville was unconscious when he entered and mercifully still dead to the world when he came out minus his right leg below the knee and half his face covered in gauze. She intercepted the stretcher-bearers about to dump him on a pallet placed on the marble floor of the Courville dining room.

"Please, the boy lives here. Could you take him to his room? I will look out for him."

"You been good to our men, Mrs. Maddox. Just tell us where to put him."

She gestured to the opposite staircase, not wanting Rufe to hear, and had March placed in his own bed on clean linens. She stripped and washed him with water from the pitcher and bowl in Addy's room and placed him in a nightshirt as tenderly as if he had been her own son. Such a beautiful youth maimed and crippled. She pulled the netting around the bed to keep the flies from his wounds. All the while, Addy played old sweet hymns.

The music grew louder as Fr. Cyprien, red-faced and grumpy, opened the door. "Last rites?" he asked.

"Not yet. Amputees often live. Though the facial wound will scar, I think it's not life-threatening."

"Rufus wants you. Tell him to beware of what he says since he has been absolved."

Espy went to her first love. He lay wide-awake, but struggling to breathe. Still, he insisted upon talking as she held his hand.

"Fr. Cyprien was not pleased by my last confession. I told him that I loved you and always would, but have never acted upon my feelings not since—I knew. And he cannot even give me penance or extort more money for the church I'm in such bad shape." He tried to laugh but choked instead.

"Don't. My father used to bait him—our father."

Rufe grimaced, whether in pain from the knowledge or from his wounds, Espy did not know.

"Do you think that when we leave our earthly bodies and go to the next world, we will be allowed to be together?"

"We will be with all our loved ones in heaven."

"Not what I wanted to hear, Espy."

"The nuns always say time and prayer takes care of all things."

"My time is up."

"No, Rufe. We will have all of eternity."

He tried to snort, but blood came from his nose. "Tilt the old chest at the foot of the bed and press on the knot in the wood. The Yankees have already taken the blankets, but the bottom is false. Give it a good tug to lift it out. There's a jewelry case. Please, humor me."

Espy did as he asked though she would rather have stayed holding his hand. She could hear a gurgling building in his chest.

"The gold and ruby ring—always meant for you. Give the rest to Addy. Tell her where to hide the box again. Let me put my ring on your finger."

"Oh, Rufe, don't." In the end, she helped him push the ring onto a finger where it fit perfectly.

"For all eternity." He could barely speak now.

"I must tell you, March is home. He is wounded, but will live."

"Love him. Love Addy. Tell them. Love you."

Rufus Courville gasped, strangling on the blood in his throat, and was gone. Esperanza Niles Maddox put her head on his chest and wept.

****

Espy did as Rufe asked. She led Addy from the piano to her father's bedside, expressed his love for her, and showed her the jewel case and where it should be hidden. She assured the girl that hearing the music had eased his passing and probably helped the sick soldiers in the rooms below. March had come home wounded, so Addy was no longer alone. She must remember that and take care of her brother.

In March's room, she gave the awakened boy some laudanum for his pain and told him the circumstances of his father's passing, how well Rufe had loved his son. March must get better and watch over Addy even though he was the younger. She watched the tears slide down the downy side of his face and also into the gauze covering the other half.

"Oh, Miss Espy, I should have stayed home like he wanted. Glenn and me, the both of us. Glenn is dead.

He rode right beside me in the charge and then he got blown up."

She'd had time to adjust to Rufe's death, to accept it, but Glenn, her little boy taken from her? Esperanza thought she might faint. She grasped the bedpost until she steadied.

"I'm glad you came home, March, even if Glenn couldn't. I have to leave now. My younger boys are at home with only old Hazel watching them. And Owney, I don't know where my Owney is—or Glenn's body."

"I heard Owney shouting orders when I came to for a minute. Then, I passed out again when the ambulance started rolling. Owney is well."

"Thank you for telling me that. You are such a fine, brave boy. Your mother would be proud. But I must go now."

She gave him a kiss for his father and for Marie-Celeste and went on wobbling legs down the stairs. An orderly assisted her as she sat on the last of the steps.

"Can I get you some water, Mrs. Maddox?"

"No, no. I must get home."

"All the ambulances are out right now collecting wounded from the battlefield since the Rebs allowed it. I don't think we can spare you an escort for a while, but I'll ask Corporal Dawkins."

"Thank you."

"Ma'am," said Dawkins, "I have no extra men to see you home. There's an old nag in the stables and I think a sidesaddle, if you ride, but it would be best if you waited."

"Oh yes, that old nag is Satan, once the best stud in the Courville stables. We were well acquainted at one time. I think he could get me home. I must go and see about my sons, all of my sons. It is only a short way and everyone knows me in Rainbow. I will not come to any harm."

Dawkins, a little flustered by her use of the word stud, said he'd have the horse saddled for a lady and brought round, but he still wished she'd wait for an escort. Mrs. Maddox reminded him of his own mother, but dark-haired and smaller. He guessed it was that same soft voice. The corporal helped her to mount. Darkness was falling.

"Go with God now, Mrs. Maddox."

"And you, Corporal Dawkins."

Rarely ridden, Satan took a while to get into his stride. Espy managed to get a respectable canter out of him. As a matron, she seldom rode anymore. She let the stallion have the lead. She closed her eyes and remembered her race to meet Rufe in the oak grove so long ago, remembered the sweetness of their love and the thrumming anticipation of her heartbeats. She leaned low over the neck of her mount and let Satan take her away.

****

High in the evergreen canopy of a live oak he had played in as a child Owney Maddox cocked his head and listened to the oncoming hoof beats. He had volunteered for sniper duty—any job to take him away from the sight of his grandmother, her sharp brown eyes accusing him and Uncle Billy of not keeping Glenn safe. She was right. He knew those woods as well as the boys and would have been a more prudent guide, but he'd been ordered to stay with his men. Women seldom understood what orders meant. Now, Glenn lay dead and his sweet mother would grieve. Her eyes would not accuse, but he could not bear to see them filled with tears.

The moon hadn't risen yet and the rider came on fast, maybe a Union courier with a pouch full of orders that could be of use to General Green. In the dark, the rider, only a black mound to his eyes hunched on the back of a large horse. Owney thought he recognized old Satan, the Courville stud. So, the Yanks had confiscated even that ancient nag. Who knew what they'd done to frail little Addy. He'd fancied her once, but his family had been dead set against the courtship. Now she wore her cousin's ring—if the Yankees had let her live unmolested. This shot was for Addy and his brother Glenn.

Owney Maddox drew a bead and hit his target square through the back.

****

Espy slumped over Satan's neck as the bullet punched through to her heart, but the stallion kept running in the night until he came to large oak across from a white frame house with yellow flowers growing on the fence. His master had stopped here often, sitting in the deep shade on the far side of the tree and watching a lady in her yard. His current rider slipped to the ground when he stopped suddenly. Satan took in her scent with flared nostrils, the same aroma as the autumn roses. Then, the smell of blood spooked the old horse, and he fled away from the tree and went to crop the green grass growing on the edge of the cemetery.

INTERLUDE

Noreen could not forgive herself for failing to recognize him sooner. How could a woman who dreamed as she did walk right by her soul mate and not see him? True, Rusty always stood in Bodey Landrum's shadow though he was the taller of the two. Bodey had the kind of looks and reputation the Mt. Carmel students drooled over onto their pristine, white parochial school blouses. Rumor said Bodey could get a girl out of one of those blouses in under fifteen seconds regardless of the fact that Mt. Carmel debs supposedly dated only St. Leo guys—not young cowboys with wicked blue eyes.

Who was Rusty Niles? Only Renee's poor cousin, red-haired, freckled, quiet around the female sex. He bore no resemblance to dashing Rufe Courville at all except in stature, but she should have looked closer and seen those whiskey-colored eyes gazing at her. Russ hadn't recognized her either, claimed he still didn't. Of course, she was no Espy Niles with a cinched-in waist and romantic full-skirted gowns, but again, her eyes were the same, big and brown. They should have seen him standing there, waiting. The times of mannerly, ardent young men and graceful, chaste ladies of eighteen had vanished. Even the well-educated and rich could be crass and crude when it came to love. Virginity no longer had any value, and no one pined forever. People now moved on, got over it.

She'd never said a word to Rusty before that party and was scared stiff to talk to Bodey Landrum. What if she had gone into the barn that night with Bodey instead of being pushed on Russ? What if she had failed to discern the gentleman inside the cowboy? Would she have had to wait another hundred plus years to find her lost love and end the family feud?

Chapter Thirteen

Rainbow, Louisiana, 1982

Noreen Courville waved good-bye cheerfully as her mother's white minivan pulled away from the curb. She was so excited about tonight she hadn't changed from her Mt. Carmel Academy uniform before grabbing her overnight bag and urging her mother to hurry up and drive her to Sally Parker's house for the sleepover. Mrs. Courville declined to get down because Mrs. Parker would keep her talking forever, but she had waited until the gate buzzer sounded and allowed Noreen to enter the courtyard of the New Orleans-style colonial. The gate kept out the Jehovah's Witnesses and charitable solicitors plaguing the subdivision, according to Mrs. Parker.

Noreen skirted the small fountain planted at its base with mounds of red begonias and ran to the front door. Sally, tall, brown-haired and much nicer than the bleached blonde crowd she ran with, waited for her. The two girls went down the central hallway and out the back, past the swimming pool, and through the oleander hedge into the next yard. Ignoring a small, yappy dog barking at their heels, they popped out onto the sidewalk and proceeded to the top of the highest hill in Red Horse Acres, so called for the two iron horse heads, antiqued a rusty-red, adorning the brick pillars at the entrance to the development. Jed Niles had built there, Noreen's mother said, so he could look down on everyone else. Mom called the house Tara-on-the-Bayou to indicate the Niles family had no taste. If she'd known the party was really being held at Renee Niles' home, Noreen wouldn't have gotten permission to go, let alone a ride over there.

According to Carolyn Courville, the Niles family consisted of vicious and vengeful liars. Being from Abbeville, she hadn't known this until she married Charles Marchand Courville the Third, but he had set her straight. One example of a Niles falsehood consisted of their saying none of the Courvilles had fought in the Civil War. Why, Charlie's great-something grandfather had lost a leg at the Battle of Frenchman's Bend, a minor affair to be sure, but the injury prevented the man from dying more gloriously at Chattanooga or The Wilderness. So what if the name of March Courville hadn't shown up on the enlistment rolls of the Confederacy. Besides, Charlie had proof positive one of Marchand Courville's cousins, Rory Donahue, died at Kennesaw Mountain, but the soldier simply did not carry the Courville name.

As for the Niles family, so many of their men had died in The War or run off to Texas to become outlaws afterwards, that much of their land had been left in the hands of widows and orphans and lost to carpetbaggers. Jed Niles had nothing to boast about. He was only a minor cattle rancher, a cowboy, who had gotten lucky in a land deal. When Noreen pointed out that her own eldest brother, Hardy, had put together the land deal and gotten very rich himself off the real estate sold, her mother always gave her one of those severe, shut-your-mouth looks.

Sometimes, being sixteen was very difficult, especially when you had a successful, grown-up brother like Hardy, another brother serving God as a priest, and a perfect sister like Estelle, valedictorian of her class and often cited as an example by the nuns at Mt. Carmel. Noreen had been a late baby in more ways than one, but very bright her mother always told her. She had been accepted into the Academy almost a year early because her birthday came in December. Most of her classmates were turning seventeen and were oh-so-much more sophisticated. Noreen felt strongly she would have been more popular if she'd been named Amber or Brandy or if she'd been allowed to dye her hair red or bleach it blonde and streaky. Her mother called those bimbo names and said Noreen had adorable short, brunette curls not to be changed.

Tonight, however, Noreen Courville meant to do something none of her siblings had done. Well, maybe Hardy had once or twice. She would attend a wild party. The party being held at the Niles house made the occasion even juicier. As Renee Niles was known to be out of control, alcohol and boys were sure to be involved. Noreen had no idea why she had been invited because only the cool girls got the casual verbal invitations to stay over at Renee's place on Friday nights. Renee tossed out the words like a challenge when they passed in the school cafeteria on Thursday, and Noreen gobbled up that challenge. The Courvilles were not cowards.

Noreen's heart beat hard as she and Sally stood before a door big enough to serve as an entry to a church. She prayed that tonight her dreams would stay away, that she wouldn't cry out the name Rufus in her sleep. Rufus was such a dorky name and Renee would to make fun of her. She'd probably accuse Noreen of being queer for an ancestor if she tried to explain. Please, please, please, let the dreams go away. "Oh Lord, hear my prayer," Noreen murmured to herself as the girls waited for a response to their knock.

Finally, a black maid opened the door to Tara-on-the-Bayou and showed the girls into a large recreation room. Renee could not be seen, but she was heard. Redheaded and known to have a temper, Renee shouted from an adjoining room. "But I want to go to Paris with Uncle Dewey!"

"You have gone to Paris before with him. It's Catherine's turn this year," Renee's mother answered.

"Cathy doesn't want to go. She wants to play softball and try to make the all-star team."

"And that is why she should go. Your sister is such a tomboy. I remember you were the same at fourteen, always wanting to ride horses and never caring about your appearance. That summer in France did you a world of good. You came back a young lady."

Several other Mt. Carmel girls lounged around the recreation room. They snickered. Kelley O'Connor couldn't stop laughing. Few of the Sexy Six, as they called their supposedly secret club, remembered Renee as a tomboy. Now, she owned the reputation of being the biggest slut of the group and hardly a lady.

"I'll tell you what, since Renee is my favorite niece, I'll take her this summer and do Cathy some other time. Maybe, we can go to Italy instead. Women love those stiletto shoes they can get in Florence. Pru, you got another beer in the fridge for your lovin' brother Dewey?" a masculine voice said.

Sally Parker elbowed Noreen and whispered in her ear. "Can you believe Renee's mother is named Prudence and her uncle is Dewey. What was their family thinking?"

Then, Mrs. Niles breezed in carrying a huge bowl of popcorn as if nothing had been overheard. She sat the bowl down on a round coffee table. "Snacks, anyone? I know y'all are watching your figures so I sprinkled on a little Parmesan cheese, no butter. Help yourselves to soft drinks over there in the bar, but stay out of the liquor. Renee's daddy will notice if any is gone. Who do we have here? Aren't you the Courville girl?"

"Yes, ma'am. Renee invited me." Noreen felt like a little black coot chick in a flock of fluffy, yellow peeps.

Prudence Niles eyed the girl. Her glance implied the Courville child could stand to lose a little weight, or at least Noreen thought so.

"We have diet drinks, too. Make yourself at home, then. I'll be in the next room, so don't make any trouble."

"Oh, no, ma'am," Noreen promised.

Pru went off to enjoy a cocktail with her brother, but her shrill voice continued to interrogate her daughter. "What's with the Courville kid being here? You know your father says the Courvilles are not to be trusted. He said he had to get every detail of the land deal down in writing before the sale, or he would never have sold out to Hardy Courville."

"Oh, I know how to treat the Courvilles," Renee snapped back.

She slinked into the rec room before Noreen's

bright blush faded. Noreen wanted to say she was trustworthy and would never say a word about anything the Sexy Six did, but she couldn't get the words out. Renee's fierce sexuality always stunned her.

The leader of the pack wore a backless sundress and no bra. Noreen could tell because of the way her well-developed boobs wobbled. Renee went to the bar and opened a can of Diet Sprite. She poured out half and added a slug of her daddy's vodka, then went to splay herself out in a red beanbag chair. Noreen could see right up Renee's short skirt to her bikini underwear. She was fairly sure Renee waxed more than her legs and was a natural redhead, unlike her mother who dyed, according to Carolyn Courville.

"I'm so bored. Anyone have any good ideas for some excitement tonight?"

"We could dress up in your clothes and you could do our eye makeup," Sally said hopefully.

When not at school, Renee outlined her eyes in black, both top and bottom, caked on the mascara and slathered on green eye shadow. Her eyes possessed an interesting shade of gray-green with little black flecks, but at the moment she campaigned hard for green contacts even though her vision had no need of correction. Noreen's mom said Renee looked like a tramp and probably was one.

"Noreen wouldn't fit in any of my clothes. She's too small at the top and too big at the bottom," Renee's pouty coral lips, outlined in a darker shade, said cruelly. "Besides, we are here to initiate little Noreen into our club. I guess we could go cruising for a guy."

"That wouldn't be right," said Kelley. "We all did it with St. Leo boys. She could get VD and then pass it to the people we date."

"After she does it, we'll be the Sexy Seven instead of the Sexy Six," Sally added brightly.

"Yes, Sal. We can all count. Let me think a minute until Noreen stops blushing." Renee sucked on one long, coral-painted acrylic fingernail. The nuns had asked her to get rid of the nails, but she refused, everyone knew.

A telephone rang in the void of silence. The black maid came into the room toting a large portable phone. "A call for you, Miss Renee."

Gee, the Niles family had a real portable phone. Noreen's mother considered them a useless luxury, always getting lost or dropped. Noreen could hear a boy's voice on the other end. She never got calls from boys.

"Yes, Cuz. I'm having some girls over. No, Eve Burns declined my invitation. Princess Eve is going to New Orleans with her daddy to see a musical at the Saenger. Not that she would have come anyhow. Eve is much too uptight. She should go right on and sign up to be a nun and not bother with college."

"Oh, I don't think Eve intends to be a nun. She wants to go to art school," Noreen piped up.

"Hush! What have you got to offer, Rusty? I'm not into raising 4-H cows anymore, but I do have a fat, little heifer over here just ripe for slaughter. Oh, Bodey Landrum's birthday party, lots of food, open bar—and Bodey Landrum. For a public school guy, he's pretty hot. Okay, see you soon."

The Sexy Six plus one looked expectantly at their leader.

"Seems like we are all invited to Bodey Landrum's

eighteenth birthday party, gang. Let's see what I have in my closet for those of you who came in uniform. Not you, Noreen. Stay just as you are. Guys have fantasies about girls in parochial school uniforms. I don't know why. Sally, I should have something for you."

Mrs. Parker monitored Sal's wardrobe closely: nothing tight, nothing clingy, nothing revealing. Sally's mother was such a drag. All the girls said so.

Leaving the dry popcorn behind, they trooped from the room up the stairs to Renee's bedroom. Renee threw open the doors to her walk-in closet and her friends began tearing a bountiful selection from the hangers like piranhas attacking a pig that wandered into their pool. Within half an hour, most of them were attired as if they were trying out for the bad girl parts in Grease.

Sally sat on the bed next to Noreen. She hadn't found anything that wouldn't get her into trouble if her mother saw the group drive by. Noreen watched Renee sitting at a makeup table overflowing with compacts, trays of eye shadow, perfumes with provocative names, and jars of brushes and cotton balls. Renee worked on making damn sure none of her freckles showed. She turned on Sally.

"Too bad you couldn't find anything, Sal, but that's okay. As I told Noreen, boys just love that Catholic schoolgirl thing. Didn't you see Rusty and Bodey on their horses under the oaks this afternoon? They couldn't take their eyes off our tushies when we went posting by in riding class. I wonder what they said to Eve? She was so red when she got back to the stables, I thought she got sunburned. Pale people like her always burn, even in March. Eve Burns, get it?"

Renee's audience laughed appreciatively. Noreen

looked around the frilly lavender and lace bedroom. Discarded clothes puddled on the floor and draped over dainty chairs and the frosted globes of the pole lamp.

"Shouldn't we pick up before we leave?" she asked.

"The maid will do it. Can't the Courvilles afford a maid?"

"We have a cleaning lady and a woman who cooks dinner and does the laundry, but my mom says a full-time maid is a waste of money."

"Jed Niles has money to waste. Too bad his brother wouldn't sell his land for subdivision, too. Now, Big Ben Barnum, the Texas oilman, owns it, and my cousin Rusty practically lives in poverty. On the other hand, Bodey Landrum has the richest step-daddy in the state. I think I need to get to know Bodey better."

"Bodey has that rodeo cowboy look going on. He even has a tiny scar on his face that he got from bull riding. He's a little on the short side though, definitely under six feet—but not short where it counts, I heard." Kelley O'Connor smirked.

She waited for Renee to giggle, but Renee growled, "When were you that close to Bodey Landrum?"

"Oh, some guy dragged me to a local rodeo on a date and introduced me to Bodey. He was surrounded by lots of girls and I was with someone else, so he's still all yours, Renee. Afterwards, Coty and I did it in the back of his pickup truck—and then he never called me again. Men are such pigs."

The group agreed. They herded together behind Renee and went out to her car, a sporty little red convertible meant to seat four. "Going over to Cousin Rusty's place," Renee shouted to her mother from the doorway.

Renee placed her four skinny blonde friends in the backseat, had Sally ride shotgun, and forced Noreen to nearly sit on the gearshift. Uncomfortable as the seating was, Noreen felt exhilarated as they cruised down the hill, out through the Red Horse Acres pillars and along the warm asphalt of the access road by the highway. Renee swung the convertible onto the long drive leading up another small hill to the Three B's Ranch. The wrought iron gates topped with three golden bees stood wide open and the lawn at the top of the hill overflowed with an impressive array of expensive cars. Renee parked between a Caddy and a Mercedes and the girls tumbled out, skirted a massive black truck with a double horse trailer and swayed the rest of the way up the hill.

Bodey Landrum stood there beside Rusty Niles sizing up the possibilities. Four leggy blondes, none of them naturally fair-haired like Eve Burns, one real redhead with nice tits, a tall girl with light brown hair who wore a school uniform, and a short, slightly pudgy brunette with lots of curls. Obviously, Bodey regarded Renee as the pick of the litter. His beautiful blue eyes passed right over Noreen and went back to the redhead. The new arrivals swarmed around the guys who led the way around the massive house to the pool area.

They were stopped in their tracks by Betsy Barnum who eyed them up and down while Renee did the introductions. Despite her obvious disapproval, Mrs. Barnum minded her manners and said, "Nice to meet y'all. Go on now and get something to drink. Bodey, the candles are dripping wax on the cake. Blow them out like a good boy."

Obviously mortified, Bodey Landrum, teenage sex god, slouched over to the cake and did the birthday routine. The guests, mostly older men accompanied by their wives or mistresses, clapped. Betsy Barnum began to cut the cake into little chocolate squares.

The girls circled the pool. Kelley pointed out the grossness of the pig's head sitting on the food table, the centerpiece for its own barbecue. A frilly ring of ornamental kale decorated the animal's neck. Its mouth held a ripe, red apple and its eyes had been replaced with green grapes.

"Poor Piggy," said Noreen, shaking her dark curls sadly, her deep brown eyes filling with tears, but the other girls had gone ahead already.

Renee shook down a college-aged bartender for a Bacardi and Coke. The rest of the group, not having the nerve, helped themselves to diet versions of Sprite and Dr. Pepper from a huge ice-filled cooler.

Noreen whispered to Sally, "Are we party-crashing?"

Sally shrugged. "Rusty's daddy used to own all this land, but he had to sell out to pay off some debts. He stills own a little piece of it, but mostly he manages for Mr. Barnum now. I guess Renee figures it's still family land and she can come here any time she wants."

Renee drew Bodey Landrum to the round table where the flock of girls finally landed. Her red hair and Bodey's cropped black curls were only inches apart as Renee planted a few choice words about the unavailability of Eve Burns, future nun, in his ears. Bodey had the most lovely blue Irish eyes, sparkling and lined with dark lashes, that Noreen had ever seen. She bet Renee leaned close enough to see that little scar they'd been talking about. Heck, Renee was all over Bodey Landrum, but Big Ben Barnum called for his stepson and Rusty to come forward by clanging a fork against a pitcher of Margaritas and Renee had to let the birthday boy go.

Big Ben put his beefy arms around the shoulders of the two boys. He spoke right up and loudly. "Bodey here was offered a scholarship from McNeese University where he plans to head up their rodeo team. I tried to talk him into A & M or UT, but he wasn't havin' none of it." Applause, hoots, and Hook 'em Horns signs came from the audience.

"I said Big Ben's boy can go anywheres he wants. He don't need a scholarship, but I do know a lad who does, Rusty Niles, a great roper and steer wrestler who would be an asset to your team. Rusty, you and Bodey are going off to college together. Let's give these boys a Hip-Hip Hooray!"

Ben Barnum held up Rusty's arm like he was a winning boxer. Russell Niles dipped his head making his reddish-brown hair flop across his eyes. Mr. Barnum shoved the boys toward the head of the food line, letting them go first. Bodey Landrum streaked back to the Mt. Carmel table as soon as he filled his plate. During the speech, Renee had wasted no time in gathering up a few stray Margaritas for her followers.

Her cousin Rusty slumped over to where his father, Ted, sat nearby neatly dressed in clean jeans, a white shirt that looked like he had pressed it himself, and a black string tie. He definitely had something to tell his dad. Noreen shoved her chair back and blocked out Bodey Landrum's sex appeal and the chattering of the Sexy Six to tune into the drama.

"It's not right. If the scholarship was for Bodey, they shouldn't give it to me."

"Don't be a fool, son. Bodey Landrum doesn't lack for money."

"We'd have money like Uncle Jed if you had gone into real estate and sold off the land for houses like he did instead of giving it away in one piece to Mr. Barnum."

"Big Ben gave me a good price and a promise not to subdivide the ranch. I'm sorry the money had to go to paying off the mortgage and the rest of your mother's medical bills, but that's the way of life. We still get to live here and I got a good job with Three B's. It don't pay to be too proud, Russ."

"I'm not proud. I'm ashamed and embarrassed." Rusty left his full plate on the table in front of his dad and stalked off toward the barns to sulk.

Bodey watched his friend go. He started to rise, but Renee Niles pulled him back to the table. She'd been pouring the Margaritas into empty Sprite cans in case Mrs. Barnum came around to check up on the group. She also poured more poison about Eve Burns into Bodey's ears—all about Eve's divorced parents and womanizing father who treated his spoiled little girl like a princess.

Noreen opened her mouth to defend Eve, but only a hiccup came out. She covered her plump, Cupid bow lips with her hands and blushed.

"Oh, drink up, Noreen. This is your night. We've all done it except you and we have two fine cowboys ready to help you out."

"I don't think I can. It's a shin…a sin, you know."

"If Catholic girls never lost their virginity, there

wouldn't be so many Catholics in the world. It's like your duty, Noreen. If you won't do it tonight, you're out of the club."

Noreen downed the contents of her Sprite can as fast as she could. "I'm almost ready. Bodey?"

"Not Bodey. It's his birthday and he doesn't want some inexperienced little virgin ruining his fun. Let's walk over to the barns and I'll give Bodey a present he won't forget."

They tried to stroll casually past the cadre of adults, but the drunkest of the girls kept giggling and drawing attention. Mrs. Barnum caught on right away.

"Where are you going, Bodey?"

"Ah, just takin' the girls to see the foals out in the pasture."

"Don't be long, you hear?"

Bodey nodded and kept on walking as if he knew all about Rusty's cousin's reputation and was in a hurry to get out of sight. The group crossed the road and headed for the nearest of the barns where a few mares in season were being boarded prior to breeding with one of the Three B's thoroughbred studs. Plenty of empty stalls full of clean rice hull bedding sat ready and waiting. Bodey slid the door open wide enough to slip the girls through and they found Rusty kicking at a bale of hay.

"Hey, Russ. The girls want to give us a present," Bodey announced happily. When he got closer to Rusty, his voice dipped, and he whispered, "That Noreen is a virgin," but she still overheard and reddened.

Russell Niles jerked his head up and appeared startled and suddenly shy. Noreen thought he wasn't bad looking, taller than Bodey and sort of lanky. His shoulders seemed strong, probably from all that ridin', ropin' and steer wrestlin'. His face, unlike Bodey Landrum's, was not really handsome, but possessed a sort of friendly, freckled charm. He had nice eyes, a lighter brown than her own and sort of speckled with gold like her daddy's good whiskey. If he must be her first, maybe this deflowering thing wouldn't be so bad after all.

Rusty's Cousin Renee busily worked out logistics. "Noreen, you go over and stand by my cousin. The rest of y'all, go back out and down the hill. Pretend to admire the horses. Bodey, you come along with me to the other end of the barn while we find ourselves a comfortable spot. Noreen, you know what you have to do if you want to be part of the new Sexy Seven."

Renee led the way to a clean stall near the rear door of the barn. She checked to be sure the walls were high enough for privacy and watched Noreen and Rusty moving into a stall near the front door. If anyone got caught, it would be them. She crooked her finger at Bodey and said loudly as if giving Noreen a hint.

"You got condoms, cowboy?"

"Sure. Big Ben told me never to leave home without 'em. There's two in my wallet," and he gave Renee Niles a big, bright grin that Noreen could see all the way at the other end of the barn.

Noreen pried her eyes off Bodey and entered the stall with her own companion. She immediately huddled in a corner and stared at Rusty's big shoulders blocking the exit. Her eyes went wide and her lips quivered.

"I've never done this before. I had to get a little bit

drunk to do it." A gentle burp passed her lips.

"We haven't done anything yet, Noreen, and you shouldn't let Renee push you into it. She's bossy and mean. Why, we don't have to do it at all. We can just say we did."

"Really? No, Renee will want some kind of proof."

Noreen's dark eyes seemed to fill her face, they got so wide. Rusty bet she thought she was fat, but the girl had a nice round figure and a pretty pink and white complexion like the china figurines his mom collected when she was alive. His dad had broken some with his clumsy attempts to use the vacuum cleaner. The rest sat gray with dust.

"Give me your panties. I'll get you some proof."

Self-consciously, Noreen removed a pair of pristine white cotton panties from beneath her plaid kilt, taking care that she showed nothing off in the process. Rusty listened for a moment. The moans and grunts from the far end of the barn were loud enough to cover his exit from the stall. He found one of the nervous mares there for breeding, raised her tail, and rubbed the crotch of the panties against the horse's behind. He crouched over and crept back to where Noreen watched, dark eyes peeping over the stall.

"Here." He offered the panties.

"Oh, yuck! Gross! I can't put these back on!"

"Suit yourself. Here." He wrapped them in a ball and stuffed the wad into the pocket of her blue, parochial girl sweater.

"I can't go back to the party naked down there, Rusty."

"Okay. Let me think. Turn around. Don't look."

Noreen heard the sound of his zipper going down,

his pants dropping. She worried that he might have changed his mind completely. A few seconds later, the sounds reversed. The cloth swished upwards. The zipper zinged to the top of a pair of jeans.

"Here, wear mine. I put them on clean before I went to the party." He dangled his tighty-whities on one finger.

Noreen took them gratefully, stepped into the leg holes and pulled the underwear up. The cotton held the warmth from his body. "Rusty Niles, I believe I want to kiss you."

She did. Her lips were soft and tasted of the salt and lime of Margaritas sipped on the sly. Rusty put his arms around her and prolonged the kiss. Noreen opened her mouth to breathe and he slipped in just a little tongue. He found his hands moving like they had a mind of their own to the pillowy breasts under the simple white blouse.

A shout came from the other end of the barn, then, an order. "You just keep moving, Bodey Landrum! I'm not finished yet."

Sounding a little out of air, Bodey called, "You need a condom, Rusty?"

"Got my own, thanks!" Russ tried to answer in the same gasping voice.

He whispered to Noreen, "Lie down and sort of swish your head in the rice hulls."

Rusty lowered himself gingerly on top of Noreen. If he wasn't careful, he'd embarrass himself. They kissed some more until they heard a shriek from Renee. Russ rolled off of the girl and instructed, "Try to look satiated, will you?"

They lay side by side waiting for Bodey and Renee

to put themselves back together. Noreen closed her eyes and breathed through half-open, slightly swollen lips. They'd been kissing hard, even French kissing, not the quick, dry, goodnight kisses she got on the rare occasions she went out with a boy.

Noreen put her hands behind her head and sighed making her rumpled white blouse gap. Rusty could see the swell of one flushed breast. He closed his eyes and tried to relax. Now that they were done, he wanted to begin. He had to get rid of his woody before Bodey and Renee came to find them. Breathe deep, Rusty. Don't think about soft lips and round breasts. Oh hell, now he did. Hoping to flatten out his erection another way, Russ rolled over on his stomach. If he were at home, he'd just beat off in the bathroom before his dad saw. That's probably what he would be doing tonight with Noreen on his mind.

Finally, the other couple came clumping toward their stall. Rusty helped Noreen up, went behind her back and was bushing rice hulls from her hair and skirt when Renee looked in.

"Well, how was it, Noreen?"

"Great, really great. It didn't hurt at all. I think Rusty Niles is the most wonderful boy I've ever known." Maybe she had overdone her enthusiasm, but she did mean it. She'd met the man of her dreams.

Bodey raised his dark eyebrows at Renee. Renee looked at her cousin as if she'd never seen him before. Then, she said smugly, "Well I guess Bodey Landrum is the best lover I've ever had, and he's going to be the best bull rider in the world."

"Bodey, Bodey Landrum! Some of the guests are leaving. You come out here and say goodbye."

Mrs. Barnum's voice sounded closer and closer to the barn. That did it. Rusty had no need to hide behind Noreen's skirt anymore. Frantically, he brushed her backside. She tossed her hair trying to remove all the rice hulls.

Bodey, though, he just sauntered out to meet his mother in the spring twilight as if nothing had happened. Renee followed him, her dress looking as if she had slept in it, her hair as full of rice hulls as if she had been showered with confetti after a premier performance.

Betsy Barnum took a good look at her son, Renee, and the sheepish couple behind them. "I think it's time for your little friends to go home, too."

****

Back at Tara-on-the-Bayou, the new Sexy Seven stampeded past the kitchen where Mrs. Niles seemed to be on her fourth or fifth little drinkie with her brother, Dewey. Those two were eating the popcorn, now doused in butter.

"Have a nice time, girls?" Mrs. Niles trilled. A stylishly thin woman, she didn't hold her alcohol well, but drank quite a bit anyhow.

"Fantastic. I really got my rocks off, Mom," Renee called back as she mounted the stairs.

"What did she say, Dewey? I didn't hear."

"Drink up, Pru. It wasn't important." Dewey, also spare, had thinning dark hair and the lined face of a hardened drinker. He took another handful of popcorn and ground it into a ball in his fist as Noreen watched, then scurried on to catch up with the rest of the girls.

Upstairs, Renee slammed the door to her room, locked it and held out her hand toward Noreen. "We want the proof. Let's see your panties."

Noreen fished the ball of white cotton from her parochial pocket and held it out. She loved Rusty Niles. If she hadn't loved him instantly, it had only taken her a minute to recognize the feelings she had for him. He was so gallant and clever.

"Oh, gross! Your hymen must have been two inches thick and you said it didn't hurt," gasped Sally.

"Maybe I was numb from the alcohol," Noreen suggested, blushing once more.

"So, are you commando under that kilt or what?" asked Renee. "Let's see."

Noreen took the corners of her kilt in her fingers and slowly raised her skirt.

"I don't believe it! The simpering little virgin got on my cousin's underpants."

Kelley O'Connor flipped her blonde hair back over her shoulders. "What did you get from Bodey?"

"A good fuck and"—Renee fished in her bodice— "his Junior Rodeo Champion belt buckle."

"For a moment there, I thought you had been outdone by sweet, innocent Noreen."

"No way. No one beats Renee Niles when it comes to sex."

She flipped the belt buckle onto her makeup table and took a bow to the applause of the new Sexy Seven.

Chapter Fourteen

Noreen had to admit she didn't much care for being a member of the Sexy Seven, though there were advantages. Their group never ate the school lunches. If Noreen appeared at their table with a tray burdened by spaghetti and garlic bread or chicken nuggets and fries, one of the girls, usually Renee or Kelley, would say, "You aren't really going to eat that!" Noreen meekly followed their lead and picked at the small side salad and the canned fruit or fresh apple offered for dessert. She dropped ten pounds in six weeks.

Mostly, Noreen kept her mouth shut at lunch because she realized that once accepted into the clique, she had taken Sally's place as the goat, the one they teased and tormented mercilessly, when they weren't shredding other girls' self-confidence with comments like, "Do you know how many split ends you have in your hair?" The topic of the day turned to Rusty Niles and why he hadn't called.

"I guess you weren't as good as you thought you were, Noreen, if Rusty didn't call you for another date. I've been seeing Bodey often and we do it every time."

"I guess not." Noreen lowered her head and dared to take a bite of cheeseburger. The question nagged at her, too. Hadn't Rusty felt the same attraction like two magnets being pulled toward each other—even if they had been forced together at first? She thought she felt his interest when he lay on top of her, kissing her really hard. Maybe that had been just the seam of his jeans.

"Don't worry, little Nory, we'll find you someone better from St. Leo's to be your second lover. If you stuck with my cousin you'd never see Paris. Rusty spends most of his time scrambling for extra college money, chasing rodeo prizes and exercising Big Ben's quarter horse racers and thoroughbreds. Russ is way too tall to be a jockey—sad because they make a bundle if they're good riders. Like his daddy, Rusty never will be more than a small scale cattleman."

"I kind of liked him, but I guess he didn't like me back." Noreen bit her dessert apple to the core.

"Oh, are we in grade school? He didn't like me back!" Kelley O'Connor cooed. "You should have called him if you wanted him. No guy is going to turn down free sex."

"Oh, my mom won't let me call boys. She says that's chasing."

"No, chasing is running them down and having your way with them," Renee said savagely.

"Okay. Well, I'm going to walk down to the stables and give Lightning my apple core. See you in French class."

That was the other thing about being in the Sexy Seven. She fled their company so often she did much more walking. Like Eve Burns, she frequently hid out in the stables during the free time after lunch. Eve was the first person she saw as she entered the ancient brick barn. As usual, Eve had her sketchpad and sat framed in the far doorway, her back against a bale of straw as she drew the horses. So engrossed, the tall, fair girl with the long white-blonde braid down her back didn't look up when Noreen entered the pleasant dimness of the stable.

Noreen found Lightning's stall and the placid sorrel gelding stuck his head over the door to greet her. She held the apple core on the flat of her hand and he lipped it up, then snuffled her for more goodies. She scratched under his forelock. Lightning was neither fast nor flashy despite his name. She appreciated this good, dependable horse who never tried to scrape her off under low branches.

Unlike her sister, Noreen wasn't much of an athlete. She didn't captain the girls' field hockey team or play lacrosse or basketball the way overachieving Estelle had, but she did love to ride. When Sr. Inez, the riding instructor who also coached field hockey and taught history, allowed her pupils a gallop across an open field, Noreen felt as if she flew toward a special destination. She would imagine a handsome man waiting for her in the oak grove that had been a trysting place for over a hundred years. Lightning always got her there safely even if she did not totally pay attention.

"Would you like to see my sketch of Lightning?" asked Eve Burns in that reserved kind of way she had.

"Sure." Noreen went to squat down beside the artist. "Hey, you even noticed Lightning's white spot. It's usually hidden by his forelock. I like that you used a sort of reddish-brown crayon for his coloring."

"It's a conté crayon, great for sketching and not as messy as charcoal. This is my mare. I did use charcoal for her so I could rub in her dapples."

"I wish I could buy Lightning. I hate to think of him being ridden by other girls after I graduate, but my dad says no. He said the pony I had when I was little almost ate us out of house and home. I cried for a week when I got too big to ride him and Dad sold him off."

"I'd hate to lose my horse. After I graduate, I want to board her near where I go to college. The Art Institute of Chicago would be great, but I think Houston is a better area for horses."

"Probably so. I wish I had some talent."

"You're in honors English and History. If I didn't have electives in art and riding my GPA would be below that A minus I usually get. It's a good thing my dad can afford to send me to art school so I don't have to compete academically. What do you want to do when you graduate?"

"I don't know. I'm sort of looking for my future."

"And who knows what that will bring?"

"Say, isn't this a sketch of Bodey Landrum? I didn't realize you knew him."

"I don't. We ran into each other out on the bridle path. I guess he was trying to pick me up. He has kind of an interesting face."

"Gorgeously handsome, I'd say. I like the way you just colored in the blue of his eyes and did the rest in black charcoal. You should show it to him. He asks about you sometimes."

"I couldn't. I wouldn't know the first thing about dating a guy like Bodey. He knows too much and I'd make a fool of myself."

"You could learn."

Suddenly, Sr. Inez's stocky form filled the doorway and cast a shadow over them. As usual, she wore a short veil over her salt-and-pepper hair and was dressed in riding attire for her afternoon classes. "The first bell rang five minutes ago. You girls had better get going to class. Noreen, stay after riding today and we'll talk about getting an early start on your social science project for next year. With some work over the summer, you could go to the state finals. A win like that would look very good on a college entrance form."

"Yes, Sr. Inez. I'd like that."

As the two girls raced to class with Noreen puffing to keep up with long-legged Eve, she confided, "My sister never went to the state finals with her social science projects. Wouldn't that be great?"

"It would. Good luck, Noreen. Try to stay as nice as you are."

****

"A boy calling for Miss Noreen Courville," her mother said in a sweet singsong voice.

Noreen nearly broke her yellow number two pencil in half. What if Renee had given her name to a St. Leo guy and told him she did it?

"Did he give a name?"

"Russell somebody. He sort of mumbled. I think he's nervous. Isn't that cute? You see, nice girls don't finish last." Carolyn Courville's wide red lips smiled brightly.

Noreen knew her cheeks turned as red as her mother's lipstick. Her heart pounded. She wanted to dash from her homework desk to the phone, but forced herself to move slowly and pick up the receiver casually.

Her mother pondered, "Russell. Do we know a Russell? Such an old-fashioned name. All the boys are Lance or Jason or Rhett nowadays. Does he go to St. Leo's?"

"Like Hardy is a normal name," Noreen dared to say.

"My maiden name. That's an entirely different thing. It shows a pride in family."

"Whatever. Rusty, hi! I was hoping you'd call."

Her mother shook her head. That was close to chasing. Clearly, this would not be a private conversation. Noreen wasn't allowed to have a phone in her own room.

On the other end of the line, Rusty Niles said with amazement, "You were? I—uh—I didn't call before because I didn't think I'd have the money to go to my senior prom, but I saved enough for flowers and dinner and a tux—if you'd like to go with me. Bodey says he's renting a limo and there will be plenty of room for us. He's taking Renee so you'll know somebody there. I mean the prom is at the public school in Opelousas—if that's okay."

"Why, I would love to go to the prom with you, Rusty! When is it? Oh, two weeks. That doesn't give me much time to find a dress."

Her mother mouthed, "No problem."

"I know I should have called sooner. Sorry. It wasn't you. I mean, you were my first choice. I just didn't know about the money."

"That's not a problem. I am sure I can find something and I'll let you know the color of my dress as soon as I get it."

"Why?"

"For the flowers, silly. They should match. Like you wouldn't want yellow flowers with a red dress."

"Okay. White goes with everything, right?"

"I am sure whatever you choose will be lovely."

Carolyn Courville nodded her approval.

"That's good. I mean, I really wanted to see you

again, but I had to work."

"I understand."

"And you can keep my briefs. I got plenty."

"Oh, why thank you, Rusty."

"Is your mom on an extension?"

"No, just nearby."

"Gotcha. Okay, then, I'll call you when I have times and such."

"Call anytime. Bye-bye."

Noreen's mother frowned. "You shouldn't make yourself so available. Play hard to get, Noreen. Now, do we know this Rusty's family?"

"Um, no. I don't think so. He goes to public school in Opelousas."

"If I had known you'd be riding all the way from Lafayette to Opelousas on prom night, I might have told you not to go. There are so many accidents on prom night, I…"

"We're going in a limo. A limo, Mom!" She couldn't help herself and jumped up and down and hugged her mother.

"Isn't that nice? Then, of course you may go. What did you say Rusty's last name was?"

"Um, Niles. Russell Niles."

"Oh my God, Noreen! The Niles men have a reputation for being oversexed and they are not to be trusted, especially in a limo, I would think. How did you meet this boy?"

"Mom, I gave my promise to go with him. You wouldn't want me to break my word or lie and say I had a previous engagement. Besides, we'll be in the limo with another couple. Nothing is going to happen, I swear. Rusty is an only child, so I don't see how his father could be oversexed, and Rusty isn't either."

"Where-did-you-meet-him, Noreen?"

"Just around."

"Come. Sit down. We need to talk. I think you are old enough to hear this. Rusty Niles' mother and I went to college together. We were sorority sisters. Maggie Durel had big dreams and she didn't marry right out of college like most of us—although she was pretty and bright enough and had lots of beaux. She got into real estate and did very well. She had her own business eventually. But Maggie got mixed up with Ted Niles."

Noreen could tell this was going to be a long, sad story, full of doom and gloom. She knew Rusty's mother had died and that was bad enough. She braced herself to listen.

"Maggie tried to get Ted Niles to sell off his land for a subdivision after his daddy died. He inherited half the ranch and his brother, Jed, got the other half. Well, he wouldn't sell, but she kept going over to his house to work on him. I guess that wasn't all they were doing. All of a sudden, sophisticated, successful, thirty-five year-old Maggie Durel is marrying this twenty-five-year-old cowboy. They just up and eloped."

"So? I think it's kind of cool she married a younger man. Mr. Niles is still sort of nice looking for an old guy. He looks a lot like Rusty." Noreen caught herself, thankful her mother hadn't noticed the slip about actually seeing Ted Niles at the Three B's bash.

"Maggie claimed she was too old for a fancy wedding, but six months later, the truth came out. They named the baby Russell after her dad. Oh, Maggie said she was getting older and wanted children for a long time, but I mean, they had to get married—at her age."

"No one has to get married. She must have loved Mr. Niles."

"In those days she had to or give up the baby. The Niles men are sneaky and oversexed and that girl, Renee, she isn't much better. I hear Jed Niles runs around on his wife, too, but you aren't to repeat that. I want you to beware. On prom night, you keep your legs crossed. Promise me."

"I promise to keep my legs crossed on prom night. There, okay? Can we not tell Daddy that I'm going with Rusty because then we'll both have to hear about how his granddaddy killed someone else's granddaddy in olden times."

"If he doesn't ask, I won't tell him. I do want you to have dates and nice high school memories, but please be careful. And after the prom, get rid of this boy before your dad finds out."

****

This was a dream come true. Noreen had dropped two dress sizes on what she called the Sexy Seven diet. Her gown was strapless, and she still had plenty on top to hold it up. With her stomach smaller, her breasts looked bigger. No matter what Renee said, Noreen thought her boobs were just as nice as the ones on the clique's leader. She didn't push them up and squeeze them together, that's all.

The gown, pure white, fell straight from the bodice to the floor. The material, all floaty and diaphanous, had an underlining so it couldn't really be seen through. Even though she had short hair, the stylist managed to sweep it up into a bundle of curls on top of her head and secure the do with pearl-headed pins matching her dress. A girl at the salon had done Noreen's makeup, too, with her mother standing nearby saying, "Not too much, not too much."

Now, all dressed and standing before the mirror, Noreen felt beautiful for the first time in her life. Her mother said she resembled the Empress Josephine and since Noreen aced history, she knew exactly what picture her mother meant. Josephine and Napoleon, one of history's great love affairs. She'd read their story in a public library book called, obviously, *History's Greatest Lovers*. Describing her dress in great detail to Rusty over the phone she told him about the Josephine connection, but he'd just said, "Uh-huh" every once in a while.

At last, she was content with being one of the petite, dark Courvilles; Courvilles came in two varieties, the reddish ones and the dark ones. The red ones tended to be tall and well built like her brother, Hardy and her dad. Female Courvilles of this type were described as statuesque. Noreen wasn't one of them. She'd always hated her curly dark hair and the brown cow eyes that seemed to go with being short.

Rarely, a tiny blonde Courville who looked like the portrait of Marie-Celeste Courville hanging over the sideboard next to her husband's picture (definitely a red Courville, and named Rufus, too) would be born, but Noreen hadn't lucked out. Now Estelle, her older sister, took after the Hardys, who were tall and brunette and dramatic looking, as did her brother, that gorgeous priest, Fr. Matthew. Carolyn Courville colored her gray back to its original shade because she claimed she didn't want Noreen to have an old looking mother even if she had given birth to the child at the age of thirty-eight. Her mother's figure was, well, generous as an opera singer, but her dad seemed to like it that way. Ancestry, such a fascinating subject—and how could she be thinking of this on prom night? Nerves, purely nerves.

The doorbell rang and Mrs. Courville fluttered out of the room to grab a camera before answering. Noreen took her place at the head of the stairs as she had been told to do. Her father took up his position at the foot of the steps. Noreen held her breath as her mother opened the door to let in a stunningly handsome young man, not too tall, but with blue eyes to die for and black hair slicked back for the evening. Bodey Landrum certainly looked fantastic in a tuxedo with a peach-colored rosebud tucked in the lapel.

"But…" said Mrs. Courville and stopped.

Mr. Courville stood right there with his hand out. Bodey shook in a manly manner and introduced himself. "Bodey Landrum, I think my stepfather does business with your law firm. You know, Big Ben Barnum."

"Why didn't you tell me who my baby girl was dating, Carolyn? Of course, I've handled many a deal for Big Ben Barnum." Charlie Courville couldn't seem to stop pumping Bodey's hand.

The truth was Good Ole Charlie Courville, as most called him, had taken an interest in every aspect of his sons' lives: academics, sports, fishing, and hunting even down to making Matt kill his first deer when his son wanted to let it go. This interest did not extend to his daughters, except for the occasional admonition to "be good and listen to the nuns." Estelle fought hard for his attention, but Noreen had given up on getting it long ago.

Having no idea where Rusty hid, Noreen wafted down the stairs as she had been coached. Bodey looked up and grinned. "You look mighty pretty, Noreen," he said in that Texas way of his. "The limo awaits. Sorry we don't have more time to talk, sir."

"No, no, pictures first," Carolyn Courville cried. She began snapping: Bodey helping Noreen down the final step, Bodey with his arm around Noreen, Bodey and Noreen going out the door, Bodey and Noreen getting into the white, stretch limousine with the uniformed driver holding the door. They were gone, finally.

"Well," said Mr. Courville, "if that boy knocks Noreen up tonight, at least I've got Big Ben as a client for life. He looks the type."

Carolyn nearly hit her husband with the camera. Besides, if Noreen did get pregnant, Charlie would have Rusty Niles for a son-in-law and it would serve him right for saying such a thing.

****

Rusty Niles, clutching a white box, sat in the far corner of the limo away from the streetlights. Noreen slid over to be beside him. The guys had picked up Renee on their way to town. She had gone with a short, tight dress of iridescent green. The gown did have thin straps, but they didn't really hold up the low-cut top Renee's breasts spilled out of. At the base of one strap, Bodey had pinned a cluster of peach-colored rosebuds. As soon as he got seated, Bodey slung an arm around Renee and let his hand dangle on one of her breasts. He used the other to rap on the shaded interior window of the limo that slid down.

"Opelousas High, Jeeves."

"Jordan," corrected the huge black man in the chauffeur's uniform. His expression seemed to say "Why hadn't he made it in pro sports? Another night, another dollar earned putting up with snotty high school kids." He raised the window and pulled smoothly away from the curb.

Rusty offered Noreen the flower box. "I'm sorry I didn't come in. It's not like I'm chicken, but considering what your mama said about me, I didn't want to ruin your evening in case your dad got mad and wouldn't let you go."

The box contained, not a corsage, but a small bouquet of pale yellow roses and tight buds set off with ferns and held together in a lacey cone. Some flowers were full-open, delicate and fragrant.

"Ah, I asked Renee what you liked and she said old stuff and riding smelly horses. So, I went to this place that has what they call 'old roses' and asked if they could make me a corsage. We walked around and looked at all the plants, and the lady said this one was called the Courville Noisette because she collected the specimen growing on the wall of the old plantation house. She's a rose rustler, she says, and she thought the flowers would be much more charming in a nosegay."

"Did you say nosebag?" Bodey chortled.

"I said nosegay." Rusty drew back his foot and kicked Bodey with the toe of his patent leather shoe.

"You said you were gay? Oh, darlin', it's gonna to be a long night for you. But don't worry. I can handle both you and Renee if you get bored."

Rusty kicked his friend harder.

"Hey, man, I won't be able to strut my stuff if you

keep doing that."

"Then get a bottle out of that case of champagne you smuggled along and shut up."

Noreen, her heart fluttering, inhaled the sweet scent of the yellow roses. For some reason their simple beauty made her want to cry. In that instant, she forgave Rusty Niles for not standing up to her parents.

"Rusty, what you did was so thoughtful. They are beautiful. I've seen them growing on the old homestead when we used to camp out there, but never knew they were named for my family."

"The rose lady said around Rainbow is the only place she's ever seen them—that old roses must be tough and hardy to survive. Some grow in the cemetery and in yards around Rainbow because women used to exchange cuttings."

"I think the nuns have one like this planted at the Academy, too. I always thought they were so lovely."

"Like you." Rusty wore two tiny yellow buds and a sprig of fern as his boutonniere. He broke off one bud and placed it among her curls in a gesture so pure and natural he had to wonder where all his awkwardness went. "The color is beautiful against your dark hair," he said as smoothly as if he'd said it before.

Noreen sighed so deeply she thought she might pop out of the top of her dress. In her dreams, one of the good ones, this had happened over a hundred years ago.

Renee rolled her eyes. "Champagne, please, before I gag."

Bodey had learned from Big Ben that only a fool shakes champagne bottles. He took off the foil and eased up the cork gently. The bottle sighed more than popped and not a drop spilled. He began pouring into real glass flutes supplied by the limo company.

"To a wild night," toasted Bodey. They clinked the glasses together.

"To the Sexy Seven," shouted Renee. They clinked and drank again.

"To old roses and beautiful women." Rusty looked deeply into Noreen's eyes, eyes like those of the hound dog pup he'd loved that had been killed on the highway.

"That should get you some tonight, Russ," Bodey Landrum quipped. "Drink up. Champagne don't keep."

Renee tossed off her drink and held out her glass for more. "Noreen, we haven't heard your toast."

"To Rusty Niles and the end of feuding families."

****

Renee and Bodey, having finished the bulk of the wine, were well lit by the time they arrived at the prom in the high school gym. Noreen and Rusty at two glasses each, stayed mildly intoxicated, mostly with each other. While Renee and Bodey bumped and ground around the dance floor, they drifted along to the slow dances, more holding each other close than actually doing any steps. Noreen held on to her nosegay and breathed in the sweet scent as she cuddled her head against Rusty's chest and listened to his heart beat. Bodey sometimes danced with other girls, ticking Renee off, but Rusty belonged to Noreen alone.

The refreshment table ran out of red punch and cookies early on. The chaperones told Bodey he couldn't make out at the table and to stop squeezing Renee's behind when they danced. Bodey grew bored and Renee testy despite frequent trips to the limo to refuel. They signaled they wanted to leave, but Rusty shook his head no.

He and Noreen stood in line to have their picture taken in a bower covered with fake wisteria. This would be their real prom picture, not the ones in Mrs. Courville's camera. They did the usual face forward pose so Noreen's dress would show and then Rusty paid extra for a shot of them holding hands and looking into each other's eyes. Noreen glowed.

"Com'on. Gotta pee-pee," Renee shouted and staggered off on heels twice the height of the shoes Noreen wore, not caring if they made her an inch taller than Bodey.

Noreen followed, hoping Renee would not throw up in the restroom. She wanted to ask her sexually knowledgeable friend something and couldn't do that if the girl was spewing.

Renee made it into a stall and slammed the door. "Jesus, I'm peeing like a stud horse."

Noreen agreed. This simple act took so long that Noreen's hands got clammy waiting. At last, Renee toddled out and began soaping her hands.

"Ah, Renee, do you think the guys expect us to have sex tonight?"

"Duh, little baby, it is prom night."

"I mean I have my period and if Rusty doesn't like that what could I do for him? You know, to keep him happy."

"Noreen, you got to get on the pill, girl. I've been taking them since I was fourteen—shorter, lighter periods or none at all if you take two packs in a row. Good for your complexion, too."

Renee looked at Noreen's pink and white china doll face. She'd gotten cheekbones since her weight loss and now had a heart-shaped rather than round face. "I'll bet you never had a zit."

"Not very often. Good skin runs in the family unless you are a red Courville. Then, you have to cope with freckles."

"The bane of my ex-shitance." Renee started powdering her nose.

"About pleasing a man if you are on the rag?"

"Oh, well, there's fellatio and the old hand job, but that won't do much for you. Sixty-nine is great if you can lie down, unless you are real acrobat, oooh, but not with a period. Go for the dry hump, I guess, and promise him you'll get on the pill."

"My mother would never sign for that and I won't be eighteen for a year and a half."

"Bummer. Then make sure Rusty has some fresh condoms. He might be just a baby cowpoke, but he won't be put off forever."

"Thanks, Renee."

The girls met the guys at the limo. Jordan, the driver, held the door for them and helped the ladies inside.

Bodey came last in the line. "Man, I need something to eat. You know the Rainbow Café, Jeeves? Take us there posty-hasty."

"Sure. Anywhere you want to go." Jordan slammed the car door extra hard and mumbled, "Mastah."

Bodey and Renee started a major make out session on the way back to Rainbow. Rusty and Noreen held hands, but watching Bodey with his hand up Renee's skirt was a little bit of an embarrassing turn-on. The hands of the watching teenagers grew sweaty. They were both relieved when the limo pulled up in front of the Rainbow Café despite the dive's reputation. Noreen had never been inside. Families did not eat here, but sometimes her father bought barbecued ribs at a drive-up window in the back. The couples got out and headed for the shabby frame building with a crude rainbow painted on the side.

She looked around the dark and smoky interior with interest. An impressive and crowded bar with a brass rail and a long mirror with about a hundred bottles of liquor sitting in front of it dominated the room. Round tables covered in checked oilcloth had four battered bentwood chairs each. There didn't seem to be a menu. A slim and pretty light-skinned colored girl dressed in jeans came to take their order.

"How come you're not at the prom, a sweet thang like you, Ja'nae?" Bodey asked.

"Gotta work. Always workin'. I tell you someday I will turn this place around, and folks will have to make a reservation to get in here. What do you want?"

"The ribs, naturally. Best in the state of Lousiana. Not sure about Texas."

"Same here," said Rusty and Renee.

Conscious of her white dress, which her mama said might do for her deb presentation if she didn't put the weight back on, Noreen ordered tentatively, "A cheeseburger and fries?"

"And four beers," added Bodey.

"I'll make that four Cokes unless you want iced tea. You know my mama isn't going to lose her liquor license to serve the likes of you, Bodey Landrum."

The waitress turned on her heels to go and Bodey pinched her tempting rear. Ja'nae slammed his hand with her order pad and strode off to the kitchen.

"Touchy, huh."

"Ja'nae won't sleep with him. We rodeo with her brother, Leon, so it wouldn't be right," Rusty informed the girls. "Leon is probably back there washing dishes. You better hope she doesn't tell him about that pinch, Bodey."

Nope, Ja'nae told her mother, an imposing black woman wearing a well-set wig. Mama Tyne sailed through the restaurant as if she were the Queen Mary docking. She slapped down a red plastic basket full of cornbread squares.

"My Ja'nae said you was out here drunk as a skunk, Bodey Landrum, and you pinched her behind. I know Miss Betsy raised you better. You eat this here cornbread and sober up. Won't have you dyin' on the way home from my place."

"Sorry. Yes, ma'am, but we ain't gonna die. Got a limo for the night."

"Wise choice. Now see here, how you gonna be a championship bull rider if you drink and ride, huh?" Mama Tyne put her hands on her ample hips.

"It's prom night. Give us a break, huh, Mama Tyne."

"If you get into any trouble tonight, Big Ben will break yo' sorry white ass, so you better eat everything I send out and soak up that alcohol, you hear."

"Yes, ma'am."

"Who was that," Noreen asked, wide-eyed.

"Leontyne Plato. Her and Pop Plato own the place. She's been tryin' to talk him out of his rib recipe since they got married. He does most of the cooking."

"Did you know this place was once a fancy restaurant, the Arc-en-Ceil, the best place in Rainbow before the Civil War? Arc-en-Ceil means Rainbow in French. The Yankees took all the fine fixtures and even the nude painting over the bar," Noreen informed them with enthusiasm.

"That's what I'd take, the nude painting. How about you, Rusty?"

"Shut up, Bodey."

"After the war, a mulatto woman named Jeanette Plato bought the place with her life savings and served meals here. Her brother, Jean, ran a general store across the street to serve all the freedmen. It's still there, too, only now it's Rainbow Liquor and Food. Isn't it cool how old these places are?"

"Okay, we all know you take honors history, Noreen." Renee yawned without covering her mouth.

"I didn't know about Arc-en-Ceil meaning Rainbow," Rusty said with love in his eyes.

"Yeah, we habla the espanol at Opelousas High." Bodey yawned, too, but had the decency to cover it.

The food came served by a young black man who could have been Ja'nae's male twin but a couple of years older. He had the long plates lined up both arms and set them down, not gently, on the table.

"Pinch my sister again and I'll saw half way through your bull rope next time you ride, Bodey Landrum," the waiter said.

"I said sorry. Jesus God, Leon. I'm drunk."

"No excuse to me. You keep your hands off Ja'nae."

"Will do, but don't expect a big tip."

"Sometimes, I could just pop you."

"Wanna go outside? I'm ready. I can take you."

Leon Plato shook his head in disgust and walked

away.

"Guess his mama don't allow him to fight."

"Neither does yours. Here, Noreen, let me cover your nice dress."

Rusty Niles tenderly tucked a paper napkin into her bodice without even trying to feel her up. Noreen sighed again. He watched her chest heave with great appreciation.

Bodey did the same for Renee by stuffing the napkin deep into her cleavage. "Eat up."

The long plates contained a full rack of ribs, a heap of slaw and a mound of steaming French fries. Noreen's huge burger dripped with mayo, shredded lettuce, thin-sliced onions, tomatoes, and cheese. She cut it into quarters, plucked out the onions, and ate daintily while watching Renee nibble tender meat off the rib bones. This was quite a production and Bodey couldn't take his eyes off of her sucking, licking lips. Neither could Rusty.

"Finish up. I gotta hit the outhouse. You girls might want to wait till we get to the motel 'cause it really is an outhouse, two in fact. Usta be one for whites, one for blacks, but now you can use either to take a crap." Bodey swaggered out a little more steady than when he entered.

"Motel?" echoed Noreen.

"Don't worry about it, honey," Rusty said.

"I'd worry if I were you, Cuz. She's not on the pill. Better ask Bodey for some good condoms. Yours are probably expired." Renee swished a last fry in ketchup and got up to wait for Bodey in the limo.

"I have my period," Noreen lied.

"I said not to worry." Still, Rusty's face turned red

at receiving this information.

Bodey returned and left a big tip to make up for his transgressions. Rusty chipped in for the food and their prom night continued.

The motel sat on the outskirts of Lafayette. Nothing fancy, the place looked clean enough but wasn't part of a chain with a reputation to keep up. The tired desk clerk didn't seem to care how old Bodey was or how long he used the room.

"Your turn to get a key," he prompted Rusty.

"I thought we'd just stay in the limo, Noreen and me. My money is running low. I didn't figure on the cost of a room."

"Idiot. The girls expect this. Don't you ladies? Look, I'll pay for it," Bodey offered.

Noreen piped up, her eyes very wide. "I've never done it in a limo before. I'd like to try that."

"Whatever you want. Come on, Renee."

As soon as the door to number eight closed, Rusty eased closer to Noreen and put his arm around her. She stiffened up. "You know I've never done it at all, Rusty. I mean, there hasn't been anyone else since I went with you in the barn. I sort of want to be a virgin when I get married like my sister. She had her first baby exactly nine months to the day after her wedding night," Noreen babbled.

"That's okay. We can just make out a little like we did the last time."

He brushed a kiss over her lips and she willingly opened her mouth for him. The kisses grew harder. Rusty shrugged out of his jacket and unhooked his tie without losing contact. Before long, they were prone on the wide, cushy leather seat of the limo. Noreen pulled his starchy shirt tail out in order to feel the warm flesh of his back. He rubbed her breasts through the material of her gown. Gradually, her skirt bunched up to her waist and Noreen could feel how much he wanted to go further—but he didn't. He just rubbed as hard as he could against her pantyhose and undies.

She began to feel all hot and sparkly down there between her legs. Her toes, freed of her high heels, tingled. Rusty jerked a couple of times and cursed, "Damn, I was afraid that would happen. Sorry." He collapsed on top of her.

Noreen ran her fingers through his nice, thick hair. The color wasn't the greatest, almost the same shade as the horse she liked to ride, but the texture felt wonderful. She couldn't stop stroking. After a while, she realized from his gentle snoring that Rusty Niles had fallen asleep right on top of her. That was fine, just fine. She held him tight and when her nether parts stopped throbbing, she slept, too.

The driver got a little shuteye for himself as well. Bodey ventured out around three a.m. for more liquid refreshment but didn't wake a soul.

By five, the great Bodey Landrum was done in. He staggered out of the motel room looking like he'd been rode hard and put away wet. Renee came after, mussed but still sexy as hell. She had small hickeys all across the tops of her breasts. Rusty checked Noreen to make sure he hadn't marked her up, but she still looked all pink and white except for a bit of beard burn on her neck.

Renee leaned over and whispered to Noreen, "So, what did you go for?"

Blushing, Noreen whispered back, "I think it was

the dry hump. I'm not sure."

Renee put back her head and, showing off her perfect white incisors and sharp little canine teeth, howled. "Judging by the way my cousin has his coat draped over his lap I think you might be right."

Bodey pounded on the window to wake up the driver. "Take the girls home, Jeeves. Now!"

Within fifteen minutes, they pulled up to the Courville house in one of the wonderful old leafy Lafayette neighborhoods. The sky was brightening, but lights were on in the hallway. Noreen shook out her dress. It didn't look too rumpled. Rusty got out with her and, turning his back, put on and buttoned up his jacket. He came all the way to the door and gave her a parting kiss, no tongue in case her parents were up, before she inserted her key in the lock. He'd retreated to the limo by time Mrs. Courville got to the door.

"Would Bodey and your other friends like to come in for pancakes? It won't take but a minute to mix up a batch."

Noting that her mother remained fully dressed in last night's clothes, Noreen shook her head. Heaven forbid if her mother ever found out one of those friends was Renee Niles. She must be really groggy to consider inviting Rusty into the house.

"Everyone is tired, Mom." The limo pulled away safely. "We went to a party afterwards."

"Well, I am so glad I don't smell liquor on your breath and you did keep…"

"My pantyhose on. Goodnight, Mom."

"Oh, what lovely flowers, a little nosegay. How original. Did Bodey get them for you?"

"Bodey was not my date. Rusty found them. He

says the roses are called Courville Noisettes because they are found on our family's old estate. That's how thoughtful he is. He didn't come in to avoid a scene with Dad last night."

"Humpf, all this sounds pretty slick to me. Remember, dear, you can't see the Niles boy anymore, so don't make promises to him you won't be able to keep. Sleep tight."

Up in her room, Noreen carefully peeled off her gown and hung it up in the plastic bag. She took the pearl-headed pins out one by one, planning to save them forever along with the yellow rosebud. When she stripped off her pantyhose, she noticed Rusty had worn a small hole in the top of the crotch. She'd wash them and nest them with his briefs.

****

Bodey Landrum thanked God he got back to the Three B's before he hurled. As it was, the driver held him up as he puked on limo's left rear wheel, keeping him from ending up facedown in his own vomit.

"Thanks, man. You're a good guy. Sorry about the Jeeves crap. I was tryin' to impress a girl and drank too much." Bodey spit, attempting to get the taste out of his mouth.

"Been there. Need helping getting to the door?"

"No, no. I think I can make it now. Here, this is all the money I got left." Bodey stuffed the bills in the chauffeur's jacket pocket. "I'm gonna recommend you to all my friends."

"I surely thank you for that, sir." Jordan used an Uncle Tom voice, but Bodey failed to notice as he wove up the front path.

****

Rusty Niles returned to a darkened house. He hung up all the parts of the tux and debated if he should try to wash out the damp spot in the front of the pants, but decided against it. The rental place probably dry-cleaned these things. He took a quick shower and tried to fall asleep, but couldn't seem to turn off his feelings for Noreen Courville. She was so pretty and pliant. Though her breasts were nice, her big brown eyes got him the most. He could look into them forever. If she hadn't let him do what he did, he would have sat there all night with his balls turning blue. No way in hell her family would ever let them date. They would have to sneak around—and yes, he had to admit it, for Noreen, he would sneak and connive and do whatever to be with her.

****

Renee Niles let herself into Tara-on-the-Bayou. No one waited up. The prom was just another all-nighter when she'd gotten four times out of a guy, but better because the guy had been Bodey Landrum.

Chapter Fifteen

School ended in mid-May. Bodey and Russ hit the road in Bodey's fancy new birthday truck pulling the matching double horse trailer. They planned to enter every rodeo they could before starting college at the end of August. Rusty wanted the prize money and Bodey craved the fame. Rusty had promised Noreen he would phone at every stop and let her know how he did. Bodey placed the calls since the one time Russ had called after the prom, Mrs. Courville hung up on him. She wouldn't do that to the stepson of a rich client.

Thanks to Cousin Renee who put pressure on Sally Parker, Noreen and Russ had been able to get together during two fictitious sleepovers. With some experienced advice from Bodey, he'd given her some pleasure, too, once he'd convinced Noreen that using hands and mouth did not rob her of virginity. They both benefited. Renee's gloating was hard to take, though.

"Oh Cousin Rusty, please, please knock up little Noreen Courville. I'll bet her parents would send her off to one of those Catholic homes for unwed mothers before they'd let her marry a Niles."

He wouldn't let that happen. Even Bodey got sick of Renee and rejoiced when she left for Europe with her Uncle Dewey. She destroyed his concentration and sapped all his strength like some kind of sexual vampire, Bodey said. Russ might have stood up for his cousin if she hadn't made those ugly remarks about Noreen, but why bother? Renee was what she was—a real bitch.

The Sexy Seven minus one received postcards from the Riviera and Venice. Bodey got a snapshot of Renee on a topless beach. She had very little covering her bottom, too. Uncle Dewey had taken the picture. He showed Rusty, but threw the thing out before his mother saw. The whole idea kind of made Russ feel sick.

The boys ducked back into Rainbow briefly in mid-August to collect their gear for college. While Rusty trundled through K-Mart with his dad and a checklist, Bodey borrowed one of his stepfather's credit cards and headed for the university in Lake Charles before Renee Niles got word he was in town. He told Russ he'd ridden broncs and bulls all summer and didn't feel as beat up as he did after a night with Renee. All Rusty desired was another night with Noreen before he left again.

With all the packing and the pledging to his dad that he wouldn't do drugs, drink to excess, or ride bulls no matter how good the money, Rusty had only one chance to get together with Noreen in the flesh. She told her mother a tale about staying after school to work on her history project which necessitated copying names and dates from the tombs in the Rainbow cemetery to check her facts. Rusty met her by the Niles monument, a pile of marble plenty big enough to hide them from the road if her dad developed an envie for Pop Plato's barbecued ribs. The disappointment came when he realized Noreen really was working on her project.

"It's entitled *The Courville-Niles Feud—Discovering its Origins*. You see, I'm going to expose why our families don't get along. When I do, the feud will be over because all that happened so long ago no one remembers. I will find proof, and you and I won't have to sneak around anymore."

"I always heard one of the Niles girls broke off an engagement to a Courville son."

"I don't believe that could be the reason. Russ, it's something darker and deeper. I've always known it, but I need evidence."

"I think they took their engagements more seriously back then. I heard once that in Scotland, folks could try each other out for a year then call it off if they didn't get along."

"What does that have to do with my project?"

"Nothing. It's just that some cultures don't think pre-marital sex is wrong."

Rusty kissed the back of Noreen's neck just below her bobbing, black curls. He wished she would sit down on the bench inside the iron fence decorated with weeping willows and lambs and let him hold her. He'd forgotten during a summer of eating dust that she smelled so sweetly of talcum and rose-scented soap. His arms went around her waist and he rubbed up against her backside hopefully.

"Tracing my family tree was easy. The Courvilles seemed to have trouble producing male heirs, or at least raising them to adulthood. Lots of daughters, few sons. Until my father had Hardy and Matthew, only one boy was born per generation, and being a priest, Matt won't have any children at all."

"You never can tell about priests. They aren't all

queer," Rusty mumbled as he nibbled on Noreen's ear lobe. She shot an elbow to his ribs.

"Show some respect. Now, Aaron Niles, he had twelve children—which I suppose is why your family has the reputation for being oversexed. His poor wife!"

Rusty undid a button and slid a hand into Noreen's white parochial school blouse. He gently massaged her soft, plump breast. He could feel her heart take up a faster beat. Now, he was getting somewhere. With the other hand, he pulled Noreen to the far side of the tomb and pinned her against its marble wall between two ornamental pillars. His lips descended for a kiss, but Noreen kept talking.

"Don't you care that your family was once the richest in the area, even better off than the Courvilles?"

"Nope, 'cause we ain't rich now so what does it matter?" He took that kiss and made it last a long time, but Noreen came up yakking.

"Look, Rusty, I can't go home without some research to show my mother. Help me finish, and then I'll show you a special place where we can be together."

He sighed, much put upon. "Give me a pencil and paper. I'll copy down the names and dates on the other side if it will get us out of here quicker."

"Aaron Niles built this tomb to look like his house at Frenchman's Bend with enough space for himself, his widow and all twelve children, but as you can tell, not all the kids are buried here. According to *The Illustrious Niles Family in the Nineteenth Century* written by Mrs. Victoria Niles Duperier, the youngest daughter, widowed in the War Between the States, an infant, Aaron Edward, and a little boy, Henry Clay, are buried in the two small graves over there next to a family friend, Cecile DeVille Cortez. A sister, Amalia, became a nun and lies buried near the Academy's founder, Mother Leontine, in the convent's graveyard. Another son, William Harrison Niles, a heroic cavalry officer, disappeared into Texas along with a nephew, Owen Maddox, and was never heard from again. I'm going to find out what happened to him, too."

"Done!" Rusty held up the quickly scrawled sheet of names and dates. "Victoria is over here with all her sisters. The first is Esperanza, killed in 1863 during the Battle of Frenchman's Bend. Olivia and Susanna and chatty Miss Vicky made it into the twentieth century, the last three all widows of guys who died between 1862 and 1865. Sad. Can we go now?"

Noreen made her way to Rusty's side of the mausoleum. "I guess the family put Esperanza's husband in here because they had the room. Owen John Maddox, physician and native of England, survived his wife by seventeen years. Victoria said her eldest sister was the only female civilian casualty of the war in Rainbow, shot down by a sniper, Union, she claims, on her way home from selflessly nursing the wounded of both sides. Look, here's the grandson who died at the Battle of Frenchman's Bend on the same day. You know, Rufus Courville died on that date, too, defending his home from the Yankees. Kind of gives me the shivers."

"We all got to go some time, and speaking of going…" Rusty wasn't about to admit getting to know his dead relatives gave him an eerie feeling, too.

"I wish we could ride horses to the place I want to show you. It's on the old Courville plantation. We'd come out here in the motor home on weekends if my brothers or Estelle had games to play at St. Leo's or the Academy. I'd ride to my secret glade on my pony and hide out if Hardy and Estelle were being mean to me."

"My dad's truck has four-wheel drive. We can get there without horses, but next time if you tell me in advance, we can ride. One thing the Niles family still has is horses."

"Big red horses like the ones the subdivision is named for. Big red horses," Noreen said again, sounding dreamy as if she were finally getting in the mood.

They raced toward Ted Niles' old but powerful Ford truck. Noreen pulled up suddenly in front of the Courville mausoleum. Rusty sighed. "Now what?"

"This is where the yellow roses grow, the Courville Noisettes. They aren't in bloom with all this heat, but they will be in the fall." She hugged herself, goose bumps rising on her arms.

"Great, I'll pick some for you then. Come on, Noreen. We don't have much time. I have to leave for college in the morning, and your mom is expecting you home by six-thirty. We only got an hour or so."

Noreen came along without hesitation then, and they piled into the old truck and raced down the street, going off-road at the dilapidated ruins of the old Courville plantation house and heading for the coulee on the edge of the property. Noreen told Rusty to park near a copse of trees completely devoured by rampant wisteria vines, thick and green at this time of year. She led him, hunched over, through an opening and out into an open glade where the late afternoon sun shone in on a thick bed of leaves and soft, pithy fallen branches.

They tumbled over together unable to get enough of each other standing up. They filled their single hour with all the satisfaction hands and lips could deliver. Lying back, Noreen cuddled against Rusty's chest when they finished.

"Jeez, I wish you were on the pill, Noreen."

"You know I want to wait until marriage."

"I surely do. At best, that's five years off. I think my balls will turn purple and drop off like rotten grapes by then."

"Will not, not if we keep this up. That's one reason why I love you, Rusty. You're willing to wait."

Russell Niles went very still. Should he say the words?

"We're awful young to be talking about marriage. Things could change."

"Don't you love me, Rusty?"

"I love you with all my heart and all my soul, Noreen."

Now where had that come from when he attempted to be sensible? Somewhere deep inside. If Bodey overheard, he'd be laughing his guts out right now.

"Because we're soul mates, Russ. Meant to be together, meant to end the feud."

"I guess. We still got a few minutes. We can just lie here a while."

The sun hung a hot, orange ball on the horizon, its light no longer visible in the dark glade when the young couple woke. They hightailed it out of there getting tangled in the dark vines and tripping over the shadowed roots. Fortunately, Rainbow's two policemen dined late at the café with their squad car parked outside. If they heard the roar of a big engine speeding by, the officers of the law didn't get up from their oyster loaf sandwiches to attempt getting the license number.

"We'll go by my house and you can call your mother with some excuse. Then, I'll get you home."

"Does this mean you are finally going to introduce me to your dad?"

Rusty hadn't thought about that. Ted Niles would be at the house, probably making one of his carefully balanced, but easy meals—Shake 'n Bake chicken with canned sweet peas, a small salad and a hunk of French bread, or macaroni and cheese with the same sides, ice cream or store bought cookies for dessert. His old man would be tired from a day of taking care of two ranches, maybe having a beer while he cooked. This was as good a time as any.

"I guess so. Here goes."

Russ turned onto a long gravel drive and parked to one side of a ranch-style home with a deep porch made of stained wood, but empty and without rockers. The place once had landscaping. Gaps in the bushes showed where the azaleas had died off. A live oak, planted around the time the house went up, did its best to grow large enough to throw some shade. Off to one side, wild morning glory vines engulfed an old aluminum swing set. The generous house site with a small barn in the rear had been carved from a cow pasture and fenced off on three sides. A few chunky black steers stared placidly at the company and returned to grazing.

Rusty helped Noreen down from the big cab. He loved placing his hands around her waist and sliding her body down the front of his, but this was no time to get excited. The outside lights flicked on.

"That you, Russ? Your dinner is cold. You'll have to heat it up yourself."

Ted Niles, tall, lean, and going white early, stood in the doorway. "About time you got back with the truck. We need to get some of the stuff packed in there tonight and make an early start to Lake Charles in the morning right after I check on the stock. Who's that you got with you?"

"This is Noreen, Dad—the girl I took to the prom."

"Oh, I didn't know you were still seeing each other, what with Rusty being gone all summer. Nice to meet you, Noreen. Do I know your daddy?"

Ted Niles eyed her as if judging a cow. Noreen had slimmed down, but her Mt. Carmel uniform gave away the fact that her daddy had more money than the Niles family for sure. From the way his dad stared, Rusty thought maybe he figured she would be a snob or the kind of girl who would hurt his son.

"I think everybody knows my daddy, Charles Courville, the attorney. I live in Lafayette."

The faint, assessing smile disappeared from Ted Niles' face. Total silence ensued.

Rusty rode to the rescue. "I was helping Noreen with her social studies project and it got late. Sorry. She needs to use the phone for a minute."

Mr. Niles didn't move from the doorway until Rusty got almost in his face. "Sure, but be quick about it. Like I said, your dinner is waiting."

The man listened in as Noreen spoke to her mother. "A friend was helping me with my project. We were hungry, so we stopped for burgers at the Rainbow Café. No, we didn't go in that place. We used the drive-up. I know I should have called an hour ago. Sorry, sorry,

sorry. I'll be home in half an hour, I promise."

"Look, Dad, I need to get Noreen home. I'll heat up my dinner when I get back, okay?" Rusty shuffled his big feet and jingled the truck keys in a hurry to end the big meeting.

Noreen intervened. "Could I use your bathroom, Mr. Niles? We've been out copying data for my school project in the graveyard with no place to go."

"Second door on the right down the hall."

****

Noreen hurried off eager to be away from his scrutiny. She found the bathroom to be tidy enough except for the ring around the tub and the toilet seat in the upright position. A couple of limp, threadbare towels hung on a rack. The sink was cluttered with cans of men's shaving cream and spray-on deodorant, but someone had cleaned the porcelain of beard hairs. A wick deodorizer emitting a faint gardenia scent sat on the back of the commode.

She should have peed back at the glade but hadn't wanted to sully her favorite place. Now, she was bursting, probably from nerves. Noreen put the seat down and tinkled. As she washed her hands, she glanced in the mirror mounted on the medicine cabinet. Oh God! She had flakes of leaf duff like huge chunks of dandruff in her hair and Rusty had misbuttoned her blouse. Her lips looked swollen and probably were because they had gone at it hard. How could she go out there and face Mr. Niles again?

"Noreen! You about done in there, honey? Are you sick?"

"No, I'm coming out now, Rusty."

She rebuttoned her blouse and shook her hair out

over the sink, washing the leaf fragments down the drain. Maybe, Mr. Niles hadn't noticed after all. Men weren't that observant. Noreen joined Rusty by the door. They started out to the truck, but Mr. Niles asked them to wait a minute. He opened a closet and making a great show of it took out a Dust Buster. First, he sucked up the trail of leaves Noreen had left on his floor before saying, "As I recall from my misspent youth, these Mt. Carmel kilts are like magnets for hay and leaves and such." Ted Niles ran the Dust Buster down Noreen's back and over her bottom while she turned a brilliant red.

"Thank you, Mr. Niles," Noreen said in a tiny voice. "We have to go now."

"Yes, you do. Get along."

In the safety of the truck flying toward Lafayette, Noreen said to Rusty, "Do you think he knew what we were doing?"

"Oh, yes. I'll have to listen to the whole lecture about respecting women and being careful when I get back—like I don't know my mother was knocked up when she married my dad. The first time I ever brought that up, he shoved me half way across the room and I landed on my backside. My mom had been dead two years. I was fourteen and didn't know when to keep my mouth shut. I knew about them for a couple of years before I said anything, ever since I had to dig up my own birth certificate to play in Little League. Their marriage license sat right under my papers. They married the second week in December and I was born the first week in May."

"I know. My mother was your mom's sorority sister. I guess they didn't keep up with each other after

Miss Maggie married your dad."

"Because she married a Niles. You see how it is. Old grudges don't die around here."

"We're going to kill this one, Rusty. Wait and see."

Noreen snuggled up under his right arm and stayed there all the way home. She got out on her own, ran up the sidewalk and let herself in quietly with a key. Even so, her mother lay in wait, looking out the window as the old truck pulled away. Mrs. Courville pounced.

"You're still seeing that Niles boy. Your father will hit the ceiling if he finds out and with his blood pressure, he can't afford to get that upset. You must break this off, Noreen."

"I haven't seen Rusty most of the summer, Mom. He went off riding in rodeos with Bodey Landrum and he leaves for college tomorrow. He drove by, saw me in the cemetery and helped me get my data. We had burgers. No big deal, okay?"

"What's this in your hair?" Mrs. Courville picked out a fragment of crumbled leaf from Noreen's curls. "Turn around."

"Oh, for heaven's sake, Mom. We weren't doing it." Silently, Noreen thanked Mr. Niles and his Dust Buster.

"Well, missy, I can't think of more lethal challenges to a girl's chastity than rodeo cowboys and college men. You won't be seventeen until the end of December. If you are up to anything with Russell Niles, your father could and would have him jailed for statutory rape. If you care about this young man, let him go."

"Jeez, Mom. Should I go upstairs and take off my clothes so you can check my virginity like we live in some Third World nation?"

Noreen sincerely believed nothing she and Rusty had done had broken her membrane, but she could be wrong. What if her mother took up her challenge? Before Mrs. Courville replied, Noreen ran up the stairs and slammed her door. She wouldn't be able to sneak any dinner. So what? Going without a meal would be good for her figure. She could always drink water, chew the gum in her purse and pretend she lived in starving Bangladesh.

****

Here it came, the lecture. Rusty's dad sat in his recliner. He'd had a beer, but wasn't mellowed by it. Rusty took a seat on the sofa just to get it over with, but the speech didn't go as usual.

"If you had burgers, I guess you don't want your dinner, son."

"I could eat again."

"Mama Tyne and Pop Plato must be cuttin' down on the meat if you still have room."

"No, sir. I'm just a growing boy is all." Rusty tried out a wobbly smile.

"Don't pee on my boots and tell me it's raining, boy. Russ, the girl is a Courville. They are cheats and liars. If you got Noreen pregnant—and don't tell me how careful you are—her family could and would have you arrested, even if it was partly her fault, because she's still in high school. You are eighteen and should know better. If they didn't want the bad publicity, Good Ole Charlie Courville would see she had an abortion or arrange a private adoption. They might even try to foist the kid off on some other guy she knows. You can't trust a Courville."

"Noreen is different. She wants to end this feud."

"Sure, she does, but she'll come around to their way of thinking eventually. I don't want you to be the one who gets hurt. Did I ever tell you what the Courvilles did to your mother?"

"I guess not."

"Well, Ole Charlie and his son, Hardy, decided this land we sit on was ripe for development. Maggie served as one of the top sales people in Hardy's new real estate firm. They sent her out here to convince me to sell after my daddy died. Your Uncle Jed had already married Pru who was none too happy with their lifestyle. She wanted finer things and ranch life didn't agree with her. They got to Jed with money. Me, I was only twenty-five and fell for the woman, but I still wouldn't sell."

"You're saying my mother used sex to get what she wanted."

Russ regretted the words as soon as they came out. The only time his father ever manhandled him, other than a regular spanking as a child was that one time he insulted Maggie Niles. Ted rose halfway out of his chair now and Rusty put up his fists because he would not to be shoved around again.

Ted Niles sank back into his seat. "I don't want to fight with you, Rusty. Just listen for a change. You know your mother had ten years on me. Her clock was ticking as they say. When she became pregnant, she wanted you so badly—and so did I. I did the right thing by her. I kept my vows. And, I loved her all the way to the end. But, the Courvilles, when I wouldn't sell, fired her and spread rumors all over town that she'd been taking money from clients to make better deals and cutting out Hardy, that she was immoral to boot and would sleep with men to close a deal. After you came along, she started her own business, but because of their stories, she didn't get the best clients."

"I didn't know that. She was a great mom. I always came first, not her job, she told me."

"True. She wanted more children. When she turned thirty-eight, she went to the doctor for a routine checkup so she could get off the pill and start on giving you a brother or a sister. That's when she found out she had breast cancer. First, they took one breast, then the other. She had chemo and radiation, a few years of remission. The cancer came back. She fought as hard as she could to stay with us, a real tiger."

"I remember some of that. She lost her hair." Russ shifted with discomfort.

"Hell, I was a young rancher with no health insurance when we married. Maggie lost her insurance with her job and had nothing to cover the pregnancy. She got another policy when she started her own business, but it didn't cover what they call catastrophic illness. I said I'd sell out to pay the bills, but among her last words were 'don't ever sell to Hardy'. So, I sold to Big Ben instead and got to keep this little bit of grazing land and the house. That's what the Courvilles did to your mother."

Rusty squeezed his eyes shut and looked away. Eighteen-year-old men did not, should not, cry.

"So you do see, son, if you keep on with this girl, you'd just as soon be spittin' on your mama's grave. Go off to college and forget her. You're young. Both of you will get over it and marry someone else. It's for the best."

Chapter Sixteen

Bodey Landrum leaned back in the old desk chair, put his feet up on the battered desk, and contemplated his new athletic shoes, still so white they reflected the late afternoon sun coming in the dormitory window. Cowboy boots, he'd found, were no good for walking around campus while hauling a ton of books in a knapsack.

He looked around again at the bunk beds, the pint-sized refrigerator with a small microwave balanced on the top, and the single sink with a mirror over it between the built-in closets, and thought for the hundredth time that Big Ben would have paid for a great off-campus apartment where he and Russ could have partied without end. But no, Rusty couldn't afford his half of the rent and was too proud to let Bodey foot the bill. Russ was like a brother to him, so he'd suffer through a year or two in the dorm until his bro saw reason.

Bodey stretched, very nearly tipping over the chair, but he had great balance and righted himself immediately. As it was, since the desks faced each other, his feet framed Rusty's dejected face. "I did my best. Wasn't my fault her mama caught on to the phone trick."

"She saw me when I dropped off Noreen. She knows now you were covering for me. I don't know what to do. If I send a letter, her parents will throw it out while she's at school."

"Why don't you break up with her? She's a high school kid, and now we're college men on a campus swarming with college women, most of them warm and willin'. I mean, Noreen doesn't even put out for you."

"She's saving that…"

"Yeah, for marriage. Most likely some other guy will come along while you're in college and pluck that cherry she keeps tucked away."

"Not Noreen."

"I'll bet I could get her to."

"Don't even say it, Bodey, or I'll knock out your shiny white teeth before the bulls you ride do. Noreen is the one woman I know who doesn't find you attractive. She says you will end up broken and alone."

"The hell she does! Why after a dozen or so years of rodeo when I'm rich and famous, I'll just cut my favorite buckle bunny from the bunch—but not before I'm good and ready."

"That's the kind of woman you want to marry? Someone who sleeps around with bull riders?"

"Maybe not, but me marrying anybody is a long ways off. While you, you got to go without sex for years if you plan to marry Noreen. That's plain crazy."

"I hope to God, Bodey Landrum, someday you fall in love with a woman who won't leap into your lap when you crook your little finger.

"Never happen!"

The telephone on Bodey's desk rang. A little steamed because Russ might consider they only had a telephone in their room because Bodey made up a story saying said his mother insisted on keeping in touch, he jerked up the receiver and answered, "Yeah!"

"Is that so? Uh-huh. Okay by me. Here's Rusty." Bodey tossed the receiver across the desk. "It's your virgin. She's at Renee's house. Renee just broke up with me. Says she can't go until Christmas without sex. Boohoo."

"Noreen, honey. How did you get our number? Renee of course. I had Bodey call the house, but your mother told him not to try that trick again. She knew we were in cahoots together. Yes, she really said that. Renee will let you use her phone? Tell her she's my favorite cousin. Every Friday at four."

Bodey shook his head, making signs that looked like beer drinking and rodeo riding or maybe girl riding.

"Friday is no good. How about Thursday at four? I'm gonna live for Thursdays, Noreen. You know that I do. Won't Uncle Jed notice the phone bills, though? Oh, he thinks Renee is still seeing Bodey. Got it. Just hearing your voice makes me want to…"

Bodey made gagging noises and slammed down his chair. He left the room to prowl for a mid-week date. Rusty would probably stay on the phone with Noreen for an hour, then take off to bus tables at the cafeteria for his spending money. By the time Bodey got back from having a good meal somewhere and a little female companionship, Russ would be hitting the books, studying animal husbandry and farm management like it was brain surgery.

Bodey took straight business management courses, which, like so many things in his life, came easy to him. He already knew plenty about animal husbandry from Big Ben. That was why he couldn't figure out Rusty's attachment to Noreen after he'd heard the whole sad story about what her family had done to Maggie Niles.

If the Courvilles bred liars and cheats like Ole Charlie and Hardy, why would his best friend want to marry into that family? Oh, yeah—Noreen was sweet, Noreen was different, Noreen was the love of his life. Rusty should look for better stock, or at least someone more fun. Why, he'd be doing old Russ a favor if he broke them up. Then, they could finish college and go on the pro rodeo circuit like they'd always planned, two pals making money and having a hell of a good time.

****

No one could say college was boring. Between his studies, his job and the rodeo team, Rusty had little time to pine for Noreen. He let Bodey drag him to parties, but generally after a beer or two, he slipped out and went back to the room, where if thoughts of Noreen plagued him, he could take care of it in private.

Christmas vacation followed by semester break came up quickly before he'd had time to think of a gift for his love that he could afford on limited funds. He'd have to find something in Lafayette, he guessed. Maybe something antique since she loved historical stuff like those yellow roses, which really wowed her on prom night. A vase she could put them in? He didn't know. On the way home sitting beside Bodey in the truck, the college things he had to take with him piled in the back, Rusty remembered an old box his mother prized, full of antiquey objects. He knew his father had given the junk inside to his mom as gift. Maybe, he could find the perfect present for Noreen in there. His dad wouldn't notice.

Bodey dropped him off at home. His dad's truck sat in the drive, the keys on the hall table. Ted was probably out seeing to his own stock. Rusty grabbed the keys, thanking God he did not have to ask for them or give an explanation. Noreen said she'd be at Sally Parker's house. She had the good excuse that she was setting up her boards for her social studies project and whole thing would be easier to transport over to the Academy from Sally's place. Mrs. Parker had given her a corner of the family room and even a small filing cabinet to keep her research organized.

Mrs. Parker greeted Rusty, whom she always referred to as "that poor orphaned boy", despite the fact that he had a daddy very much alive and opposed to the Courvilles. Mrs. Parker, a neutral party, played bridge with Noreen's mother and tennis on Pru Niles' court. Her looks were neutral, too, not too tall or short, too thin or fat, medium brown hair and hazel eyes neither brown nor green, but a forgettable blend of both. Her best trait was her desire to mother everyone and offend nobody. Her worst—a tendency to talk too much.

"Look who's here to visit, Sally. Rusty Niles. I swear Rusty, you've grown another inch since you left for college. Hasn't he, girls? And so cute with those freckles and red hair."

Rusty, his freckles obscured by his red face, stepped away in time to avoid a pinch on the cheek. "Hi, Sally, Noreen. Nice project board." He peered at it closely to avoid Mrs. Parker's fingers.

"Why don't I bring in some cold drinks? Diet Coke for the girls, I know. How about you, Rusty?"

"I take my cola straight up, ma'am, but Dr. Pepper if you got it. Thanks."

"Such a polite young man. I can see your daddy taught you manners after your poor mother died."

"Yes, ma'am."

"Refreshments coming right up." At last, Mrs. Parker bustled away.

Rusty pulled Noreen into his arms and gave her a kiss that left Sally Parker wide-eyed with envy. Sal had never considered Rusty Niles to be either handsome or sexy, not like his friend, Bodey, and let Noreen know it. Now, Rusty lifted Noreen off her feet to raise her to his lips and held on to her like he'd never let go. One solid minute passed before they came up for air. Sally gave a thumbs-up to show she was impressed.

Noreen, a little breathy, said, "Oh, I've missed you, too, Russ, but let me show you my project. You won't believe what I've found! When I started pasting up the pictures of the two family lines, I noticed something odd. I copied the old portraits from different books and labeled them on the back so I wouldn't forget who was who, but when I went to mount the first one, Aaron Niles, I picked up a picture of Rufus Courville by mistake. Both were painted at about the same age, maybe thirty-five. If it weren't for the change in clothing styles, they could be twins."

"Yeah, I guess I see the resemblance."

"Here are the portraits of Maxime and Marguerite Courville, supposedly the parents of Rufus. My family still owns the original miniatures they might have exchanged at marriage and this small one of their eldest son, Francois. All three look kind of dark and delicate and very French. Get that little goatee on Maxime. But Rufus, who ended up with the estate, looks exactly like Aaron Niles. That's my proof some hanky-panky went on between Marguerite and Aaron. That's what caused the feud. So, it's no wonder Esperanza Niles was forbidden to marry the man who was her half-brother."

"You're saying we are some sort of cousins? That makes me kind of uncomfortable." Rusty shifted his weight and dropped his arm from Noreen's waist.

"Don't be silly. The Courvilles and the Niles family haven't ever intermarried, even in the female lines as far as I can tell. Most of my Cajun friends still have relatives who married their cousins not all that long ago. It's been 160 years since Rufus Courville was born. I think we are safe from all accusations of incest even from a hard-ass like Fr. Cyrus. Every time I confess to lying to my parents, he really lays on the penance."

"Good thing I haven't spent much time in church since my mama died, or he'd get me for impure thoughts every time. I guess our children won't be monkey-faced idiots with strange diseases, then." His arm went back around Noreen's waist and he would have swooped in for another kiss if he hadn't been warned by the clinking of cans and glasses of ice on a tray.

"Here we go. Drinks for everyone and a basket of pretzels to tide you over until dinner. Would you like to stay Rusty, Noreen?"

"No, ma'am. Thanks just the same. I promised I'd drive Noreen home."

"Yes, we need to get going. We'll just take the drinks in the can. Thank you, Mrs. Parker. And for giving me the space to work on my project. I want to surprise my parents."

"Glad to help you, dear." Mrs. Parker trailed them to the front door and buzzed them out of the courtyard. She waved as Rusty lifted Noreen onto the truck seat.

"Now why can't you find a nice boy like that, Sally?" she said to her daughter.

Rusty overheard and smirked at Noreen. "See, I'm a catch to everyone but a Courville."

He pulled slowly from the curb. As soon as they were out of sight, he gunned the engine. "I figure we have about an hour in the glade before the sun goes down this time of year."

Fortunately for them, the local cops had set up their speed trap on the other side of the highway. As it was, Rusty nearly took out two nuns crossing the street in front of the Academy. He veered the truck around the old Courville place slowing enough in the turn to notice some construction was going on.

"Your family is fixing up the old place?"

"Hardy and Estelle are. Estelle said she is bored with staying home with two babies and never using her brain for more than figuring out how to get a raisin out of my nephew's nose. She badgered Dad and Hardy until they agreed to renovate the plantation house for a bed-and-breakfast and wedding reception place. Estelle really got to them when she mentioned that the interior designer who fixed up Frenchman's Bend was making a nice profit. It is tons of work, though. I think it will be a success because the house is haunted, you know. Tourists love that."

"Who rattles the chains—Rufus Courville?"

"No, but he did die there, probably in that same massive bed still standing on the second floor. The netting and draperies are all rotted and the mattress is gone, but Estelle thinks she can restore it and use the room as bridal suite. No, our ghost is a young woman, all pale and blonde. She plays the piano in the night exactly as she did for the wounded soldiers housed downstairs during the war. When I was a child, I was sure I heard her and once I saw this sort of misty figure walking toward the bayou. That's where they found Adelaide Courville's body floating after she got word her fiancé had been killed in battle."

"Cool. Ghosts are cool." Rusty urged the old truck across the terrain to the wisteria thicket.

"She still got to be buried in the Courville tomb because the Mother Superior at the Academy said Rainbow's own sweet Ophelia had been deranged with grief and unknowing when she slipped and fell into the bayou. I guess God didn't see it that way because Addy still haunts the plantation."

"I thought her name was Ophelia."

"You weren't listening, Rusty Niles! Ophelia is a reference to Shakespeare's *Hamlet*. She was Hamlet's girlfriend and she went crazy and drowned herself. Mother Mary Frances wrote *The Founding of Mount Carmel Academy and the Town of Rainbow with notes on its First Families*. They loved to use classical allusions in those days."

"We did *Macbeth* in public school, Miss Honors English. I only know about the witches and the toil and trouble. Come on, we're here."

They dashed through the short tunnel into the glade, ghostly and skeletal now with the leaves gone from the vines and the dead trees beneath them showing through. Rusty had Noreen's blouse open and bra unsnapped in seconds. He buried his face in the warmth of her breasts and suckled them like a baby frantic for food. He did get his jeans and underwear down before he exploded all over Noreen's softly curved belly. She didn't have a chance to take him in hand. He bet this never happened to Bodey, but then, he guessed Bodey had never been in love. Relieved after months of waiting, Rusty took more time satisfying Noreen and then cuddled her in his arms.

"About Shakespeare. We're just like Romeo and Juliet, aren't we, Russ?" She murmured into that patch of auburn hair on his chest.

"Don't say that. They both died."

"We won't. We won't—because I believe we are the souls of Rufus Courville and Esperanza Niles come again, given another chance to be together because it wasn't their fault their parents had sinned. I've had dreams about them all my life. I know this is true."

"Noreen, I love you, honey, but that's just nuts. Besides which—if it were true—I should be a Courville and you should be a Niles."

"I think we had to be born into opposite families so we could understand the other side."

"Right. You're crazy and you read too much, but I love you all the same." He bent his head to kiss her hair. "We need to get going. Gets dark early this time of year and I want to be sure I have you buttoned up the way you should be."

"I love you, too, Rusty. Our families might have a hard time getting used to this idea, but that won't stop us this time."

"No, no, it won't."

"Still, you'd better drop me off on the corner in case Daddy came home from work early."

****

When Rusty walked in, his father was sitting at the kitchen table reading the newspaper. Ted Niles looked up, a peeved expression on his face.

"I meant to drive over to the Rainbow Café and get us some ribs tonight to celebrate your finishin' up your first semester of college, but my truck was gone when I got in from the barn. Where'd you hare off to?"

"Oh, ah—Bodey had some trouble with his truck. We went to get a part."

"That truck is brand new. Big Ben should of gotten him a Ford. Interested in those ribs?"

"Yeah, the works. I want fries and slaw and cornbread, too."

"Don't they feed you in college? You look thin." Ted Niles canted his head. "Or maybe you've grown some more."

"College food is nothing like Pop Plato's ribs. And, yeah, I guess I've grown some. I could use new jeans for Christmas, maybe some long-sleeved shirts."

"I'll take you to the mall and let you pick out what you want at Penney's. I've missed you, boy. Want to ride along for those ribs?"

"No. I think I'll unpack and take a shower."

"A shower this early?"

"It's sticky out for December."

"A bit. I'll go get dinner, then. You're eighteen now, nineteen in the spring, so have a beer if you want one. I'd rather have you drink here than on the road."

"Thanks, Dad."

As soon as the truck rattled onto the blacktop road, Rusty headed for his parents' bedroom where the bureau top sat still cluttered with his mom's figurines of elegant ladies from other eras holding out the skirts of their ball gowns. Dust grayed the porcelain folds of their dresses. One reminded him of Esperanza Niles from the portrait on Noreen's board, dark-haired with big Spanish eyes and yellow roses tucked in her curls. Rusty could have given Noreen that for Christmas if his dad hadn't broken the head off and glued it back on again. He knew the little statues cost over one-hundred dollars each because his dad had taken him along to the fancy jewelry store to get his mom one each year before her birthday and anniversary. When he had the money, he'd get Noreen a new one just like that.

Rusty opened the bottom drawer of the dresser and found the antique box among some scarves and evening bags that had been overlooked when his dad cleaned out the closets and took his mother's clothes to the Good Will. The edges of the box were worn and a few scratches marred the top, but it had a nice cherry finish. The scratches happened when the interior designer who bought Frenchman's Bend pried up some rotten floor boards and found the small chest. He'd returned the box to Rusty's family because, he said, it held family letters and jewelry.

Uncle Jed and Aunt Pru were only interested in new stuff, but his mother had loved the box and its contents. He'd been maybe eight when his mother first showed him the small chest and only cared that it had a secret compartment which the designer had shown them since he knew all about antiques. Very disappointing to his third-grade mind, the secret drawer held merely letters, not treasure. Still, he recalled his mom getting teary-eyed when she'd read some of them to him. Mushy stuff. Maybe the chemo had made her weak and sentimental.

Rusty shined the box a little with one of the scarves. He could put some stain on the scratches and polish it with a paste wax to make the wood glow. Older now and a veteran of high school woodshop, he appreciated the beautiful dovetails holding the box together without nails and the even more cunning button hidden in the carving of a rose that sprung the secret drawer. He pushed the button. The compartment stuck it was so jammed with letters, but he eased it open. Noreen would love this.

Rusty intended only to compact the letters a little more so they wouldn't get caught in the drawer. He felt around on the inside and found a note that had gotten crumpled in the back, caught in the works, a scrap of paper with a few sentences. He smoothed it out intending to put it in one of the bundles. Despite the fancy script, the faded ink and browning paper, the words leapt out at him.

My Dearest Espy—I love you with all my heart and all my soul. No one can come between us. Meet me in the oak grove this afternoon after the dinner hour. Your most devoted—Rufe.

That same frisson he'd felt in the old cemetery made him shiver. He shook off the chills. This was just the kind of crap men said when they wanted to get a woman into bed. No, it wasn't. He had to admit, he wouldn't say anything like that unless he intended to marry the girl. Neither would Bodey. He put the note on the very bottom of the stack of letters and pushed the drawer closed. No sense in giving Noreen more wild ideas. What he needed was a really good Christmas gift and yikes, her seventeenth birthday came right after that.

He opened the top of the jewelry box and took the items out one by one. A nice set of what he thought were garnets set in gold filigree that hadn't lost its shine in over a century—earrings, necklace, brooch and ring—maybe a gift from a doting husband long ago. He held up another pair of earrings that looked like small drops of blood and had more luster than the garnets. Real rubies? He didn't know.

Another brooch rimmed in gold had a glass face containing a lock of hair. Creepy. He fingered a set of combs made of mother-of-pearl from the days when women had lots of hair to pin back. They'd be useless to Noreen, but she'd love them because they were really old. When he moved the combs out of the box, he uncovered a second ring, gold again, and set with a row of vibrant red stones. Looked like it could use a little cleaning. Black gunk and dirt filled the crevices, but this was a fine enough piece to be an engagement ring, better than anything he'd ever be able to afford.

Rusty had a vague memory of his mother wearing both the rings on her slim, elegant fingers until she'd gotten so thin the jewelry would fall off and she'd been afraid to lose them. She loved rings. He wondered why she'd never had the rubies cleaned. Too expensive, maybe. She'd worn her wedding ring on a gold chain toward the end. Swiping a hand across his eyes, he gathered up the contents of the box and took all the loot to his own room. He'd sort out what to give Noreen when later on.

****

Rusty took the jewelry box over to Bodey's place to stain and polish. Miss Betsy, bearing freshly baked cookies, walked in on them while they worked in the barn's shop and exclaimed over what a wonderful job they did with that old chest. He'd asked her to keep it a secret until Christmas passed. By then, Noreen would have her present and if his father noticed the box was gone, it would simply be too late.

He'd decided to give her the box and letters and the garnet necklace and earrings for Christmas. The ring and brooch, he'd save for her birthday. The ruby drops and the ring with red stones he wanted to save for a really special occasion, though having them made him uneasy. He'd get both cleaned and appraised first.

Bodey mocked him. "That will be the day, bro, when I go around looking for special jewelry for a girl when she'd be just as happy with any old thing from the mall."

"You may be great in bed, Bodey, but you will never understand women."

"Like you do."

"They want to have things no one else has. They want to know you went to some trouble for them."

"Oh, I bow to your superior wisdom."

Bodey salaamed his way backwards toward a cooler holding only soft drinks. Miss Betsy wasn't nearly as easy going about liquor as Ted Niles and Big Ben, but she did bake a great chocolate chip cookie. Bodey popped the top from a cola and stuffed a cookie into his mouth.

"When I ask Noreen to marry me, I'll give her this ring." Rusty held up the golden circle, its red stones shining despite the dirt in their settings. "It's unique like her, and it's an antique so she'll have some of that old, new, borrowed, blue stuff taken care of."

"Like that's your responsibility. Aren't her bridesmaids supposed to do that?"

"Give me a cookie. I think we're done here. I'm

going to wrap the box and put it under the truck seat. As soon as we can get away together, I'll give it to her."

"And then she'll put out for you."

"I'm not asking her to."

"Rusty, Rusty, Rusty, you are a sad excuse for a man."

****

Russell Niles knelt beside his father at St. Leo's as people in their aisle squeezed past them to go up to the communion rail. Christmas Eve and Easter Mass were the only services Ted Niles made his son attend. The rest of the year sort of slipped by and the two never went to confession. While they waited for the regular attendees to take the host, Rusty thought about Noreen probably worshipping with her family at the big cathedral in Lafayette.

He had her gift all ready. After Mass, his dad would insist on going to the Christmas Eve party Big Ben Barnum always threw. Big Ben and Miss Betsy weren't big on religion, but they never missed a chance to celebrate. He could probably get away for a drive Christmas day after dinner at Uncle Jed's house but wasn't sure about Noreen. Maybe, Renee would call for him and arrange a place for them to meet if she had any holiday spirit in her hard heart.

The organ blasted out the opening chords to a familiar carol and people got to their feet. After another fifteen minutes of the usual hoorah, the priest and altar boys marched out. The congregation followed. Sure enough, Ted said he had to put in an appearance at Big Ben's bash and pointed the truck toward the Three B's. Rusty knew his dad would stay at the party until the last drunk went home. He'd check the pasture gates to make sure no one had tampered with them, the farm pond for cars that might have swerved off the drive, and the barns for couples who needed to go home to their own beds. All these events had happened in the past. Rusty would probably be drafted to drive the most tipsy home if they'd come alone or without a designated driver. Big Ben always paid him well for the service.

"Here you are, boy! Bodey's broodin' out by the pool because there ain't any pretty young gals around, but help is on the way. Your Uncle Jed and his girls are comin' and my lawyer is bringing his family right after church. Mind parking cars for the folks? It's getting crowded and I don't want my guests to have to walk up the hill." Big Ben, as effusive and generous as ever, tucked a fifty into Rusty's coat pocket.

Rusty stripped off the jacket to his one and only suit, left it in his dad's truck parked over by the barns and got to work helping women in high heels, party dresses and fur wraps from low-slung sports cars or substantial sedans. He took the keys from the men and found spaces for the cars. Renee, looking like a thousand-dollar hooker, arrived with her family and smirked when her father gave Russ a tip, calling it "a little Christmas cash." Rusty parked their big van next to his dad's old truck.

He returned to the front of the house in time to open the car doors for the next arrivals. A statuesque woman in a full-length mink coat slid out. The night was a little chilly, but not nearly cold enough for this extravaganza of fur, Rusty thought, paying scant attention to the wearer. The woman inhaled sharply. Rusty glanced up to see if he'd caught the coat in the door and realized he'd just assisted Mrs. Charles

Marchand Courville the Third. Noreen, her older sister, Estelle, and Estelle's husband exited the back seat while he stood there frozen and humiliated.

"Come along, Noreen. Let's get in the house where it's warmer," Carolyn Courville prompted her daughter.

The group began to move toward the front door blazing with twinkle lights twined in greenery. Noreen dawdled behind.

Rusty whispered, "Meet me by my dad's truck over near the barns as soon as you can. I have a present for you."

"Noreen!" Mrs. Courville shrilled. "Come say hello to Mr. Ben."

"My favorite lawyers come to call!" Big Ben boomed, pumping the hands of Good Ole Charlie and his partner, Estelle's husband. He gave Carolyn Courville a bear hug for good measure and told Noreen that Bodey sat out by the pool looking for company his own age.

Fifteen minutes later, Rusty saw Noreen circling the house from the pool area and heading toward the barns. He deserted his duties, letting the well-off drop their wives and park their own vehicles for a change.

"Get in the truck. It's getting a little cold. You look mighty pretty, Noreen. I think these might go with your dress." Rusty offered her the box wrapped in holly-sprigged paper and topped with a red stick-on bow he'd gotten at the drugstore.

Noreen, dressed in a long-sleeved, high-waisted red velvet gown, wore small pearl earrings with a matching strand at her throat above the crimson lace bordering a square neckline. She attacked the wrapping paper like a little child on Christmas morning and revealed the box, its polished wood shining in the glare of the barn's security light.

"Oh, this is lovely—and old, I think."

"It's got dovetails. You like dovetails, right? Open it."

"Rusty, what wonderful jewelry! Garnets and gold for me?"

Noreen plucked out her pearls as she spoke and inserted the earrings. "Put the necklace on me, Russ." Noreen turned the truck mirror down to see how the red stones and gold filigree looked against her white chest. She dropped her pearls into the box next to the set of hair combs, which she picked up and held to the light.

"These are beautiful, too. However did you afford antique jewelry, Rusty Niles? You shouldn't have."

"You are wearing the Niles family jewels, Noreen. That designer found the box when he renovated Frenchman's Bend. I cleaned it up for you."

Noreen could not hold her knowledge in any longer. "I know this box."

"Oh, come on. Not more of that reincarnation junk."

"It's not junk, but no. I read in *The Illustrious Niles Family in the Nineteenth Century* that the body of Esperanza Niles Maddox was found by her colored servant under the oak across from her house. Her husband, a doctor, had valiantly volunteered to serve in the Confederate medical corps and was gone from home. Only her two youngest sons remained at her house with their old mammy. Ramona Niles, her mother, came to help lay out the body, took the boys into her care and, I quote, 'removed a small chest of valuables belonging to her daughter to Frenchman's

Bend lest the Yankees return and ransack the empty house.' Mrs. Niles hid the box but passed away in her sleep before the war ended, telling no one where she'd buried the chest."

"Wasn't buried. Ramona stuck it under some floorboards. Look, this is the best part. Press the center of the rose ornament."

"I know what will happen." The secret drawer popped open.

"These are old letters from Rufe Courville to Esperanza Niles. They really did have a thing going on. You can use them to document your project."

"Oh, Rusty. These are better than jewelry. I can't wait to read them. I don't have your present with me. Tomorrow, meet me in Girard Park on the bridge over the pond at three. I'll tell everyone I'm taking my nephews to feed the ducks."

"I still have your dad's keys. We'll put the box under the front seat of your car, and you can get it out later. But hey, don't I get a Christmas kiss?"

Noreen leaned in, crushing her velvet skirt and not caring one bit.

****

Renee Niles stretched way across the table to pluck a candied pecan from the bowl in front of Bodey. She wanted to be real sure he knew what he was missing. Her short, skin-tight black dress rode up in the rear showing off the tops of her dark stockings and the bottom of a red lace garter belt. Several middle-aged men escaping their wives by sitting out near the pool gawked and swigged at their drinks, giving her great satisfaction.

"I thought we were over, Renee, but I see the

offerin' is still on the table," Bodey drawled. "You want to go out to the barn?"

"I'm seeing a St. Leo's guy now. He's head of the debate team and wants to go into politics and be governor someday. I could be First Lady of Louisiana."

Bodey snorted. "He'll marry some frigid, politically-connected bitch and keep you for a mistress more likely."

"At least his career won't be over in less than ten years, Bodey Landrum—if you last that long riding bulls. I'm not interested in you tonight, but you know what would be fun? You could put the hit on Noreen. I saw her sneak around back to meet Rusty. He probably has her all warmed up for you. Look, there she is coming back all mussed up. Bet you a blow job you can't make it with her."

Bodey's blue eyes turned sharp. "Bet I can. I might be doing old Russ a favor. He shouldn't be so hung up on a girl at our age."

Bodey stood up. He wore a dress shirt and sports coat over jeans held up by a brand new rodeo prize belt buckle that glittered in the festive lights. He swaggered over to Noreen on his ostrich skin cowboy boots.

"Hey, Noreen. Why don't you sit with me until Rusty is free? Better yet, let's go over here away from the crowd. I can tell you what Rusty would really like for Christmas and how you might go about doing that for him."

"Really? I already have a gift, but I don't think he'll like it very much."

"Let's just scoot behind this here life-sized nativity scene Bets paid a fortune for. I think the folks who delivered it left some extra bales of straw back there."

"He wants straw?"

Bodey rolled his eyes. "No. He wants an experienced woman who knows how to please a man. I can show you what you need to learn."

Noreen stopped dead in her tracks, but they were close enough to the fake stable for Bodey to jerk her into the shadows behind the creche. Renee Niles watched the back wall of the plywood stable begin to shake hard. Maybe Bodey really had nailed Noreen against it. She saw her cousin coming over to her table. This was going to be so good.

"Have you seen Noreen?"

"Sure, she's behind the manger scene making it with Bodey. We have a bet that she wants him."

"No!"

Rusty charged around the pool and behind the creche. Its flimsy walls shook even harder. In her mind, Renee pretended that the Virgin Mary looked alarmed and the Baby Jesus cried because of the ruckus. Soon, other guests took notice, among them Uncle Ted who was picking up trash from the tables and Mr. Courville who worked on a plate of sweet-and-sour cocktail weenies while schmoozing with some of his clients.

The stable wall collapsed taking out St. Joseph and two worshipful shepherds. Miraculously, the two young men swinging at each other missed the Virgin and Child. Renee imagined the Three Wise Men were outraged at this behavior and their life-sized camel spooked. She enjoyed watching little Noreen trying to tug up the zipper on the back of her dress that the nimble-fingered Bodey had gotten down to her waist. Hmmm, she would have thought Bodey Landrum would be the better fighter, but Rusty came out on top and pummeled his best friend hard. Maybe fighting for someone you loved did give a person an edge.

Ted Niles dropped his trash collection on the floor and headed for the fight. Mr. Courville choked on a weenie when one of the men in his circle said, "Isn't that your daughter trying to get her dress back on?"

Renee howled with laughter as a doctor in the group positioned himself behind Mr. Courville and popped that weenie out. The thrashing fighters rolled over and splashed into the shallow end of the heated pool where candles shaped like poinsettias floated in the steam. The waves sent up swamped the fragile flames. Ted Niles went in after the boys, cowboy boots, good suit and all, and tore the guys apart. He shook his son by the collar like a half-drowned puppy.

"Stop this! Bodey is your best friend. Don't let that little slut come between you!"

"She's not a slut. Noreen was trying to fight him off."

Bodey spit out a mouthful of bloody water. "I was just tryin' to show you Noreen ain't nothin' special—for your own good."

Russ took a roundhouse swing at Bodey and clipped him good on the jaw. Bodey went down with a tremendous splash that splattered on Charlie Courville's expensive tailored suit just as he was removing his jacket to cover his daughter's bare back.

"Ted Niles, keep your oversexed son away from my daughter! Same goes for you, Bodey. Son of a client or not, I see this sex maniac friend of yours has rubbed off on you. If either of you raped her, I'll see you in jail!" Mr. Courville's face grew empurpled with rage.

Ted Niles dragged his son out of the pool by

locking both arms behind his back. Rusty elbowed his father in the stomach and freed, headed straight for Noreen and hugged her to him.

"Did Bodey hurt you? I'll kill him if he did!"

She clung to his wet shirt. "I'm fine. Nothing happened. Just believe I didn't encourage Bodey. Oh, please believe me."

On his own, Bodey slogged out of the pool. Renee sauntered over and handed him a cocktail napkin to wipe his face.

"Your nose is bleeding and I do believe you'll have a shiner and a swollen jaw tomorrow," she assessed.

"I been injured worse in the rodeo ring. Russ, you were right. Noreen doesn't like me—at all. Man, I'm so sorry," he appealed to his friend.

Rusty's long, lean body suddenly jerked back as beefy Mr. Courville, six feet tall, but carrying a lot of extra weight, hauled him out of Noreen's arms.

"Get your filthy, cowherd hands off my daughter, you bastard! I won't tell you again." Good Ole Charlie gasped, dumped Rusty on his ass and clutched at his chest.

Mrs. Courville, a late arrival as she had gone to get her mink before coming out, raced to her husband's side, the nitroglycerin tablets already removed from her sequined evening bag. "Open wide, Charlie. Get them under your tongue. There you go."

Nearby, Ted Niles sat doubled over in a chair. Slowly, he toppled to the ground. Big Ben watched his ranch manager drop.

"You, Doc, over here. Come on! He's got good insurance. I seen to it."

The same physician who had given the Heimlich to

Charlie Courville knelt down next to Ted Niles. He tossed car keys to his wife and asked her to get his bag from the Mercedes.

Ted came to. "I'm fine. High blood pressure. I know I shouldn't lose my cool. My daddy died of a heart attack at fifty-two. I watch my weight. Do hard, physical work."

"You need to be on medication, regardless. I'll give you some samples, but I want to see you in my office. Liz, when do we get back from the ski trip?" he asked his wife who had delivered the medical bag.

"The twenty-ninth."

"Make an appointment for the thirtieth, then. Don't skip it," said Dr. Bouchard with the authority of a rising young heart specialist who looked every bit the part, trim and hawk-eyed, steady of hand and voice.

The doctor listened to Ted's heart, checked his blood pressure to make sure it was coming down and dispensed the samples along with his card. Meanwhile, Rusty and Noreen coupled together again, holding each other so tightly not even a straw from the wrecked manger scene could have gotten between them. Renee laughed silently. They were so like puppets with their strings tangled together.

Ted Niles shook his head as if to clear it. "Rusty, son, you have to let her go now."

Estelle Courville Simone moved over to her sister. "Baby, Mom wants to take Daddy to the hospital. We have to go now. Don't put up a fuss, okay?"

"Rusty?" Noreen said plaintively.

"Noreen, I believe you. I believe in us." He kissed the top of her head. "Go on now. They won't stop us. No one can come between us."

Renee Niles watched the Courville family form a phalanx around Noreen as if they were marching her off to execution. She sidled up to Ted Niles while a bereft Rusty, shaking either from the cold air on his wet body or his anger at Bodey, watched his girlfriend leave.

"Can I get you some water, Uncle Ted, or something stronger?"

"No, thanks, honey. But you can promise to tell me if Rusty and Noreen get back together. We have to nip this thing in the bud."

"I'll do my best, Uncle Ted."

Renee Niles knew she was a liar, but never a snitch. She really, really wanted to see how this drama played out and would make sure Noreen and Rusty had all the opportunities she could provide for them to screw up their lives. The cowherd and the Mt. Carmel girl—priceless.

****

"Noreen, go straight up to bed," Carolyn Courville ordered her younger daughter. "This has been such a terrible night. That Niles boy almost killed your daddy."

Noreen, halfway up the stairs, turned on her mother. "He did not! Daddy almost killed himself with too much good food and liquor and being too stubborn to have by-pass surgery."

Noreen trembled with anger, making the garnet earrings shake and glitter and the matching necklace heave on her chest. Mrs. Courville cocked her head. "Weren't you wearing pearls tonight? Where did you get that jewelry? I've never seen that necklace before and it looks expensive."

"I got it at the mall. The earrings looked better with

my dress than the pearls, so I changed them. No big deal." Noreen covered the necklace protectively with her hand.

"Noreen, please tell me you aren't shoplifting. I cannot take much more tonight."

"I'm not shoplifting, Mom. You never notice anything about me unless it's something bad!"

Noreen tore up the stairs and punctuated her exit with a door slam. Mrs. Courville, shocked at the outburst from her sweetest child, stood at the foot of the staircase and called after her, "That's just not true, lovey. It's not!"

After her mother retreated to her room for the night, Noreen crept down the stairs and out to the family car. She carried the precious box with is cargo of letters back to her private space and read them one by one, tears streaming down her face exactly as they had more than a century ago.

****

Carolyn Courville asked her family to link hands around the table on Christmas day. "Dear Lord on this most holy day, we thank you for this bounteous feast, this fine home, the comfort of family and friends gathered around us. We thank you, also, for making Charles Marchand Courville the Third see the necessity of having a quadruple by-pass—that he should have had two years ago—tomorrow morning. Although we miss our husband, father and grandpa very much, we trust in you to allow him to live for many Christmases to come. Amen."

Big, red-haired Hardy Courville, sitting in his father's place, rose to carve a perfectly browned bird. His lovely blonde wife, Amanda, sat to his right with his four stair-step children, two strawberry blonde daughters and two strapping sons ranging in age from four to ten sitting next to her. To his left sat Estelle and her husband, Burgess Simone, who would have to carry the law practice while his dad remained hospitalized, with their two sons in high chairs wedged between them. At the end nearest his mother, the miscreant Noreen was positioned across from Fr. Matthew. Maybe brother Matt, either as a priest or a wise relative, could get through to the ninny whose illicit romance had almost killed their father.

Hardy tore off the turkey's leg and put it on the plate of his clamoring eldest son, a true blond like his mother, but big like his dad. Proud as he was of his perfect family and thriving business, he had no desire to become the Courville patriarch because of the actions of his goofy, romantic baby of a sister.

The plates were filled to overflowing and the contents eaten with relish by all but Noreen. Dinner finally at an end, the mothers wiped their small children down, released them and followed in their wake to the living room where new toys awaited. Noreen rose, but Hardy waved her back to the table.

"Mama, I think we should take our coffee into the living room while Fr. Matthew and Noreen have a little talk."

Hardy walked his mother to the dining room entrance and drew the pocket doors closed behind them. Over the sideboard, the portraits of Rufus Courville and his pretty wife, Marie-Celeste, seemed to listen with interest as Fr. Matt cleared his throat, sipped his coffee and cleared his throat again.

"Noreen, I'm saying this as your brother, not as a

priest, okay? You're only seventeen, or will be this week. You are much too young to be forming permanent attachments yet."

"You're just saying that because Rusty is part of the Niles family."

Fr. Matt held up his hand. "I'm not. I don't know the young man in question, but I've often thought this hatred between our families should stop. I suppose it won't until God is good and ready to do something about it. This is not in our hands. Okay. I'm going into priest mode now. You know you should wait to have sexual relations until marriage, don't you? Marriage is a long way off for you. If you keep this up, young lady, you are sure to stumble."

Noreen wondered if French-kissing and dry humping and lots of other pleasures counted as stumbles, or if only doing it qualified, but she didn't ask. Her favorite sibling, Matt appeared tired and worn down by the priesthood. At only thirty-one, he had small lines by his eyes and a few gray hairs in that thick, black mane of his. Being handsome and a priest must be very wearing, she thought.

"We haven't had sex yet. We are waiting for marriage. But don't you see, if I married Rusty, we could end the feud. We're soul mates, maybe more than soul mates."

"Soul mates, well. You know, you might have made this feud worse with your antics. What if Dad had died last night? Noreen, little sis, please finish high school, go off to college, look around at your options. I wish I hadn't rushed off to Indiana to study for the priesthood, but Mom and Dad were so proud of that scholarship. I locked myself in and couldn't back out."

"Do you hate being a priest?"

"No. I enjoy helping others, but I could have done that another way."

"Fine, so you enjoy helping others. You don't know anything about being in love, Matthew Courville."

"I do, Noreen. Please, be careful not to hurt your family in your haste to be with this boy. Fight your feelings. Struggle with what you want, then in the end if you are meant to be with him, I'd say it is God's will. I'll be on your side."

"Thanks, Matt. I am struggling not to give in every inch of the way." Noreen got up and came over to kiss her brother's cheek. "If you are in love with someone, I hope it works out for you, too."

She slid open the pocket doors. "I know you all want to go see Daddy and take him his gifts. The kids won't be allowed in, so how about if I take them to the park to feed the ducks? Seeing me will only raise Dad's blood pressure, but tell him I love him anyhow."

****

As the six Courville grandchildren fed, chased or got pecked by ducks coming from all over the pond to feast on stale bread and leftover dinner rolls, Noreen and Rusty locked together in the gazebo. She exclaimed over receiving the rest of the jewelry suite for her birthday. He had been less excited about the stack of books she'd presented to him, a reprint of *The Illustrious Niles Family in the Nineteenth Century*, the history of Rainbow by Sr. Mary Frances which she had copied and bound at the college book store, and a genealogy of the Courville family her aunt had complied and self-published.

When they came up for air, Rusty said, "Now, I don't want you to think this ring is an engagement ring."

"Oh, I never thought that." But she had.

Rusty watched her face droop with disappointment. "I'm saving something better for that—when the time comes that we can be open about us. This is sort of a pre-engagement ring, part of the Niles family jewels, remember?"

"I do. I marked the page where Victoria Niles Duperier talks about the box. I'm sorry I only got you books. Bodey told me what you really wanted, but you know we can't do that yet."

"I know. Don't listen to Bodey—ever. The books are great." He flipped the pages of the Courville genealogy and stopped at a picture. He asked, "Who's this dude with the big white beard and the profile of an eagle?"

Noreen suspected he only feigned interest to make her believe he liked the books. "That's Marchand Courville, Rufe's son. He lost a leg and had his face scarred at the Battle of Frenchman's Bend when he was only sixteen. He grew the beard to cover the scars and would only be photographed from his good side, according to family legend. Still, he did wed at twenty-nine to a spinster of twenty-seven named Adele Charles. You know, so many young men were killed in that war the women had no one left to marry."

"So this Adele had to settle for a guy with one leg," Rusty commented, obviously trying hard to show interest.

"He still had the leg that counted." Noreen felt herself blush, but Rusty chuckled.

She balanced the Courville genealogy on the railing of the bridge. "See here. They managed to have six children, but only the last one was a boy, born in 1888, the first of the Charles Marchand Courvilles. He married in 1911, had a son the next year and two daughters later. His son of the same name married in 1930, had my dad the same year. Then, he left his wife and son behind to fight in World War II even though he was a little too old. He made it home and conceived my aunt who is just a few years older than Hardy. Isn't that funny?"

"Sure is. I'm glad one of us can figure that stuff out. Me, I'm just a dumb cowboy, or what did your dad call me—a dirty cowherd?"

"You're not dumb, Rusty Niles. I know you got straight A's your first semester of college."

"Yeah, well, in animal husbandry and agricultural management. Bodey helps me with my math and I help him with his English comp. He is a good roommate, but I guess I'll have to find another one. He can afford an apartment, anyhow." Rusty threw a stone into the pond and ruffled some feathered friends.

"You don't have to ditch Bodey on my account. He knows now he can't break us up. In fact, I'd like you to stay friends with him just to show him we were meant to be. He can be best man in our wedding."

"Noreen, you are a wonder."

The sound of Estelle's younger boy taking a header into the water interrupted their kiss. The mallards took off, but fat white Peking ducks continued to circle the shrieking youngster as if he competed with them for breadcrumbs. Rusty raced off the bridge, surged down the bank and stretched out a long arm to draw the child to safety. The kid had swallowed some pond water, but not enough to kill him. No time now to tell Rusty about the proof she'd found in the letters. Noreen comforted her nephew and wrapped him in a blanket from the car.

Rusty beamed at her. "Ten years from now, I'd like to see you holding our son that way."

"Don't count on that taking ten years, Rusty Niles," Noreen said. "Don't count on that at all."

Chapter Seventeen

Bodey could hear Noreen's sweet, chirpy voice all the way over on his side of the desk. He stuck the eraser ends of two pencils in his ears, making Rusty chuckle, and tried to continue concentrating on Business Math II, but he could still hear the part of the conversation taking place in the dorm room.

"I think it's great you won at the state social science fair, honey. What did the judges have to say about your conclusions on the origins of the feud? Oh, Sr. Inez made you take out the part about both families being descended from the same man because you had no real proof other than those pictures. Yeah, folks painted in those times do sort of look alike. So, Sr. Nessy wouldn't go for exhuming bodies or testing DNA?" Rusty joked.

"Sure, I'd give a blood sample. I'd give you a whole pint. I'd give you my heart. Oops, already have."

Bodey winced and tried to block the conversation by standing his textbook up in front of him. Sometimes, he was sorry Rusty had forgiven him at Noreen's prompting. His roommate made that very clear.

"I'm glad Rufe's love letters clinched it for you. At least, you could still say that part of the feud might have been caused by Esperanza Niles breaking up with him, poor dude. You think reading the letters softened your mother up a little. Well, that's good news."

Bodey waggled the pencils in his ears and looked over the edge of the textbook. "Man, you do not have to repeat every word she says. I do not need to know this stuff."

"How's your daddy doing? Great. Mine, too. He claims he takes his high blood pressure medicine every day. Tell Sr. Nessy that should be proof enough they are related what with Aaron Niles stroking out somewhere in his early fifties. Sure, I read the books you gave me. I never knew I was descended from Nathan Niles, the cattleman. I can't believe he and his twin married sisters named Violet and Lily. Let's not name our kids after flowers, okay?"

Bodey groaned. "No, name your first born after me for all I have suffered."

"I can't believe you asked Sr. Nessy if she believed in reincarnation. She gave you the party line, huh? Catholics work out their sins in purgatory, then go on to heaven. Do you think this is purgatory, honey? I do, every day we are apart."

Bodey knocked his forehead gently against the desk. Three more years, he had three more years of this to endure before he and Rusty could hit the rodeo circuit and have some good times on the open road. With luck, Noreen would ditch Russ when she found someone else close by at Southwestern in Lafayette this coming fall. Chances would have been even better if Noreen had gone to LSU like Hardy and Estelle, but since Christmas, her parents had second thoughts about letting their baby go too far from home. Three more years—Bodey could only hope for a breakup.

****

Three years passed pretty fast, Bodey found out.

The Oil Bust finally drove Big Ben to close up his mansion in Rainbow, sell off the racehorses and retreat with Betsy to his ranch in Texas. Now, Bodey went home for the holidays to Fort Worth. Russ joined his dad who was still a caretaker at the Three B's and allowed to lease the acreage and the barns at a bargain rate for his cattle.

Just as well because Noreen and Rusty were still together and got on Bodey's nerves whenever they managed to link up. Since Noreen got a car for her Academy graduation present, they hooked up more often than Bodey could tolerate. If he and Russ were rodeoing anywhere within easy driving distance, Noreen showed up. Being the good friend that he was, Bodey let the couple have the privacy of the little tack room in the back of the horse trailer to do whatever they wanted. They'd already broken the struts on the fold-down cot once, but still claimed they weren't having sex. It just wasn't natural. When Rusty gave Noreen his college buckle for Best Roper, Bodey knew he had to take action to free his best bud before it got too, too late.

The middle of August came along, chasing Noreen back to college classes for her senior year. Bodey and Rusty, intent on making some money on the circuit now that they had turned professional, were at the top of their divisions at this particular rodeo, but Bodey knew he'd take the bull riding and bump Russ from winning the overall competition. He'd done it time and again, all because Ted Niles made his son promise not to ride the bulls. Must be nice to have someone who cared so much about you, but hell, like not screwing Noreen, these promises kept Rusty back from something he should have—at least on occasion.

Bodey made a bad landing during the bareback bronc competition and knocked his head hard against the ground. The doctor on duty said he had a mild concussion, and yes, he could ride the bulls if he wanted, but Bodey would feel like his head was coming off. Naturally, he meant to ride and beat Rusty for the overall prize again. Or maybe not. That fall might have been responsible for knocking a whole new idea into his head. Noreen was back at college already and too far away to visit this weekend. High time for Russell Niles to be King of the Rodeo.

The doctor knew his business. Three seconds into his ride, Bodey did feel like his brains were about to blow out his ears. Making no great sacrifice, he loosened his hand from the bull rope, toppled to the ground and staggered toward the sideboards while the clowns and bullfighters distracted the beast from goring him.

He could hear the announcer saying, "What a shame. Failure to complete this ride drops Bodey Landrum into third place in the bull riding competition and takes him out of contention for the overall crown. Riding with a concussion from a spill yesterday was probably not a good idea for this promising young cowboy. Better luck next time, Bodey."

Bodey gave the crowd a wave and a smile, thanked the bullfighters and went to beg a painkiller from the doc. Rusty would take the overall and deserved a hell of a party. Bodey made sure that happened. After he got his painkiller, he spent the rest of the afternoon inviting barrel-racers and buckle bunnies to a party in a suite at the nearest hotel. He used up a month's worth of winnings to stock the bar and order party trays of spicy chicken wings, nacho grandes and stuffed potato skins.

The suite filled up and overflowed into the hallways. Russ stayed on the phone in a bedroom yammering about his triumph to Noreen at her sorority house where Renee footed the bills for their calls. That was okay because Rusty's lengthy conversation kept the second bedroom free. Bodey served his friend three beers while the talking went on. Out in the sitting area the solid food disappeared fast. Bodey had stoked up on potato skins himself.

When Rusty finally emerged slightly buzzed to join the crowd, Bodey held up a shot glass of amber Jack Daniels Black Label and toasted, "To the best damn All-Around Cowboy I know." He held out a full glass to Rusty before tossing back his own.

"Rusty, old pal, we both turned twenty-one last spring. Time we live like men, drink like men and love like men."

Clueless, Rusty said, "Haven't you been doing that for years?" The girls hanging on Bodey giggled.

"But you haven't. You may have beat me today, but I say—I say I can beat you tonight. I'm going to drink you under the table, Rusty Niles."

Bodey poured another round while the half-sober women and men surrounding him chanted, "Drink, drink, drink."

Rusty conceded at number four and staggered off to the bedroom to lie down. Norma Jean Scruggs, up and coming young barrel-racer acknowledged to have the best tits on the circuit, wrapped her long length around Bodey and tickled his cleft chin with the end of her long, black braid.

"You think the other bedroom is open, Bodey?"

"Sugar pie, between the painkillers and the whiskey, I'm about to puke. With this concussion, I ain't riding nothing for a few weeks. Why don't you go on in and entertain Mr. All-Around? Here, take these condoms with you. Knowing Rusty, he doesn't have any. You might even have to put them on for him."

Bodey lowered his voice. "Russ might be a virgin."

Norma Jean's arched black brows shot up. "No foolin'? He's not gay, is he? I don't want to have to worry about that HIV shit."

Bodey put his hand over his heart. "Rusty is waitin' for marriage. Ain't that sweet?"

"It is, kinda. But, I do love a challenge."

Norma Jean's blue eyes glittered as she strutted off to take on Rusty Niles. Full of regret for what he had just given away, Bodey watched her go in jeans that looked like they'd been painted on her bodacious ass. Another succulent young woman took Norma Jean's place at his side. Unfortunately, he'd meant what he said about the concussion. Maybe she'd be amenable to something that didn't take much motion. He took the hand of the bleached-blonde with the perky breasts and led her toward the other bedroom.

****

The party broke up around four a.m. Bodey managed to get some sleep before the noise of Rusty barfing up his liquor woke him. He had a Bloody Mary all mixed from last night's leavings, right down to a wilted stalk of celery from the tray of wings, when Russ, looking like death, came out of the bathroom.

"Hair of the dog." Bodey handed him the drink.

"Make the next one a Virgin Mary."

299

"Speaking of which, how was your night with Norma Jean? She didn't come out of there until three in the morning."

"Norma Jean. I was with someone named Norma Jean?"

"Yes. You remember—long legs, tight buns, big tits, long black braid you can wrap around your hand."

"Oh, God! I called her Noreen."

"More than once, I heard. She made you do over for that. What a punishment."

"I cheated on Noreen. God, oh God. I have to tell her."

"Are you crazy? Confession might be good for the soul, but it doesn't do a thing for relationships."

"I have to tell her, Bodey."

"Okay, then. Don't say I didn't try to stop you."

"I have to do this in person. Can I borrow your truck?"

"Russ, you're talkin' about a two day drive from here and back again. Most everybody will be movin' out about noon for the next competition. We'd have to board the horses somewheres, too."

"I'll drive day and night and get back in time for us to make the next show. I swear."

"Not in your condition. Here, take one of my painkillers. We get a free breakfast buffet with this room and I'm going to take advantage of it. If you can keep some eggs and toast down, I'll drive half the way, then you take over. Puke in my truck and I'll put you out by the side of the road, you hear?"

"Thanks, Bodey. I know I can always count on you."

Yes, he could. Within forty-eight hours, Rusty

would be free to go on the rodeo circuit with Bodey Landrum for the next ten years—or as long as they both lasted. No wedding next June, no trailer in Ted Niles backyard, no pitter-patter of little feet before his friend turned twenty-three. Bodey Landrum had just done Rusty Niles a big favor—and so had Norma Jean Scruggs.

****

When Noreen noticed Rusty sitting on the front steps of her sorority house with his head hanging between his knees as if all his dreams had fallen out on the sidewalk, she shoved her heavy history books at Renee who carried none and raced to him. Bodey had to admit his friend looked pitiful. Shit, Renee spied him leaning against his big, black truck parked under a live oak down the road. She took a detour in his direction.

"What's up? Rusty never comes here because he knows the other girls mock Noreen for dating a cowboy. Besides, the two of them are still hiding out from Noreen's family. Can you believe that?"

"Won't be a problem anymore. Wait for it."

From their vantage point, they watched Noreen burst into tears. She turned her back on Rusty. He put his arms around her and spoke quietly into her ear until she stopped sobbing. Then, Rusty Niles got down on his knees and pulled a ring box from his pocket. He assumed the posture of begging. Even the rundown heels of his cowboy boots seemed contrite. Bodey had to look away. Any minute now, Russ would be on his way back to the truck, probably shedding some puppy love tears of his own. Good thing his best buddy remembered to bring along the remainder of the Jack Daniels.

"I do not believe this," Renee said. "He's proposing right here and now. I thought he would for her twenty-first birthday. At least, that's what he told me. They really think they are getting married in June. I wish we could turn up the sound and hear what he's saying."

"Oh, something like this—I slept with another woman when I got real drunk, but I called her Noreen. All I remember about her is her long, black hair. Please forgive me, sweetheart. You are the only woman I will ever love. What a total wuss I am," Bodey mimicked. "I added the last sentence. He's been rehearsing that speech for the last two hundred miles."

"I don't believe this! She's accepting the ring. I would have kicked him in the nuts and gone inside."

"Remind me never to propose to you, Renee."

The newly engaged couple headed their way. Noreen held out her hand and showed off the antique band set with rubies, cleaned and glowing in the hot September sunshine.

"What, you couldn't afford a new diamond, Cuz?" Renee said in a voice tinged with envy.

"This ring is part of the Niles family jewels," Noreen answered. "I love it."

Bodey began to laugh and pounded the side of his truck with a fist. "Yeah, you got his jewels all right."

"Bodey, when you're done abusing our transportation, could I borrow the truck? Noreen's little Civic can't go off-road and we want to get to our special place."

Bodey laughed harder, tears forming in the corners of his sharp, blue eyes. "Special place. They've got a special place. Noreen, Rusty is a cheatin' bastard. Don't you hate him?"

"I forgave him, Bodey Landrum, because our love is greater than one mistake made when he was drunk at a party—given by you. Now, may we have the keys?"

"Oh, my pleasure. Take my truck. Take my best friend. Take everything I got."

Bodey and Renee watched the couple drive off in the Silverado.

"Do you believe in true love, Renee? I think it's all crap."

"Yes, I do, Bodey. But people like us don't deserve true love."

****

In their special place surrounded by the leafy cathedral of wisteria vines, Rusty laid down a thick blanket. Reverently, he took Noreen's clothes off and she undressed him. They lay down and looked up at the small piece of the warm, blue heaven above them.

"I can't believe you forgave me, sweetheart. I can't believe you want to do this now. Oh, hell, I don't have any condoms. Bodey probably has some in the glove compartment. Let me get my jeans back on. I'll just be a minute."

"Stay. I've been thinking about this moment for a long time. I'd rather lose my virginity here than in some tiny cot on a cruise ship or in a motel room. I started taking the pill last month, and now that the moment has come, I don't want anything between us. I was going to tell you at Christmas when I turned twenty-one and no one could stop us anymore," she lied.

No way would she lose Rusty to some loose woman on the rodeo circuit. She was sure he had been good in bed—and tender. No woman could resist that.

By May when she graduated, five years of loving Rusty might be just another part of her past if she didn't make this happen now. If she did have another period, she would go on the pill next month and make her claim the truth.

Rusty began stroking her body all over, making her ready as he had so many times before without going any further. He made sure with his fingers that she was wet and primed. Before he entered her, he said, "Noreen, you honor me with your body," and plunged in, not wanting to prolong any pain. She made a small sound.

"Did I hurt you?"

"No. Go on. I don't want to lose you."

"Noreen, honey, I'm so swolled up, there's no chance of that."

"I mean to other women. I can't lose you. Not to Bodey's tricks or my parents' disapproval."

"I'm so sorry about Norma Jean."

"I don't want to hear her name ever again. I want you to shout Noreen!"

"Noreen, Noreen, Noreen!" He shouted so loud that a flock of birds hiding in the thicket took off and left a few white feathers floating in the breeze above them. He kept going until she clenched around him and whispered, "Oh, Rusty."

They stayed in the glade, repeating the moment, until the mosquitoes came out at dusk and drove them away.

****

"About time you got back. Jesus, I had to ask Renee to take me for a burger. Got to meet some of her sorority sisters, though. I think I changed some minds about datin' cowboys, but they drank up all my Jack Daniels." Bodey didn't appear to have suffered from either starvation or lack of attention during the wait.

"Yeah, well. Noreen and I need some time together. You go on to the next rodeo without me. I'll meet you at the one after that even if I have to take a bus. Renee will drive me out to my dad's place."

"You'll lose your entry fees and a lot of points just when you got on top."

"Bodey, it's time you realize rodeo doesn't mean the same to me as it does to you. Sure, I like it fine for now. Mostly, I want some money to set up a home for Noreen and maybe buy back some acreage from Big Ben. I don't want to be on the road all the time staying in your horse trailer when I can't afford my share for a room. I do want to be with the woman I love."

"Shit, you sound like that king of England who gave up his crown for a divorcee, only Noreen doesn't have that much experience."

"She does now. That's why I can't leave her for a while. I don't hit and run like you do, Bodey."

"That's because round-heeled girls pop right back up again. I don't need to stick around."

"You go on. See you in a couple of weeks."

"Oh, get in the truck. I'll drop you at your dad's house before I hit the highway, and I'll take care of your horse while you stay here slobbering over Noreen."

"You're a friend, Bodey."

"Yeah, I got you laid three times in three days."

"Oh, way more than that, my man, way more."

****

Noreen Courville never intentionally cut her

305

classes. During her sophomore year, she'd had the flu and missed a week, but that was the only time. Now, she failed to show up five days in a row plus the weekend. Two of her profs sent messages to the sorority house to see about their star pupil. In a shaky hand, she replied with notes saying the flu had gotten her again.

Her mother had been right of course. Once a woman experienced sex she wasn't likely to give it up again. She and Rusty spent so much time in the glade, coming out only for sustenance at the Rainbow Café, that they were both covered in chigger bites and had to do tick checks before putting their clothes on again. At night, they used the back of his daddy's truck or cheap hotel rooms.

Noreen had never been the kind of girl who kept track of her "safe days" on a calendar as some of her sorority sisters did, or who carried an assortment of condoms and a large tube of spermicidal jelly in her purse like Renee Niles. Having lied to Rusty about being on the pill after he'd been so honest with her, she could hardly ask him to use a rubber now. No, Noreen's only protection was prayer after each day long orgy ended, begging God and Jesus, the Virgin Mary and Mary Magdalene, the four biggies, that everything would work out for the best.

Rusty left in the middle of the second week after they'd first had sex. He vowed to be true and to beat Bodey again and seize the All-Around. Noreen said she believed the first and didn't care about the second. She wanted him to be safe. In December, they would announce their intentions to their parents and defy anyone who tried to stop them from marrying. She drove him to the bus station and followed the lumbering Greyhound until it turned off on I-10 toward Texas.

Noreen had no time to worry or cry. She needed to catch up on classes and attend Sunday dinner at home. She'd pledged her mother's sorority only to get out from under her parents' thumbs and gain housing she could slip in and out of easily. This convenience meant wearing silly ribbons on her head and enduring humiliating initiation pranks, all for love of Rusty.

In the worst rite of passage, she, Sally Parker and Renee Niles were left stranded thirty miles away wearing old-fashioned housecoats, flip-flops, and curlers in their hair. Noreen had been petrified by the clients of the roadside casino in Crowley who stared at the three girls when they came outside for a leg stretch between bouts at the slot machines.

Renee took over commanding Noreen to shed her blue housecoat out behind the casino and switch it with the orange flowered one Renee wore. Renee stripped off the polka-dotted I Love Lucy headband, shucked her curlers into a dumpster and raked her hands through her red hair. She'd tied the headband around her waist to make the blue housecoat less baggy, unbuttoned until the top of her black bra showed. Carefully choosing a place against the casino wall free of urine, chewing tobacco and broken glass, Renee kicked off her flip-flops, leaned back and drew one long, naked leg partially up the other so the housecoat gaped almost to her crotch, and waited.

The first man who accosted her, she asked for a ride to Lafayette. He was pleased to oblige, thinking "a ride to Lafayette" meant something else entirely. As they got into the car, Renee called the other pledges from hiding. All three piled into the back seat and gave the sucker directions to the sorority house. The sorority sisters who were supposed to double back and pick up the girls once they suffered enough embarrassment returned in a panic a half hour after their pledges.

All three girls duly became full members in a ceremony involving many candles and girlish vows. Beautiful and clever as she was, Renee won no popularity contests with the rest of the young women and bullied Noreen into becoming her roommate at the sorority house. After all, she offered to pay for Noreen's calls to Rusty. Noreen told her mother that roommates were assigned and she'd had no choice. Her family never invited Renee to partake of the Sunday dinner Noreen attended each and every weekend.

If Rusty performed nearby, Noreen would get in her little Civic on Friday afternoon and drive until she got to him. She'd leave as early on a Sunday as she had to in order to make the dinner appearance. With Rusty and Bodey touring west Texas, New Mexico and Arizona right now, all the contact they would have for the next few months would be the phone calls charged to Renee's bill. Noreen's father had his daughter's bill sent to his business address as another way of checking up on her along with the mandatory Sunday dinners.

The nausea began about three weeks after Rusty left. Crying jags and the inability to concentrate on her schoolwork followed. Noreen did not need a test to diagnose her pregnancy. She knew. When she upchucked two Sunday dinners in a row, her mother asked if she was bulimic. Noreen said, "No, just stressed about mid-terms." She would have to learn to vomit more quietly.

Nothing escaped Renee's sharp observation. "Knocked up, huh?"

"I think so," Noreen whimpered.

"With your puking and crying all the time, I'm not nearly as amused as I thought I'd be. Want to get rid of the baby before it's too late? You must be at least two months along by now." Primping for a date, Renee gazed into a mirror and carefully covered her freckles.

"You've had an abortion?"

"Hell, no! I'm not all sappy about love. If the guy doesn't have a condom, I put one I brought along on him myself. I have driven two of our sorority sisters to that clinic in Texas, though."

Noreen put her hands over her belly as if Renee would force her to abort right then and there. "I want my baby."

"But does Rusty?"

"We're engaged. We were going to get married in June. It's just that I told him I'd gone on the pill so I wouldn't lose him to Norma Jean Scruggs."

"From what Bodey told me, Norma Jean makes you look like the platter of crudities next to a plate of frosted brownies. No one wants nice, healthy broccoli when they can have rich, dark chocolate. So, the operative word here is 'were' as in 'were going to get married in June'. That kid is coming out in May. When are you going to break the news to my cuz, the guy stupid enough not to use a condom no matter what you told him? I'll bet Bodey never fell for that."

"I'll wait until Christmas. We planned to face our parents then, so he'll be braced when he comes home."

"Oh, how I'd like to be a spider on the wall when that happens," Renee said while applying a second glossy coat of lipstick. She picked up a kicky little bag filled with cosmetics and condoms and slung it over her shoulder.

"I do have to say, Noreen, your breasts never looked better, but nursing will ruin them." She left her roommate to her misery.

Noreen lay across her bed in the sorority house. The place had gone quiet with most of the girls out on dates. Evidently, morning sickness could last all day. She took some crackers from a pack in her night table drawer and nibbled.

The only good thing about her condition so far was the complete cessation of her troubling dreams. They disappeared as if pregnancy were an anecdote to nightmares. She'd expected them to go away once she exposed the reason for the Courville-Niles feud. The families were supposed to acknowledge their relationship and embrace their kinship, right? Well, that hadn't happened. Her family still hated all of the Niles, Rusty especially.

Now, she'd screwed up royally and appeared would be rewarded for her condition as if she'd done something right by hastening her marriage to Rusty—once he knew. He'd come through for her. So tired, her eyelids grew heavy. Why not slip into a blessed and dreamless sleep?

Chapter Eighteen

Carolyn Courville noticed right after Thanksgiving that her youngest daughter had put on weight again. That dress Noreen wore to dinner was a trifle tight in the bust and across the belly, but as a good mother she would not nag, not after the bulimia scare. As Christmas approached, Noreen went up a dress size, undeniable when they shopped for holiday clothes. Mrs. Courville pondered how to mention the gain without upsetting her child who had been awfully weepy as her finals approached.

"This one doesn't fit either. Look, Mom, I don't really want a new dress. I need to meet my friends at one for a study group."

Noreen hung the party gown up on the hanger of the dressing room and began to squeeze herself into her loosest jeans. Frankly, she'd be glad when the truth came out and she could purchase some maternity clothes. So far, she'd gotten by with big sweatshirts and oversized tees her mother regarded as examples of sloppy dressing and letting herself go—just when she should be dressing more professionally for student teaching in the spring.

"Could we have a light lunch first? Could we talk about your future? I know you'll want to teach history for a few years before settling down with the right man and you need to dress the part. We'll go to the sales in

January, maybe take an exercise class together. What do you say?"

"No to lunch, but thanks. We will talk, but not today. Got to run."

Noreen checked her watch. Rusty's bus was due in from Dallas where he had been dropped off by Bodey. She had only half an hour to cross Lafayette with all its traffic and be there on time.

Of course, an accident on Johnston Street congested traffic and by the time she detoured to the station, Rusty sat there alone with a dirty duffle bag between his feet. His smile when he saw her could have lit the dark corners of the place, driving off the drunks and homeless people hiding in the shadows. She knew he'd notice her weight gain and blurted that out first.

"I've kinda pudged up, Rusty."

He held her close. "Didn't notice. You feel like you did that first night in Big Ben's barn. Want to go to our special place?"

"I do. We have to talk—about what we're going to say to our parents."

"After we get some loving done. I been gone four months and no Norma Jean Scruggs took your place." He kissed her tenderly and deeply making a granny who boarded a bus with a sack of wrapped gifts sigh and a jealous, pimply teenager shout, "Get a room!"

They headed out for the glade, but had to park the Civic beside old plantation house now called the Le Rosier Courville Bed and Breakfast. The winter had been mild so far and the yellow noisette roses trained anew up the side of the building still bloomed. Their dainty likeness graced the sign by the entrance. Their light scent perfumed the air.

"Since I don't have a truck, I guess we'll have to hike out to our place. Estelle sure did a great job fixing up the house," Rusty said as he admired the creamy stuccoed walls and the elegant rebuilt outer staircases to the second story.

"Want to go inside? I have a key. I help Estelle when a wedding is booked here. She pays me."

"Sure that will be all right?"

"Rusty, my family has owned this house for nearly two-hundred years. We aren't trespassing."

She tugged his arm until he followed her up the staircase and trailed her into a bedroom full of antiques: a massive armoire, an old chest, and an enormous canopied bed with a veil of mosquito netting draped over it for a romantic look.

"Now we're talking." Rusty lifted Noreen up on the high bedstead hiding a modern mattress and box springs beneath a crocheted spread and cotton sheets with a thread count of four hundred. No biting insect or poking stick would ruin their pleasure here.

"Are you thinking what I'm thinking?"

"I doubt it. Rusty, dearest Rusty, I am pregnant."

His face paled so quickly his smattering of freckles seemed to stand out in relief against his skin. She watched as Rusty Niles reached deep down inside himself and pulled up a half smile. He swallowed hard, put his bottom on the bed next to Noreen and placed his arm around her, hugged her tight.

"Well, I always wanted to be a father. I guess I'm just following in my daddy's footsteps by getting an early start, is all. When?"

"May, I think. I haven't been to a doctor."

"You need to go. Didn't you tell me I was related

to the doctors who run the Maddox Obstetrical and Pediatric Clinic and the folks who own the Niles Department Store in Opelousas? Maybe we can get a discount on the delivery and a crib." He released a small laugh as if the joke were on him.

"You don't hate me? Rusty, I lied about being on the pill. I had no time to get some before you went back on the road and I knew Norma Jean would be waiting for you. I wanted to bind you to me. I know that was unfair."

"Honey, Norma Jean waits for no man. I was just a pebble beneath her boot on her way to somewhere else. You forgave me and said you'd be my wife. I forgive you and say I'll be a good father to this child. We just have to move the wedding up a notch. No sense putting off telling our parents. We'll do it tonight."

"Rusty, could we stay here for a while and make love?"

"Now you're thinking what I'm thinking."

Noreen folded back the expensive bed coverings with care before they rolled onto a mattress more comfortable than feathers or moss had ever been. Time slipped away until they rested in each other's arms, half asleep and well pleased. Noreen's eyes opened. She rolled onto her back and placed a hand on the small mound of her abdomen

Alarmed, Rusty said, "Did I hurt the baby? Was I too rough?"

"No, but you did stir him up. Russ, I felt the baby move for the very first time—like angel wings fluttering inside me. They used to call this the quickening in olden times, the sign that the baby lives and possesses a soul." She instantly regretted making a history lesson of this special moment, but Rusty didn't seem to mind.

He placed his large, freckled hand next to hers. "Can I feel it?"

"Probably not. He's still so little, but he's in there growing, our baby."

Noreen covered his hand with her own and closed her eyes again. She hummed along to the faint music coming from the parlor.

"What's that tune, honey?" Russ kissed the curls on the top of her head.

"*Aura Lee*, maid of golden hair, an old Civil War song. You know, Elvis sang it with different lyrics, the Love Me Tender song.

"Did Estelle or the cleaning lady leave a radio on?"

"I don't think so. I believe someone is very happy for us. She plays for the newlyweds sometimes—the ghost of Addy Courville."

****

After Noreen changed the sheets and remade the bed, double-checked that the bathroom installed in the former sitting room was immaculate after they had soaked in the big, claw-footed tub together, she ran out of excuses not to go straight to her parents. On the way past the Rainbow Café, she begged Rusty to stop. He humored her, but said, "I don't know how you can eat when you know what we have to do tonight."

He drove into the gravel lot, helped Noreen from the car and held on to her elbow as they crossed the uneven gray boards of the sagging cypress entry. A hand-lettered sign on the checkout counter said, "Seat Yourself." They did.

Ja'nae Plato sauntered over. "Hey, Rusty, when did

you get back in town?"

"Just this afternoon. I plan to stay."

"What, no more calf roping or manly steer wrestling?" She gestured toward the bar mirror where pictures of Bodey on a bull and himself chasing a calf on his big, red horse were taped up.

"I have other manly things to do. What about you?"

"Almost finished with my business degree. I tell you things are going to change around here."

"Do what you want with the furnishings, but leave the food alone."

"Think salad bar, Rusty."

"Like I said. Give me a slab of ribs with fries and slaw."

"Same here," Noreen added.

"Whole or half slab?"

"The whole pig if you got one."

"Why, I remember you from prom night long time ago. You and Rusty are still together. Figure that."

"Forever together." Noreen flashed the ring that spent more time in her pocket than on her finger, thanks to her family's prejudices.

"That's a beauty. The whole pig, huh?" Ja'nae Plato went away laughing.

Noreen apologized for her greed. "The first few months I couldn't keep anything down. Now, I could eat the entire hog at one of Big Ben's boucheries."

"I guess you and Bubba need your nourishment." Rusty patted the small bulge of her tummy under the cover of the checked tablecloth.

"Please do not call this child Bubba, ever. The relatives did that with my aunt's son before he was born and they still call him that."

"I'd name him after my dad if his real name wasn't Theodore Roosevelt Niles the Second."

Noreen didn't mean to, but the giggle came bubbling out. "You are kidding me."

"Nope. Names like that are a family tradition. Remember Andrew Jackson Niles from my illustrious family tree?"

"He had no children of his own, never married. Old Andy had a house full of women to take care of after the war and raised his widowed sisters' kids. Victoria said in her book that he had suffered an early disappointment in love. I wonder who broke his heart?"

"Knowing you, you'll find out someday. Maybe he was gay."

"I don't get that feeling about him. Besides in those days, he would have married anyway. Who were you named for?"

"My grandfather, Russell Durel. Please, I do not want a junior with that name."

"How about Rufus Courville Niles?"

Rusty shuddered. "Rufus is definitely a name that should be retired."

"You have lots of great names in your family tree like William Harrison Niles."

"Oh yes, Wild Billy. He took up quite a few pages in the history of Rainbow and then disappeared into the west."

"I found him and Owen Maddox, too. With all that's been going on, I never told you. I even have a picture of him with his bushy beard and cavalry hat with the cock feathers tucked in the side. It's on a Wanted poster from the Texas archives. There's one of

Owney, too, all slit-eyed and unshaven. They apparently had trouble adjusting after the war and went rogue, robbing banks and stagecoaches. Then, they disappear again."

"Gone and forgotten by everyone but you." Rusty smiled in the way that said he loved her anyway, history nut or not. That only encouraged Noreen to go on.

"I found Billy's obituary in the Tucson, Arizona, newspaper, I think. The names used are William Henry Harrison, no relation to the late president they said in the obit, survived by Niles Owens, his partner in a ranch. There's a formal photo of Bill Harrison, noted local cattleman, with a big, white mustache and full head of white hair. I swear it's the same man as the one on the wanted poster. He greatly resembles March Courville in old age. Evidently, he and Owney used their ill-gotten gains to set themselves up as partners in a cattle spread and died respectable."

"Not exactly Jesse James then, robbing from the rich and giving to the poor. I like the name Jesse. How about Jesse Ted if we have a boy? You can name the girls, but not after flowers."

"Deal."

By the time Ja'nae brought the steaming, sticky slabs of meat to their table, Noreen was almost happy.

****

Noreen belched and covered her lips with her fingertips. "Sorry. Heartburn. Nerves. Could we go somewhere for Tums?"

"I think we should get this over with."

Rusty parked the Civic squarely in front of Charlie Courville's house—where he wasn't welcome and didn't think he ever would be. Noreen seemed to take forever getting out of the car, unsnapping the top of her jeans and adjusting her T-shirt, making sure her stomach didn't show too much. No sense in having her father go ballistic too early in the conversation, he guessed.

Rusty rang the doorbell. He could hear Noreen muttering a soft, little prayer. "Please Lord, let my mom be the one to answer." But her luck for the day had run out. Charlie Courville filled the doorway with his bulk, took one look at Rusty Niles and said, "You!"

The door came slamming closed but bounced off of a cowboy boot stuck across the sill and a forearm made strong from roping and wrestling calves. Noreen, hidden behind Rusty, shuddered against his body. He wasn't a shy high school boy anymore, but a man full-grown and not likely to be intimidated.

"Sir, we have to talk." Russ drew Noreen forward and tucked her under his arm.

"Say what you have to, then go." Charlie Courville held the door halfway closed.

"I love your daughter. We've been engaged since September, and we plan to get married soon."

"Is my daughter pregnant?"

They heard her mother's voice. "Charles Courville, we will not discuss this on the sidewalk! Let them in at once."

Mr. Courville backed up slowly like a bull still looking for a chance to gore a downed rider, Rusty thought. Mrs. Courville wrestled her husband for the door handle and invited the couple in.

"I'll get coffee, and we will sit in the den and discuss this like civilized people."

319

"No coffee for me, Mom. We just ate." Noreen placed a hand over her lips and suppressed another burp. Her mother looked at her, an odd expression crossing her face. She knew. Rusty sized her up—for or against him?

He replied, "Me neither. I want to say what I have to say and go."

Rusty followed Mrs. Courville into a room clearly designated as Charlie's turf being filled with leathery furniture and trophy buck heads mounted on the walls. He sat in the deep chair Carolyn Courville gestured to, his legs tucked in and his hands gripping the arms in case he needed to spring up and defend Noreen at any moment. Charlie Courville, eyes red with hatred, assumed a similar stance in an identical chair directly across from him.

They looked for all the world like two football linemen facing off, youth and speed on one side, experience and weight on the other. LSU memorabilia scattered around the room enhanced the image. Noreen on the couch with her mother emitted a nervous laugh.

"To answer your question, sir, yes, Noreen is pregnant. We didn't plan for things to happen this way, but she is. We were going to marry in June, but we'll be moving that up a bit."

"So you aren't here to ask for my permission?"

"No, sir. We planned to tell you when Noreen turned twenty-one, but this is Louisiana. You know we could have married a lot sooner."

"But you waited until I paid for her college education. How good of you."

"I've been saving up money for a travel trailer so we'd have a place to live while I was on the road. But now with the baby, I thought maybe it would be best to put a single wide on the back of my daddy's property and settle down."

Noreen's mother sucked in her breath. College educated Mt. Carmel girls did not live in any-sized trailers on anyone's property. They married doctors and lawyers and business executives. The old Janis Joplin song began running through Rusty's head. Noreen let loose with a silent fart, barely noticed. The air was ripe enough with testosterone already.

"It's a good thing you've given this some thought, young man, because I don't plan to pay for Noreen's last semester of college or her expensive room and board in that so-called sorority house. Might as well be a bordello since my daughter got knocked up while she lived there. Even better you don't plan to ask my permission because you will never, ever get it!"

Charlie Courville rose halfway out of his chair and Rusty tensed to move. He'd backed Bodey in more than one fight and figured the old man was soft in the middle and would go down easy if he knocked the wind out of him. Mrs. Courville, a referee without the striped shirt, came between them.

"I am sure you don't mean that, Charles. We're talking about our youngest daughter and our seventh grandchild. We'd like to see them have a lovely wedding and a nice home, now wouldn't we?"

"No, we wouldn't. I will not pay a cent for any farce of a wedding, not a penny to bring a Niles bastard into the world. Look at your daughter, Carolyn. She's already showing. You expect me to walk her down the aisle all dressed in white while my clients snicker behind their hands?"

Full of Pop Plato's ribs and four months worth of baby, Noreen's belly pooched out. She was unable to suck it back in. Rusty felt a surge of pity for both women as Carolyn Courville gazed sadly at her daughter. She assessed the livid color of her husband's face, then pressed him back into his chair using both of her hands.

"Charlie, dear, you know what the doctor said. Your heart may be like new, but with your blood pressure, you could still have a stroke. Calm down. Let's discuss some alternatives."

"I'll give these two sneaking, lying fornicators some alternatives. If you want my help in getting you out of this mess, Noreen, you will agree to give up the baby for adoption. Drop out of school for a semester, have the kid and finish up during the summer on my dime. I know several attorneys who can arrange a nice, quiet transfer of the child to a good home. The adoptive family will pay for the birth and all the legal fees. Otherwise, you can go live in a trailer with your—your saddle bum!"

Noreen couldn't hold any part of her body in any longer. Another fart escaped, a belch popped out, and she exploded into tears. Rusty unfolded from his chair. He'd grown since that fracas in the swimming pool and now topped Charles Courville by a good two inches. He knew he was all long, lean muscle, too.

"My dad and I own a cattle ranch. It's small, but we raise some of the best beef around here, the kind you eat at Ruth Chris' Steakhouse with your cronies. I'm proud of that and my family name. We've been on this land since 1822. A family member and three sons-in-law died for the Confederate cause. Noreen taught me that. I have nothing to be ashamed of. This child will have my last name even if we have to get married by a justice of the peace in the backyard of my daddy's house. Come on, Noreen. We don't need their help, sweetheart." Russell Niles gathered up his first and only love and steered her toward the door.

Noreen said nothing, but her mother went into full cry. "Charles Marchand Courville the Third, we are not giving our grandchild away to a good home like some kind of pound puppy! Do you understand me? "

They didn't hear Mr. Courville's answer as Rusty closed the front door behind them. In the car, Noreen continued to cry until they were half way to Rainbow. When she finally looked out the window, she said, "Rusty, please, let's not tell your father tonight. I don't think this is good for the baby—or for me."

"We'd best get it over with. If my dad throws us out, too, we'll get a motel room for the night and look for a place to stay tomorrow."

"I can always go back to the sorority house if your father objects. I'm paid up until the end of December no matter what my father says."

"Noreen, honey, I don't plan on spending another night of my life away from you. Get used to the idea."

"I can get used to that. I've been dreaming about being with you for years, but Rusty—do we have to get married by a justice of the peace in your daddy's backyard? I've always wanted to be married in the nun's chapel at the Academy. I think my brother would preside. We don't have to have a fancy wedding, but..."

"Honey, I was just saying that. I have enough saved up to pay for your last semester in college. No one is going to claim you had to give up your education because of me. I should have enough left over for a simple wedding. If your brother would marry us, I'd consider that an honor. We'll still have to go see Fr. Cyrus, I guess, to get permission to use the nun's chapel instead of St. Leo's."

"We aren't doing very well at ending the feud, are we, Russ?"

"Give it time, sweetheart. Let's see how it goes with my dad."

****

"Hey, Dad," Rusty called out as he opened the door of the ranch house.

"That you, Rusty? I didn't expect you home for another day or two. I'm makin' some scrambled eggs. You want some?" Ted Niles appeared grasping a small skillet full of jelling eggs and a spatula. "What's she doing here?"

"Dad, Noreen and I are getting married."

The skillet dropped to the floor. Eggs splattered on the walls.

"Dad, don't have a stroke, now."

"I think we should all sit down," Noreen said in a small voice since there was no other female to intervene.

"Like spittin' on your mother's grave, Rusty."

"Dad, Noreen is pregnant."

"She tricked you just like I said she would."

Noreen, as shaky as those eggs on the floor, wobbled against Rusty. "We should sit," she repeated in an even tinier voice.

"Dad, her father threw her out. He treated her just like he treated Mom—who was pregnant when you

324

married her. Did she trick you? Did you love her, or me, any less?"

"Of course not!"

"Down," said Noreen faintly. Her knees buckled as the whole, awful scene turned to blackness.

In her unconscious state, Noreen dreamed she lived in a trailer with twelve screaming, redheaded children. She shivered as a sharp scent like ammonia in a million urine-filled diapers passed under her nose. What she heard as she came around was Rusty's low, steady voice saying, "We'd like to stay here until the baby comes. I can pay some room and board. Noreen will help with the house, but I want her to finish college. I think I've saved enough for that and she has a car in her own name to commute."

"Son, you're only twenty-three. Don't you want some freedom first like Bodey Landrum?"

"I want Noreen."

"Maybe you should consider Charlie Courville's offer. Both of you and that baby would have better lives."

Suddenly, all those screaming babies in Noreen's dream coalesced into one small boy with his mother's dark curls. "Rusty, don't let them take Jesse Ted!"

Noreen opened her eyes. Her head rested in Rusty's lap, her body stretched out on the worn plaid sofa in the living room. Rusty capped a bottle of ammonia and said, "She's back in the discussion. I sure hope this stuff didn't hurt the baby."

"Just a quick whiff, not enough to do that, I don't think. You're going to call the baby Jesse Ted?" Rusty's dad stared at the bump of Noreen's belly.

"Only if we have a boy. You always said you

wouldn't wish Theodore on anyone, but this will be your first grandchild. I sort of wanted to carry on the tradition of naming him after his grandfather."

"Jesse Ted, huh?"

"Jesse Ted Niles. His mother will be Noreen Niles in only a few weeks. She won't be a Courville anymore."

"The Courvilles will probably hate her as much as they hate the rest of us. Okay, you two can stay. I don't want your money. You can work for me and Noreen will keep house and go to school. That will be enough."

Rusty laid Noreen's head carefully on the cushions. He got up and held out his hand. Two tall, lean men shook. Then, Ted Niles embraced his son, the first good to come out of the whole situation. "Jesse Ted Niles, huh."

****

Noreen, exhausted, spent the night spooned against Rusty in the narrow bed of his childhood, a far cry from the magnificent four-poster at Le Rosier Courville. She woke surrounded by a décor of 4-H trophies and rodeo prizes. Wrapped in Rusty's plaid bedspread, she wondered if Mrs. Niles had had a thing for Scotsmen as plaids seemed to be everywhere in the house. She heard Rusty in the shower next door, a comforting sound she wanted to hear for the rest of her life. Her stomach rumbled, "Feed me," a constant problem since the nausea passed.

Noreen covered her nakedness with yesterday's clothes and wandered out to the kitchen. She'd slept later than she intended. Ted Niles had gone already to work around the ranch, his breakfast dishes left washed and stacked in a drainer. An old, gold-colored dishwasher matching a stripe in the plaid kitchen curtains sat under the counter, but Ted evidently didn't use it for his small collection of Melmac dishes and K-mart cutlery. Noreen poured out orange juice and made toast for herself and Jesse Ted. It wasn't enough food to feed her raging hormones. She put some eggs on to boil and made coffee for Russ, though she didn't intend to drink any herself.

Rusty walked in freshly shaven and wearing a clean, blue shirt and jeans smelling like a spring breeze according to the claims on the box of dryer sheets sitting on the old washer in a corner of the kitchen. He sought her out for a long kiss while the eggs cooked to a soft boil. He sat down to decapitate his breakfast and dip his toast into the gooey center only to find their breakfast had hard-boiled while they fooled around.

"What are we going to do, Russ?" Noreen asked as she scooped out spoonfuls of egg and spread them on her bread.

"We'll go see Fr. Cyrus today and get a date for the wedding. Afterwards, we'll drive into Lafayette and collect your things from the sorority house, bring 'em here and start planning."

"I can't see Fr. Cyrus like this—in dirty clothes and with no makeup on, my hair all messed up."

Rusty sighed. "The sorority house first, then Fr. Cyrus. But you know Noreen, you look just as pretty without all that stuff."

"Another reason I love you, Rusty. Let me polish off this second egg and we'll get going."

****

Renee Niles lounged on one of the twin beds with the matching Laura Ashley spreads and worked on repairing the chips in her plum-colored nail polish. She barely glanced up when Noreen, looking like she'd slept in her clothes, which was close to the truth, came into the sorority house room they shared and started emptying her side of the closet.

"Out all night with Cousin Rusty? Once you two get going, you never seem to stop."

Noreen ignored the comment and threw one back. "I thought you'd be gone home for Christmas by now."

"Oh, Uncle Dewey is staying over. Since his wife and daughter left him, he seems to be at our house all the time."

"Isn't he the uncle who took you to Europe twice and other things? Don't you like him?"

"I don't like his 'other things'. I think I'll hang out here for most of the break. What about you? Has your love ended the Niles-Courville feud yet?" Renee snickered.

"My dad said I was on my own if I didn't give the baby up for adoption, so we're moving in with Rusty's father and getting married."

"Oh, I call maid of honor! I introduced you. Red isn't my best color even though it is the Christmas season. What do you think of emerald green or midnight blue for the attendants' dresses?"

"I was going to ask Estelle to be my matron of honor. Besides, the wedding will be very small, whatever we can afford."

"As if Estelle's husband will let her come, let alone be in the wedding party. Burgess might as well be Charlie Courville they are so close. Sally Parker will want to be a bridesmaid. Kelley O'Connor is going to LSU and belongs to the same sorority. We could reassemble the Sexy Seven. That would be cool."

"I can't afford six attendants."

"Nonsense, all of us can pay for our own dresses. Bridesmaids are the one thing you can afford. So what do you think—emerald or dark blue?"

"I don't know. Maybe a deep green if you can find something in a hurry. Look, I have to clean up. We're going to see a priest. Could you start hauling my stuff down to the car?"

"Only if I can be maid of honor."

"For heaven's sake, Renee! I want to ask my sister first."

"Will Bodey Landrum be best man?"

"I suppose so. He doesn't know about the wedding yet."

"Or the baby is my guess. We always figured you and Rusty would get yourselves in trouble one day given the chance."

"Thanks for the good wishes, Renee. Now haul this pile down to the car."

Noreen pulled a bulky white cotton sweater from a drawer, chose a demure gray pleated skirt reminiscent of her old parochial uniform and black flats from the heap of clothing she'd dumped on Renee. Fr. Cyrus was a known grouch and a stickler for tradition. Why aggravate him by arriving at his office in jeans and an untucked shirt?

****

Fr. Cyrus's stare nailed Rusty to his chair. The priest had the face of a bulldog with a flatulence problem and a bald head fringed by a ring of iron gray hair. He peered at the couple through wire-rimmed spectacles and wore a clerical collar that seemed much too tight. His favorite sermon, given at least twice a year, dealt with the sins of Eve, a woman, being redeemed by Christ, man and God in one.

The girls at Mt. Carmel dreaded giving him their childish confessions because his penances were twice as hard as those of other priests. Every time Fr. Cyrus heard Renee Niles' confession, he'd drag out his "woman as the root of all evil" sermon and up the ante on Hail Marys and Our Fathers yet again.

"So, you young people wish to marry. Do you feel you are ready for this grave responsibility?" Fr. Cyrus asked, implying they were not.

"Yes. We're ready," Rusty Niles answered while trying to meet the priest eye to eye.

"We'd like to marry within the month," Noreen added in a timid voice as she tried to hide the bulge under her sweater.

"Let me see. The banns will have to be read three times in church. You'll require marital counseling. Lent is coming up early this year. I don't marry people during Lent."

"The first week in February would be fine with us—before Lent. And, we'd like to be married in the nun's chapel with my brother, Fr. Matthew Courville, presiding with your consent," Noreen said softly.

"We'll take all the instruction you want to dish out. We'll start now." Rusty added.

"Why the unseemly haste? Is there is a child on the way? Answer me!" Fr. Cyrus said slamming his hand against the desk and making both of the young people jump.

"Yes, sir. I'm the daddy and I want to do the right thing."

"So you will, right after Lent."

"But I'll be seven months along by then, can't you..."

"You should have thought of that before you sinned. I'll pencil you in for mid-March. You may go now."

Noreen, shaken, let Rusty help her from the chair and out on to the main street of Rainbow.

"Could we walk over to the Academy? I'd like to visit Sr. Inez. She's usually in the stables around this time."

"Whatever you want, honey. Say, have you ever considered becoming a Methodist?" As always, Rusty made her laugh.

Sr. Inez was not about, but they sat cuddling on a bale of straw, taking in the comforting scent of horses, hay and grassy manure until she arrived. Noreen poured out her heart to the chunky nun who wore riding pants and her usual short veil over cropped, thick salt and pepper hair.

"Fr. Cyrus is being arbitrary. The man is a born misogynist, the kind of priest who drives young people away from the church—in my most humble opinion. Let me sic the Mother Superior on him. She's no pushover. We'll see what we can do about the date and place of your wedding. There, I see Sr. Helen passing by. Let me speak with her for a moment. Mother Bridget Claire values her input."

Noreen and Rusty waited, framed by the brick archway of the old stable built by the generosity and lust of Aaron Niles. Sr. Helen, the aging art instructor who had mentored Eve Burns, glanced over at them and nodded.

"He can't treat one of our girls this way, the old prick. Father, forgive me, I meant to say priest, but the word just popped right out. I'm going to pray to our founder, Mother Leontine, and ask for her intervention. Why look at them, Nessy, a young woman with child and a man who cares for her sitting in a stable. They could be the Holy Family themselves and Fr. Cyrus would play games with them."

"We'll do all we can for them, Sr. Helen, all we can."

****

That troublesome young couple had stirred up the nuns at the Academy. Fr. Cyrus in a huff entered the rear gate of the old cemetery and cut across the graveyard on his way to have it out with the Mother Superior of Mt. Carmel. He refused to walk all the way around to the front gate of the Academy and waste precious minutes of his time because of this interview. Only he had the authority to set the date and place of the Courville-Niles wedding.

The priest hurried past the humble graves of black people and reached the grand tomb of the Niles family. He paused to catch his breath. The descendants of Aaron Niles were no better than small farmers now and could not lord it over him, no matter how rich and influential those people had been in the past.

Out of the corner of his eye over by the nun's cemetery, Fr. Cyrus caught sight of an imposing nun in a full habit, completely covered as she should be, as all women of the church should be, not romping around in knee-length skirts and even slacks. She must be visiting from abroad where they had more respect for tradition, Fr. Cyrus concluded. He hailed her with a stentorious,

"Peace be with you."

"And also with you, Fr. Cyrus Martin, but you shall have no peace if you delay the wedding of Noreen Courville to Russell Niles. This feud is ending in God's good time and through the means of an unborn child. You will not interfere." Her voice came across clear and commanding even from a distance like church bells ringing.

He started to fold his arms over his barrel chest to assert his authority, but the nun came closer, floating across the grass, her feet unseen beneath her long robes. She towered over him and glowed with a strange backlight—an aura, a halo? Her eyes of steely gray were solemn and piercing and her voice implacable. Fr. Cyrus felt his genitals shrivel in his pants. He tripped over a small headstone buried in the grass and fell to his knees before the vision.

"Pray to be weaned of the sin of pride in your place in life and your manhood, Fr. Cyrus. You know not the will of God."

The stately nun vanished just in time. The priest nearly wet his pants. He got up and swiped at the grass stains on the knees of his black trousers. He knew that face from where? A check of his watch confirmed his lateness for his appointment with Mother Bridget Claire. He jogged the rest of the way to her office and arrived red-faced and sweating.

Mother Bridget Claire, come over from Ireland, was stout of body, firm of will, and greatly practical. For all that, she had a smile so bright it encouraged the weak and warmed the strong to their tasks. She did not waste a smile on Fr. Cyrus but instead took in his condition with her shrewd blue eyes. The two of them had locked horns before and he had won more often because he was the priest and she was the nun.

The priest who came before her today hardly resembled the bullheaded man she often dealt with. He shook and jabbered and stabbed a finger toward the full-length portrait of the academy's founder, Mother Leontine, hanging on the wall. At first, Mother Bridget Claire assumed he disparaged the great nun, but that was not the case at all when he made himself clear. After Fr. Cyrus left her presence, she sent one of the novices to find Sr. Inez and Sr. Helen.

"The two of you will be pleased to know the Courville-Niles wedding will take place in our chapel the first week in February with Fr. Matthew Courville presiding," the Mother Superior said in her pleasant brogue. "I might add, the Blessed Mother Leontine has performed a miracle and that hardhearted priest will attest to it in writing."

****

Having any event on an early February day in Louisiana is risky. The weather may be warm and benevolent, or might pour gray sheets of cold rain to kill the party. Noreen Courville was pleased with her wedding day. The sun shone down encouraging the pink magnolias planted near the chapel to open their thick, cupped petals and causing the purple and white winter pansies lining the walkway to turn upward like a thousand happy faces.

Noreen stood on the threshold of the chapel, her arm linked to Ted Niles. She'd found a dress very similar to the one she'd worn to the prom—simple, white and high-waisted, its folds draping softly over her five-months belly. The seamstress had sewn a short fingertip veil to one of the mother-of-pearl combs from the old box of jewelry and the hairdresser tucked it into her dark curls. The last of the Niles treasures, a pair of ruby drop earrings as pure a red as fresh blood, hung from her lobes. Rusty matched this wedding gift with a huge bouquet of roses of the same color. Noreen felt like the first pregnant Miss America winner holding them. She would have preferred another nosegay of yellow Courville Noisettes, but they weren't in bloom.

She credited Renee Niles for being an excellent maid of honor when Estelle had failed to come through for her. Renee ran down the Sexy Six and parted them from semester breaks in Aspen and Cancun to assist with the wedding of their seventh member. She made their attendance seem like a holy obligation. A natural bully, Renee imposed her will to get all the bridesmaids dressed in deep green in a simple pattern of her choosing and sewn up in a hurry by the equally intimidated seamstress. Each would carry a single red rose plucked from the bridal bouquet.

Since Rusty could come up with only Bodey, who was missing a major rodeo involving most of their friends to be here, and Leon Plato as groomsmen, Renee proclaimed she would march out with Bodey. Leon could escort Sally Parker and the other four would double up in the final procession. No arguments! Surprisingly, Renee adhered to the old-new, borrowed-blue checklist and forced her own recently purchased blue silk garter belt on the bride who had planned to wear maternity hose.

"Let's make an effort to be a little bit sexy on the wedding night, Noreen," she'd chided, shaking her head. "Some men do find pregnant women desirable, go figure."

Rusty picked out the rings, a wide band for him, a narrow one for her, each with a simple engraved pattern sort of matching her antique engagement ring. Noreen knew the words on the inside of hers read "My One and Only Love", along with their wedding date. His had the only anniversary date engraved in case he forgot it.

The nuns took charge of the music, which included a lovely rendition of Ave Maria. The chords of the wedding march sounded now as the last of the Sexy Six stutter-stepped down the aisle. Ted Niles, feeling the arm he held tremble, said, "You and Jesse Ted ready to go?"

Noreen nodded. She stepped forward and focused on Rusty beaming at her from the front of the church. Other than her brother, handsome in his priestly garments, not a Courville sat in sight, none among the groomsmen standing at the altar, none among the guests seated in the pews. With the colors of the Niles' stained glass windows jeweling her gown and Ted Niles proudly standing in as a substitute father, Noreen walked down the aisle to "join the enemy" as Charlie Courville said when she'd asked him to give her away.

The nuns of the Academy placed themselves on both sides of the aisle, hiding the paucity of well-wishers. A smattering of Noreen's sorority sisters showed solidarity on the bride's side. Jed Niles, his wife and their younger daughter, who had never gone to Paris but was a senior star on the Academy softball team, sat in the second row reserved for the groom's relatives.

The service included a full communion with Fr. Matthew assisted at the altar by a newly humble Fr.

Cyrus. Bodey joked that this was a way Catholics got out of Sunday Mass so they could fish or golf, but Noreen ignored him. At the very casual rehearsal dinner held at the Rainbow Café, Bodey seemed intent on punching out as many verbal jabs toward Noreen as he could. The best man remained grim-faced throughout the ceremony. She cared not a bit. In one swift, sweet hour, Noreen Courville became Noreen Niles.

Ted Niles planned to take everyone who wanted to go afterwards to a good restaurant in Lafayette with a large buffet. The bridal couple had reserved one night at the Hilton, no honeymoon because classes were in session, and Noreen was determined to finish her history degree by May. Despite being married in 1987, a supposedly liberated decade, she'd had to postpone her student teaching thanks to an administration who thought a pregnant woman in a high school classroom not to be a good idea. Hell, Bodey said, probably half the girls in the class would be pregnant, too. His opinion, a rare defense of Noreen, carried no weight.

After the final blessing, Fr. Matthew made an announcement to those gathered before him. "All are welcome to attend a reception at Le Rosier Courville, a gift to the bride from her sister who was unable to attend today. Turn left at the gate and follow Main Street until the bend where the road becomes Courville Lane. You can't miss the old place, and I hope to see all of you there. And now let us rejoice for the newly married Mr. and Mrs. Russell Niles."

Applause and a burst of organ music signaled the recessional. Tears flowed down Noreen's cheeks. She could not stop them. Rusty wiped them away with a fingertip as they stood outside in the sunshine accepting best wishes.

"Crying?"

"Estelle doesn't hate me after all. That's two down and the rest of the family to go."

****

Obviously, Estelle had spent all morning at the old plantation home. The glossy dining room table that could seat twelve had a three-tiered wedding cake centered in its middle, each layer adorned with small red rosebuds and tiny fern leaves. The cake was surrounded by plates of triangular sandwiches with four different fillings, and a spiral cut ham ready to be loaded onto fresh rolls and heaped with adjacent condiments. Two black women from Rainbow, whom Estelle hired regularly to help at events, smiled and circulated with trays of bite-sized crab cakes and pecan-crusted chicken nuggets.

The oldest of the nuns sat in the twelve chairs arranged around the room and sipped a pale, pink beverage Bodey dismissed as "Lemonade, got no kick," prior to returning to the Academy in the nun-mobile to pick up another load of Sisters. A double champagne cooler held the bottles for toasts once everyone assembled. Estelle had done as nice a job as she would have for a paying client, and in terms of the Courville family, that meant a great deal.

After his final ferrying trip to the convent, Bodey Landrum filled a plate and slipped out to the back verandah to get away from the religious folks cramming the room. He looked down the back lawn to the gazebo by the bayou, and over to the refurbished cypress barn with its silvered timbers that contained no animals, but was available for hayrides and hoedowns according to the brochures resting on a side table.

Noreen came thank him. "I appreciate your bringing the Sisters back and forth, Bodey."

"Why else was I put on this earth? Must be nice to know you come from a place like this, know who your people were way back."

"I guess. Rusty didn't know much about his family until I showed him the documents. You could always do a genealogy. We all come from somewhere."

"Not me. My mother's family threw her out when she came up pregnant after a drunken party with some rodeo bums and couldn't even give them my daddy's name. Betsy says I look just like him, though. Must have been a handsome devil."

Bodey shook off his gloom as two of the Sexy Seven wandered past with their blonde heads close together, reminiscing as they strolled toward the gazebo. Those Irish blue eyes of his picked up some sparkle and shifted from the gorgeous young women to the barn and back.

"Bodey Landrum, you stay away from my bridesmaids!"

"I couldn't teach them anything they don't already know. I thought maybe Eve Burns would be in the weddin'."

"Eve? I haven't seen her since we graduated from the Academy. Her father lost his luxury car dealership in the Oil Bust, sailed off in his yacht and was never heard from again. Eve finished school on a scholarship. Sr. Helen helped her get into art school in Houston. She had to give up her horse and left it at the Academy. That's all I know about Eve."

"Too bad. That was a sweet little mare."

"Yes, I used to envy Eve, but not anymore. Now I have Rusty and he's all I want."

"Yeah, you won."

"This isn't a game, Bodey. Russ and I are two souls who have waited a long time for each other."

"Right. Well, Rusty is my best friend and like a brother to me. We were going to hit the high road and get rich and famous on the circuit. Now, I got to do that alone."

"I'm sure you will—if you give up carousing and womanizing and keep your mind on your career."

"Noreen, you can suck the fun out of anything."

Renee Niles swayed by, her dress fitted tighter than the other bridesmaids. "Have you seen how they've fixed up the barn for parties, Bodey? Want to explore?"

"Got to go, Noreen. Best to you and Russ and little Bubba."

"Jesse Ted," Noreen shouted after him.

****

Rusty Niles rubbed his hand over the smooth, waxy surface of the carved posts on what Estelle called the Courville marriage bed and looked down on his bride. Noreen had passed over all the suggestive, peek-a-boo lace garments gifted to her by the Sexy Six and chosen a simple, almost transparent, white batiste nightgown with little yellow roses embroidered on the yoke. She said her gown matched the bed. The deep golden petals of dried Courville Noisettes lay scattered on the sheets and gave off a heady scent.

"I never thought I'd see you here like this. I believed we'd have to elope."

"You saw me here just a few of months ago."

"Not as man and wife. We waited five long years."

"Longer than that."

He wasn't about to argue with her. Rusty eased himself down naked beside Noreen and ran his hand over her breasts where her darkened nipples showed through the sheer material. He cupped his palm and gently massaged her belly, smiled when he felt a faint response to his touch from the baby.

"I guess I'm not too tempting," said Noreen, suddenly uncertain.

"You are more beautiful to me than you will ever know." Rusty flicked the ruby earrings she continued to wear and ran a finger down her neck, past the sensitive side of one breast and on down her side to her small red-painted toenails.

"I didn't get you a gift, Rusty, with money so tight and all."

"Sweetheart, you have given me Jesse Ted and all the days of your life. And you are about to give me the best wedding night a man ever had." When he came back up, he took the nightgown with him.

Chapter Nineteen

Noreen bobbed across the stage in her cap and gown to accept her college diploma. So what if people thought she was obese. She'd finished college before the baby came. Faltering a little going down the steps on the opposite side of the platform, she fell out of the line of black-robed graduates and headed toward an exit. Her eyes searched the stands for a head of auburn hair. Rusty hadn't stayed where she spotted him earlier sitting next to Ted Niles and leaning over the balcony railing to take her picture. Her big brown eyes, desperate, scanned the crowd and came across a row of people she didn't expect to see—her brother Matt in civilian dress, Estelle and Burgess, Hardy and his wife, her parents. She'd sent them all invitations, of course, but received no response. Her mother half rose and waved tentatively, but Charlie forced her back into her seat. Noreen could not appreciate the miracle of their presence right now.

While the long-winded speeches went on and on, Noreen felt her belly bunch up under her gown, more of those pesky Braxton-Hicks contractions that sent them running to the hospital once already. By the time she hauled herself up the stage steps using the shaky metal railing for support, she experienced some real pain. Right after accepting a handshake from the dean, something gave way. A trickle of liquid rolled down her leg. This was it. Jesse Ted had signaled his arrival, but where was Rusty?

She saw movement in the crowd just before she went through the doors. Someone in too much of a hurry to take the stairs dropped from the second tier railing and landed in a neat tuck. Two security guards went in pursuit. Rusty ran full out to meet her in the lobby.

They wasted valuable time explaining Noreen had gone into labor to the guards, but at last, they let Russ race across the vast parking lot to get the car. Ted Niles arrived to put a comforting arm around his daughter-in-law. She could feel his excitement through his fingertips about Jesse Ted's arrival.

Before Rusty returned with the car, Noreen found herself enveloped in Courville women, her mother, Estelle, and Hardy's wife, Amanda, all asking her how far apart the contractions were, had her water broken, where was she scheduled to deliver? The Courville men hung back, staying away from the alarming puddle forming on the floor.

"I'm supposed to deliver in Opelousas, but I'm not sure I can get there now. You know, I told Rusty he was related to the doctors who own the Maddox Ob-Gyn Clinic up there. When I went for my first checkup, I took along the genealogy I prepared for my final Louisiana history project—the one where I tracked down Captain Billy Niles and Owney Maddox. They really did give us a family discount. Oh! That was a good one." Noreen hunched over her stomach and tried to take three cleansing breaths.

"If I deliver in Lafayette, I don't know how we'll pay for it."

"Don't you worry. Your father will pick up the tab," Carolyn Courville asserted.

"The bill for this baby is her husband's responsibility." Charlie Courville crossed his arms and sank his chin back into his great bull neck as if he were intimidating a client who wanted to weasel out of a real estate deal with Hardy. Burgess Simone and Hardy mimicked his stance, but Matthew Courville stepped forward.

"I'd help you financially if I could, but…"

"You can baptize the baby for us, Fr. Matt."

Noreen's brother gave her a painful smile. "Maybe."

Ted Niles spoke up. "We don't need your help. Noreen is a Niles now. We take care of our own, so hold on to your wallet and go. Je-Te, the b-baby come."

Suddenly the name Ted had repeated with such joy over the last few months would not come out of his mouth. His left arm, wrapped around Noreen's shoulders, fell limp at his side. One long leg began to fold under him. Fr. Matthew caught him under the arms before he hit the concrete. Carolyn Courville said, "He's stroking. Give him this aspirin if he can swallow."

"Aspirin is for heart attacks, for Christ's sake, woman," Charlie Courville bellowed. Noreen began to cry. Aspirin wasn't going to solve this problem. Ted Niles had given Rusty and Noreen his room with the adjoining bath and gone to sleep in the old single bed surrounded by his son's trophies. He'd helped the young people clean out the third bedroom Maggie had used as her office, hauling a computer so slow and antiquated it was only good for gathering dust, to the dump along with the old real estate files he'd never gotten rid of.

He hadn't said a word when Noreen "baby-proofed" the house, packing up all of his wife's figurines in newspaper and storing them in the attic. When his daughter-in-law got rid of all the plaids in the house, covered the sofa in red, and put up new drapes, he hadn't protested. Now he couldn't. She suspected he lived mostly to see Jesse Ted come into the world.

Rusty dashed toward them, not knowing who to help first, but Fr. Matt held on and got Ted to the car, riding in the back seat with him while Noreen sat carefully on a blanket in the front. Good thing they were only a mile from the Lafayette hospital and got going before the graduation crowd let out. Noreen said a silent prayer that her father-in-law would live to hold his grandson in his arms.

****

Maybe he could have gotten Noreen all the way to Opelousas before the baby came, Rusty thought, as he made yet another trip from the maternity ward to the floor where the stroke victims were housed, but then, he couldn't have monitored his dad. His father had a health insurance policy, a pretty good one as it turned out, thanks to the generosity of Big Ben Barnum. Russ was insured through the rodeo association, but that wouldn't help with the delivery bills. He'd pre-paid the Drs. Maddox all he could. Maybe, they would give him a refund since he couldn't use the discount now.

According to Carolyn Courville, who had been very mothering to him, his dad could make a good recovery with therapy. She kept up with all the latest information on strokes because of Charlie's high blood pressure, she explained. Her husband sat not saying a word, drinking old and bitter coffee in a corner of the waiting room.

Hardy and Burgess had gone home to pay off babysitters while Amanda and Estelle took turns sitting with Noreen when Rusty went to check on his father. This was as chummy as Rusty had ever been with the Courvilles. He wondered if a tiny baby could make the amiability last. Noreen, glowing with sweat, insisted the birth of her son would bring an end to the feud. The women of her family had come down hard on her side now, coaching her every step of the way, and telling their own scary birth stories between Noreen's contractions. When the females started in on that, Rusty wished he were in a bar somewhere chugging down a beer with Bodey.

He took a seat by his father's side and prayed. "Dear Lord, save my dad. He gave up everything to raise me, and now I need and want his help with my own child. Bring him back to us and let his life be better than ever. He deserves it. Amen."

****

Hardy's wife left the labor room to get a cold drink with an "I don't want to tempt you" tossed at Noreen who could have only ice chips. Estelle stayed by her sister's side, coaching her breathing through each contraction and making small talk.

Centered on what went on within her body Noreen barely listened until she heard Estelle say, "You know you were always the quiet, sweet, almost invisible one in the family before you got hung up on Rusty Courville. All the rest of us competed for Daddy's attention. I guess that's why I married Burgess. He's just like Dad. No wonder our father picked him out for me, shoved Burgess at me as soon as I graduated from college. Now, I think I should have had the guts to do my own choosing like you did."

Noreen's eyes widened. She'd braced for a captive lecture about the lack of sense she'd shown in loving Rusty and getting pregnant, and here her flawless sister admitted to a mistake of her own.

"Another contraction, honey? Deep breath, now let it out between your lips. That's good. I was going crazy staying at home with two small kids and doing the perfect business wife thing. Amanda has that down pat, but I couldn't do it. The renovation of the old Courville place saved my sanity. I've almost made enough money on the business to buy Hardy out. I could leave Burgess and move to Rainbow, fix up another old house in town and send the boys to St. Leo's."

"Leave Burgess? Get a divorce?" A hard contraction hit Noreen low in the gut. She panted through it. No meds for her. They cost too much.

"Yes. He's as inflexible as Daddy. He hated letting me start my own business. Said it took my time away from home and family, and he is a good provider—like we don't live in 1987 when wives can have careers, too. But, Hardy saw the profit in the deal and got Daddy on his side. Burge didn't have a chance. Only my name and Hardy's are on the mortgage for Le Rosier Courville."

"W-won't Hardy object to your dumping Burgess? He's as old-fashioned as Dad and might not sell out to you." The contraction ended, and Noreen took another deep breath.

"If he does, I'll tell Amanda about his philandering

and he might end up in divorce court himself. Burge told me he and Daddy and Hardy regularly take clients to those men's clubs. Burge claims he only has few drinks and watches, but Hardy and Dad pay for lap dances. Burge is such a stick, that's probably true."

"Dad pays for lap dances?"

"Yes, but only Hardy ever goes farther. I don't know what Mama would do if Dad stroked out in one of those places. Maybe his high blood pressure keeps him faithful, but Hardy has no restraint. I should tell Amanda anyhow. He could give her AIDS."

The door to the room opened and the lovely and charming Mrs. Hardy Courville, a former Academy girl, returned to the bedside. "Why don't you take a break, Estelle? Get something to drink. I'll coach for a while. After all, I've been through natural childbirth four times. I know when to pant and when to breathe."

Estelle took her up on the offer and Amanda settled gracefully into the still warm chair at Noreen's side. "How far apart are the contractions now, Mommy?"

"Five minutes."

"Still have a little way to go."

"You did this naturally every time? I think this will be my one and only."

"It's your first child. Gets easier, but always hurts. Always hurts. Noreen, this may not be the best time to bring this up, but we never see each other. That awful Renee Niles told me Rusty cheated on you, and she couldn't believe you were going to marry her cousin anyhow. I called her to find out what color flowers you were having so I could use the same on the cake. Did you like the red velvet recipe? I guess you didn't know I made it since you never sent a note. With all the children in school now, I have so much time on my hands. I took this course in cake decorating and I do several very fancy cakes for the nun's spring festival bake sale every year. Yours was my first wedding cake."

"The cake was delicious and beautiful. We both love red velvet. Sorry, I didn't know you made it. Communications with the Courvilles have been nonexistent up until now." Noreen gritted her teeth as another contraction started. Amanda wanted a fricking thank you note at a time like this?

"Breathe, relax. I only mention Rusty's cheating now because it isn't too late for you. You could probably get your marriage annulled before he does it again, before you have more children."

"He cheated on me one time when he was drunk and far away—and under the influence of Bodey Landrum. I forgave him. Amanda, Rusty waited five years for me to grown up and finish college. I can't begin to tell you how great he is, but right now, I wish he'd used a condom."

"He didn't use a condom with that other woman?"

"No, with me. That's why I'm lying in this bed and feeling like I'm being cut in half with a wire."

"Hardy cheats on me, regularly, I think. Everyone believes I'm blind to his philandering, but I have four children to raise. I won't do that in a broken home. Until death do us part. I'm not naïve. I've had myself tested for AIDS. So far, so good. In my heart, I try to forgive him. I keep wondering why I'm not woman enough for Hardy. I must try to be as brave as you are and endure."

"Bullshit! If he cheats on you all the time, the fault

is his. You can tell him I said so. Now get the damned doctor. I want to know when this will be over. Go!"

"Dear, I think you've gone into transition. Fr. Matthew is out in the hall. He just got back from visiting some of his sick parishioners. I'll send him in to pray with you until I find the doctor."

"I don't want prayer! I want to be delivered!"

Amanda exited in a rush. Fr. Matt entered, stumbling as if he'd been pushed. "I don't know much about this kind of thing, but Amanda said to tell you to pant. And, I'm supposed to pray with you about getting an annulment? Is that the pain talking?"

"I don't want an annulment! Can't any of you understand I love Rusty? Where is my sonofabitch husband? Why isn't he here! "

"I do understand. Believe me, when I tell Mom and Dad I'm leaving the priesthood for love, all the heat will be off of you two and directed at me."

"What! You're telling me this now?"

"Actually, I told you years ago when our parents asked me to speak to you about Russ. I've struggled with my feelings nearly as long as you."

The contraction waned. Noreen focused on her brother. "Mattie, are you in love with another priest? Are you gay?"

"No. I just lack your courage. Susan and I have been working together trying to better the lives of the rural poor. She's a social worker. She helps those living in poverty to manage their money, improve their homes, start small businesses making crafts. I've never met a better person and I love her deeply, but I can't speak up until I leave the priesthood."

"What if she doesn't feel the same and you've

ditched your vocation for nothing?"

"I'm not sure I ever had a vocation. Mom and Dad were so proud when I showed an interest in the priesthood and got that scholarship to go to Indiana. I realize now I fulfilled their dream, not mine. I've never been aggressive like Hardy. I didn't want to follow Dad into law or start up some cutthroat business, so I let myself be pushed into the church. I do like helping people. I can still do that even if Susan won't marry me."

"Poor Mattie. Oh, Goddamn! Here comes another one." Noreen sucked in some air and started to puff it out. "I want Rusty. You get that low-life cowboy down here to hold my hand. Now! Where's that fucking doctor?"

Looking shocked by the words spewing from the mouth of his sweet, gentle little sister, Fr. Matt backed from the room as if he had to keep an eye on the demon possessing her and went in search of Rusty Niles.

****

If Bodey could see him now, he'd never stop laughing. Rusty jogged along beside the gurney, his auburn hair covered by a paper shower cap, his feet encased in booties. The flimsy, disposable gown he wore over his street clothes flapped open in the back. He never once let go of Noreen's hand.

Then, they were under the glaring lights of the delivery room and the birthing process accelerated. Push, push, push. Stop pushing. Raise her shoulders, Daddy. Help her to push. Rusty took a moment to realize he was the daddy the doctor talked about.

He raised Noreen up and whispered, "Give Jesse Ted a good shove now."

His sweet, little Noreen grunted like a linebacker and pushed until her face turned red.

"Here we go, and it's a boy!" the doctor called out as if a touchdown had been scored thanks to Noreen's efforts.

Jesse Ted Niles lay on his mother's stomach, filling a good set of lungs with air, while the doctor cut the cord and delivered the afterbirth. Rusty Niles wasn't squeamish. He'd helped deliver calves and seen barn dogs eat their afterbirth, but this situation made him a little weak-kneed. He was the father of a son, a well-endowed son, who had his mother's dark curls plastered down by white gunk at the moment. Wait until he told Bodey.

"Wow, you can sure tell he's a boy, Noreen."

"Oh, that swelling goes down," one of the nurses informed him.

"Twenty-two inches, eight pounds, nine ounces, and broad-shouldered like his dad. We have some stitching to do down here, but your wife will be fine, Mr. Niles."

"Thank you. Thank you, God, for that."

****

Charlie Courville balked and snarled about donning a paper gown for a visit to his daughter and grandson. "I won't bother if I have to look so ridiculous. I have plenty of grandchildren and do not need another one, especially this one."

Fr. Matt put his gown on without protest. He gave his father a "What would Jesus do?" kind of look. Charlie saw the answer would be, "Force this stubborn old man bodily into Noreen's room." His own son, the gentle priest, did not have to lay hands on the man because his wife did it for him.

"Come along, Charles, and see the new baby. One can never have too many grandchildren."

She clamped on to one of his arms and Estelle took the other. Fr. Matt followed, cutting off any last minute retreat. Amanda Courville rose from a chair near the bedside, vacating it for the grandfather.

Noreen, her curls as plastered down as her son's by sweat, held out the blue-wrapped bundle containing her sleeping child. "Want to hold Jesse Ted, Daddy?"

Charlie Courville didn't hold out his arms until his wife discreetly pinched the flesh above his elbow. He jerked forward and before he knew it, he gazed into the round, red face of a newborn wearing a tiny stocking cap.

"Humpf. What kind of dumbass, cowboy name is Jesse Ted?"

Russell Niles' face colored up. Noreen placed a hand on her husband's arm to quiet him.

"Well, Daddy, Amanda has already used Charles Marchand Courville the Fourth and Carolyn Ann for two of her children. We both liked the name Jesse."

"A fine Biblical name," Fr. Matt added.

"Ted is for Rusty's dad. You know, the man who took us in and might be downstairs dying right now? The man who would give anything to hold this baby."

"Right. Fine." Charlie Courville struggled with the words. "How is your father doing, Russell?"

"As well as can be expected. They want to run more tests in the morning. With therapy, he could be good as new in six months. So they tell me."

A nurse bustled in. "Everyone must leave now except the father. We have a breast-feeding lesson to give."

The men surged toward the door, Charlie Courville almost forgetting to return the baby to Noreen's arms. He came back to the bedside and put his burden down.

"He's a beautiful baby, Noreen. I know you will be a fine mother just like your own. I guess Russell will make an okay dad. I can see he cares about you very much."

"Thank you for saying that, Daddy. Come visit as soon as we get home."

Charlie Courville hustled out of the room. Damned if he would shed a tear in front of the cowpoke.

Rusty watched the nursing lesson, smiling a little when Noreen said the baby pinched. The nurse left them alone for a while.

"He sucks my breast even harder than you do, Russ."

"Don't make me jealous. I could watch the two of you all day."

"Rusty, do you think the feud is over?"

"Maybe not entirely, but pretty damn close."

****

Rusty asked for a cot in order to stay in the room and bring the baby to Noreen when Jesse Ted needed feeding. He clumsily changed his son's first diaper at five in the morning. He'd been told because of the lack of insurance for his wife and baby, the new family would have to vacate the room by ten after he made arrangements for payment of the bill. Thank God, they would take a credit card. He hoped his maximum would cover the costs.

When Russ sat in a cubicle going over the bill and realized they had been charged extra for the cot, the packet of diapers, hell, even the plastic water pitcher, he despaired of ever getting out of debt. Another charge would come from the doctor, he knew. His father must have felt this way, overwhelmed, when Maggie died. The only difference, this debt was payment for life brought into the world, not taken out of it.

Rusty took a thin wallet from his hip pocket and withdrew his single credit card, one he'd gotten in college, one with a five-thousand dollar expenditure limit. If he got home right quick, he could call the company and ask for an extension. He held out the card to the clerk.

"Do you have any questions about the bill?" asked the clerk, a kindly middle-aged woman who often saw that stricken expression on the faces of people without insurance.

"No, ma'am. I guess not. You do take credit cards?"

"Yes, but your bill has been covered. Mr. Courville left a note." She held out a piece of hospital stationery. Rusty read the words with disbelief.

"This is a gift for the baby, not a loan. Don't even think about rejecting it. No grandson of mine should start out life in debt. Make sure you keep his life that way. Charles Marchand Courville III"

"I love giving people good news. I so rarely have the chance," the clerk said as she watched a smile cross the face of Rusty Niles.

"It's good new all right. Excuse me. I have to go tell my wife the feud has ended."

Chapter Twenty

Ted Niles sat hemmed in by fancy throw pillows on the red sofa in his own home. Carolyn Courville brought the cushions along with baby safe houseplants and infant toys when she'd practically moved in with them for two weeks following the birth of Jesse Ted. He'd seen her face when she looked around the simple ranch-style house. She was probably estimating how far down the social ladder her daughter had fallen. Ted would give the woman some credit for her first words to Noreen. "Sweetie, the baby's room is simply charming."

After that, Mrs. Courville showed up every day with embellishments from Pier One and Dillard's in the mall. She'd even brought groceries like he and Rusty couldn't afford to feed their family. The power of speech was returning to Ted Niles, but he choked every time he had to say "thank you". Sometimes, he wished the feud had never ended. At least, Noreen got back on her feet and the shower of visits and gifts had slowed from a downpour to a drizzle.

"Ready to go, Ted?" Noreen held her purse, cars keys and the baby.

He nodded.

"What did the speech therapist say—use it or lose it?"

"Y-yes." Hell, he wanted to go. All he did the

whole blame day was sit and watch CNN.

"Would you hold Jesse Ted for me while I put his seat in the car?"

Ted Niles started to nod again, but slowly forced out the words, "Yes—I would like—to hold—Jeshe, Jeshe—Jaaay Teee."

"Here you go, then."

Noreen tucked the baby into the crook of his grandfather's good arm and bustled off to strap in the infant seat. Knowing that his grin sat a little lopsided on his face, Ted smiled at the tiny boy. Jesse peered up at him, seemingly fascinated by the white streaks in grandfather's auburn hair. With effort, Ted moved his weak hand over to the baby and let him wrap little fingers around his big knuckle.

"You got a g-good grip, J.T. Be a roper like your daddy, not a b-bull rider. Too dangeroush."

His words always came out easier when he spoke to the uncritical child. Jesse held on tight, focused his eyes on the moving lips and opened his mouth in a sweet, gummy smile.

"Noreen, Noreen! Come see!"

Noreen dashed into the house in a panic. "Did you drop him, Ted!"

"N-no. J.T.'s smilin'."

"So he is. Just look at him. I can't wait to show Rusty."

She lied, he thought. Earlier today he'd heard her laugh out loud when she was in changing the baby's diaper. He bet Jesse Ted had smiled for her then, and now he had gone and ruined her surprise for Rusty. He spoiled their new life together. He should fall down and die and get out of their way.

Noreen scooped up the baby. "You are such a big boy now. Ted, do you need help getting up?"

"N-no."

He positioned himself behind the walker and pulled up. Carefully, he reached for his old Stetson hat on the arm of the chair and jammed it on his head. Clump-step, clump-step, all the way to the door. Ted waited while Noreen secured the baby in his seat, then slid into the front of her small car. Noreen put the walker in the back and got into the driver's seat. She checked to make sure he was buckled in. He fumbled with the latch and she completed the task for him.

"S-sorry to be a b-burden to you."

"You're not. This is just our time to get to know each other better."

His daughter-in-law was so damned cheerful. She'd given up a chance to student teach in the fall to take care of him. Ted had never been a cussing man, but he found he swore a lot in his mind now. Who wouldn't when his bedroom looked like the photo in a nursing home brochure? Rusty had rented a hospital bed, the walker, a shower seat, and worst of all, a potty chair so his father wouldn't have to try to make the trip down the hall. Ted wet himself a couple of times without telling Noreen. No way would he let Noreen diaper him, too. He needed to pass away before this latest humiliation overtook him.

"Here we are," Noreen chirped. "It was so nice of the physical therapist to schedule you at the same time as Jesse's checkup. Afterwards, we can go out to lunch. So nice to finally get out of the house, right?"

"R-right."

They repeated the ritual with the walker and the

baby seat. Ted managed to get down to the clinic's door. He jammed the walker into the opening he made with his good hand instead of using the button for handicapped help and got stuck.

"I wish you had waited for me, Ted." Noreen held the door open just as a member of the staff moved forward to help. Ted clumped through.

"I see we have a feisty client on our hands," the therapist said. She was an older woman with thick, dark hair threaded with a little silver and clipped back at her nape. Her large, brown eyes held a mischievous glint. "I like to work on the tough ones."

She put her hands on her rounded hips, molding the baggy blue scrubs she wore into a more feminine shape and assessed her new patient with her eyes. "Mona Veazey. So happy to meet you at last, Mr. Niles. Your daughter-in-law told me all about you over the phone." She held out a hand more competent than dainty.

Ted took the chance and shook it with his good hand, hoping his damaged side wouldn't collapse and leave him in a heap at her feet. Probably, Noreen had told this woman he was a difficult patient. Mona Veazey had a warm, strong grip and probably a very nice body under that sack she wore. Now where had that thought come from?

"The receptionist will give your daughter-in-law the forms to fill in. You can come with me. This time, I'll get the door." The therapist held open a swinging door leading to a series of curtained cubicles and a workout area packed with gym equipment and other strange objects that looked like bizarre instruments of torture from an old science fiction movie.

"Can you get up on the examination table, Mr.

Niles?"

He prepared his answer and said, "Yes," decisively. With the help of a small step stool, he managed. This first part went easy. She asked him to press against her hands with his arms and legs in various positions and wrote down numbers on a sheet of paper attached to her clipboard. Next, she showed him a series of stretching and strengthening exercises and ran through them one by one, making note of how many reps she wanted him to do. Some of them hurt like hell, but he didn't utter a word.

"I see you are the strong silent type, Theodore. May I call you Theodore?"

"N-no. Hate that name."

"Why? It means 'gift of God', you know. While my name, Moooo-na, sounds like a ghost wailing in some old, crumbling mansion."

"Ted." He couldn't help but smile lopsidedly

"Ted, you've got quite the wicked smile there, cowboy. Okay, ten minutes on the bicycle."

"Can't ride a b-bike—or a h-horse."

"Sure you can. When I'm finished with you in a few months, you'll ride that bike like a champ, saddle up and mount a horse or anything else you want."

"A woman?"

He felt a flush crawl up his face. All his life, Ted Niles had been respectful of women, always burying deep his cruder side, but the word had just come out with nary a stutter. He'd treated Maggie like a lady, and after her death, he'd devoted himself to raising Rusty and running the ranch, hardly giving the female sex a thought or a try. Now, he'd offended his therapist. Obviously, the stroke had done more than cripple him.

Something inside struggled to get out.

Mona Veazey put her hands on her hips again, threw back her head and laughed with infectious joy. The smock pulled tight across soft, large breasts. Ted felt the urge to rip open those snaps and pull her down on an exercise mat. He was going truly insane.

"Yes, even a woman, you devil, you. Now get on that bike."

He did his stint and was rewarded by being hooked to a machine that made his muscles jump with small, zinging pulses. Afterwards, Mona wrapped him in hot towels to improve his circulation. He'd had to take his jeans off and was relieved the towels were thick because he had a boner for Miss Mona.

"Next time, cowboy, wear gym clothes and athletic shoes, not jeans and boots, you hear."

"Yes. W-what kind?"

"Well, shoes with good arch supports for one. And those little tiny running shorts. You got nice legs, Ted."

"S-so do you."

"Short and stubby, actually. Baggy pants cover a lot of flaws. Here, I have a present for you." She held out a red rubber ball. "Squeeze this night and day, as often as you can, to get your grip back. Put that left hand to work. Pick up small objects like Cheerios. Need help getting dressed again? If not, I'll see you in two days."

"That's a d-date."

****

"Noreen, I'm missin' my last day of therapy."

"No, you aren't. We won't be more than ten minutes late at the most. Believe me, you don't want to be in the car when J.T. has a poopy diaper. He smells worse than a cattle barn in the summertime."

Miss Mona said he was making an amazing recovery, probably because he'd do anything for her. He thumped the three-toed cane he rarely needed anymore and waited impatiently by the front door. He wore a tucked in T-shirt, long tan shorts and white athletic shoes. Looking in the mirror today, he thought he appeared fit for his age, worthy to be seen with someone like Mona.

"Noreen, we're late!" His speech had cleared up in a hurry, too.

"Just get in the car, Ted. Mrs. Veazey won't chew you out. I think you're her favorite patient."

Ted stopped halfway out the door. "Did you say Mrs. Veazey?"

"Sure, Mona Veazey. Your therapist, Mrs. Veazey. Do you feel all right? Ted, are you having another stroke? Can you answer me?"

"No. I'm good. Just all this time I thought she was single."

"Oh, I see. A little crush on your therapist, huh?"

"Mona says patients get crushes on nurses, not on physical therapists, because they equate their therapists with pain."

"Equate. Wow, you had no trouble getting that out. She has done wonders for you. I am sorry, Ted. That eighteen-year-old receptionist they have at the clinic calls her Mrs. Veazey all the time. I thought you knew."

"I'm always in the back room. She doesn't wear a ring."

"Probably would get in way of her work. The brochure in the office says she and her husband founded the clinic in 1967. I know you're fond of her, but you'll get over her just like you did this illness."

"You didn't get over Rusty."

"Rusty and I are soul mates. I've told you that before. I swear we are Esperanza Niles and Rufus Courville come again."

"Then, you should have been born in the opposite families or a different sex or somethin'. That's just crazy stuff, Noreen."

"You have no idea what God can do if He wills it."

"I can't argue with that, but we're still late."

Noreen got Jesse settled in his seat. He kicked and burbled and smiled up at her, as happy a six-month old as any on the face of the earth, his granddad thought, until the sun got into his dark eyes and he squinted them down to little slits and frowned.

"When you look at me like that, I could swear you are the image of Owney Maddox on those wanted posters, J.T."

"What did you say, Noreen? Something about wanted posters."

"Not important. What's that you have?"

"Nothin'." Ted threw the baby name book Noreen and Rusty had used to pick out a girl's name onto the dashboard. "Let's go and get this over with."

****

Mona Veazey appeared as impatient as Ted. They could see the therapist pacing the office through the glass walls when they drove up. For a man in a hurry, Ted took his time getting out. He paused to address his daughter-in-law. "Noreen, I know I'm not a prize patient. You've been like the daughter I never had, right there helping me all the way. I thank you for that with all my heart."

Before Noreen could say something mushy, get all teary-eyed or claim they were related in another life, he abandoned his cane in the car, drew himself up to his full six feet plus and walked straight to the door.

Mona greeted him almost distraught. "I've been waiting so long for you, Ted. I thought you had gotten in an accident. Maybe been killed. You know this is our last chance. How could you be so late?"

"Pardon me, Mrs. Veazey. The baby had a poopy diaper. I'll get started on my stretches right now, ma'am. After today you won't have to bother with me."

"And then twenty minutes on the bike, transfer to the treadmill and end up with the hand weights. If you do all that in good time, I'll give you a farewell massage."

Oh, he did love those massages, but he wouldn't tell her so now. When she bent over him, he smelled the faint scent of gardenias. She said she wore dusting powder because some of the patients objected to perfume. Sometimes, when she worked really close, those big, soft breasts of hers brushed against him and filled him with a lust like he hadn't felt since in his twenties—and shouldn't be feeling now.

He did his exercises as if he were training for the Olympics. On the treadmill, he cranked up the pace and ran for a while to take the edge off his unruly hormones. Mona caught him and chewed him out. What did he need with such a bossy woman, anyhow?

"Are you out of your mind? Do you want to injure yourself again and have to start all over?"

"Maybe."

"Ted, I don't know what's wrong with you today. Skip the weights. You can do that at home from now on. Let me give you that massage."

He lay facedown on the padded table as Mona put lotion on her hands and began rubbing his legs all the way up the thigh. He'd never feel her touch again after this. Losing her was like losing his power of speech all over again. Today, he had intended to tell her how he felt. Good thing he'd found out about her marital status in time before he made a damned fool of himself.

"Ted, I know something is wrong. Want to talk about it?"

"I don't know. Sometimes, I feel like I've been punished all my life for things I never did. I got my wife pregnant before we were married. She was an educated businesswoman, older than me, but I tried my best to be a good husband and father. I saw her through a long illness, but she died anyhow. I was a good husband to the land, too, but I had to sell off most of the spread that had been in my family for more than a century to pay the medical bills. Almost lost my son by being stubborn about his wanting to marry Noreen. Never cared for her family. But, I fixed that one in time. Now, I feel like I'm losin' something else that means the world to me."

Ted didn't expect the sharp slap across his backside.

"Did you just spank me?"

"You bet I did. I can't abide self-pity, Ted Niles. You want to hear a sob story? I'll tell you one. I married Darren Veazey right out of college and gave birth to five daughters in eight years. One set of twins in there, for your information. Do you know how much trouble girls are—boyfriends and squabbles and always wanting everything new? In the middle of all this,

Darren wants to start his own clinic, so we take out a second mortgage on the house. Ten years later, we're finally doing great and my husband is diagnosed with ALS—you know, Lou Gehrig's disease. No matter how many times I gave him a massage, he still wasted away before my eyes and died a terrible death. I had to sell the clinic to one of those big medical chains to get my girls through college. At least, I can still work here. So, don't tell me about tough lives and losing things."

Mona kneaded his shoulders so hard it became almost painful, and yet, also arousing. "You're a widow."

"Didn't I just say that, Theodore Niles?"

"Do you like to dance? Can you do a Cajun waltz? I hear dancin' is great for stroke victims. Would you go with me to the Rainbow Express tomorrow night?"

Her touch grew gentle as her hands moved down his sides. "I'll go anywhere you want to go, Ted."

"I looked up the name Mona in the baby book. It means the The One." He wished he could see her face when he said that.

"That's me, the one and only Mona." Her strokes turned ticklish as her fingers played over his ribs.

Ted Niles flipped over, sat up suddenly and took her hands in his. He didn't care if the towel fell off his lap and she saw how much he wanted her.

"All my life I've been missin' something, someone, even when I was married. Noreen thinks she and my son are reincarnated lovers, and that's why they fell in love so quickly. Crazy, huh?"

"Not so crazy. I've been right here waiting, Mr. Niles. What took you so long?"

A word about the author...

Once a librarian, now a writer of romance, Lynn Shurr grew up in Pennsylvania Dutch country. She attended a state college and earned a degree in English Literature. Her first job really was working in a burger joint. Moving from one humble job to another, she traveled to Europe and across the United States, finally buckling down to get an M.A. in Librarianship.

She found her first reference job in the Heart of Cajun Country. For her the old saying, "Once you've tasted bayou water, you will always stay here" came true. She raised three children not far from the banks of the Bayou Teche and lives there still with her astronomer husband.

When not writing, Lynn likes to paint, cheer for the New Orleans Saints and LSU Tigers, and take long road trips nearly anywhere. Her love of the bayou country, its history and customs, often shows in the background for her books.

She is the author of the popular Sinners sports romances, a new series, The Roses, and a single romance title, A Trashy Affair.

Contact Lynn at:
www.lynnshurr.com, lynn.shurr@yahoo.com or lynnshurr.blogspot.com

~*~

Other Lynn Shurr titles
available from The Wild Rose Press, Inc.:
THE CONVENT ROSE
A WILD RED ROSE
A TRASHY AFFAIR
GOALS FOR A SINNER
WISH FOR A SINNER
KICKS FOR A SINNER
PARADISE FOR A SINNER
LOVE LETTER FOR A SINNER